Mark Mason was born in 1971. He lives in London.
What Men Think About Sex is his first novel.

What Men Think About Sex

Mark Mason

timewarner
paperbacks

A *Time Warner* Paperback

First published as a paperback original by
Time Warner Paperbacks in 2002

Copyright © Mark Mason 2002

The moral right of the author has been asserted.

Permission to quote from *My Wicked, Wicked Ways*
by Errol Flynn has been granted by William Heinemann,
publishers, and G.P. Putman's Sons, proprietors.

A CIP catalogue record for this book
is available from the British Library.

ISBN 0 7515 3287 8

Typeset in Berkeley by M Rules
Printed and bound in Great Britain
by Clays Ltd, St Ives plc

Time Warner Paperbacks
An imprint of
Time Warner Books UK
Brettenham House
Lancaster Place
London WC2E 7EN

www.TimeWarnerBooks.co.uk

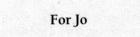

For Jo

Sunday 18th April

4.45 p.m.

Let me start by explaining what Tim is not. He is not my 'best mate', whatever that phrase means. I do not know his birthday, nor his middle name, nor exactly what part of the country he comes from. I do not know how old he is, although I seem to remember that it's either a year older or younger than me, either twenty-nine or twenty-seven. There is no element of 'look at us, we're real lads' to the relationship. Rather, Tim is someone with whom I work in the London office of an internationally successful computer software company, and who, it has dawned on me over the last eighteen months or so, shares my attitudes to quite a few things. We tend to laugh at each other's jokes, to have seen the same films, to enjoy drinking the same drinks for approximately the same amount of time before we get drunk. And, most recently, we have found ourselves in agreement about something else that has given rise to this little enterprise. But more of that in a minute or two.

On the general disposition front, then, Tim and I share common ground. But physically there are differences. He is about an inch over six feet tall, although he says he doesn't know the exact figure. As if. Any man who has even the slightest chance of being six feet tall and claims not to know for sure is lying. I, on the other hand, am three inches short of that mark. Two and a half on a good day. His dark hair is receding, but in a way that lends him an attractive maturity, a bit like Bruce Willis before he went for the shaven psycho look. My fair hair is staying put. Tim's default setting is slim, whereas my figure can tend towards 'healthy'. No more than that, of course. All these factors are pertinent to the enterprise I mentioned. But as I say, I'll come to that shortly.

Our work is quite specialised, and although it keeps our interest a detailed explanation of it would be exceedingly dull, so suffice it to say that we design and develop bits of computer trickery that allow sad people with personal organisers to exhibit techno-superiority over you at parties. Sorry about that. I can only plead in our defence that, like the guy who invented the nuclear bomb, we only come up with the technology, we're not responsible for its subsequent use. Our office is a pleasant enough place to work, with quite an interesting assortment of people as colleagues, and in the absence of the sawn-off or the six numbers it's as good a way as any of paying the mortgage. And as of last Tuesday, it got a hell of a lot better. Because into our office has flown (quite literally – she's on attachment from our San Francisco office) Clare Jordan.

Little is known yet of Clare Jordan, as the week has been quite busy, and opportunities for conversation few and far between. But on one thing Tim and I are in full agreement. Clare Jordan is sexy.

Now sexy is difficult. All week long I've been trying to work out what makes someone sexy. But it's very, very difficult.

Pretty is easy. Pretty is a fresh face, bright eyes, soft hair, an innocence that perhaps you fancy, perhaps you don't. Pretty is Audrey Hepburn in *Breakfast At Tiffany's*.

Good-looking is easy. Good-looking differs from pretty in that you have to fancy good-looking. We've now moved on to the sexual rather than the merely aesthetic. Good-looking is pretty plus you want to take them to bed. This is not to say, of course, that all men will agree on whether a particular woman is good-looking. Nor is it true to say that all men have a 'type'.

Horny is easy. Horny is not necessarily good-looking. In fact, the best sort of horny is not conventionally good-looking, because horny is just you want to take them to bed, whether or not they're good-looking, and if they're not good-looking the wanting to take them to bed has the added value of mystery. Sigourney Weaver is horny.

But sexy. Sexy is difficult, and maybe that's why it's so wonderful. The best-looking girl in the world can stop being sexy the moment she says her first words to you, if they are words that fail to interest you. Sex can be many different things, but the best sex is in the head as well as the underwear, and that's where sexy comes in. Like good-looking, sexy can be different things to different people. Again, that's why it's so great.

How, then, do we describe Clare Jordan? I'd say that she is mildly pretty, certainly good-looking, not really that horny. But none of those really get to the heart of it. The only word that hits this particular nail is 'sexy'.

But *how* is she sexy, you ask? The best answer I can give you is that I didn't notice her sexiness for four days. That's how true sexiness works. Attention-grabbing cleavages produce instant reactions. But true sexiness takes its time. It creeps up on your consciousness, it worms its way into your brain, and before you know it . . . wham.

I have a feeling that were you to ask Tim this question, he would simply regale you with a physical description of Clare. Well, I can do that if you want. She's five-nine (I'm very well placed to spot when people are that height), she has a good figure that doesn't quite qualify for 'curvy', and the length of the skirts she has worn on each of her four days in the office shows that she knows how gorgeous her legs are. Her shoulder-length hair is a slightly darker brown than that of her eyes, which shine almost to the point of sparkling. They always seem to be smiling, even when she isn't. Her petite nose is perfectly straight, her lips definitely kissable without being 'full'. You can tell by her bearing when she walks that she's aware of her height, but not so proud of it as to appear conceited. She obviously knows that she attracts men, but carries it off with the quiet confidence of Cameron Diaz rather than the pouting sensuality of Marilyn Monroe.

Those details, though, still don't tell you why she's sexy. You could put someone else in that body, and the sexiness would be missing. Equally, Clare could inhabit another body, and her sexiness would still be there. As I say, the fact that you can never fully explain 'sexy' is what makes it so magical.

Halfway down Friday evening's second pint was when the subject first arose between Tim and myself. The end of the third pint would have been the discussion's natural finishing point. But In Löwenbräu Veritas. Forget apples falling on heads – true inspiration comes dissolved in alcohol. As Tim and I swam in the comforting warmth of our discussion about Clare's sexiness, and while the girl herself completed her unpacking on the other side of London, a seed was sown. And the idea for the Clare Jordan Five And Three-Quarter Feet Handicap Stakes was born.

The exact provenance of the scheme remains, and is, I fear, destined to remain, drowned in the advanced drunkenness of Friday evening. I do, however, remember two key moments. The first was a mock court proceeding, in which Tim delivered a closing speech to Her Honour Lord Justice Jordan as to why he should be the one sentenced to be taken from this place, and back to her place. Then he encouraged me to do the same. The other moment of clarity is him shouting (don't worry, it was a loud pub, we weren't making fools of ourselves) 'give me a C' – I obliged – 'give me an L' – ditto – and so on. Looking back on it, I'm sure that was where the idea started. That was, in every sense of the phrase, the initial point.

Confirmation that the idea was a reality (in fact, technically the race has already started, so if you're in a gambling mood place your bets and place them quickly), came at Tim's flat yesterday afternoon. In our booze-fuelled enthusiasm we'd arranged the meeting to formalise matters. But even as I made my way round there, the hazy outline of our proposal was flashing the phrase 'non-starter' at me in big red neon lights.

It was just after three o'clock that I found myself seated on Tim's sofa, mug of coffee in hand, my host standing before me, ready to open proceedings.

'Gentlemen,' he announced grandly, 'we are gathered here today to commemorate the inauguration of the Clare Jordan Five And Three-Quarter Feet Handicap Stakes.' Tim paused, not just to let the full weight of this historic moment sink in to all those present (i.e. me and him), but also to bend down and fetch from underneath his television cabinet a large folded piece of paper.

Very solemnly, wearing a Black-Rod-meets-newsreader-about-to-do-a-train-crash-story expression, he unfolded the paper and Blu-tacked it to a space on the wall vacated specially for the occasion by Al Pacino (Scarface incarnation). It was about eighteen inches wide, and a good three and a half feet long. The paper was divided vertically into two columns, headed 'TIM' and 'ROB'. Down the left-hand side were the letters 'C', 'L', 'A', 'R' and 'E'. Below that was a large blank space, headed 'Rules'. Laid out before me as starkly as this, the details of the plan seemed appalling. For the very good reason that they were. The red neon lights flashed even more brightly. No way could we do anything like this.

Tapping a random point on the piece of paper, Tim said: 'We drive the Land Rover into the square.'

A light-hearted moment, which given my sense of unease was more than welcome. Auto-pilot guided me to the reply: 'Piazza, Arthur, piazza.'

Obligatory *Italian Job* reference out of the way, Tim returned to his serious demeanour. 'Now then, gentlemen, as we are all well aware, the Goddess In Human Form hereafter referred to as "Clare" has recently been the subject of some admiration, not to mention primal lustful yearning, from the Humans In Human Form hereafter referred to as "Tim" and "Rob".'

He turned to me. Still not entirely convinced that Tim wasn't joking (*surely* he couldn't be serious about this?), I maintained a silence.

'And so,' he continued, 'the judges – Tim and Rob – have decreed that the contestants – Tim and Rob – shall each compete for the right to be the first to try and win Clare's hand, and indeed such other parts of herself as she might deign to be winnable.' At this point Tim turned to face the chart. 'Furthermore, the judges have also decreed that the nature of the competition should reflect the prize itself. Accordingly, the rules shall be as follows. Tim and Rob shall each attempt to sleep with five girls, the initials of whose Christian names shall be,' he tapped each letter as he slowly enunciated them, '"C", "L", "A", "R", and "E". Whoever shall complete this task first shall be deemed the winner. If an expensive dinner date between him and Clare Jordan transpires, it shall be funded by the loser.'

Tim stood back from the chart and turned towards me. By now my lack of comment was becoming uncomfortably obvious. Tim sat down next to me on the sofa, sighed, and took a sip of his coffee. I had to say something. But what? The obvious first comment bubbled up in my mind: *Funny as you've been in writing it all up, Tim, now's the time to end the joke.* But what would he say to that? Clearly he *wasn't* joking. So would ambivalence on my part be seen as fear of the challenge?

There was another factor, though. Something more than a mere worry that to withdraw would be seen as an admission of an inability to pull. It was the thought that maybe sleeping with five girls (or at least trying to) would be a contrast with the landscape of my recent sex life. This was painted six months ago, when I found myself on the wrong end of an ultimatum involving an engagement ring. Loving Sarah as I did, and loving the time we spent together, it was a very unpleasant moment when I realised that I couldn't bring myself to make that final step. Not even as I walked away from her flat for the last time, clutching the toothbrush that I'd kept there. Why not? No tangible reason presented itself, but I knew that I just couldn't. And while I felt sure my decision was the right one, losing Sarah knocked me sideways with rather greater force than I thought it would. If you want the truth, it still hurts. For a while I didn't even notice other girls, didn't want to notice them. The desolation that shrouds you after loss became, almost, a comfort blanket. Misery was the tax I felt I owed to my memories of Sarah, and now I'd got used to being miserable. Too used to it. Perhaps the Clare Jordan Five And Three-Quarter Feet Handicap Stakes was my exit visa from unhappiness? After all, the prize was only the chance to ask Clare out for a date. There was no guarantee that she'd want to sleep with either of us. We would be competing for the right to approach her, not for the girl herself.

But while part of me was attracted to the race in this way, another part thought that . . . well, that you just don't *do* things like this.

I tried to say as much to Tim. But, curiously, what came out of my mouth was: 'I've thought of a problem.'

'What?'

'We go to the same pubs as each other,' I found myself saying. 'And the same parties. We meet a lot of the same girls. We'll probably end up competing against each other for the same "C", the same "L", the same "A" . . . We'd just be setting up a direct clash that could ruin the chances of either of us completing the course.' Was this an attempt on my part to kill the proposal in its tracks? Or did I genuinely see it as a glitch in the plan that needed ironing out? Did part of me want to engage with the idea? If, for the reasons of male pride and excitement, I was beginning to come round to it, I can offer no excuse. All I can do is be honest with you. Those reasons were there.

Tim reflected on my statement. I reflected on it too. Even Al, staring mournfully up from his new home on the carpet, if a man firing a machine gun can ever be said to look mournful, seemed to be reflecting on it.

And then the 'engage with the idea' part of me took over. 'Got it,' I shouted. 'One of us has to do names. The other has to do *places*.' (Look, I'm not saying I'm proud of what happened, I'm just telling you that it did.)

Confusion crossed Tim's face. 'What, like Carlisle, Liverpool, Alaska . . . ?'

'No, no, no. Well, yes. I mean, they could be placenames. But they could also be car, lawn, arrivals lounge. Or couch, lay-by, arboretum . . . that sort of thing.'

Inspiration lit up Tim's face. 'You could do car and lay-by in one go.'

I thought for a minute. 'Nah, that would be too easy.' Now that my interest had been seized I found myself ignoring my misgivings. Even though I knew, in my heart, that we were never actually going to do this, I really wanted to get it right. 'We have to be rigorous. I mean, you could do it in a car in a lay-by on the A23 and claim you'd done the first three letters. Each letter has to be a separate incident.'

Tim's turn to mull. 'Agreed,' he said after a while. 'But if the contestant doing that option has to find five girls *and* get them into five places he's got a more difficult task than the other guy, who just has to find the girls. So he should have to do five separate incidents, as you say – *but* each incident shouldn't have to be with a new girl. It could be one girl in five places, or two girls in two places each plus . . . well, you get the idea.'

'Reasonable. Reasonable. But then again, he could just find one girl and sleep with her in five different parts of London – like Chelsea, Lambeth, Archway – and win like that. That'd be *too* easy, wouldn't it? So only, say, one of the places should be allowed to be a geographical placename. And the other four have got to be approved by both judges. Otherwise that competitor will go for doddle options like carpet, lounge, armchair . . .'

'Fair points,' said Tim. 'Well made.'

'And we have to do the letters in order, right?'

'Sure.' He gulped the last of his coffee. 'I think we've also got to define the rules concerning Clare Jordan herself. Like – no asking her out for sneaky dates.'

'No inviting her along to collective social functions without asking the other contestant first.'

'No mysterious flowers, "you've got a secret admirer" notes, or anything like that.'

I nodded my agreement.

'Right,' said Tim. 'That's the rules sorted. It just remains to decide who's going to do which option.'

At this point we lapsed into silence, trying to outguess each other. Exhausted by my creative spasm, I let the outrageousness of all this wash over me. I was sitting here, working out whether I preferred an attempt at sex with five girls of preset initials, or at sex in five places with preset initials. Disgraceful behaviour, I know. But deliciously appealing as well. Shamefaced, I couldn't help but be drawn to the calculation. We'd set up the handicaps so that each contestant should have the same nominal chance of winning (that's what handicaps are there for, of course) . . . but surely one option had to have an advantage over the other, however marginal? I set about listing in my mind the various factors that mitigated the level of difficulty presented by each option, so that I could carefully and scientifically assess which . . .

'I'll go for names,' said Tim suddenly, with great confidence.

Shit. Here I was, agonising over my decision in the minutest detail, while Tim had plumped for an option with the absolute assurance of one who knows he could walk either of them. I could hardly argue, say 'no, I want names, you have places', could I? That'd blow the whole equal-difficulty theory out of the window. If I was happy that the Clare Jordan Five And Three-Quarter Feet Handicap Stakes was a level playing-fie— racecour— oh, you know what I mean – if I was happy about the rules, why was I bothered which option I got? Secretly, though, each of us knew, and each of us knew that each of us knew, that Tim must have had a reason for preferring 'names'. But what was it? How confident is he of victory in this ignoble enterprise? What are his assessments of our respective merits vis-à-vis the . . . Oh, look, what I'm trying to say is, has Tim shagged more women than me or not?

I know, in my heart of hearts, that the answer's yes. Don't get me wrong, I'm sure Tim and I are in the same sort of league. More than the Pope, not as many as Peter Stringfellow. But that covers a multitude of sins, and although I'm no saint, Tim's a bigger sinner than me. I'm sure of it. I'm happy enough with my (and get ready to cringe, because this is rather a vulgar expression) 'strike rate'. But there's an easy charm about Tim, which you've either got or you haven't, and which means that he'll have struck more than me. I can't know that for certain, of course, but I'd put money on it.

Just ask him, you say? Are you *mad*? Boys don't talk about things like that. Well, all right, some do, but they tend to be the sort who enjoy burping and farting in front of each other. Boys like Tim and myself, though? *Oh* no. We'd never ask each other how many girls we'd slept with. We'd be too scared about the other guy's score being higher. Or rather I would. Tim, I'm sure, is confident that his score would be higher.

So perhaps that was his reasoning: Tim thinks that 'names' is more difficult, and he's confident in going for that because he knows he's better at pulling than me, and wants the challenge? Whatever – that's how it's worked out. So can I do this? Can I put myself into the saddle for the Clare Jordan Five And Three-Quarter Feet Handicap Stakes?

THOUGHTS REGARDING THE CLARE JORDAN FIVE AND THREE-QUARTER FEET HANDICAP STAKES

I freely admit that this isn't big, and it certainly isn't clever. But smallness and stupidity don't stop something being exciting. At least not for males in their twenties. As St Augustine said, 'Lord, make me virtuous – but not yet.' You may think that a fourth-century Christian philosopher sits rather uncomfortably in a discussion like this, but that quote is right at the heart of it. We know we'll settle down one day. We're not after a score like Peter Stringfellow's. After all, look what everyone thinks of him. Sixty-something men sowing wild oats are a ludicrous sight. Mick Jagger does it because he can afford the paternity suits. Although even he must be contemplating a vasectomy by now.

So why, you ask, do you want to do it? Why do young men want to sleep with lots of girls? There's no doubt that they do. To quote the poem at the beginning of Errol Flynn's autobiography:

> *Come, all you young men with your wicked, wicked ways,*
> *Sow your wild wild oats in your younger days,*
> *So that we may be happy when we grow old.*
> *Ah yes! Happy and happy when we grow old.*

Yes, you insist – but that was Errol Flynn. Do *you* want the chance to sleep with lots of girls? Yes, I do. Why? Well, I will get round to answering the question truthfully, I promise. But first let me say a few words about the practicalities, as they strike me, of the Clare Jordan Five And Three-Quarter Feet Handicap Stakes.

Which are that there's every chance it won't even work. The simple truth putting the going at heavy to improbable is that pulling is like getting drunk and getting to sleep: when you're trying to do it, you can't. For those of you with your Rule Book of Life to hand, you'll find this one in the same section as 'buses always come in threes' and 'the toast always lands buttered side down'. And if pulling when you're trying is difficult per se, the chances of me, with my recent lack of form, pulling five times with one or more girls in the right places, in order, make Lord Lucan winning next year's Derby on Shergar look odds-on.

But anyway – I promised you an attempt at an explanation for why young men want to put notches on their bedposts. So here it is. Inevitably this will involve a fair amount of generalising, but if Germaine Greer can do it then so can I.

It's not that men enjoy sex more than women do. Physical desire and the enjoyment of its fulfilment are suits held pretty evenly by the sexes, as far as I can tell. There's just as much rev in the female 'phwoarrrr' elicited by a George Clooney poster as there is in the one a bloke gives when he sees Kylie Minogue. It's not a question of libido, it's just a question of how that libido's dealt with.

Anthropologists will tell you that men want sex with as many partners as possible because it maximises the chance of reproduction. There may be something in that, but my preferred explanation owes more to Gary Lineker than Desmond Morris. It's simply a question of scoring. As many times as you can, within reason. Whereas women tend to worry that they might have slept with too many people. I once compared partner-counts with a female friend who was several years older than me. We both came up with numbers quite close to ten. Years later, in an alcohol-induced moment of honesty, we discovered that she'd halved her true count and I'd doubled mine.

No man's dying words have ever been 'I wish I'd slept with fewer women'. Sad, depressing and sordid – but, I'm afraid, true. Even John Betjeman. Hardly your archetypal think-with-his-balls merchant, I trust you'll agree, and yet asked in his twilight years if he had any regrets, he replied, 'Yes, I wish I'd had more sex when I was younger.'

I'm not saying that any of this reflects terribly well on men. I know it doesn't. Maybe I'm seeing all this in so much detail because I haven't thought in these terms for such a long time. My post-Sarah depression closed down the whole debate for me, and only now are the myriad aspects of male sexuality repermeating my thinking. And, boy, are some of them unappealing. But I hope you agree that there's no point me being anything other than honest. Men do have this side to their nature.

Equally, though, it's only one side of it. Our creed isn't 'lad-dism' (Christ how I hate that word). Our lives aren't one long course at the University of Look At The Arse On That. Men may be immature enough to want as many sexual partners as reasonably possible, but they also understand that sex is like bridge – the more you do it with one particular partner, the better you get at it with them. (Actually, I've never played bridge, but I'm guessing that's true. It's got to be, hasn't it?) Similarly, sex *isn't* like golf, something you're either good at or not. It's not a skill, it's an interaction, and so the quality of it depends on who you're doing it with. And moreover when a relationship's developing, and the eight-letter word 'feelings' is progressing towards the four-letter word beginning with 'l', blokes will not lightly run off with someone else just to increase the score by one. 'Infidelity' translates very impre-cisely between the languages of Male and Female, but once a bloke has defined it he tends to stick to it.

Monday 19th April

6.20 p.m.

Quiet day in the office. Noses a lot further away from the grindstone than last week, thank God.

It felt quite strange being in Clare's presence after what happened yesterday afternoon. Reminded me, for some reason, of schoolday pranks where a derogatory note is stuck to an unwitting victim's back, the note in this case being over three feet long with her name down one side and mine and Tim's across the top. Did the race feel like a tribute to her sexiness, or an affront to it? Maybe a bit of both.

Noticed something new about her today. Whenever she settles back in her chair to read something, she pushes her hair behind her left ear – but only uses her third and fourth fingers, rather than all of them. Still no real information about her, though. She's not been out for a drink with us, and has that knack some people have of joining in conversations without really giving too much away about themselves. This is easier in her case as the desk she's been given is a little way down our open-plan office, about twenty feet away from the block where Tim and I sit. She can join in those conversations she wants to, and pretend not to have heard those she doesn't.

But I did get to speak to her on my own this morning. At the coffee machine, which is right down the other end of the floor, out of earshot. Tim and I both spotted that she was on her way, but he was on a phone call. A few grams of adrenalin shot through me as I registered that this turn of events made me excited. Quickly forming the questioning thumb-and-index-finger gesture that is Accepted Officese for 'coffee?', I set off for the machine at a steady pace to make sure I caught up with Clare, but not so quickly that it was obvious what I was doing. I composed myself into an appearance of one who is interested in the person he finds himself talking to, but not overly so. Or at least I tried to. Inwardly my interest meter was way past 'overly' and flicking into 'obsessed'.

'You needed a caffeine top-up as well?'

'Mmm,' she said, just before the mug touched her lips. (I've never felt jealous of a mug before.)

I had to say something else quickly, before she set off for the return journey to her desk. 'Hope our English coffee is all right for you. I know how good the American stuff is.' A bit naff, and now that I think about it not even true, but just within the confines of not sounding stupid.

'Oh, it's lovely,' she said, in her West Coast accent that's relaxed enough to be sexy without slowing to an actual drawl. What's her life like over there? My imagination conjures up a snapshot of a huge house overlooking the Pacific, a father whose invention of some revolutionary gadget made him millions, and a mother playing exquisitely on the piano.

Over Clare's shoulder I could see Tim, still phone-anchored to his desk, desperately trying to crane round the group of people who'd stepped into his sightline to Clare and me. Tee, and indeed hee.

'Whereabouts in America are you from exactly?' I asked, framing it (I hoped) in a tone of friendliness rather than anything more forced.

'Blah-blah. It's a town just outside San Francisco.'

Now, obviously she didn't say 'blah-blah'. It's just that at that moment she turned her head slightly, and a gentle waft of her perfume floated over. For a second I was lost in the pure sensation of being close to her. Anyway, it doesn't matter. The town's name isn't important. My mouth was open, ready to deliver a reply (not sure what that reply was going to be yet, but ready to deliver it anyway), when Clare's head turned again, this time a lot more sharply (top-up waft, just as hypnotic as the first), and with an 'Oh, that's my phone,' she was hurrying off to her desk. Damn. Oh well, a brief audience with sexiness is better than no audience at all, especially when you're the only member of that audience. And even more especially when your rival in the Clare Jordan Five And Three-Quarter Feet Handicap Stakes is otherwise engaged. Rival? For the first time Tim stopped being merely Tim to me, and took on the role of rival. A few more grams.

I reflected on how Clare had seemed during our . . . well, I can hardly call it a chat, can I? She'd said sixteen words, four of which had been about her phone ringing, one of which I didn't even hear, and one of which was 'mmm', which I suppose you've got to put down as a noise rather than a word. All right then, during our exchange. My overriding impression was of her tone. It seems to discourage any further questions. Not rude, not even formal – she's perfectly friendly – it's just that something lets you know that she'll tell you what she wants to when she wants to. Short of giving her a questionnaire to fill in I don't really see what I can do.

When Tim finally got off the phone, I replied to his impatiently whispered (one might almost say curt), 'Well?' with a, 'She didn't say anything, really,' that implied not the literal meaning of 'she didn't say anything, really' but the mysterious, cryptic meaning of 'she didn't say anything, really' that people use when they've got something to hide. A mite pathetically, I found myself enjoying the advantage I held over Mr Attractive. Knowledge is power. And as far as I'm concerned, Tim thinking I've got some knowledge, even when I haven't, is still a bit of power. Which is handy, because believe me, when Tim gets the bit between his teeth I'm going to need every bit of power I can lay my hands on.

This, it hit me, was the first minor skirmish in our battle. And I was relishing it. Despite my awareness of how crude this race looks when committed to paper (either by Tim on Saturday, or me now), I just couldn't help relishing it. Six months of despair were being thrown from my shoulders. *I'm up now*, I thought. *I'm on my feet, bouncing along*. Please don't begrudge me that.

We went to the pub for lunch. At first it was just going to be Tim and me, which would no doubt have allowed him to press me at greater length about the coffee machine episode, but then Simon piped up that he thought he'd come along as well, so that was the end of that. Simon is Welsh, but he doesn't seem to mind, he just gets on with life as best he can. At heart he's a great bloke, genuinely funny, presentable if not good-looking, and bloody good at his job to boot. But he never seems to get as much out of life as he should. Simon's is always the last umbrella still up after everyone else has realised it's stopped raining. I've heard a number of girls (okay, it's not a large number, but it's still a number) express the thought that he's quite attractive, in his way. His humour, usually self-deprecating, is a large part of the explanation for this, because if he's going to attract a girl who likes men taller than her (as a lot of them seem to) then she can't be any more than five feet five point nine recurring.

Anyway, this is all academic, as Simon has for a fair number of his twenty-six years been engaged to Michelle. From his rare pronouncements on the subject, it seems that Michelle is a childhood friend from the valleys, and that the engagement just emerged through mutual parental collusion, like some bizarre Celtic arranged marriage. The only one of us in the office who's ever laid eyes on this mythical Welsh creature is Tim, who bumped into Simon and his intended on Oxford Street one Saturday afternoon.

He talks of it in reluctant tones. She is pretty nondescript-looking, apparently, but then as Tim said, so was Rosemary West. Simon on duty with Michelle, it seems, is Office Simon minus the witticisms about how boring his life is. With her it's scratched agonisingly across his face just how tedious that life is. And it stays there, unspoken, as they work their way around the shops. The itinerary, length of stay in each shop and final purchases are all dictated by Michelle. Simon's role is to carry the bags and drive the car. Husbands, for that's what he will be when she decides the time is right, aren't for having fun with. Having fun is what she does with her girlfriends, at their coffee evenings. Coffee evenings, for God's sake. A load of girls in their twenties, and they have *coffee evenings*. Simon doesn't know exactly what goes on at them, because he has to get out of the house every time it's Michelle's turn to host one, but they don't sound like the wildest bunch of girls in Streatham.

We went to our Lunch Pub, a little old-fashioned Victorian job in a winding backstreet between Charing Cross and the Embankment, which for lunch purposes we prefer to the teeming Über Bars of Covent Garden and Soho. I stuck to Coke, as daytime drinking, quite apart from wiping me out for the afternoon on sunny days like today, depresses me.

Anything alcoholic before six on a work day always feels like the first foot on a slope that is strewn at the bottom with our Lunch Pub's Regulars.

Simon got the first round in.

'That bloke,' he said, indicating an LPR in the corner, 'just asked for a triple vodka. No tonic, no ice, just vodka. And the guy behind the bar told him they're not allowed to serve triples, but if he wanted he could have a double and a single and pour them into the same glass himself.'

We all laughed at this.

'Mind you,' continued Simon in his gentle burr, looking at the LPRs, 'it's not that bad a life, is it? I sometimes think that would suit me. Triple vodka for lunch, couple of doubles for tea, nice bottle of Thunderbird for supper.'

'Yeah, right,' said Tim sarcastically.

'No, I'm serious, like. The booze'd cost me about the same as Michelle's IKEA habit, and I wouldn't have to traipse round for three bloody hours deciding which vodka I wanted.'

That was it. Tim and I launched into our failsafe device that always rescues Simon from the Land of Maudlin. We started to sing the theme tune from M.A.S.H. After about the third line, he admitted defeat.

'All right, all right,' he laughed. 'I didn't mean it. My life is without fault. It is one huge cocktail of fun and delight. Just pretend I never said anything.'

There then followed a discussion as to whether or not it would be sick to request in your suicide note that the theme tune from *M.A.S.H.* be played at your funeral (consensus – didn't matter, as your relatives probably wouldn't play it anyway). I said I wanted the theme from *The Simpsons* played at my funeral, on the grounds that everyone likes *The Simpsons* and it would help cheer them up a bit. Tim picked the *Star Wars* theme for similar reasons. Can't remember what Simon opted for.

Right, Sainsbury's calls.

10.10 p.m.

Got back to find Helen on the phone. It was one of her 'I just don't know if I like him enough' calls.

'Oh, we had a really lovely time, Trudi, a *really* lovely time . . . we went to this beautiful restaurant near his flat, this Italian place, candlelit, you know, and the food was *gorgeous* . . . I mean he's such an interesting guy, and he was telling me about the year he spent in Cuba, and it sounded really *fascinating*, you know? . . . and at the end he put his hand on mine, and the way he looked into my eyes, it was really . . . but, oh, I just don't know, Trudi, I just don't know if I like him enough.'

Quite what my flatmate wants from a man before she *will* like him enough I've not yet managed to work out. From the number of rejections handed out so far I can only assume that it's something minor like the ability to walk on water. The offers are always there, because she's quite pretty, although not that sexy, and not at all horny. (Precisely the reason I chose her from the applicants wanting to subsidise my mortgage; I knew I wanted a woman, but I didn't want a woman I'd fancy, because that would get too complicated.) Helen's five-fiveish, slim (because her build in general is slight, rather than because she works at it), with dark hair that's always cut short but attractively and the freshness of complexion you still take for granted when you're twenty-four. While she sifts through the offers for Mr Perfect, though, she's content to busy herself with whichever 'philosophy of life' she's heard about last, usually from the telly, or a 'really interesting' person she met at a party, or sometimes just from a guy handing out leaflets in Covent Garden.

WHY I SOMETIMES WISH I WAS A WOMAN

I do, you know. A woman like Helen, anyway. I don't mean the feng shui and the energy pebbles – you can keep those. No, I mean the approach to sex. Received Wisdom on this subject is that men don't get emotionally involved in sex and women do, which is why they always end up getting hurt. But when you come to think about it, that's the wrong way round. Or at least it is if you take Helen as your example of womanhood, and me as your typical man. She enjoys all the exciting stuff – meeting him, wondering about him, giving him her number, wondering whether he'll call, getting asked out on a date by him, wondering how the date will go, deciding what to wear for the date, wondering whether she's worn the right thing for the date, going out on the date, wondering whether she wants to take it any further . . . and then deciding that she doesn't. End of discussion, no one got hurt, goodnight Skegness.

Whereas I do take it further. And so catapult myself headlong, yet again, into a state of uncertainty. Who's feeling what here? Are we as cool/excited about this as each other? Is it a One-Night Stand, a Quick Fling, a Proper Relationship, or what? And if it's a Proper Relationship, is there a sell-by date stamped on it anywhere? And even if I've got my answers all written out, I'm still trying to sneak a look at her exam paper to see if she's on the same wavelength. And if she's not, how do we go about reconciling the differences? It's a bloody nightmare.

Mind you, not even girls like Helen go through their *whole* pre-the-perfect-man life without having the odd fumble. I know from odd references in her conversations that Helen's tied a couple of beaus in her dim and distant. So surely she's got to take a risk at least once in a while? There's the worry of getting burned, of course – I know that. But there's no real harm in getting mildly singed, is there? Someone like Helen shouldn't be *entirely* wasting her sexual prime. Even I can see that.

Tuesday 20th April

6.35 p.m.

As if to prove the saying about all good things, today Graham's absence from the office came to an end.

If Graham was on Ricki Lake, the caption at the bottom of the screen would read 'Graham – bit of a wanker'. From the tip of his South Park tie to the uneven edges of his feeble moustache, everything about him screams the fact. Graham calls e-mails 'electric letters'. Graham puts 'meister' at the end of people's names ('Ah, it's none other than the Robmeister'). Graham says 'low' when you say 'hi' to him. He persists in this relentless behaviour because he thinks it's his only chance of getting any attention from us. Whereas the truth is the other way round – if he wasn't so tiresome, we'd stop not paying attention to him.

We don't mind him being out with us. 'Not as such', to quote a common Grahamism. For one thing, so desperate is he for social acceptance that he's always one of the first to get his round in. And also any group situation from which Graham is absent generates the same sort of disappointment you get at Scotland failing to qualify for the World Cup so that you don't have the chance to see them lose to Costa Rica. No Graham, no option of rescuing a flagging conversation by focusing on the butt of everyone's ridicule.

He told someone on the phone this morning, 'You have to watch out for me, I'm a bit mad.' Oh please. Whenever anyone says that you've got a cast-iron guarantee that the very last thing they are is mad. Vincent Van Gogh was mad, Jimi Hendrix was mad, Peter Sellers was mad. Graham is just a pest.

This afternoon there was a Significant Development.

You'll be able to guess, I'm sure, in which field this Development occurred. But I have a *distinctly* uneasy feeling that it was more to Tim's advantage than to mine.

Everything started well enough. Miss Jordan got back from a late lunch (who with?) during a general chit-chat between Simon and myself about music. As she was passing our desks, Clare heard him mention Madonna.

'I just love her last couple of albums,' she said, stopping between us. Instantly I felt on edge, controlled by that power which great beauty has to simultaneously attract and frighten you. What can I report of how Clare appeared to me? Well, a simple detail is that she was wearing a new pair of shoes. Or at least new to us. Black, like most of her others, but a noticeably higher heel than before, which accentuates the back of her calves. Tim seemed untroubled by the attraction/fear dilemma. He wasn't so much mentally undressing Clare – she was still facing Simon, continuing her Queen of Pop discourse – as mentally ripping every last stitch of clothing from her with all the tenderness of a gorilla. I wanted to talk to her, though. Eventually I managed to edge my way into the conversation.

'It's incredible now when you see Madonna's first *Top of the Pops* appearance, isn't it? What was she performing? Was it "Holiday"?' Stupid thing to say, of course – Clare wouldn't know about *Top of the Pops*, what with being on the other side of the world and all that. But Simon picked up on it, he thinks it was 'Holiday', for what that's worth, and soon enough the conversation was a three-header.

Which, needless to say, rapidly became a four-header. Tim's first couple of forays, praise for R.E.M. and criticism of Bryan Adams, met with a satisfying lack of acknowledgment from Clare. But then his admission to liking 'the odd' Bob Dylan track caught her attention.

'Really?' she said. 'You like Dylan? We'll have to call you "the hippy" from now on then, won't we?' And before Tim could reply, she was back off to her desk.

Initially, this sent me over the moon. Tim's been made to look stupid by Clare, but Rob hasn't, therefore game and at least set to Rob. But the more I thought about it, the more it struck me that what we witnessed in those three short sentences might, just might, have been the first signs of flirtiness from Clare Jordan. And it's not something that I'm enjoying being struck by. Because the question arises: who was she flirting with?

Was it Tim? Or me? Was it Clare ribbing Tim to goad him into a response? A response that she didn't give him time to deliver, but then of course that's all part of the game, isn't it? Or was it her ribbing him to align herself with me? Using Tim as a joint target to develop a bond with Rob?

The unease I'm feeling at the moment leads me to suspect that the latter option can be filed under 'wishful thinking'.

Oh hell.

Not much else of note in the office today, other than a fax from Jane. It was a flyer she picked up at her gym, about activity weekends, one of which is doing a parachute jump. She'd rung the place up; the more people she can get together the cheaper it is, so did any of us want to go?

I think I've decided I'm going to do it. Should be a laugh, and anyway I like Jane. Although she's only a year or two older than us, she's already a partner at the advertising agency that our marketing department use. Most of the people who work for her are stylehead ad-posers who cope with their frequent periods of mid-morning weariness by licking the edge of whichever credit card they were out with last night. But Jane just drinks (lots, often without discernible effect, or maybe that's just because after the same amount of alcohol as her I couldn't discern a bull elephant at five yards). Jane has fun. She's a no-frills, no-bullshit girl from a small village outside Leeds who came to London and found she was good at her work, and who twelve years later is doing very well indeed.

Jane does everything to the max. Including sex. And before you leap in to proclaim me a sexist bastard, those are her words, not mine. She takes enormous pleasure in detailing her sexual adventures, sometimes with people I know, often with people I don't. Only last week she was telling me (with great enthusiasm) about what she'd done (with great enthusiasm) when she and a guy on her table at an awards lunch had got bored and checked into the Dorchester.

Jane makes it perfectly plain that the offer's there. She's made it plain to me, to Tim, to James, who works with us, as indeed does James's girlfriend Lucy, which explains the wary eye whenever Jane's out with us, and not only has she made it plain, she gives us constant reminders. Standard Jane greeting: 'Hello *gorgeous*,' followed by a huge kiss, always on the mouth, never on the cheek. I have often tried, for a challenge, to get Jane to plant her kiss on my cheek, but her mouth always tracks mine like a satellite that can only re-enter the earth's atmosphere at its allotted point.

I've never taken up the offer though. And it's not that I don't fancy her. I do. Well, a bit, anyway. Jane indulges in excessive use of a lipstick that's so red it makes her shortish auburn hair seem almost black by comparison. She is overly proud of her breasts, which, although large, don't particularly turn me on (why do women always assume that bigger is necessarily better in that department?), and she wears tops that reflect that pride. Jane's cleavage is the shop window of her availability.

She's not unfanciable. It's just that I don't like the thought of everyone I know getting a post-match report. If I don't swap details with Tim, I don't want them swapped on my behalf. So Jane's a good laugh, but that's as far as it goes.

Needless to say, Graham was the first to reply that he'd do the parachute jump, followed by plenty of comments about how he'd often thought of joining the Paras. Tim told him he's got marginally more chance of joining the Corrs.

11.35 p.m.

Just back from dinner at Chris and Hannah's.

Let me explain about Chris and Hannah. Chris is a financial adviser, and Hannah is 'Purple Rain'.

Now let me explain the explanation. Chris first. He's the best sort of financial adviser, namely the sort that doesn't advise you about finance unless you ask him to. As it happens I did ask him last year, and he was very helpful, but that's not the point of this story. When he's off-duty he stays off-duty, and confines himself to the roles of Hannah's Boyfriend and One Of My Best Mates. For instance, he never tires of me asking him about the 1981 Headingley Test match, when Ian Botham beat the Aussies single-handedly, and which Chris attended as a ten-year-old schoolboy. He always seems to remember a new detail about something his dad said to him, or which four crashed over the boundary right in front of their seats, or which of Dennis Lillee's swearing fits he managed to lip-read.

And Hannah being *Purple Rain*? It was Our Song, in as much as you can have one of those during a last-year-at-college fling. That's not 'fling' as in 'regrettable error', by the way. The few weeks we spent together were very happy ones. I've never forgotten the day we went to the Sir John Soane museum after staying up all night at a party where we'd drunk ourselves sober. The fact that we both got equal enjoyment from both activities told us something about how much we had in common. And there was our shared love of *The Muppets*. Hannah did a perfect impression of Miss Piggy saying 'Kermeeeet', while I could just about muster a passable Fozzy Bear. But work and family circumstances meant that we didn't see each other for a while after the end of college, and somehow when we did meet up again it never seemed to blossom into anything more. We always stayed friends, though. And so now I've got Chris as a friend too. If anything, he's become even more of a friend than Hannah.

Got round there just as *EastEnders* was starting, so neither Chris nor I were allowed to speak to Hannah for the first half-hour.

'What is it with this programme?' he whispered as we decamped to our end of the room. 'If I'd had the sort of day at work she claims to have had, the last thing I'd want to watch would be a load of cockney misfits screaming abuse at each other.' Hannah's the office manager at a design firm, by the way.

'God knows,' I replied. 'I think it must be a "grass is browner" sort of thing – you watch it to remind yourself that however much stress and hassle you're going through, at least you don't live in Albert Square.'

Chris and I then spent a fair chunk of the programme trying to make Hannah giggle, but she pretended not to notice us. Eventually, when the doom-laden drums signalled the end of tonight's angst-fix, she went through to the kitchen, and unveiled what we were having for dinner: lamb with a red-currant sauce.

'This is gorgeous,' I said after my first mouthful.

'Mmm, it's wonderful,' added Chris. 'Top marks, darling.'

Hannah insisted on pulling her customary not-really-sure grimace. She always does this. It's not false modesty; there's no chef equivalent of 'what, this old thing?' going on – it's just that she loves cooking to the extent of being a perfectionist about it, and so she's never entirely happy with any of her creations.

We all talked about what we'd been up to. Funny, isn't it, that when you try to list the things you've done recently – new things, unusual things, not just the gone-to-work-paid-the-bills-done-the-shopping things – you realise you haven't done that much. I mean, we go and see new films with new plots, and buy new CDs with new songs, but usually they're new films with the same stars, and new CDs by the same bands.

This accusation of sameness, though, could not be levelled at the Clare Jordan Five And Three-Quarter Feet Handicap Stakes. (It's one of the few accusations that couldn't.) With a sense of trepidation, I mentioned the race to Chris and Hannah, and gave them a quick outline of the rules. Not surprisingly, they both stared back at me in amazement.

Hannah studied my face for clues. 'You are joking?' she asked hesitantly.

All of a sudden I felt very uncomfortable. 'Er, I'm not sure. I don't think so.'

She put down her knife and fork in disbelief. 'That is an *outrageous* idea.'

'Yeah, well maybe that's part of its attraction,' said Chris, suddenly quite defiant. 'Especially for Rob. He's been such a miserable bastard, moping around for the past six months. Something like this will be a laugh.' He turned to me. 'Sorry, mate. But you have.'

'I can't believe you've just said that,' said Hannah. It was obvious that she was seriously put out. 'That was one bloke intellectualising about another bloke getting his end away five times.'

'Oh, come on,' I said. 'It's not as th—'

'No, I will *not* come on,' she shouted. 'How can you even contemplate something like that?' And then, as if she couldn't bear to look at us, she addressed her next comment to the lightshade. 'Only the male mind could have come up with that sort of idea.'

'Oh don't be like that, Han,' said Chris. 'Can't you see why Rob's going to find the challenge tempting? Blokes have an internal switch that's activated by vanity. The vanity of finding women who want to sleep with them. And very few men ever disconnect it, not completely. I'm not saying they always act on it. But the switch is usually there to be pressed.' Chris suddenly realised where he was leading himself, and started to backtrack. 'Not that . . .'

'Don't bother, Chris,' said Hannah, giving him a look that could have withered grapes on the vine. 'I know precisely what men are like.'

Everything Chris had said was true, but nevertheless he hadn't made a very good job of defending me. I decided to have a go at the job myself. 'It's not as though I'm going to hurt anyone, Hannah. I'll enjoy the competition, for sure – but I won't go dragging any innocent bystanders into the fray.'

'You can't say that. How can you ever be certain what people are really feeling?'

'Well, of course I can't be *absolutely* certain,' I said. 'But I'll be really careful.'

'Ooh, you'll be "really careful",' she sneered. 'What do you want, a medal?'

We all stewed in a horrible silence. Then Chris topped up our wine glasses, and gradually, once we'd got on to less provocative topics, the evening returned to something approaching civility. But on my way home, the truth of Hannah's viewpoint kept dogging me. It's all tied in with responses and what triggers them. Have you ever noticed how often women will be attracted to a man if he's (a) gay, or (b) holding a baby? That's women's innate good sense guiding them along. Both those things prevent them trying to sleep with him. Women are preset to find attractive those men they won't be able to make physical advances on. This leaves them free to get on with enjoying the cerebral, personality aspects of what they find attractive about him, the mentally sensuous as opposed to the physically sensuous. Blokes (at least this bloke) are more than aware of the mentally sensuous aspect of sexual attraction – it's just that they are more inclined than women to be led by the physical aspect as well.

This state of affairs makes life pretty complicated at times. When you're confronted by the Clare Jordan Five And Three-Quarter Feet Handicap Stakes, for instance. An idea, as Hannah so correctly points out, that could only have sprung from a masculine brain, and which will only appeal to a masculine temperament. But understanding that fact isn't going to alter it. Mitigating its effects may seem a second best to not being like that full stop, but it is better than not caring at all. Isn't it?

FURTHER INITIAL THOUGHT REGARDING THE CLARE JORDAN FIVE AND THREE-QUARTER FEET HANDICAP STAKES

I think it only fair to point out, at this early stage, that anything that may follow will not, repeat not, contain luridly anatomical descriptions of sexual encounters. This is because, contrary to what you may have heard, men don't go around swapping intimate details about their bedroom endeavours. It's women who do that.

I've got a sneaking suspicion that some of you won't believe me on this. So can I attempt to illustrate the point by telling you about Lois? (Not her real name, and you'll see why.) Lois was a girl I went out with for quite a while. One afternoon, we found ourselves in bed, and in the enthusiasm of the moment (which was both substantial and mutual), Lois cried out, 'I'm just your slave.'

Things like that don't sound funny at the time, of course. But it sounds funny now. It even sounded funny immediately after the event, as Lois and I cuddled in post-coital bliss, laughing about what she'd said. Tempted as I was to take her remark as confirmation of my elevation to the status of Sex God, in reality I knew that our enjoyment of the occasion was down to our feelings for each other.

Cut to a couple of nights later. Lois and I are round at her place, sharing a bottle of red wine with her friend Maxine.

'Nice wine,' says Lois.

'Mmm,' agrees Maxine. Then, looking straight into her glass: 'Are you a slave to this wine, Lois?' They both collapse in giggles. I turn the colour of the wine. Every last detail of the other afternoon has clearly made its way post-haste to Maxine's eager ears.

Now I could no more regale a male friend with explicit

details of bedtime comments, positions or measurements than fly to the moon. But you can guarantee that, as well as filling in her girlfriends on the venue, attire and general conversation details of a date, a woman will, sooner or later, and it's probably sooner, get round to reporting on any sexual element it may have contained.

But this won't be like that. Just thought I'd better get that clear from the outset.

Wednesday 21st April

6.50 p.m.

MEMO TO BILL GATES

Two new bits of software for you to invent. Stop pissing about with spreadsheets and new fonts, get these babies sorted, and you'll finally, once and for all, extinguish any last threat of competition you might still be facing.

The first is an extension of the 'right click' properties device, which lists information about people on a firm's e-mail system: what room number they work in, what telephone extension they're on, their full job title, that sort of thing. It's very impressive, and occasionally quite useful. But what we *really* want listed in 'properties' is the stuff that we *really* want to know about people. Like: marital status, and if unmarried whether they're living with anyone. If not living with anyone whether they're seeing anyone, whether it's serious, or whether they're the sort not to count a quick bonk back at the office after a particularly heavy Friday evening in the pub as proper, got-to-tell-him-about-it infidelity. Also, and maybe this is the more advanced stuff you could put in the update in a couple of years' time: whether or not she fancies you.

While you've got the Microsoft boffins looking into that one, perhaps you could devote your personal attention to my second request. Again, it's a further development of already existing gizmology, so I'm sure it won't be too difficult for you to crack. How about a version of 'undo' which allows you to undo the corrections people made to an e-mail before sending it to you? You get the e-mail, open it up, and then work your way back through all the things they thought about saying to you before they sent the edited version.

At this point, Bill, perhaps I should explain the particular circumstances that have led me to contemplate the invention of these bits of software. Today I was in the fortunate, nay electrifying position of having to send Clare Jordan an e-mail. It was just some technical gumph about American specifications, and all she had to do was send it back to me with the blanks filled in. She did that, but she also put a note at the top: 'Rob – here are all the answers. I think they might be useful to the hippy as well. Do you want to forward them on to him? C.'

As soon as I read that my stomach gave a little jolt, and yesterday's debate about the flirting significance, if any, of her 'hippy' comment kicked back into full swing. Did the e-mail constitute her flirting with me, in that it was the two of us sharing a joke about Tim, or with Tim himself? Or was she flirting with neither of us?

The properties software would have been invaluable here. I could have right-clicked on her name in the 'sender' field, scrolled down to 'properties – flirtatiousness', and looked up the answers to all my questions. And with the undo thing I could have clicked away and seen whether Clare had originally put her full name instead of the more intimate 'C', whether an 'x' or two had ever been there after the 'C' (all right, all right, but a boy can dream, can't he?), and whether 'the hippy' had ever been a simple 'Tim'. All of these things would let me gauge where she was operating on the flirtiness scale.

Or rather they'd let me know where she was operating on *my* flirtiness scale. Because her scale might be differently calibrated from mine. In fact I'm sure it is. She's a girl, for a start, and their scales are metric, while boys' are imperial. Or is it the other way round? Either way, I just wish Europe or someone would standardise the bloody things once and for all, so we can all know where we stand (or lie down). Save a lot of confusion and disappointment.

Mind you, having everything spelled out for you like that would also take half of the fun out of things, wouldn't it?

On second thoughts, hold that research, Bill.

7.15 p.m.

Just in case you're in any doubt – of course I didn't forward the e-mail to Tim.

I'm worried enough about him as it is, what with both of us still to make our first move in the race. Only three days into it, of course, and he's not had a chance to proposition anyone whose name begins with 'C', except maybe our office cleaner Cheryl, and that's unlikely, as Cheryl's not so much the mature woman as the mature woman's mother. But, nevertheless, there must be some plans forming in that devious mind of his. And sooner or later social occasions will arise (i.e. the pub), at which numerous unknown females with random initials will be present. And how long a female will remain unknown to Tim is difficult enough to predict at the best of times.

Thursday 22nd April

8.40 p.m.

POSSIBLE REASONS WHY CLARE JORDAN HAS STILL NOT BEEN OUT FOR A POST-WORK DRINK

As discussed by Tim and Rob. Tonight. In the pub. When no one else was listening.

1. She doesn't like any of us.
Unlikely. Unless she's very good at hiding her feelings when she's in the office. And if so, why would she have got involved in that conversation about music on Tuesday?

2. She doesn't like Graham.
Of course she doesn't. None of us *like* him, 'not as such'. But that doesn't mean we storm out in protest if he joins us in the pub.

3. She's still jet-lagged.
Very, very unlikely. She's been here over a week now. And anyway, even if her body (stay calm, Rob, just write the words and stay calm) does still think it's in San Francisco, seven o'clock here will be eleven in the morning for her, so that's when she should be at her most awake.

4. She fears that her barely controllable passion for Tim would, under the influence of even the smallest amount of

alcohol, break embarrassingly free of its chains and force her to leap on him in an unabashed display of physicality.
One of us disagreed with this proposition.

5. She has social contacts in London not known about by any of us in the office, and with whom she has been spending her evenings.
What – *all* her evenings?

6. She has social contacts in London not known about by any of us in the office, and with whom she went out on one of her first evenings in the country, thereby meeting a man with whom she has since been conducting a torrid affair.
Don't do that to me, Tim. Don't even say things like that.

7. She has a boyfriend back in America, who each evening receives a lovelorn telephone call from lonely London.
Don't do that to me, Rob. Don't even say things like that.

8. She just hasn't felt like going out for a drink on any of the nights in question.
That sounds better. Shall we cling to . . . decide logically and rationally that that's the correct answer? Agreed? Good.

I like sharing this uncertainty with him. It's a bit of a leveller. Tim may be stronger when it comes to the race itself, but in the Kingdom Of Clare Jordan we are both equally blind. (Minor worries about who she was flirting with in that e-mail aside.)
   What I don't like is what happened when four or five girls came into the pub, and passed our group on their way to join some friends. One of them stopped to let a guy through who was carrying a tray of drinks. As she waited, next to Tim, he

struck up a mini-chat with her. Couldn't hear how he started it, as I was on the other side of our group talking to James and Lucy, but the usual magic was worked and he had her talking within seconds. Forget computers, he should be in double-glazing. She didn't stay more than about a minute before rejoining her friends, but the warning was there for me all the same. Moves will be made. Successes will occur. Can I keep up with him?

Saturday 24th April

11.50 a.m.

What was that I was saying on Thursday?

Last night, post-work drinks (which yet again failed to be graced by the presence of Miss Jordan) progressed, with a gradually decreasing cast list, to the point where it was just Tim and me, in a pub near Seven Dials. Not long after we got there, a group of girls came in. There were about half a dozen of them, in their early twenties, maybe even late teens, and while they were all, in their varying degrees, good-looking, and while pride and care had obviously been taken in their appearance, I didn't really find them attractive. I couldn't imagine myself being interested in them, or indeed them in me.

The two nearest us were both on their mobile phones. No doubt they were each telling friends where they were, but Tim elected to undertake a strategic misunderstanding of the situation. He put his mobile to his ear and said to me, in a voice just loud enough to carry to the girls: 'They're on the phone to each other, look.'

Even as my reflexes took over and caused me to lift my own phone to my ear, I was trying to disobey them. Don't encourage him, I told myself. Don't play along with his ruse. His chat-up lines are dangerous enough on their own, without you helping him out. But no, my reflexes were having none of it.

'Yeah,' I said into my phone. 'They're trying to pretend they've got friends.'

'Sad, isn't it?' replied Tim. The girls twigged what we were doing, and turned to face us. 'There they are, no one to talk to but each other, and they're doing it on the phone.'

The girls started to giggle. One of them, quite a short but feisty-looking blonde, finished off her call, and came over to us. She took Tim's mobile from his hand, examined it for a second, and then handed it back.

'You don't want to start talking about mobile phones when you've got one as crap as that,' she said.

'Oooh,' said Tim. 'Get her.'

A smile broke across her face. Already the assumption was there that this conversation was between her and Tim. Having performed my function as Tim's straight man, my services were no longer required. I hate it when that sort of thing happens.

A set of introductions then took place in which I felt like the kid brother who was about to be offered a tenner to go down the cinema. The mobile-phone girls were called Susie and Vicky, and once he'd chatted briefly to them Tim worked his way into the middle of the group. All I could hear as he did so was the music from *Jaws*.

I was left in a pleasant but dull conversation with Vicky. She told me about her job in a bank, I told her about personal organisers. And all the time a large dorsal fin was circling around in the middle of the girls, and a cello was going 'dum-dum' nineteen to the dozen. Tim talked to them all, but after a few minutes he seemed to latch on to one girl in particular. I couldn't hear what he was saying, but whatever it was she was laughing. My stomach tightened.

'Looks like she's enjoying herself,' I said to Vicky.

Vicky looked across. 'Oh yeah, she always does. That's my cousin. She's up from Maidstone for the weekend.'

Even though I had a nasty feeling I wasn't going to like the answer, I had to ask the question.

'What's her name?'

'Celia.'

In my mind *Jaws* fast-forwarded to the point where the kid's happily paddling around on his inflatable, unaware that the shark's right underneath him. And just as at that point you're screaming at the screen, 'MOVE, you're about to get killed by a fucking great shark!', I wanted to yell out to Celia that she should get away from Tim immediately, because she really didn't know the danger she was in. But of course that wasn't right. By the look of things Celia was only too willing to play the part of Tim's next victim. And that brought it home to me: Tim was really going for it. He was really setting the Clare Jordan Five And Three-Quarter Feet Handicap Stakes in motion. With a sense of shock, I realised that Celia wasn't the one in danger – I was. Danger of falling behind in the race. And there was nothing I could do about it. I had to watch helplessly as Tim plied her with charm and alcohol.

About ten minutes later I reached the end of my pint. Vicky's colleagues had turned up, and she'd started talking to them. The well-known phrase involving the words 'spare' and 'wedding' came to mind. I headed for the door. Passing Tim, I said: 'I'm off. See you soon.'

He broke off from the latest sentence that had Celia in its spell. 'Yeah, see you mate.'

My steps, which contained not a trace of spring, took me towards Shaftesbury Avenue. Heading the other way were a couple, walking arm in arm. As they got closer, I couldn't help staring at the woman. What made me do it? Despite her height (five-ten or so), neither her looks nor her figure nor her age (forty-two?) would earn her a place on any catwalk, those tyrannical institutions which presume to dictate what men find sexually appealing. But she was very, very horny. With the fullness of her lips, with the intelligence in her face, with the quintessential calm of one who is totally sure of herself, she filled my imagination (in just the brief moment before she was gone) with thoughts of a cottage in the Lake District, rain lashing against the windows, a log fire, a long talk, a bottle of port, and lots and lots of sex.

Many women of her age are starting to think about plastic surgery. They couldn't make a bigger mistake if they tried. Cosmetic surgeons are the enemies of true beauty. They worship at the temple of Perfection, when perfection is the least sexy thing in the world. That's why the women in *Penthouse* leave you cold. Every line around this woman's eyes had been put there by experience, experience which she'd give back to you in conversation, in bed, in everything you did together. They made her more attractive, not less, because they showed you that she'd lived, she'd discovered things about the world, she had things to say that would interest you, make you think, make you want to spend time with her. There was depth to her, a capacity to fascinate, which is the sexiest thing I know. She attracted me in a way those girls in the pub never could. The feeling she gave me was what sex is really all about, not the Clare Jordan Five And Three-Quarter Feet Handicap Stakes.

And yes, I know that all of this sounds like so much flannel from a trailing competitor. But can I say it without fear of you thinking I was merely envious of Tim's success? I certainly couldn't say it to him without that fear. Of course I was envious, but what I said just then was true in its own right as well. I promise you.

1.10 p.m.

He's just called. Suggested a committee meeting. Might as well get it over with, so I'm going round there now.

4.30 p.m.

The chart was already up in Al Pacino's place by the time I got to Tim's flat.

'Gentlemen,' he announced, standing there in an old T-shirt and an even older pair of tracksuit bottoms. Had he been wearing them last night, Celia wouldn't even have looked at him, and he wouldn't have been about to say what he was. 'This is the first meeting of the Clare Jordan Five And Three-Quarter Feet Handicap Stakes committee. It has been called to record the progress of one of the contestants. Which occurred, as it so happens, in this very flat. Last night. And, for the record, this morning as well.'

With that he turned to the chart, uncapped the black marker pen he was holding and slowly, neatly wrote the name 'Celia' at the top of the column headed 'TIM'. With each letter I was reminded of how I felt exactly a week ago, when he had first unveiled the chart to me. At first I felt slightly ashamed that, by my presence on the committee of this race (and indeed in the race itself), I was condoning the act of sleeping with someone because her name began with the right letter. But then I thought back to Celia in the bar last night. No one made her come back to Tim's flat and sleep with him. There are lots of reasons for sleeping with people. She obviously had hers, and Tim had his. Not just that her name began with 'C', either. I'm sure he really did fancy her.

'Good night, then, was it?' I asked Tim nonchalantly, deter-mined not to show any annoyance.

'Thoroughly enjoyable.'

'When's the engagement notice appearing in *The Times*?'

He laughed. 'I might discuss that with her tonight.'

'Eh?'

'She and Vicky – that's her cousin—'

'Mmm, I know,' I interrupted, casually trying to imply that more of a bond had developed between Vicky and me than was the case. I suppose you might call it an infantile gesture towards keeping Tim on his toes.

'Yeah,' he continued, 'they're going out on the town again tonight, before Celia goes back to Kent tomorrow. She said she might give me a call when they know what they're doing. Fancy coming along?'

The chart, with its five empty spaces in my column and four in Tim's, yelled out to my competitive streak. The best way of getting rid of your frustration that Tim's taken the lead, it cried, is to get straight back up and carry on fighting. Rise to the challenge. Seize the day. And indeed a girl, if you can.

'Yeah, sure. Where shall we meet?'

'Somewhere in Soho? Slug and Lettuce on Wardour Street?'

We're meeting there at eight.

Sunday 25th April

3.50 p.m.

Slug and Lettuce was packed last night. Bad, in that it took an age to get served at the three-deep bar. Good, in that the place offered ample enticement for my sexual interest to be awakened. (Or, as Tim phrased it with his customary delicacy: 'Fuck me, Babesville USA or what?')

'What time's Celia getting here?' I asked him.

'She hasn't called yet,' he replied, trying to feign indifference but incapable of resisting a glance at the door.

'Oh, right.'

'I bet they're still putting their make-up on. You know what girls are like.'

'Mmm.' I allowed myself a little smile.

By the time we reached the end of our first drink, Celia still hadn't called. This was something I couldn't help feeling smug about. 'She's obviously had a better offer.'

'Don't be stupid,' snapped Tim, obviously agitated at the thought that he might not, after all, be able to parade his conquest before me.

'No, you're right,' I said calmly. 'What could be a better offer than you?'

His jaws clenched involuntarily. 'It's your round, Rob.'

'Yes, of course, sorry.' Laughing, I went to the bar.

Twenty minutes later, even Tim had accepted that his acquaintanceship with Celia wasn't going to be renewed.

After a graceless comment to the effect that the evening wasn't missing much by this, he declared his intention to 'find another field to plough'. The absence of Celia, I realised, meant that he was free to progress to 'L', should the chance arise. Maybe it'd have been better if she *had* turned up.

I tagged along with him, and together we succeeded in starting a few preliminary conversations, curtailed either by boyfriends getting back from the bar, screensaver faces appearing when we started to bore them, or a combination of the two. It was weird, chatting people up again after such a long break from it. But once I'd managed to fight my way past the craving (still there, even now) to fall again into Sarah's reassuring embrace, I found that it was enjoyable. Forget success or failure – just making the attempt was like a ray of sunshine into all the blackness of the past few months.

By about half nine the fourth pint of Kronenbourg was nearing its Waterloo. Tim, I was heartened to see, had coped with the alcohol far less comfortably than I had (still tired from last night?), and he set off, noticeably unsteadily, for the Gents. As I waited for him to get back, I spotted a girl on the far side of the room. She was in her late twenties, with third-vertebra-from-the-top-length chestnut brown hair. Somehow she didn't seem very interested in the three girls she was standing with, and as her attention wandered around the bar she noticed me looking at her. A split second's gathering of my courage allowed me to hold her gaze. Nodding towards her companions, I gave an inquisitive raise of the eyebrows. She answered by stifling a cartoon yawn. Nerves gripped me as I realised that this was a chance. Furthermore it was a chance when Tim wasn't around. Could I take it? The chart, and in particular the five empty spaces underneath my name, flashed into my mind. And for one crucial instant those spaces got the better of my nerves. I went across.

'Boring night, then?'

'Tedious in the extreme.' She said it with a smile that gave me a little more confidence.

'Oh dear. I'm Rob, by the way.'

'Zoe.' She extended a perfectly manicured, nail-varnish-free hand. Something about her manner helped put me further at ease, and although my next question was the time-lessly uninspired 'What do you do?', it didn't sound too awkward. She worked in the press office of a record com-pany. Drawing on my limited understanding of that industry, gleaned mainly from Jane, who once had a short affair with quite a senior executive at one of the major labels, I started chatting away to her. Meandering, exploratory opinion-swaps, initially about bands, then footballers, then God knows what else. Soon, my nerves by now firmly on the back foot, we'd settled into chatting mode, and I was getting more confident by the second. After a while she offered to get us another drink (ignoring her friends, who seemed to have established a breakaway round of their own). Things were going well. Time was flying.

Unfortunately, I noticed while Zoe went to the bar, so was Tim. Unable to locate me when he got back from the Gents, he'd bought himself a vodka and tonic. It had sent him hurtling spectacularly over the cliff-edge of drinking. He was careering randomly around the bar, trying to engage people in conversation. It had gone beyond any attempt to pull. Now Tim was content merely to talk to people, irrespective of their sex. Most were amused enough to watch him, taking evasive action if he veered too close. But a few looked annoyed, and the ear-pieced Neanderthals on the door had, I noticed, started to take a worrying interest in him.

As Tim's mate I owed it to him to lend a guiding hand. As Tim's rival in the Clare Jordan Five And Three-Quarter Feet Handicap Stakes I owed it to myself not to jeopardise things with Zoe. Compromising, I decided to spare thirty seconds for him, before she could get back from the bar.

I hurried over. 'Tim, for fuck's sake pack it in with the Oliver Reed routine, will you? You're going to get thrown out if you carry on much longer.'

'FuckinellitsRob. Wairvuebinyacunt?'

'Talking to a very nice young lady, thank you for asking.'

Tim broke into an evilly conspiratorial grin. 'Whurishee?' He then span round through a full three hundred and sixty degrees, looking for the likely object of my affection. In fact he did about five hundred and ten degrees, before realising that he'd missed me on the way past, and turned slowly back again until he found me.

'She's getting me a drink,' I replied, before realising that any more talk about Zoe might cause Tim's competitiveness about the race to rear up again. 'Look mate, why don't you just go and have a sit down over there,' I indicated a spare seat at a table in the corner, 'and I'll come and check on you in a bit.'

He looked at me, drunken confusion furrowing his sweaty brow, until he alighted on the crucial snippet of information he needed: he was very, very drunk, and I wasn't. Therefore I should be trusted on all policy matters from now on in.

'SurethinRob. Juspoynemeinrydyrecshun.'

It was quite touching, really, his childlike faith in me in this, his hour of need. Putting one arm round his shoulders I guided him over to the table, positioned him in front of the chair, and let him fall on to it. For a second I thought I heard the sound of splintering wood, but no, it was all right. He just sat there, slumped near enough to the vertical to remain upright, content merely to contemplate the arrangement of beer mats in front of him.

'Sorry about this,' I said, turning to everyone else at the table. 'He's feeling a bit weary. As weary as a newt, in fact. If he starts playing up just slap him a couple of times. If that doesn't work try shooting him.'

And with that I legged it back across the bar, arriving at the space next to Zoe's group of friends just before she did. Thankfully, neither she nor they seemed to have noticed my involvement with Comedy Bar Drunk.

I found myself starting the next phase of our conversation at a deliberately marked point. 'So do you get to go out with lots of famous rock stars then?'

'Do you mean "go out with" or do you mean "go out with"?'

'Either.'

'Well, I "go out" with a few, yeah. After-gig parties, that sort of thing. But "go out" with them? Don't be silly. They're all completely obsessed with themselves.'

The glass hit her lips a fraction of a second after she'd finished speaking, and she held my gaze as she drank. Did I sense an implication that she preferred ordinary blokes? Blokes like . . . Could I allow myself the thought? Blokes like *me*? She turned towards me slightly, her arms falling to her sides. My last mouthful of lager had managed to elbow my trepidation aside for a few seconds, and I leaned into her. She didn't retreat. Before I knew what had happened I'd leaned all the way and kissed her, at first tentatively, expecting her to pull away at any moment. But then her mouth opened under mine, her tongue pushed back against mine, I took the quarter-step necessary to bring our bodies together, and we carried on kissing. I could sense her friends watching us out of the corner of their eyes, giggles replacing their conversation. After a while she pulled away, not sharply, but markedly enough to tell me that the kiss was over.

All of a sudden I'd lost the power of speech. It had been just over two years since I'd kissed a girl for the first time. (You know who that was, of course.) And now the shock, the strangeness, and – yes – the pleasure I got from doing it again had frozen my brain. While I struggled to get it working, I looked across to check that Tim was still slumbering safely in the corner. *Shit!* He'd moved. There he was, lurching about on the far side of the room. He stopped next to two girls, who stubbornly (and very wisely) refused to acknowledge his presence. So on he moved, in search of fresh victims.

Oh sod it, he'd have to fend for himself this time. Even guardian angels don't run away from a girl who's just kissed them. Especially when the bloke they're looking after is their opponent in the Clare Jordan Five And Three-Quarter Feet Handicap Stakes. Tim was on his own now.

I turned back to see that Zoe had moved across to her friends. They were all draining their drinks and gathering up their stuff.

'You off, then?' I asked, hoping for an invitation to accompany them.

'Afraid so,' replied Zoe.

No invitation then. Uncertainty clasped my heart.

'Oh, right. Can I take your number? We could go out for a drink some time.'

By now all three of Zoe's friends were past me on their way to the door. She kissed me quickly, lips firmly closed this time.

'Sorry, I don't give my number to strangers in bars.'

'But—'

It was no use. She was off.

Arse. There's many a slip 'twixt bar and bed, but this was just plain out of order. One minute it's full-on snogging without even knowing my star sign, the next she's off into the night. Leaving me (could it get any worse?) with the task of chaperoning London's Drunkest Man back home. Tempted as I was to take out my colossal disappointment on Tim by letting him get his head kicked in, I realised that that would just be childish. So I went over and yanked him away from the group of Brylcreem-and-bumfluff Essex lads who were his latest targets (and who, by the looks of it, were going to be far less sympathetic than his previous ones), marched him towards the door, muttered something to the bouncers about antibiotics, and shoved him out on to Wardour Street.

No chance of a cab within three hundred yards of there at that time on a Saturday night. So I set our course north, towards Oxford Street. The only way to cope with Tim's virtually dead weight was to stand behind him, propel him violently forwards, wait for his momentum to die down, then propel him again. A sort of horizontal human yo-yo.

The result of this was as unpleasant as it was inevitable. The one merciful detail was that it happened just as Tim had reached a small side street, thereby saving the oncoming pedestrians from the full horror of his efforts. While the pavement's redecoration was being completed, I waited on the opposite side of the street. Stewing in my pissed-offness, I aimed a kick at a discarded Coke can.

'Aimed' was the operative word. Missing it by a couple of inches, my foot carried through and expended its considerable momentum on the next object in its path – a brick wall. Collapsing in agony against the same wall, I undertook one of my occasional attempts to break the world record for consecutive swear words without repeating yourself. (This is a record held by my father, on the legendary Sunday afternoon when his lawnmower broke down seven times in an hour and a half.) I usually manage about eleven. You can guess most of them, I'm sure, but I always know I'm in trouble when I get to 'shite', which, as it's merely a corruption of 'shit', doesn't really count as not repeating yourself.

Exhausted, both physically and verbally, I slid in a pathetic lump to the ground. There I lay, waiting for the throbbing in my right big toe to subside, for Tim to finish his retching, and for a huge asteroid to come hurtling out of space and put me out of my misery.

After months of wandering an emotional and physical wilderness, I'd pulled myself together and hitched a ride back into the sexual Big City. And what had happened? It had chewed me up and spat me back out in a matter of minutes. Why had Zoe just walked off like that? She seemed to be enjoying our conversation enough. She'd definitely enjoyed our snog. Surely the least she could have done was give me her number?

Why do girls do that sort of thing?

5.20 p.m.

Look, I'm sorry to go on about this, but it's really bothering me. Why *do* girls do that sort of thing?

Flirting Without Intent. That's what it is. One of the most heinous crimes in the world, and practised almost exclusively by the female half of the species. It's barbaric, it's degrading, it's almost inhuman. A poor, defenceless man is led mercilessly up the garden path, at the end of which he is robbed of his dignity, and abandoned with nothing to his name except a burgeoning erection and a deep sense of frustration. The experience of suffering FWI has been known to traumatise men for days.

What's the point of flirting with someone when you know you're not going to do anything about it? And, more particularly, what was the point of Zoe flirting with me last night when she knew she wasn't going to do anything about it? The cruelty in her eyes as she walked out of the pub was wounding, almost physically wounding. These were the same eyes that only minutes before had been staring at me over the top of a whisky glass, beckoning me on to unimaginable heights of sexual pleasure.

Cow.

6.15 p.m.

Still fed up. What is it about this time on a Sunday that makes it so depressing?

Songs Of Praise doesn't help. Why do the TV companies *never* put anything decent on at this time? It's their scheduling blind spot of the week. Or are they part of the conspiracy? Do they deliberately keep it all God and athletics from Gateshead just to keep us pissed off? Yes, they say, you can have your cool Channel Four film premiere later on. But just for now we're going to keep the viewing so crap as to be unwatchable, forcing you to contemplate the gloomy dusk settling on the world, dragging your soul down with it. A reminder that this Sunday twilight comes around again and again, and you can never escape it. Whatever you do in the week, however much you achieve, this godforsaken time of the weekend will come relentlessly around again, a never-ending reminder of life's essential futility.

And my bloody toe still hurts.

6.25 p.m.

I've had enough. I'm calling Chris.

6.28 p.m.

Hannah answered. They both said I could go round.

10.40 p.m.

Arrived there to find Hannah in the kitchen masterminding some lasagne, and Chris in the hallway bleeding a radiator. Remembering what Hannah can be like if you disturb her during the crucial part of a recipe, I opted to sit on the stairs and chat to Chris.

Effortlessly he managed to turn that fiddly little bit at the end of the radiator with one hand, hold a bucket with the other, and engage with my points about Darren Gough's bowling, all at the same time. I wish I was practical. I couldn't bleed a radiator to save my life. I don't even know *why* you bleed radiators. Yet there was Chris, going about it as though it was the easiest thing in the world. To some people, I guess, radiators just come naturally.

Soon Hannah shouted that dinner was ready, so through to the dining room we trooped. The lasagne was lovely. Both Chris and I said so. But after the inevitable nit-pick (fraction too dry, apparently), Hannah changed the subject: 'Why did you sound such a misery-guts on the phone? What's up?'

I guided her and Chris through the events of last night (sparing them, in view of where we were, the full details of Tim's unwellness). I could see Hannah tensing in disapproval.

'What, she wouldn't even give you her phone number?' asked Chris incredulously.

'No.'

'She snogged you, and then wouldn't even give you her phone number?'

'No.'

'Not even her *phone number*?'

'No.'

'Unbelievable.' Chris took a slug of his wine. 'Why do girls think they can get away with behaviour like that?'

His indignant tone only served to heighten my sense of injustice. 'Flirting,' I declared, 'should be viewed as a contract you can hold someone to. Legally binding, if you like.'

'Try getting them to see it that way. Whereas if you fail to deliver on even the *tiniest* detail of something you've promised them, they go bloody ballistic. Like if their parents are coming round for dinner and you get back from the pub two minutes later than you said you would.'

'It was twenty-five minutes, actually,' said Hannah quietly. Written all over her face was a 'well, Rob, if you will get involved in something as objectionable as this race then you can't grumble about the consequences' comment, but she refrained from saying it out loud.

'Apart from the legality aspect,' I continued, ignoring her, '*why* do women flirt with men when they don't mean it?'

'I suppose,' said Chris after some thought, 'it's a bit like the old joke about why dogs lick their balls.'

'Because they can? I've never understood that joke. Well, I understand it, but I've never agreed with it. The last thing I'd want to do is lick my own balls. What a revolting thought.'

'Good point,' he replied. 'Just because you can do something doesn't mean you'll get pleasure out of it. For instance,

I *can* stab myself in the leg with a steak knife, but I don't go round doing it all the time.'

We both looked across at Hannah. She was smiling. It was the Hannah Smile, which is quite an annoying, knowing smile that she always does when she understands something you don't. And as the Doctrine of Female Intuition dictates that women understand lots of things that men don't, she does the Hannah Smile quite a lot.

'What?' asked Chris. 'What are you smiling at?'

'You two,' she laughed.

'It might be funny to you,' I said, 'but it's deadly serious to us.'

'Look,' she said patiently, 'girls flirt with blokes without meaning anything because it amuses us.'

'But *why*?' said Chris and I together, like the sort of six-year-olds who respond to every question with a further question.

'Because it lets us know how superior we are.'

We now turned into the sort of six-year-olds who remain sulkily silent because they know the grown-up is right.

'Men,' continued Hannah, 'have just about got the world sewn up. They're most of the politicians, nearly all of the judges, they control the biggest businesses, and they start all the wars. The only thing we poor little girlies have got going for us is the certainty that you lot think with your dicks, so we're going to get as much fun as we can by taking advantage of it.'

Still we sulked.

Hannah leaned back in her chair. 'So now we've got that cleared up – Chris, you can tidy the plates away, Rob, you make the coffee.'

Monday 26th April

2.10 p.m.

Tim this morning – what a sight. Having spent yesterday recovering from Saturday night's excess, he had the quiet pallor of an unexpectedly widowed young woman. A quick exchange of e-mails confirmed that he hadn't eaten a thing. His digestive system refused even to talk to him until about eight last night. Then he thought he might risk a bite or two. No food in the flat. A similar amount of cash in the wallet. Figuring that recourse to the Bell's bottle of discarded coppers might irreparably damage relations with his takeaway pizza place, and still not sure if the feeling in his stomach was hunger arriving or nausea departing, he opted for a food-free Sunday.

Of course this meant that by lunchtime today he was absolutely Hank Marvin. The Lunch Pub option was rejected out of hand. After Saturday night, apparently, he now realises that alcohol is the Devil's Urine, and refuses to patronise anywhere that 'peddles' the stuff. (I'll give it until six-thirty tonight at the latest.)

We found one of those 'coffee is a way of life' places on the Strand. You know, the ones that do a million types of coffee, none of which are called coffee. There's mocha, and latte, and cappuccino, and espresso, and macchiato (didn't he used to play right back for Juventus?). But just ask for a cup of coffee, and they look at you as though you're talking Chinese.

Tim had a Rustic Cheddar sandwich, a Chicken Caesar sandwich, an Apricot Danish, two Luxury Praline Chocolate bars, a bottle of Lightly Carbonated water and a Double Tall Latte. His change from fifteen quid was of insult-to-charity-tin proportions.

'The last thing I can remember,' he said, eyes narrowed as he painstakingly trawled the memory banks, 'is sitting down at that table, and finishing a white wine that someone didn't want.'

'But you don't drink white wine.'

'I know. But the lager and the vodka wanted some company, so they got together and distracted me. Anyway, what happened after that?'

I filled him in on my rescue act, the challenge he'd left for Westminster City Council, and the cab I'd levered him into on Oxford Street. But that was all I told him; he didn't seem to have any memory of Zoe, and I certainly wasn't going to give him any more ammunition by telling him about her. So I changed the subject. To something that had been worrying me, and no doubt Tim as well.

'Where's Clare today? Did she have a meeting or something this morning?'

'Dunno. The office certainly misses something when she's not around, doesn't it?'

'Mmm,' I said sombrely.

'That backside, for one.'

I cringed. I wish he wouldn't talk like that about the woman I . . . the woman I think is that sexy.

'Hey, I've just remembered,' said Tim suddenly, sitting up quickly and reaching into his jacket pocket. 'I got this in the post this morning.' He pulled out a letter. 'It's an offer they were doing the other week, when I bought that new video recorder. If you went for the more expensive model you could put your name in this draw for a load of prizes. And I've won a weekend for two in Amsterdam. Fancy it? Flights and hotel paid for. All we have to stump up is our spending money.'

'Weekend for two? We won't have to share a room, will we?'

'Nah, I've looked at the small print. We can have separate rooms if we pay an extra forty pounds. So if you want to be accurate, all we have to stump up is our spending money plus twenty quid each. Come on, it'll be a laugh. I think we can assume after Saturday night that Celia won't be interested in sharing it with me. And in case you haven't noticed, Rob, Amsterdam begins with the same letter that you'll find slap bang in the middle of a certain girl's name.'

Clearly he was winding me up. The implication was that by turning down the chance of a free trip to a place beginning with 'A' I'd be running scared of the challenge again. But quite apart from that, there was the simple consideration that it was a free (or nearly free) weekend away. The Clare Jordan Five And Three-Quarter Feet Handicap Stakes was a side issue; self-interest on its own was sufficient grounds for accepting Tim's offer. 'Yeah, OK. Cheers.'

'Great. I'll give them a call this afternoon, find out when we can go. There's one of those "subject to availability" clauses.'

2.45 p.m.

We've just overheard one of the people Clare works with – she's ill. Not coming in at all today. I'm coping with this cloud of disappointment by reminding myself of its silver linings. For instance, although it means I can't engage in any further efforts at establishing a rapport with her, it also means Tim can't advance his cause either.

Actually, that's about as far as I've got with silver linings. The cloud is just too bloody big. Or rather the worry that the cloud isn't the cloud it appears to be is just too bloody big. By which I mean: is she really ill? Has her boyfriend flown over from America? Is she spending time with a new boyfriend she's already found over here? Where is she today? What is she doing? With whom is she doing it?

Tim says he's sure she's just ill. I'm sure he's right.

2.50 p.m.

Tim says perhaps she is throwing a sickie after all. What does he know about anything?

3.50 p.m.

Tim's just called the competition people. Apparently it's the weekend after next or we have to wait until July – everything between now and then's gone. It's a bit soon, but neither of us have got anything planned for that weekend, so we might as well go for it. After all, it's something to look forward to. Takes my mind off the current absence from the office.

3.53 p.m.

He's now sent me an e-mail: 'That does, of course, only give you a week and a half to do "C" and "L".'

I think everyone else would notice if I broke my chair over his head.

Tuesday 27th April

11.15 a.m.

Still no Clare.

Further musings between Tim and me as to the real reason for her absence from the office. Pretty much the same conclusion as yesterday. In other words we haven't got a single clue to go on, but plenty of time to worry about it.

Then again, the mystery is, in one way, making this all the more exciting. You could even say it's making Clare all the more sexy. Maybe that's the answer I was searching for the other day, when I first told you about her. 'Sexiness is the thing you don't know.' Yeah, I like that. That tunnels somewhere near the heart of the matter. It's a bit like the old line about the shot of a closing bedroom door being sexier than the most explicit porn film. 'Sexiness is the thing you don't know.' I'm going to remember that one.

10.40 p.m.

We all met Jane tonight, to give her our deposits for this parachute jump. Final roll-call of Intrepids from the office is self, Tim, James, Lucy (I don't think she was overly keen – the deciding factor must have been the thought of her boyfriend spending a weekend away with Jane), Graham and Paul. Paul is a decent enough bloke, a couple of years younger than the rest of us, but always good value because he's the King of Trivia. Whatever you're talking about, Paul seems to know an interesting little fact about it. He once told me, for instance, how the 1966 World Cup Final would have been decided if it was still level at the end of extra time. (Toss of a coin.)

Simon declined the invitation in the end. I think he was put off by having to ask Michelle for permission.

We met Jane in the Dog and Duck, one of the last places left in Soho that's no-nonsense enough to satisfy her northern bluntness.

'Hello, look at all these big, handsome men come to see me,' she boomed across the crowded pub as we entered. James instinctively placed a pacifying hand on the small of Lucy's back.

We split into two rounds for drinking. Jane and Tim were first up to the bar. Our table was near enough for me to be able to hear what they were saying.

'How's your love life then?' she asked, eyes-a-twinkling, as they waited to get served. A typically subtle specimen from her repertoire of openers.

'Dormant,' he replied, with a hammed-up expression of misery. She probably guessed he wasn't telling the whole truth. As his opponent in the Clare Jordan Five And Three-Quarter Feet Handicap Stakes, I definitely wished he was.

'Oh, that's such a waste, strapping young lad like you,' said Jane, going along with the joke while squeezing Tim's arm. Tim laughed, not pulling away, but then not reciprocating the contact either. Clearly he didn't want to be rude. Neither, though, did he want to encourage Jane's attentions too much. 'Well,' she said, taking her hand away, 'I'm sure it won't be long before some lucky girl gets hold of you.'

While all this was going on, I noticed Lucy watching Jane. 'The way she makes her breasts heave like that is incredible, isn't it?' she muttered to me.

'Yeah.' Then something occurred to me. 'Hang on, Luce, if I'd said that you'd have called me a typical man and accused me of being fixated by breasts.'

'Yes.'

'So why is it OK for you to comment on a woman's body, but not me?'

'Very simple, Rob. I'm a woman, you're not.'

I started to formulate a reply about how unfair this was, but then thought better of it. There are, I suppose, worse injustices in the world.

Once Jane was back at the table, and had divvied out the drinks, she set about explaining everything. 'I've booked us in for the first weekend in June. We have to be there by eight o'clock on the Saturday morning.'

'Where is it again?' asked Paul.

'Some airfield in Leicestershire. Right in the middle of nowhere. The directions have got lots of village names in them, things like Something Parva and Lower Wotsit. Looks like it'll take an age to find it.'

'And we've got to be there for eight in the morning? Christ, we'll have to set out on the Friday night.'

'The training takes all day, apparently. If the wind's OK you can do your jump last thing on the Saturday, but they say that's pretty rare at this time of year – something to do with summer thermals – so it's odds on we'll have to camp over until the Sunday.'

'Camp?' said Graham. 'SplenDEEDO! I can use my mountaineering tent. It's a professional one. Cost a fortune.'

We all looked at him. This was typical Graham. Why the *fuck* had he got a professional mountaineering tent? Any expedition foolish enough to include him in its ranks would collapse within hours, its morale sapped to buggery by his incessant stream of terrible jokes.

Graham must have mistaken our bewilderment for envy, because he hurriedly added: 'But I'm afraid it's only a one-man tent, so unfortunately I won't be able to offer to share with anyone.'

'I'm sure I speak for the group,' said Tim, 'when I say how devastated we all are by that fact, Graham.'

'We've got a tent, haven't we, darling?' said Lucy.

'Have we?' James looked puzzled.

'Yes, you remember – that one your brother gave us after he went to Glastonbury that year. Said he never wanted to see the damn thing again, brought back too many memories of dodgy burgers and chemical toilets. We put it in the loft, said you never know when you might need something like that. And here we are.'

'So that's you three sorted, then,' said Jane. 'The rest of us can hire them at the place. They do them for about a tenner a night, I think. And talking of money, cough up everyone. I've got to get those deposits in the post tomorrow.'

Collective retrieval of wallets and purses. James wrote out a sixty-quid cheque for himself and Lucy, and as he handed it to Jane I noticed it was a joint account. Scary. Very, very scary. The sight of two names below an amount box always sends a little shudder through me. Commitment can be a beautiful thing, but does it have to be so brutally expressed? Can't you retain at least some aspects of your privacy, your individuality? Having someone else's name on my cheques would be like swapping half of my DNA for half of theirs. (And yet, thinking about it, wasn't I close to some sort of commitment, if not a joint bank account, with Sarah?)

Jane had taken out her purse ready to receive all our dosh, and it was lying open on the table. Sitting next to her, I peered down at all her credit and store cards. Their zitty silver initials looked back up at me in neat little rows. And I noticed something that made me – in very quick succession – curious, then thoughtful, then animated.

'Is Jane your *middle* name?' I asked in an offhand way, but making sure that Tim heard as well. His brain was alert to the danger in an instant. He sat bolt upright, and tried to peer across at the cards himself, but a cluster of pint glasses in front of Jane's purse was blocking his view. Somehow I managed to contain my growing sense of exhilaration.

'Yeah, it is,' replied Jane. 'I've always hated my real first name. Even as a child. I've got a dotty old gran who still uses it, but apart from her everyone's always called me Jane.'

'What is it, then?' I asked, shooting Tim a loaded glance.

'Oh, I can't tell you. Really, it's horrible.'

'No, come on, Jane,' said Paul, unwittingly coming to my aid. 'What is it?' By now Tim was looking seriously concerned.

'You'll laugh, I know you will.'

'No we won't. Promise.'

'Abigail.' Jane's reluctant mumble was like that of a child forced to apologise to a classmate. I grinned at Tim, barely able to suppress my amusement. And then, worrying that the others might notice, I took a long, calming drink of beer.

'What's wrong with Abigail?' asked Paul.

'Yeah, I think it's a lovely name,' added Lucy.

There were reassuring murmurs of assent from the others around the table. Except me and Tim. We were staring at each other, our eyes conducting a silent conversation. Mine were gloating, teasing him: 'Hey hey, Tim's got his "A" all lined up here, ready and waiting for him. So the question he's got to ask himself is how much does he want to win? What is he prepared to do for the sake of the Clare Jordan Five And Three-Quarter Feet Handicap Stakes?' His were burning defiantly, furiously back at me: 'No fucking way, sunshine. If you think I'm going to sleep with Jane just for the sake of this stupid bloody competition you've got another think coming.' I felt a little guilty at considering Jane in these terms as she sat right next to me, but it's not as though Tim's actually going to do anything with her. He's always resisted Jane's advances, and the race isn't going to make him change his mind now. But until he can find another 'A', I've got something to needle him with. Our wind-up capabilities are now a little more evenly matched.

Later on, Tim and I walked to the Tube together.

'Abigail, eh? Well, well, well. That's handy, isn't it?'

'Fuck off, Rob. You know full well that I'm not going to have sex with Abigail. I mean Jane.'

'Come on, don't dismiss it out of hand. It'd be silly to narrow down your options unnecessarily at this early stage.'

'I'm not narrowing them down. This one isn't even an option to begin with.'

'Oh, I don't know. I think we could find that as time progresses Tim might become strangely drawn to the possibility of sleeping with Jane. I mean Abigail.'

'Rob, my "A" is going to come from somewhere else. Anywhere else. I am not going to sleep with her. End of story.'

That counts as 'mildly rattled' at least, don't you think? And for what it's worth – which, yes, I know isn't much, because this race is hardly the most wholesome entertainment in the world – but for what it's worth, I found that I was enjoying myself.

Wednesday 28th April

2.40 p.m.

Clare still ill. (Or whatever the real story is . . .)

I really do miss her. Yes, OK, I miss her legs (or, as Tim insisted on calling them today, her 'pins') – but also I miss her . . . I miss her *being* here.

3.10 p.m.

There's a glint in Tim's eye. One with which I do not feel entirely comfortable. He's been text-messaging someone, on and off, for the past half an hour.

I bet I've got the same feeling he had last night when I asked Jane about her name. Not that I'm going to give him the satisfaction of asking him about it, of course. No doubt all will be revealed soon enough.

6.45 p.m.

Have just got back home to find Helen ironing her bunny rabbit pyjamas. After spending so much of the afternoon thinking about the Clare Jordan Five And Three-Quarter Feet Handicap Stakes, it was a bit like running into Julie Andrews in a Thai brothel.

Thursday 29th April

2.50 p.m.

I knew I was right to be worried about Tim's texting.

Got in to the office this morning to find a message on my voicemail: 'Morning, camper. Tim here. Bright and early, on my way into work. Might take a while, though, as I'm on my way into work from Wimbledon, and you know what this District line can be like. Anyhow, I was ringing to propose a spot of lunch. How about that place we went to on Monday? See you presently.'

My spirits sank. No diploma from detective school needed to spot the clues here. Why was he on his way in from Wimbledon, and why was he suggesting we go to the Coffee Place rather than the Lunch Pub? The second one was easy enough – he wanted to keep our conversation secret from everyone else, so therefore it was going to be about the Clare Jordan Five And Three-Quarter Feet Handicap Stakes. And the first? Well I couldn't yet know the specifics, but a girl was no doubt going to be involved. A girl whose name began with a particular letter, usually found somewhere between 'k' and 'm'.

So the morning dragged twice as much as normal. And the way mornings have been dragging without Clare here, that's saying something.

Tim kept me in suspense until we were sitting down in the Coffee Place. (Drink Of The Day was Monté Bianco, by the way. Couldn't be arsed to work out what that actually is, so I had a cup of tea instead.)

'You're probably wondering why I suggested lunch,' he said.

Of course I wasn't. And he knew it. 'Funnily enough, Tim, I rather fancy that I've got an inkling why it might be.' The coating of sarcasm on my words was just a bit too obvious, I realised. The last thing I wanted to do was let him think he'd got to me. So with a superhuman effort, I managed to revert to affected disinterest. 'My bet is that this is a meeting of the Clare Jordan Five And Three-Quarter Feet Handicap Stakes committee, and that somewhere in Wimbledon lives a girl whose name begins with "L".'

By fronting him out I'd managed to steal a little of his thunder. But, nevertheless, when he said the name it still shot a tiny dart of annoyance into me.

'You're right – Lisa, as it happens.'

I took a bite of my Avocado and Pistachio Wrap to compose myself. 'Nice girl, is she?'

'Very nice. Just as nice as when we were going out together a couple of years ago.'

'*WHAT?*' I shouted, causing several people to turn round. Lowering my volume control, I carried on. 'You slept with an ex-girlfriend?'

'Yeah. Why not? There's nothing in the rules about that.'

Perfectly true. Funnily, though, I found that I wasn't really bothered about what was and wasn't in the rules. The thing that was getting to me was . . . well, it was what I feel about Clare Jordan. I wanted to yell at Tim, who was now staring out of the window, that I find her sexy in a way that goes far beyond his superficial titsandbummery, that my appreciation of her is far more deeply rooted than his. But what would I have been claiming by this? That I'm somehow better than he is, just because I see things in Clare that he can't, and because I can see why some people might disapprove of the Clare Jordan Five And Three-Quarter Feet Handicap Stakes? I'm still taking part in it, aren't I? I'm still bothered that I'm two–nil down.

Suddenly Tim's attention was caught by something on the other side of the Strand. You could almost see the light bulb appear over his head.

'Now *that* is an idea. An idea for getting girls. It could work for both of us as well.'

I followed his gaze, but couldn't work out what the cause of his inspiration was. The only buildings in his line of sight were a discount bookshop, a chemist's and a tourist-trap Italian restaurant. The link between any of these and an ability to attract girls remained a mystery to me.

'What? What is an idea?'

'Ah, you see but you do not observe, Watson. Come with me, and all will be revealed.'

We crossed the first half of the Strand, traffic keeping us on the small central reservation for a few seconds.

'There,' said Tim. 'See it yet?'

'No. Give me a clue.'

'As we look from here, it's between those two lamp posts.'

Nothing. Nothing that could possibly have anything to do with attracting the opposite sex. The three establishments mentioned above, plus, from our angle of approach, about two feet of Tesco Metro. And unless Tim was planning a mass seduction campaign involving expensive pâté and maraschino cherries, I didn't see how that could be involved.

Dashing between a couple of buses, we reached the other side of the road.

'You must have it by now?'

I looked around. 'No idea. Come on, what are you going on about?'

'Over there.' He pointed. And there it was – a phonebox. So commonplace that I hadn't even noticed it. As we approached it, I got the first horrific inkling of what Tim had in mind. Inside the phonebox was plastered, as are so many of central London's phoneboxes, with brightly coloured cards advertising the services offered by various women, all of them only a short walk away.

'Yes Tim, very funny.' I refused to believe that he was even half-serious about this.

'No, come on,' he said earnestly, opening the door. 'Hear me out.'

We wedged into the phonebox, and peered round at the cards.

'"Tie and tease, aim to please,"' said Tim. I followed his gaze to the top-right hand corner, where said slogan was emblazoned in flirtatious red italics across a phone number.

'That's very customer-orientated of her and all that Tim, but really, this is scraping—'

'"Slim, leggy blonde, new in town."'

The blonde in the photo was certainly slim and leggy. She was equally certainly not the woman who awaited anyone foolish enough to ring the telephone number on the card. I relayed this fact to Tim.

'You seem to know an awful lot about the subject,' he said.

'I read an article about it in the *Standard* once.'

'Likely story.'

'Even the ones that have got "genuine photo" on them aren't the real girl. You get round there, you're confronted with some toothless geriatric ogre, you complain that the card said "genuine photo", and they say yeah, that's right, it's just a genuine photo of someone else.'

'All those O and A levels,' mused Tim. 'These girls should be at university, not selling their bodies.'

'Tim, what the bloody hell are you going on about? You're not seriously suggesting that either of us buy our progress in the Clare Jordan Five And Three-Quarter Feet Handicap Stakes by calling any of these numbers, are you? Quite apart from the small matter of self-respect, it may be easy for you to pick out a name, but I'm doing places, remember? . . . Oh, is that your game? This option's a doddle for you, but nigh on impossible for me.'

'No, don't be stupid,' he replied. 'I'm not suggesting that we call any of *these* prostitutes. I'm saying that this is the ideal solution for next weekend. Where are we going then? And what is that city famous for?'

Slowly his reasoning started to dawn on me.

'It's all much more respectable over there,' he continued. 'Almost part of the Amsterdam experience, if you like. I can find a girl whose name begins with "A", and you can pick any girl you like, because the place will begin with "A".'

I couldn't believe I was hearing this. Even if Tim was willing to pay for sex just to get on in the race, I certainly wasn't. I've got nothing against the oldest profession, it's just that I myself don't want to use its services.

But that wasn't what Tim was driving at. 'Oh, hang on a minute,' he said. 'I think there's a problem with that . . . what is it? . . . just can't quite put my finger on it . . . oh, of *course* – Rob hasn't done his "C" or "L" yet, has he? Silly me.'

Here we go, I thought. Another bout of mockery. I just wasn't in the mood for it, so settling for a dignified, 'If you've quite finished being a complete arsehole, shall we get back to work?', I set off towards the office, accompanied by a quietly chuckling Tim.

3.30 p.m.

'True strength,' goes the old proverb, 'is shown not by never falling, but by rising each time you fall.'

Surely I can rise this time? Tim might be the naturally gifted one, but I can graft. There were initial signs of success on Saturday night, for example, in spite of the fact that Zoe turned out to be Flirting Without Intent.

Besides which, I've had a brainwave. If you can't beat them, nick their tactics. Tonight I shall be placing a telephone call.

7.40 p.m.

Call placed. Message left. Reply awaited.

Friday 30th April

11.25 a.m.

Ladies and gentlemen: Clare Jordan Has Re-Entered The Building.

In a trouser suit.

She's never worn one of those before.

She seems a bit subdued. Hardly looking up from her desk, working away at catching up on e-mails and the like. This is making her even more attractive, in much the same way that at a party you notice the person sitting on their own not saying anything rather than everyone else making all the noise. Tim, I can tell, is disappointed that she's wearing trousers. But in a strange way I think they're sexier than her skirts. Her legs being hidden from view adds to the anticipation, like knowing there's a great present wrapped up for you under the Christmas tree. But will either Tim or I ever get to unwrap the present? Or has Santa already delivered her to someone else?

2.50 p.m.

A few minutes ago, when Clare made a phone call, I found myself fervently hoping (as, I realised, I now do on all her phone calls) that she wasn't going to start with that classic giveaway, the 'hi, it's me' greeting.

She didn't.

But God knows what I'll do if she ever does.

I think I'd be able to stop myself going over to her desk, ripping the phone out of her hand, and saying, 'Who is this, please? And what is the precise nature of your relationship with Clare Jordan? Because if it involves duvets, I must request that you cease all contact with Miss Jordan forthwith.'

Just able to stop myself.

3.05 p.m.

Enough about Clare's telephone calls. My one of last night has just been returned.

Thankfully Kate called my mobile while I was on my way back from the loo, which meant that I could nip up on to the roof (where the smokers go) and chat to her in private. Five minutes or so of our lives' recent headlines, followed by an arrangement to fill in the details on Sunday afternoon, when we're going to meet up. As I pressed the 'end' button and put the phone back in my pocket, I realised that I felt nervous. Will I really try to go through with this? Zoe had been a complete stranger – but this was Kate.

Yes, those were the tactics I was talking about nicking. Kate is an ex. An ex that I've slept with once or twice since we split up.

Some of you, I notice, are giving me a disapproving look. I rather feared you might, so I've been thinking about how I could best respond. And what I've arrived at is this: men have the ability to differentiate between various types of sex. It can be the expression of a tender, sincere love – but it isn't always. It's not that blokes don't think there's an emotional aspect to sex; it's just that they don't think there *has* to be one. So even if you still feel something for an ex, you can sleep with her again without there being any expectation of you getting back together. That may not be a very comfortable message, and I know it doesn't make us look very grown-up – but I'm afraid it's the truth. And anyway, me going to bed with an ex also means she went to bed with me, so I don't think I should take all the blame.

Whether or not that convinces you of the advisability of what I'm doing, I don't know. On the way back down to the office I had some fairly hefty doubts myself. But when I got there Tim started whistling *Tulips From Amsterdam*, and all of a sudden I felt incredibly galvanised.

Saturday 1st May

10.25 a.m.

Helen's gone out shopping, so it's just me, a bowl of Frosties and kids' TV.

Don't feel quite so keyed up about tomorrow without Tim and his puerile taunting. (Which I suppose means that I'm puerile for being affected by it, but at least it got me over my nerves.)

Have tried distracting myself from my worries by thinking about the inspiration for the race herself. How is she spending her Saturday morning? Are the transatlantic phone lines buzzing? Can't be – even if she has got a boyfriend, it's the middle of the night in America. And why would a man, on his own, in bed, at 2.30 a.m., possibly want to listen to his girl-friend on the other end of a phone line . . .

So now I need something to distract me from the distraction.

Sunday 2nd May

8.20 p.m.

As the Tube stations paraded themselves before me this afternoon, my mind flitted back over my past with Kate. Farringdon found us in bed together for the first time since we'd split up. After six weeks of amicable 'it wasn't working, let's still be friends' peace, one summer evening's tequila intake persuaded us both that although It might not have been working, our libidos still were. The sex was as good as it had always been. Indeed, if anything, the fact that it was technically now illicit added an extra veneer of excitement. Morning-after awkwardness hung in the air, but only until Kate and I went to say 'sorry' at the same time, and we burst out laughing. She wore my dressing gown to visit the bathroom, there was not so much as a cuddle (let alone a kiss), and the incident, we agreed, was to be written off as nothing more than a drunken mistake. You could even say, looking back on it, that it was the last time we made love during our relationship rather than the first one after it.

By Barbican, though, my first doubts had showed up. Our next sex had been a few months later, after a party at her flat. Twice I'd mentioned getting back home, and twice she'd told me not to be so boring. We ended up being the last two left, and . . . well, you don't need to know the details. (Sorry. I did warn you at the beginning of all this that graphic descriptions wouldn't be forthcoming.) Now, the male mind (and indeed the male conscience) can, as I said the other day, split sex up from its emotional implications. The sex Kate and I had that night was great, but I was perfectly capable of enjoying it on a 'fun between friends' basis rather than expecting it to lead to us getting back together. I knew as I walked away from her flat the next day that our sex hadn't been meaningless (it wouldn't have been as good if it had) – but neither had it meant everything.

Equally, though (and this is where my doubts showed up), I knew that just because men can paddle in such waters (call them shallow if you must – I won't argue with you), women, I assume, usually don't. Kate didn't suggest after that night (or indeed ever) that we give our relationship another go. My conscience was happy to take her silence as confirmation that she too classed the sex as fun and nothing more. But did she really? Was she secretly hoping for more? And how did that affect how I saw this afternoon?

As we pulled into Moorgate, I had a moment of wishing that I could be one of those guys who doesn't mind hurting girls. In terms of increasing the score it's ideal: you shag them, you go and find the next one to shag. Tim operates like that. More than once I've heard him lying to women who at the time supposed themselves to be his girlfriend. If I could play things that way, this afternoon would be no problem at all. Say or imply whatever it took to get Kate's consent; quick call on the mobile to Tim when she wasn't listening; agree a location beginning with 'C'; engineer it so that that consent was acted on in that location.

Even before the train set off again, however, I knew I was glad not to be that sort of bloke. By Liverpool Street, my sense of morality was lying slumped opposite me, exhausted by its efforts to keep on the straight and narrow. Leave it up to Kate, it was telling me. Just see how this afternoon goes. No point worrying about all the decisions in advance.

We'd arranged to meet just outside the Tube station and go for a walk round Spitalfields market (Kate lives near there). As usual she was late. It was quarter past one before she came bounding up. Not that the run took anything out of her, as she spends a lot of time in the gym, a habit left over from her training as a dancer, before the financial realities of showbiz persuaded her into a career as a legal secretary. Her face is pretty in a thin, angular way – great cheekbones. And her hair today looked closer to blonde than the fair it used to be. Part bottle, she said when I commented on it, part two weeks in the Spanish sun. I didn't ask who the Spanish sun had been shared with.

We spent a while wandering around the stalls. The packed-out market (the weather was glorious today) turned us into slow-motion pinballs, shunted wherever the crowd's flow dictated. Some of the stalls were the same as three years ago, when we used to come here virtually every Sunday. Some had changed. But the general product range was essentially the same: lava lamps, garish Mexican clothing, cheap CDs. After a while the crush and the tat started to annoy us (why did we used to go there so much? I suppose it must mean we were at least a bit in love, to be that blind), so we went for a drink.

'What do you fancy?' I asked Kate as we stood at the bar.

She gave the tiniest hint of a grin, the slightest quizzical tilt of her head.

'You know what I mean,' I smiled. 'What do you want to drink?'

'Half a lager.'

'Right. Now go and grab that table in the corner before anyone else gets it.' As she went Kate brushed her hand gently across the lower part of my back. It took no fewer than four deep breaths to return my heartbeat to normal. It wasn't so much the minor sexual frisson of the moment that had affected me, more the moral debate that that frisson had restarted.

I got her a half, and a pint for myself, and took them over to the table. Having put down her flirting marker, Kate reverted to normal conversation – asking about work, that sort of thing. I told her about going to Tokyo (with the firm, about four months ago), and James's now legendary performance of *Karma Chameleon* in the karaoke bar. I updated her on Simon's entry for Most Half-Hearted Engagement Ever. But I did not mention the arrival of Clare Jordan. The omission, of course, was deliberate. And the more I realised it was deliberate, the bigger my seed of guilt grew. Tell her about Clare, Rob, and you'll tell her about the Clare Jordan Five And Three-Quarter Feet Handicap Stakes. Tell her about the Clare Jordan Five And Three-Quarter Feet Handicap Stakes and . . . well, that didn't even bear thinking about.

The pint and a half became two pints in Kate's round. She filled me in on her work news. Still at the same firm, but switched to working for a different partner, who treats her a lot better. Now that I was listening rather than talking it meant I was no longer deliberately omitting the Clare information. But that was just a technicality, and my conscience knew it – so still the seed grew. By now it was a small sapling.

Before I knew it we were nearing the end of our second drink.

'I think I'm a bit hungry,' said Kate. 'Fancy something to eat?'

'Yeah, why not?' We spotted a blackboard listing the Usual Suspects of pub food (gammon and chips, chilli con carne, steak and mushroom pie, you know the sort of thing). Kate went for a chicken burger, while I opted for the ploughman's lunch.

I went to the bar to order our food, and while I was there got another couple of pints.

'I haven't told you about my new tattoo, have I?' asked Kate when I got back.

'You haven't had another one?' She knew I'd never been convinced by her tattoo, which she'd had done just after we started going out together. It was a weird astrological symbol, a star exploding out of what was apparently some lucky constellation from the other side of Saturn, but which looked to me like a bottle of Dettol. It was located where the back of her left hip started to become the top of her buttock.

'Yes, as a matter of fact, I have,' she said. 'Without Mr Boring around to moan at me I can have all the tattoos I like, remember?'

'I'm not Mr Boring,' I countered. And then, almost without realising that I was upping the bidding a little: 'It's just that with a body as beautiful as yours I don't see why you need to plaster pictures all over it.' She flushed a little at the compliment. 'And even if they're acceptable now, what are they going to look like when you're sixty?'

'I can have them removed by laser if I go off them. And anyway, the new one will still look pretty – it's a tiny flower.' She paused for a drink of beer. 'You haven't asked where it is yet.'

'All right. Where's your new tattoo, Kate?'

'Guess.'

I laughed. 'Well, let me think.' I surveyed her cropped T-shirt, her trousers that reached no further than halfway down her shins, and her sandals. 'I can't see it, so I would guess that it's . . . on the back of your right knee.'

'Don't be stupid.'

'All right then, where is it?'

At that point the guy behind the bar brought our food across.

'Thanks,' we both said. I took a mouthful of bread and cheese while I waited for him to retreat out of hearing distance. But before I could swallow it, Kate spoke.

'So what's your romantic situation at the moment then?'

Oh, I see. The question remains unanswered, does it? That, coupled with the nature of Kate's new enquiry, made my spine tingle. It also grew another couple of branches on the Guilt Tree.

'I haven't got one,' I said. 'How about you?'

'The same.'

There was a momentary, and slightly uncomfortable, silence, which Kate broke by asking me where I'd bought my trainers. For the rest of our time in the pub we chatted about this and that. But the terms of engagement had shifted. Hanging in the air now, I felt sure, was the assumption that we could well end up in bed together. I felt my mobile phone through my trousers. Could I, at some point, get away from Kate, call Tim and sort out a 'C'? Could I really do it? His version of 'Tulips From Amsterdam' echoed round my memory. There was no doubt about it, I definitely wanted to get started in the race. But was that desire strong enough to distract me from the Guilt Tree?

After we'd finished our food, we wandered back out into the sun. The market was winding down now, and one or two stallholders had started to pack up. We meandered through the thinning crowds, pleasurably woozy from our drinking. Our steps began to trace what we both knew, although neither of us said, was the well-worn route to Kate's flat. After a few minutes, when we'd turned from Brick Lane into one of the quieter side streets, she said, just as though the thought had entered her head that very second: 'Oh, you never guessed where my tattoo was, did you?'

At this my spine got another tingle, at least two more branches (heavy ones at that) grew on the Guilt Tree, and something else started to happen that I'm not going to tell you about but you can probably guess. I stayed silent, torn between a desire to get on the phone to Tim, a feeling of being a complete shit who should just walk away without another word, and a need to explain to Kate what this was all about.

No, that's unfair. This wasn't *all* about the race. OK, the Clare Jordan Five And Three-Quarter Feet Handicap Stakes was the immediate reason I'd met up with her. But she and I had done this sort of thing before anyway. If Tim and I hadn't started this stupid race, and I'd just happened to meet up with Kate today, and we'd had the day we'd just had, then exactly the same thing would have happened. The first word of that sentence, though, was the operative one, and I knew it. Tim and I *had* started this stupid race, and I *hadn't* 'just happened' to meet up with Kate today. The Guilt Tree was now spreading its branches all over me, blocking my vision, pulling me down to the ground, slowly beginning to strangle me.

I stopped dead in my tracks. 'Kate, I've got something to say.'

She'd carried on for a couple of steps, and so turned to face me. She saw straight away from my expression that the boozy flirtatiousness had come to an end, and that I was about to say something serious.

'You *are* seeing someone at the moment, aren't you?' she asked.

It hadn't even occurred to me that this was the obvious assumption to make. 'God, no.' I paused. 'It's a bit more complicated than that.'

She looked confused, lost now that the game had suddenly been interrupted.

'Look,' I said, 'I'll come straight out with this, and if you want me to leave after I've said it then just say so and I'll go.'

I took a deep breath, stared at a point on the ground about three feet behind Kate and a foot to the side of her, and went for it. 'Tim and I both fancy this new girl at work, and her name's Clare, and we've set up this competition to decide who can ask her out first. Tim's got to have sex with five girls whose names begin with "C", "L", "A" and so on, and I've got to have sex in five different places which begin with . . .'

My voice trailed away. My obvious distress at explaining the race to Kate told her everything she needed to know about her proposed involvement in it. I could sense her staring back at me, but still didn't have the courage to look up. All I could do was stand there and wait for her reaction.

The perfect punch, boxers always say, has two defining qualities. I'd always longed to know if they're true. One, it drops you straight down on the vertical. It's not a force that lifts you up and launches you ten feet across the room, as Hollywood punches always do. It's an impact on your brain that stops it telling your legs how to stand up, so that they just buckle underneath you and you drop. And two, it gives you the best feeling in the world as you complete that drop; sounds perverse, but because your brain accepts that it's encountered a haymaker it knows there's no point in fighting back any more, so you simply relax and feel wonderful. When you wake up in hospital, of course, your jaw can move in seven different directions and you feel as though you've been hit by a tank. But at the time, in the second or two it takes you to hit the canvas, you feel utterly at peace and free from pain.

If I ever find out whether those two things are true, I'll let you know. Because Kate's punch was far from perfect. It was also, however, far from feeble. Because I was staring at the ground, and because her fist came in from shoulder level (a hook rather than an upper cut), I didn't see it until the very last moment. Connection occurred on the bony bit of my left eye-socket, and all I can say is that I was far from at peace, and as enslaved to pain as I think I've ever been in my life. Without knowing why (I think it must have been the shock), I fell to the ground, my left hand clasped over my eyes, my right hand over my left. For about thirty seconds I stayed like that, content to commune with my new friend, the pavement.

Eventually I looked up. Kate was standing about ten yards away, surveying me with a look half of worry that she might have hurt me quite badly, and half in hope that she had hurt me quite badly. She was rubbing the back of her right hand.

'Are you all right?' I asked. The pain as I spoke was incredible, but I felt it wiser to ask about Kate first, in the hope that she'd feel guilty.

'I think so,' she replied rudely. And then, realising that it would be unreasonably sullen not to return the enquiry, 'You?'

'I'll live. I think.' Although if this pain wasn't going to subside soon then perhaps death might be preferable.

I clambered to my feet. 'I'm sorry, Kate.'

'So am I,' she said. 'I shouldn't have hit you. But did you really think that I'd—'

'No,' I interrupted her, 'don't say it. No, I didn't think . . . that. I'm sorry. Really I am.' I hoped she realised I'd been guilty only of a misjudgement, rather than not feeling anything for her. But the look of anger on her face didn't do much to feed that hope. 'I'd better go.'

'Yeah.'

'I'll see you, then. I'll ring, I promise.'

'Oh fuck off, Rob.'

As I walked back to the Tube, my eye having settled down from pain to a constant throb, I felt thoroughly, comprehensively pissed off. Glad ... no, scrub that – I was too despondent to feel anything like gladness ... relieved that nothing had happened with Kate, but also annoyed that nothing had happened with anyone.

Am I *ever* going to get off the mark in this bloody race?

Monday 3rd May

8.10 a.m.

This is not good news.

This is definitely not good news.

There is no way, within the context of the Clare Jordan Five And Three-Quarter Feet Handicap Stakes, that a black eye can possibly be construed as good news.

Well, not black really. More a dark red, touching on purple in places, with the odd hint of green. But the effect is still the same. Not only will it severely reduce the chances of Clare fancying me (and being realistic, what are those chances to start with? Someone *please* tell me), but there is every danger that questions will be asked. Awkward questions. Especially with Tim around.

Oh Christ.

Options:

1. Call in sick.
No way, Pele. I am *not* leaving Clare Jordan alone with an unsupervised Tim.

2. Make-up.
Could ask Helen to put some on for me. But very risky. A fraction too much and one of the runners in the Clare Jordan Five And Three-Quarter Feet Stakes gets laughed off the course amid rumours of cross-dressing. And even if Helen gets it

right now, you have to top that stuff up throughout the day, don't you? No, forget it.

3. Sunglasses.
I can't believe I've even written that down.

What the *hell* am I going to do?

9.40 a.m.

I don't often get visited by divine flashes of inspiration on the Monday morning tube journey into work. But boy was that a divine flash. Thank you, thank you, thank you. All I've got to do now is keep my head down (literally), and wait for the right moment.

9.50 a.m.

Tim's just got in. Wait until he finds out what I've got up my sleeve (or rather, on the side of my face).

10.05 a.m.

Still got my head down, still waiting for the right moment.

10.17 a.m.

Right moment is now. Here goes. Wish me luck.

10.26 a.m.

The scene is as follows: Clare Jordan is at the printer, which is halfway between her bit of the office and ours, waiting for what is obviously a very long document to finish printing out. Yours truly, for the first time this morning, raises his head from an intense period of concentrated reading, for most of which his forehead has been cradled in his left hand, and picks up his mug.

'Anyone else for a coffee?' I ask, standing up from my desk.

'Yeah, I'd love one, please,' says Lucy. And then, as I move across to take her proffered mug, 'Oooh, Rob, what have you done to your eye?'

That's it. Everyone looks up. Clare looks across. I take a couple of steps back and just happen to execute a half-turn, so that she becomes part of the natural audience for my carefully planned off-the-cuff reply. 'Is it showing that much? I didn't think it was. It happened yesterday. I was at Spitalfields market,' (I thought it best not to make any unnecessary changes, so that my acting skills stayed fresh for the crucial bit), 'just looking over some stuff on a stall, when all of a sudden there was a shout from somewhere, and three lads came rushing towards me, their arms full of jewellery boxes. The stallholder they'd nicked them off was chasing behind, yelling his head off. By the time I'd realised what was happening two of them had gone past me, but I managed to catch the last one by his neck. He gave me a bit of a whack. Nothing too serious, though. Soon the stallholder caught up, and between us we managed to pin the guy down until the police showed up.'

The original version of this speech, as drafted in my head on the tube, contained the phrases 'seven or eight, I'd guess', 'no one else did a thing', and 'leathered the lot of them', but since then I've toned it down a bit for credibility's sake. Murmurings go round of 'that was really brave', 'well done, Rob', 'pity a few more people don't do that sort of thing', etc. None of these comments come from Tim, who, I notice out of the corner of my eye, is regarding me with a mixture of confusion and suspicion. I pass it all off with an 'it was nothing really' (the only true thing I've said so far), and turn for the coffee machine before anyone can start tripping me up with questions. Barely able to believe that the first phase has gone to plan, I'm approaching the second with about as much terror as one man can feel while still remaining conscious.

As I reach the printer, Clare takes a look at my eye. Smiling back casually (or as casually as I can manage at that moment, which I have a horrible feeling is not very), I slow down. I try to change my speed without it being too noticeable, but from somewhere I'm sure I hear the sound of a gearbox being crunched.

By the time she speaks I have stopped completely. 'Ow, that looks really sore.'

Speech proves rather more difficult now. Even more difficult than it normally does with Clare, as stupidly I've only planned my earlier account of the incident. Thinking of something specific to say to her didn't occur to me. You *idiot*, Rob. The first reply that occurs to me ('not as sore as the back of my head is from Tim's eyes burning into it with mistrust and jealousy') is rejected. I opt for a bog-standard, 'It's not that bad actually.'

Clare's sympathetic smile persists, but she doesn't say anything. Suddenly it feels like she's an actress waiting for her co-actor to remember his next line. And so from somewhere my brain picks out another comment: 'I think it looks worse than it feels.'

Good God. That didn't sound too bad.

'You were so brave to do something like that, you know.'

It takes me a split-second to recover from the fact that Clare Jordan has just put the words 'you' and 'brave' into the same sentence and addressed them to me. But once I do, I realise that this means the second phase is beginning to happen. Confidence puts one arm round my shoulder, and encourages me to try speaking again. 'Didn't really think about it. Before I knew what I'd done the guy's struggling to get away from me, and . . . bam.' I jerk my head back, not too theatrically, but just enough for Clare to envisage how the punch landed on me. By now Tim's stare is about to set fire to my hair. And, to my amazement, I'm beginning to enjoy this.

'No one would ever try and tackle someone like that in the States,' says Clare, her eyes widening in horror at the thought (but still managing to keep their smile – how *does* she do that?). 'The kid would probably have been carrying a gun.'

'Oh, some of our kids over here carry guns too,' I say, before realising that the pudding is now in real danger of getting a few too many eggs. 'But no, you're right, it was certainly a much lower-risk thing to do in London.'

Now that I've finished on a self-deprecating note, politeness dictates that Clare has to build me up again. 'Don't be too modest – you still got a nasty bruise for your trouble.'

'Yeah, well,' I switch to a corny American superhero accent, and give an equally corny salute, 'justice was served.' Clare laughs. Still not entirely convinced that I'm not dreaming, I decide to quit while I'm ahead, and set off for the coffee machine in an exultant daze.

Tim is *not* a happy bunny.

All right, he may be an unhappy bunny who's two letters ahead in the Clare Jordan Five And Three-Quarter Feet

Handicap Stakes, but nevertheless, progress of sorts has been achieved here.

10.45 a.m.

Three minutes ago Tim went to the Gents. Two minutes ago I got a text message: 'Dear Capt. Courageous – we never had a comm. meeting to confirm Lisa. How about 7, tonite, at mine?'

If that wasn't proof that I'd got to him, then nothing was.

A minute ago I sent a text message: 'But of course.'

10.30 p.m.

Tim supplied me with a beer when I got round to his flat, and then took great delight in writing Lisa's name on the chart.

'Lisa,' he said. 'Lovely Lisa. What a lovely ex-girlfriend is Lovely Lisa.' I wondered whether there'd been any tears in Wimbledon over the last few days.

He turned to me. 'You seen any ex-girlfriends recently, Rob?'

I swallowed hard. Obviously his suspicions had reached a more advanced stage than I thought. But there was still a way out of this – admitting to spending the afternoon with Kate didn't in itself contradict my robbery story.

'As it happens I did see a girl at the weekend that I used to go out with. Her name—'

'She twatted you, didn't she?'

It was no good. My attempts at framing the most convincing denial I could muster took that fraction of a second too long.

'I *knew* you were telling porkies this morning,' continued Tim triumphantly. 'You'd no more jeopardise your personal safety for the civic good than I would. Jewellery boxes my arse.'

I decided to come out all guns blazing. 'There was nothing,' I said, my righteousness so indignant you could almost taste it, 'in the rules of the Clare Jordan Five And Three-Quarter Feet Handicap Stakes about not lying. And so my audience with Clare was perfectly legitimate. As, therefore, was her admiration for me.'

'All I can say, Rob, is that if you're that desperate to impress her then you've got no chance.'

'Desperate, am I? So not like the guy who spent ages last Friday afternoon talking on the phone to someone who clearly didn't exist, so that he could delay his leaving for the pub until after the rest of us and so get left in the office on his own with her?'

'An effort which was foiled by your having "forgotten" to send an e-mail so that you had to turn your computer back on?'

'Yeah, well.' I took a sip of my beer. 'Fire with fire.'

Tim sat down, and indulgently stretched out his legs. 'Oh well. I'll just have to content myself with looking forward to the weekend. Amsterdam here we come. That's "Amsterdam" beginning with an "A". But of course that fact is only of use if one has already done "C" and "L". Four days to go, Rob. Four days to catch up. Otherwise you won't be able to take *advantage of Amsterdam.'

Tuesday 4th May

If all is fair in love and war, then I don't suppose I've got many grounds for complaint about what someone does in a war *about* love. (Or something not unrelated to it.)

But I'm not very happy about this.

I could sense that Tim was in the mood for some sharpness of practice this morning. After last night that was no real surprise. There was a feisty glint in his eye, a certain gloves-offness about him. Something was lurking in the depths of his imagination. It broke the surface at about half-eleven.

'Oh, I've been meaning to ask, Rob,' he said, slightly louder than was necessary for his voice to carry just to me. 'You heard anything more about that thing at Spitalfields?'

I froze. My typing, my gum-chewing, my breathing – everything stopped. With a little gulp to get it all started again, I scrabbled around in my mind for a realistic-sounding answer. 'Oh, erm, not really, no. The police sent me a letter saying . . .' Saying what? Commending me for my bravery? Don't be stupid, Rob. They don't hand out George Crosses for legging up a teenager who's had it away with some stuff down the market. Saying what, then? '. . . saying that if it goes to court, would I be prepared to act as a witness?'

I forced myself to concentrate on my computer screen with a kind of 'I'm far too busy working to be led astray by such inconsequential chat' look. Within seconds an e-mail was on its way to Tim: 'WHAT ARE YOU FUCKING PLAYING AT?'

His reply was almost instant: 'A dirty trick about a dirty trick isn't really a dirty trick.'

Hard to argue with that. I've taken it as a warning shot, a reminder that it's never wise to push one's luck.

And what of Clare herself today? Well, to address the merely physical, she was wearing her dark red skirt. Although this is a fraction longer than most of her others it hugs her legs even more tightly, which makes my pulse race even more quickly. That tells you a little of how she made me feel. Nowhere near the whole thing, but just a little. The rest of it isn't grounded in vital statistics, it's grounded in daydreams, which is why I'm scared of telling you about it. I might sound silly. There's one dream, for instance, of us kissing, very softly, on the steps of the British Museum. Don't know why there, it just appears in my dream like that . . . Oh, I told you I'd sound silly.

Wednesday 5th May

10.55 p.m.

What have you been thinking, as you've read your way through these scribblings, about the Clare Jordan Five And Three-Quarter Feet Handicap Stakes? I only ask because I myself have flicked through them tonight, and they've put me in mind of a story I once heard.

It concerns Aldous Huxley. He awoke one night, very suddenly, with an absolute and total conviction that he had just dreamed the central truth of the universe. Reaching for his bedside notebook, he jotted this truth down, and then went back to sleep. In the morning he read what he had written:

> *Higamus hogamus,*
> *Woman is monogamous,*
> *Hogamus higamus,*
> *Man is polygamous.*

There was, you'll note, no explanation as to why the sexes differ in this way. Simply a statement that they do. No indication as to whether men's propensity towards promiscuity is genetic, or cultural, or what the hell it is that causes it. And that's my point. As I've read about Tim and myself setting off on our race, the question has kept coming back to me: what allows you to behave in such a manner? Why are men the way they are when it comes to sex? But if Huxley's rhyme is the central truth of the universe, the fact it had to be visited on him in a dream shows how insoluble it is by human reasoning. I wish to God it wasn't, because perhaps then I could undertake some practical steps to fundamentally change this side of my nature, rather than just having to rein in its consequences all the time.

Thursday 6th May

3.40 p.m.

More taunting from my opponent about being the wrong side of 'C' and 'L' for the weekend's 'A' to be any use. In the form of a Post-it note on my desk: 'Completely Laughable Clown Loses Chance of a Lifetime.' I ignored him. All I had to comfort me in my frustration was the slightly petty observation that the 'o' and 'a' didn't fit.

6.50 p.m.

Thought for a minute that I was being eyed up by a girl on the Tube home tonight. But three things persuade me that I wasn't:

i)   My general exasperation at Tim having done 'C' and 'L' when I haven't is making me desperate for the tiniest signs of someone (anyone) fancying me.

ii) This desperation had probably reached a crescendo due to the fact that the Tube was waiting at Covent Garden, whose first letter . . .

iii) Her boyfriend got on at Green Park, and gave her the
     most passionate kiss you've ever seen.

I wish I could tell you I'm not bothered by this. But I can't,
because I am.

Saturday 8th May

3.40 p.m.

In view of the relatively early start that was in store for us, Tim and I might have been expected to bail out early from last night's post-work drinks. But he wasn't going to leave before me, as it would have meant forgoing some quality piss-taking time. His catchphrase for the evening was 'Cor, lumme!', which everyone latched on to, despite being unaware of the significance of its initials. This only served to heighten my suffering, and in turn increase my determination not to leave before him, as I would then have been seen to give in to his taunting.

Consequently we stayed out later than anyone else. Just about everyone had started the evening (with one noticeable exception – the by-now customary absentee maintained her nought-per-cent record), but by ten o'clock just the hard core remained: me, Tim, James and Lucy. Pasta-ed up, we had made our way to the Pitcher and Piano on Dean Street, in readiness for the second half's drinking.

The first round in there was mine.

'Three bottles of Beck's and a white wine, please,' I said, when (at last) I managed to get served.

'How many friends are you with?' asked the girl behind the bar.

Why did she need to know that? 'I'm sorry?'

'I said, how many friends are you with? How many people are you buying drinks for?' She was in her mid-twenties, with long brown hair pulled back tautly from her forehead and temples, revealing bright green eyes in an oval face. Her expression was completely neutral, giving no clue as to why the hell she was asking me this question.

'Well – three.'

'Three bottles of Beck's and a white wine,' she said, counting on her fingers. 'That's four drinks. So where's mine?'

Bloody hell. Her face was still on 'pure deadpan' setting, but there was no mistaking what she'd said. This girl had asked me to buy her a drink. My initial reaction was to laugh. I often do this when I can't think of anything to say. A cogent rationalisation would be that it gives me a bit more thinking time, but the truth is I'm just nervous. With a wave of my hand, I indicated the row of bottles behind her. 'You tell me.' I was (and remain) quite chuffed with that one. Not only the line itself, but also the way I managed to deliver it, namely with a poker-faced suggestiveness that was nearly as assured as hers.

'I'll have a think while I get the others,' she said, moving across to the beer fridge. Now I had passed the opening test without making an idiot of myself, nerves cascaded into the pit of my stomach. This girl had made a pass at me. The last time anyone had done that, pre-Sarah, was . . . well, have you got a five-year diary handy? I don't remember thinking specifically of the Clare Jordan Five And Three-Quarter Feet Handicap Stakes, or indeed of Clare Jordan, at this point; I was probably too shocked to perform such advanced reasoning.

'Right, there you go,' she said, putting the drinks in front of me. 'That's thirteen pounds seventy, please.'

'What about yours?' I asked, slightly confused, and sounding less than cool. (It usually happens sooner or later with me.)

'I've taken for it,' she replied, 'but I'm not allowed to drink on duty, so I'll have it later.' Then, for the first time, she broke into a smile. It reassured me that despite my last comment she was still interested in me. I proffered a twenty-pound note, which thankfully she took quickly enough to avoid noticing how much my hand was shaking. Soon she was back with my change.

'I'm Rob, by the way.'

She smiled. 'Julia.'

'How many drinks have you got stored up for later?'

She looked me straight in the eye. 'Just the one.'

Another influx of nerves. Any more and my stomach would go on strike. I decided to try some slightly less loaded conversation, and came out with, 'How long have you been working here?', which was unloaded to the point of being bland, but Julia didn't seem to mind. She said about three months, and then asked me where I worked, and for a couple of minutes we swapped information about ourselves, which was good because it calmed me down. Soon, though, she had to get back to serving. Feeling pretty pleased with myself, and having registered for the first time that here was a situation with a bearing on the Clare Jordan Five And Three-Quarter Feet Handicap Stakes, I made my way back to the others.

'Where the fuck did you get to?' asked Tim, as I shouldered my way through to the sofas they'd nabbed.

'Sorry,' I said, handing out the drinks and sitting down next to him. 'Got chatting to the girl who served me.'

'Oh really?' grinned Lucy, as she nestled cosily against James on their sofa. Tim, I could sense, had started to feel a little worried.

'Yes,' I replied in a deliberately arch 'what-me-guv?' tone. 'Just had a nice chat, that's all.'

'Yeah, right Rob,' laughed James.

I maintained my Fifth Amendment smile. Tim, I was sure, had worry coursing through his veins by this point, but now it was his turn to hide behind a façade of unconcern.

'So?' said James.

'So what?' I asked.

I was keeping up the pretence just a little too long now. 'Come on, Rob, just tell us what she's like.'

'Not much to tell, really. She's called Julia, her parents live in Devon, she's a receptionist at a TV production company, and she's working here in the evenings to pay off her debts from film college. Wants to be a director in the end. Oh, and she's one of three children.'

I tipped my head back to take a swig of beer. Looking down again I saw two dumbstruck faces, and a third struggling to maintain its composure.

'Not much to tell?' said Lucy. 'Jeez, Rob, apart from her inside-leg measurement I think you've got the lot there.'

There followed a mild teasing session from James and Lucy, which served only to massage my ego even further. Tim, I could tell, was hating it. He changed the subject as soon as possible.

As James and Lucy downed their drinks, it became clear that these were their final ones of the night, the ones that had bred not a desire for more alcohol, but a desire for each other. Hands strayed a little further up thighs, and whispered comments grew a little more frequent, until Tim and I told them to either behave, or go home where they could conduct their business in private. Laughing, they chose the second option.

'Right,' I said as soon as they'd gone. 'It's my round.'

Fortunately Tim had a mouthful of beer as I said this, which meant that he was precluded from pointing out what we both knew: it wasn't my round, and I was only saying it was so that I could go and talk to Julia again. By the time he was free to speak, I was halfway across the room, heading for the end of the bar where Julia was serving.

She handed her last customer his change, and came across to me. 'Back so soon?'

I flushed a little at her pointing out how obvious I was being. For a moment I thought about explaining how two of my friends had left, and concocting a story about the other one having run out of money, but then decided that I might as well concentrate my efforts on the job in hand. 'I thought it really wasn't fair that you only had one drink lined up for you. After you've been working so hard. So could I have two bottles of Beck's and . . . whatever it was you went for before.'

She grinned. 'Thank you.' She fetched the beers. I paid, and as she handed me my change her fingers brushed briefly against mine. 'You are going to hang around and see what drinks I've chosen, aren't you?'

'Of course.'

I really couldn't see what I'd done to attract Julia so much. Brad Pitt produces this sort of reaction in women, but it's not exactly what I'm used to. Not that I was complaining, mind you, especially after the last few months. As I rushed back to Tim I was scarcely able to contain myself.

'I suppose you'll be wanting to sort out the challenge then?' he asked, taking his Beck's. He was looking decidedly narked at the way things were turning out.

'Challenge?' It took me a moment to work out what he was driving at. 'Oh, yeah. Judges' meeting, right?'

He nodded. 'Convened.'

'I'll start.' I thought for a few seconds, feeling simultaneously elated and daunted. This was the first time we'd got down to this level of detail, and I suddenly realised how safe I'd felt being stuck without an opening in the race. Failure didn't really mean anything until you'd had a chance of success. Lack of opportunity was dull, but it was also comfortable. Now I was committing myself in a way that I hadn't done before to the Clare Jordan Five And Three-Quarter Feet Handicap Stakes.

'"Couch"?'

Tim shook his head. "Fraid not, old bean. Quite apart from the fact that it's far too easy, "couch" is an American term. We have sofas over here.' Obviously he wasn't going to make this easy for me. 'I'm prepared to allow you "cistern".'

'Fuck off. She'll think I'm some sort of pervert.'

He laughed. 'All right, all right, I'm only joking.'

'How about "chair"?' I asked hopefully.

He looked back at me in mild derision, not even bothering to reply.

'Fair enough. A bit on the easy side, I suppose.'

'How about,' he said, after a sip of his beer, 'how about – and I really don't think you can object to this one – "cinema"?'

I didn't give a toss whether Tim thought I could object to it or not, it was whether I thought I could object to it that counted. But as I considered the suggestion, it seemed about as easy a 'C' as I could hope to get out of him. My nightmare scenario, which had come to me in the fraction of a second before he spoke, was 'cab'. There's difficult, and there's 'in your dreams'. I decided it was safer to accept 'cinema' than risk pushing him into suggesting anything harder.

'All right. Done.'

We finished our drinks in record time, and near-silence. I still couldn't really believe that this was happening to me. Happening to me? All right – couldn't really believe that I was doing this.

'Well, I shall leave you,' said Tim as he put down his bottle, 'to your sudden and hitherto unknown interest in the Pitcher and Piano's closing-time routine.'

'Rightio.'

He made for the door, but after a few steps turned round and came back.

'Of course even if you manage it, you still won't have done "L".' Inspired by my earlier trick, he'd left it until I had my mouth full of beer, rendering me incapable of response. But as I watched him depart for a second (and final) time, I wasn't worrying about his snide put-down. Instead my concern was how to get a girl who, although evidently interested in me, had only just made my acquaintance, into a cinema and . . . oh my God.

I sat and waited for time to be called, and then a further age until the place was cleared. The bouncers avoided me (I'd seen Julia pointing me out to them), and as soon as she could get away from the bar she came over to me, a something and tonic in hand.

'Cheers.' She clinked her glass against my beer bottle.

'Cheers. Is that gin or vodka?'

She lifted it to my nose, and the unmistakable scent of juniper told me that this was a G&T, and moreover one that was heavy on the G.

'Thanks for this,' she said, before downing about a third of it in one go. 'God, I needed that.'

'Long night then?'

'Yeah, and everyone I served seemed to be a complete arse-hole.' She turned to look at me, and gave a wicked smile. 'Oh sorry – not *quite* everyone.' And then, without even waiting for her gaze to linger, she leaned across and kissed me full on the lips.

'Good,' I said. 'You had me worried there.' I don't know

how I managed to come out with anything that coherent, as the amazement I felt right then, at my first first kiss (if you discount Zoe) in over two years, was incredible. Especially with the added spectre of the Clare Jordan Five And Three-Quarter Feet Handicap Stakes to confuse matters. For a fraction of a second I thought of Clare herself. If my feelings for her are really that strong, I thought, shouldn't I be trying to do this with her instead? Shouldn't I just throw my cards on the table and see what she says? But then there was the pleasure (very real pleasure) that Julia's kiss had brought me . . . She was laughing now, and edging a little closer, and then she was kissing me again, more passionately this time. Clearly there was no messing about with her. And I was more than content to be swept along on the tide of her straightforwardness. It was a tide that continued with her next question.

'What do you want to do? Fancy going to a club or something?'

As it happened I didn't. My overriding thought was that I wanted to go home with Julia and take her to bed right now. There'd been a warmth in our kisses, something about the feeling between us that made me feel sure that Julia and I would get on well together, in bed as well as out of it. As I said before, sex isn't a skill you can have and brag about. It depends on who you're doing it with. And sometimes you just know, don't you?

Going straight home with Julia, though, wasn't much use in the race. But even without that constraint, I just wasn't in a clubbing mood, and this, I think, helped inject my reply with something approaching authenticity: 'I don't know about a club. Tell you what though, I wouldn't mind going to see a film.'

I held my breath, praying that it hadn't sounded too weird a thing to say at this time on a Friday night.

Julia slapped the sofa excitedly. 'Brilliant idea! I haven't been to a late-night film for *ages*.' She took another gulp of her gin and tonic. 'Wait there, I'll just say goodbye to everyone and get my bag.' And after giving me another quick snog, she bounded off upstairs to the staff changing room.

I sat perfectly still, taking deep breaths in an attempt to persuade myself that this was really happening. Of course, you always feel a nervy excitement when you're on a promise and haven't yet realised that promise. This, though, was even worse, because of the logistical challenge presented by the race. And I had started to work my way towards it. A tiny part of me, I suppose, felt the teeniest bit uneasy at what I was doing. But most of me was thrilled to hell with it. Julia was clearly a willing partner, and if – *if* – I could manage to pro-ceed to the required point once we were in the cinema, then it was only the venue that the race would have influenced, rather than the deed itself.

Julia came back with her bag, and we set out, arm in arm, for Leicester Square. Because we stopped several times on the way to resume our snogging (which, after the last six months, made me feel like a trembling adolescent again), it took about fifteen minutes before we found ourselves in front of the multiplex, its listings screen flashing at us, pimping the films on offer. Three of them had still to begin their last showing.

And it was only now that I realised how important the choice of film was. The first one was the latest Hollywood blockbuster, the sort of film that costs three times the Gross Domestic Product of Cameroon, most of it spent on explo-sives. It was called *Ultimatum*, but I can't remember whether the star was Stallone or Schwarzenegger. (That says it all, really, doesn't it?) This was to be avoided at all costs. Not only would it be the busiest film (when a deserted auditorium was top of my list of priorities), it would be so bad as to make for compelling viewing, and I didn't want any danger of Julia's attention being distracted by it.

Having said that, I had little fear that she would be tempted by such a movie, what with her serious interest in cinema. But the other two both looked possible candidates. One was a French film, *La Ferme De La Desolation*, which was in black and white and subtitled. Its poster contained a quote from a review: 'Stunning . . . a bleakly challenging study of depression in a rural community.' Well I had a big enough challenge already, thank you very much, and the last thing I needed was it getting ruined by the sound of cows mooing and the distant hiss of gas as an impoverished farmer tried to end it all. But perhaps it would appeal to Julia? It's hard to read subtitles while you're snogging; maybe she'd cool off and insist that we watch the film? God, please no. The other option looked much more suitable. Called *Small Town*, it was one of those understated American jobs, starring Steve Buscemi and a load of people you've never heard of. Set in a bar in the middle of Arizona, where everyone mumbles into their beer and hardly anything happens. Although I normally quite like this sort of film, tonight it was much more conducive to what I had in mind, namely not watching the film.

Sure enough, they were the two that Julia mentioned. How was I going to tip the balance towards the American one without appearing a philistine? Julia fancied me, that was obvious enough, but she might lose interest in me if I ventured the opinion that the reasons you shouldn't see any film that's French, subtitled and in black and white are that it's French, it's subtitled and it's in black and white. What could I say? The film student in her was rising closer to the surface with every second, I could just sense it . . .

And then a voice from behind us came to my aid. 'Jocasta saw that, didn't she?'

Julia and I turned round. A decidedly bohemian-looking couple in their mid-forties were examining the poster for the French film. He was wearing a wine-stained corduroy jacket, she had hair that crows could have nested in, and they both radiated the arty type's complete lack of concern about how others might see them. (I'm quite envious of it, if you want the truth.)

'Yah, she saw it at the NFT,' replied Corduroy to Hair. 'Said it was awful, absolutely awful. Completely failed to get to grips with the subject matter.'

I looked at Julia. 'Well, who are we to argue with Jocasta?' I whispered.

She giggled. 'All right, let's see the other one.'

What I wanted to do then was rush over to Corduroy and Hair, thank them profusely for their help, and ask them to pass those thanks on to Jocasta, as and when they saw her next. What I actually did was go over to the ticket window with Julia, and ask for two to *Small Town*.

'Where do you want to sit?' came the tinnily miked-up reply. 'Front, middle or back?'

I turned to Julia. 'Back?'

'Where else?' she said, reprising her wicked smile.

My heart started to pound, and not just because a sexy young girl had grinned suggestively at me. It was pounding because I was now in the position any sportsman dreads: winning line in sight, no one capable of beating you except yourself. Could I hold my nerve? The pressure was terrifying.

We went through to the cinema, Julia buying us a small vat of Coke on the way. We picked the very back row, which because of the way the wall tapered contained only half a dozen or so seats, and sat near the end furthest from the aisle. Scattered around the auditorium were a few couples, and one or two larger groups of friends, but still the total number of people in there was so low that everyone could have had a row to themselves. Good. The atmosphere was as it always is in late-night cinemas, where people behave like schoolchildren who know the teacher's a pushover. There was lots of chattering and laughter, and no one took a blind bit of notice of the trailers. All in all, it was the perfect ambience to accompany further snogging by Julia and myself. So that was what we did. Our hands still hadn't made much more of an exploration of each other's bodies than James and Lucy had done earlier. But there was no doubt that if things carried on as they were, my first step in the Clare Jordan Five And Three-Quarter Feet Handicap Stakes was only a matter of time.

Soon the noise from the trailers came to an end, and we broke off from our embrace to see the 'This is to certify . . .' classification sign appearing. Julia, who was sitting on my right, shifted in her seat so that she was facing the screen a bit more, but still kept her left hand on my thigh. My right hand was in a reciprocal position on hers. Taking a huge gulp of the Coke that she'd just passed me (we were about halfway down it now – only another four gallons or so to go), I looked around. There was no one sitting anywhere near us. Great. I could sense an unspoken agreement between Julia and me that at even the most minuscule dip in the film, carnal activity would be resumed. All in all, I failed to see what could possibly go wrong now.

'Oh no, I've forgotten my *blasted* spectacles.'

My head shot round. The whispered comment had come from someone standing at the end of our row. Through the darkness I could just make out that it was Hair, talking to Corduroy as she rummaged in her handbag.

'No, it's no use, darling, I really have forgotten them.'

'Oh, that's such a bore.'

'We'll have to stay as far back as we can,' she muttered. 'I simply won't see a *thing* if we sit near the front.' And with that she began peering into our row, seeing if there were two seats together. I also counted the seats between me and the aisle. There were three.

Have you ever had, simultaneously, the contradictory desires to scream in an uncontrollable rage and blub softly in utter helplessness? I have. As Hair turned to Corduroy (who was standing a couple of rows further towards the front) and indicated to him that there were seats free in the back row, I felt like doing both those things. And then, when it occurred to me that it's impossible to do them at the same time, I felt like standing up, edging along the row towards Hair, and whispering: 'One more step and you're fucking dead. Granted, I appreciated your help out there, and indeed that of Jocasta, in swaying the balance when it came to which film Julia and I should see. But that does not give you the right to come marching in here, sit down next to us, and completely ruin any chance I've got of having sex with her during the film. Don't you know there's a Clare Jordan Five And Three-Quarter Feet Handicap Stakes on?'

But people don't respond very well to that sort of thing. Certainly not people who are as blissfully unaware of others as these two were. Already Corduroy was climbing back up towards our row, and within half a minute he and Hair would be sitting down just a couple of feet to my left. And once that had happened you could rate the chances of Julia and me consummating our passion at somewhere between zero and nothing.

In a feeble attempt at consoling myself, I took an enormous slurp of Coke.

The Coke.

The giant carton of Coke that I was holding in my left hand.

I'm going to say this to you without feeling the slightest
need to apologise: I am proud. Proud of the idea that came to
me in that cinema last night, with just seconds to spare.
Perhaps it seems petty to you. Childish. Pathetic, even. But all
I can say is that you weren't taking part in the Clare Jordan
Five And Three-Quarter Feet Handicap Stakes. You hadn't
had Tim on your case for days on end. You hadn't got yourself
to within millimetres of getting off the mark, only to be
thwarted by a complete stranger forgetting her glasses.

And so you can't possibly know how eye-poppingly pleasurable it was to subtly (but swiftly) stretch out my left hand
towards the middle of the three empty seats, push it down
slightly with the lip of the Coke carton, tip that carton so
that every drop of liquid in it soaked into the seat cushion,
and then quickly bring my hand back to my side. Trust me.
You really can't. Perhaps the aspect I'm most proud of was my
calculation that only by putting the middle seat out of action
could I guarantee keeping Hair and Corduroy out of our row.
Either of the end ones and I'd have left them two dry seats
together. But as soon as Hair sat down on that middle seat, she
shot straight back up again as though it had been wired
directly to the mains.

'Urrrghh,' she said in disgust. 'That seat is sodden,
*ab*solutely sodden.'

Corduroy reached down and felt the seat for himself, confused as to how it could be wet. That sort of thing used to
happen at Beatles concerts, he was no doubt thinking – but in
a cinema?

'How strange,' he murmured. 'Oh well . . .' And off they
went to find another row.

I took a few seconds to get myself together after all this,
and then turned back to Julia, ready to pick up where we'd
left off. She was watching the opening credits, which were

flashing up over a shot that panned from one end of the bar
to the other, taking in about thirty bottles of Budweiser and
fifteen ashtrays. Putting my head on her shoulder, I kissed
her ear. She emitted a soft, contented moan, and gave my leg
a slight squeeze. I kissed her again, a fraction more passionately this time. She moved a little closer. I kissed her a third
time, and . . .

'No *way*.' Julia sat up straight, and took her hand off my
thigh.

'What?' I said, pulling myself up from the half-horizontal
position I'd collapsed into after the sudden disappearance of
my support.

'Greg Boulton.' Julia pointed at the screen. 'Greg Boulton.
He came to do a talk on our course. He was fascinating.'

I looked at the credits, and just managed to pick out said
name before it faded away, together with the half dozen or so
others above it. 'I wonder how many lines he'll have?' asked
Julia, talking more to herself than to me.

Oh no. Not this. *Please* not this.

'I'm sure he won't be in it for a while,' I said, desperately
trying to crane across so that I could resume contact with Julia's
ear. 'And even when he is I'm sure it'll be a really small part.'

'That's exactly why we've got to keep an eye out for him.
Don't want to miss him.'

I had another couple of goes at reawakening Julia's
amorous instincts, but although she reached out and took my
hand, it was clear that until this Greg guy had asked Steve
Buscemi for a light, or whatever challenging dramatic role it
was he had to perform, nothing further was going to happen
between us. By now my frustration was becoming almost
unbearable. After six months of being laid off, my libido was
back at work with a vengeance. Forget the race, I just wanted
to consummate my passion for Julia for its own sake.

'Great use of flashbacks, don't you think?' she said after a while.

'Yeah. Really good.' Oh come on, Greg, for crying out loud get into this film will you?

'But they shouldn't be concentrating on Buscemi's character so much.'

'No. I was just thinking the same thing.' Greg, will you hurry *up*?

Twenty more minutes of the slowly revolving fan, unshaven men smoking in silence, and Buscemi and the barman arguing about cashew nuts. Oh, and the occasional flashback of course. And then:

'That's him,' said Julia suddenly, tightening her grip on my hand. 'Greg. He's the guy who's just walked in.'

'Oh yeah. He looks great. Really good . . . stubble.' Now just ask where the restroom is, Greg, and *piss off*. I edged myself closer to Julia, ready for another attempt at getting her attention back.

Greg ordered himself a drink. I put my arm around Julia's shoulder. Greg went across to a table in the corner. I put my other hand on Julia's knee.

'Hey,' said the barman, 'weren't you in here about a month ago?'

Jesus wept.

Greg thought for a moment as he looked around the bar. 'Yeah, I do believe I was.' I fucking knew it. 'On my way to the deal then. Now I'm on my way back.' I took my hand off Julia's knee. Go on, Greg, tell us all about the deal. I know you're going to. Use as many flashbacks as you like.

I felt like crying.

'He's playing it *so* well, isn't he?' said Julia.

'Mmm.'

'Great interaction with the barman.'

'Majestic.'

As Greg talked the barman through the deal, one of the guys playing pool realised that he'd once been in prison with Greg's business partner. For a while there were flashbacks from the flashbacks, and under normal circumstances I'd have been struggling to keep up. But these circumstances were not normal, they were maddening, to the point where I really couldn't care less about who'd embezzled whose money. I just wanted to carry on kissing Julia's ear, and then her neck, and then . . . But the film had got her now. She was as enthralled by it as I was by her.

After another quarter of an hour or so, Greg left the bar. Cheers mate, I thought, hope you're happy now. If you ever need a kick in the balls, you know where to come.

By now Julia's head was resting on my shoulder. In a way this made the frustration a little easier to bear, as it meant I couldn't try kissing her ear even if I'd thought it would have got me anywhere. More from the pool player, who was related (don't ask me how) to the barman. Julia moved her head a fraction, to get more comfortable. The pool player was being ignored by the barman. I knew how he felt. Julia still hadn't got quite comfy enough, so she twisted in her seat a bit and repositioned her head again. Giving up on the barman, the pool player started on at Buscemi, who in turn restarted the cashew nut argument.

Julia lifted her head slightly. 'Oh, not this again.' The feeling of her warm breath on my ear refired all the frustration that I'd been trying to come to terms with. It was torture.

Still Buscemi went on about the cashews.

Julia lifted her head again. And again I felt her breath on my ear.

But this time she wasn't talking.

I turned towards her. Our lips met.

And I'm afraid that's where your imagination has to take over. Because, as I said before, it's girls who tell you the details, not boys. What I will do, though, is give you some bits of advice, just in case you're contemplating having sex on a cinema floor. Don't do it if you have even the slightest history of back trouble. One wrong move in those conditions and they'd not only have to call you an ambulance, they'd have to take out two rows of seats before the ambulancemen could get to you. Stay on snogging until your eyes have had a chance to get used to the darkness. Any attempt at removing items of clothing (either your own or your partner's) before you can see what's happening could very easily result in you having an eye out (either your own or your partner's). Finally, and glossing over both the stickiness of half-dried Coke and the question of *why* anyone takes satsumas to the cinema, never underestimate the resilience of M&Ms. Just how much pain they can inflict before finally caving in under your weight is nothing short of miraculous.

What I'll also tell you is how it felt afterwards, as Julia and I lay on the floor, gradually coming to terms with the fact that soon we'd have to tidy ourselves up and climb back into our seats. It felt outrageously satisfying. Not just because I'd finally managed to get started in the race, and not just because we'd done this within a couple of hours of meeting (I didn't know how many times Julia had done anything like this, but somehow I sensed it was more than me). No, part of the satisfaction came from how good it felt to be close to someone again. The sex hadn't just been something Julia had gone along with. She'd wanted to do it every bit as much as I had. And that felt exciting.

But, of course, the fact that I'd cleared my first hurdle in the Clare Jordan Five And Three-Quarter Feet Handicap Stakes was there as well. As Julia and I cuddled up in our seats, I couldn't help but feel smug that in having sex with her (something that brought me lots of pleasure in itself, and which I'd have wanted to do anyway), I'd managed to achieve that feat as well. Just wait till I told Tim in the morning. OK, he'd still be able to brag that I couldn't use Amsterdam for my 'A', but at least . . .

Hang on.

Julia and I were going to have sex again tonight. The way she was nuzzling my neck made that clear enough. So who was to say that that couldn't be in a place beginning with 'L'? I could actually catch Tim up tonight, before we went away. Not that I wanted to use the Amsterdam option, of course; my incentive here was the joy I'd get from shutting him up about not being able to use it.

'I'll be . . . back . . . in . . . a minute,' I said to Julia, interspersing my words with kisses.

In the Gents, I was straight on the phone to Tim. His mobile was switched off, so I dialled his home number.

I got the answerphone. 'Tim, it's Rob . . . pick the phone up . . . I know you're there . . . Tim, will you pick the phone up . . .' The little shit. 'Come on, stop fucking about and pick up the phone.' Even if he'd been asleep, he must have woken up by now. 'Tim, I *know* you are there. If you do not pick up the phone you are being a coward, and running away from the Clare Jordan Five And Three-Quarter Feet Handicap Stakes.'

That got him. 'All right, I'm here.'

'Good. Now then – I've done it.'

'Ooh, what a surprise. And there was me thinking you were ringing up to tell me that your attempt had crashed to the ground in flames of abject failure.'

'Glad you're taking it so well, Tim.'

'Don't get too fucking cocky, Rob. You have, after all, only managed to do "C". Which, I think you'll find if you check the spelling of the name "Clare", still leaves you one letter behind me. And therefore *still* not eligible to use our destination tomorrow, or should I say today, as your next step.'

'Yeah, well, that's what I'm ringing about.'

Tim went silent, the line crackling faintly as he digested what I'd said.

'Come on,' I said. '"L". Let's get an "L" sorted. Now.'

Still he didn't reply. He was clearly getting over his horror at realising there was nothing in the rules about not doing two letters on the same night.

Eventually he spoke. 'All right. Make me an offer.'

I'd only managed to come up with one idea. 'Lounge' and 'living room' were way too easy. I had to open with a slightly more realistic offer, but I wasn't at all sure that my idea fitted the bill. Crossing my fingers, I went for it: '"Lilo".'

'What?'

'"Lilo". Helen's got a blow-up bed that she keeps in the cupboard in the bathroom for when her friends stay over . . .' My words petered out as I realised it was a complete no-hoper. Anything in my flat was too simple.

'Now we'll start the serious suggestions, shall we? Here you go – "lighthouse".'

'Ha fucking ha.'

'"Lamp post".'

'Makes it rather hard to stay in the shadows, that one, doesn't it?'

'All right, then, you come up with one.'

The annoying thing was that I couldn't.

'Got it,' said Tim. '"Lift".'

I considered it. Lifts were common enough in central London, although quite how I could get myself and Julia into any of the buildings that contained them at this time of night was another question. But at least it had the advantage of being indoors. And in the absence of any better 'L' of my own, I thought I might as well accept.

'OK then, you're on.'

'Right, see you at the airport. When you've failed.' And before I could reply, he put the phone down.

Back in the cinema, I racked my brains for places that had lifts, and would be open in the early hours of a Saturday morning. Hotels, of course. No one would stop us going past reception. But how would I explain that to Julia? No, it needed to be a building that I could have a decent cover story for wanting to visit . . .

Got it.

'Do you want to come back to mine tonight?' I whispered to Julia.

'I was wondering when you'd ask,' she smiled. 'Come on, let's go now. There's no point watching the rest of this.'

As we strolled through the crowds in Leicester Square, assessing where we'd stand our best chance of hailing a cab, I put my hand into my trouser pocket.

'Damn,' I said, stopping dead.

'What's wrong?'

'I've left my keys at the office.' As my motivation for this piece of acting I recalled the despair I'd felt at the sight of Greg looking around the bar. 'What an idiot. I'll have to pop in there and get them.'

'It doesn't matter,' said Julia. 'Your office isn't that far, is it?'

'No, only five minutes or so. And come to think of it, I'll be able to call us a cab while we're there, so we'll probably get home quicker anyway.'

'Good. Come on then.'

We negotiated the Charing Cross Road, and soon enough were standing outside the locked doors of my building. As I swiped my card to let us into the deserted lobby, I ran through the next few moves to make sure I'd got the timing right. Mild snogging as we waited for the lift, progressing to heavier snogging once we were on the way up, followed by an impulsive stab at the 'halt lift' button and a 'come on, I can't wait until we get home, let's do it right now'. If that didn't appeal to the outlandish streak that Julia had already exhibited in the cinema, then I didn't know what would. But even so, the anxiety I was feeling about getting this right was almost crippling. From a standing start less than four hours ago, I was now within touching distance of drawing level with Tim. If I could manage it, he would be pissed off beyond belief. But if I didn't, his 'can't use Amsterdam' gloating was going to return in spades, and if it had been irritating before, now it would be almost insufferable.

The time available for mild snogging was curtailed to nothing by virtue of the fact that both lifts were waiting empty at the ground floor, their doors open. Fortunately, though, our office is on the tenth floor, so that gave us enough time once we were on our way up to accelerate rapidly through the passion gears. Julia was only too happy to respond in kind, and as I lowered my head to kiss her neck, a glance across at the little red indicator light told me that we were just past floor seven. Excitedly I reached across to the panel of buttons, already anticipating not just the thrill of more sex with Julia, but the joy of being able to cut Tim down to size at the airport. I homed in on the 'halt lift' button . . .

Which wasn't there. *FUCK!* Only now did it strike me that you never see those buttons in real lifts. They're always in movie lifts. Hannibal Lecter uses one in *Silence of the Lambs*. But they never put them in the lifts that you and I, as opposed to fictional characters, use. Why would they? What possible reason could you have for wanting to stop between floors?

Many factors go into the design of a modern office building, but the Clare Jordan Five And Three-Quarter Feet Handicap Stakes isn't one of them.

The lift reached the tenth floor and opened its doors with an emphatic ping. Julia broke off from our clinch and stepped out. Trying hard not to cry, I followed her.

'You might as well wait here,' I said. 'I won't be a minute.'

I followed the corridor round into our now-darkened office, making sure that I closed the doors behind me, went to the very far end of the room, took off my jacket, folded it up, put it over my mouth, and then, when I was sure I had provided myself with every last bit of sound insulation possible, I let out a cry of raw, unadulterated torment.

This formality out of the way, I walked back down the office, sat in my chair, and switched on my desk lamp. What the hell could I do now? The lift was going to deposit us straight back down into reception, and nothing I could do on the way would stop it. The doors would stay open, meaning that anyone passing the glass-fronted building would be able to see straight into the lift. Julia might be adventurous, but she wasn't an exhibitionist. (And even if she was, I certainly wasn't.) Could I somehow jam the doors open on the tenth floor, I wondered? My eyes started to flit around the office, looking for anything long enough to do it, before I realised that I'd still have to explain to Julia why I was so keen for us to have sex in that particular place. Spontaneously stopping the lift because you couldn't wait a moment longer to ravish her would be a compliment; asking her to hang on while you propped a broom-handle between the doors would smack of deviancy.

And then, as I stared at the photocopied list of useful numbers sellotaped to my monitor, it hit me. Trevor might – just might – be the answer to my prayers.

Trevor is our building's overnight security guard. We sometimes see him in the pub, when we're having a drink after work and he's having one before it. He is thirty-eight years old, drives a Ford Cortina, and has West Ham's crest tattooed on one forearm and Bobby Moore's face on the other. More important than any of these things, though, is the fact that Trevor will do just about anything for a pint of lager.

I phoned the control room. After about ten rings (I wonder if he was watching one of the 'videos' that he often offers to lend me), Trevor answered.

'Hello. Security.'

'Trevor, it's Rob.'

'All right, mate, how you doin'?'

'Not bad. But not brilliant either.'

'How d'ya mean?'

'You might be able to do me a favour. There's a big drink in it if you can.'

'Fire away.'

'Can you stop the lifts?'

'Eh?'

'The lifts, can you stop them, whenever you want to?'

'Er, yeah, I think so. Hang on, I'll check.' I waited, praying that Julia wouldn't wonder where I'd got to and come looking for me. 'Yeah, I can power them off individually.'

'What about the intercom thing that lets you talk to who-ever's in the lift?'

'Oh, that'll still work.'

I looked heavenwards, and mouthed a silent 'thank you'.

'Right, Trev, here's the plan. In a couple of minutes one of those lifts is going to start heading for the ground floor. You stop it before it gets there, wait until you get a call from the alarm button, and then say over the intercom something like "don't panic, we're in touch with the lift company, they're getting back to us to tell us which code we need to reset the computer, we'll have you on the move again soon". Then leave it about fiftee— twenty minutes, and start the lift up again.'

Trevor gave a throaty little chuckle, which I assume meant that he'd worked out what was going on. 'Yeah, no problem.'

'Trevor, I love you.'

'I'd rather have the drink.'

I laughed. 'You can have as many as you want.' I was about to put the phone down, when something occurred to me. 'Oh, Trev – that audio link you've got with the lift – there isn't a video one as well, is there?'

He gave an even throatier chuckle, which *definitely* meant that he'd worked out what was going on. 'No, don't worry. No video link.'

'Right. Stand by that off switch.'

'Standing by.'

Pausing only to flick the Vs triumphantly at Tim's chair, I went back out to the lifts.

'You took your time, didn't you?' said Julia.

'Sorry. I couldn't find the keys for ages. Turned out they'd fallen down the back of my desk.'

I pressed the call button. The right-hand lift, which was the one we'd come up in and which had returned to the ground floor, climbed back up and opened its doors once again. Letting Julia in before me, I happened to glance up at the indicator light above the other lift. And I saw, to my horror, that instead of being stuck on 'G', it was descending: '13', '12', '11'. Oh shit, someone in one of the companies above us must have been working late. And I knew what was going to happen next. Sure enough, before it could show '10', the light changed to a flashing horizontal line.

'What are you waiting for?' said Julia, as the doors of our lift started to close.

I stuck my arm between them. 'I've just remembered that . . . that . . . that I forgot to book that cab.'

'Oh it doesn't matter, we can get one on the street.'

'No, really, you can never get one round here this late. It really will be quicker to call one from here.'

She came back out of the lift. 'All right then, whatever you think's best.'

'Won't be a sec.'

Back at my desk, I hit redial on the phone.

'Trev – wrong lift.'

'What?'

'You've stopped the wrong bloody lift.'

'Well how the bleedin' hell was I to know? You said stop the next lift. And that was the next lift.'

'I know, I know, I'm not blaming you. But can you just restart that one, and stop the next one?' Then, as insurance, I added: 'It'll be coming down from the tenth floor.'

He sighed. 'Fine, fine. Whatever you say.'

'Thanks Trev. Remember – big drink.'

'Don't worry, I'll remember.'

Then I called our cab firm, who said it'd be about twenty-five minutes before they could get a car to us, would that be too long, and I said no, funnily enough that'd be about perfect. By the time I got back to Julia the left-hand lift was showing 'G' again; whoever had suffered that brief imprisonment was now free again. Our lift soon appeared, and we got in. The light showed the progress of our descent: '10', '9', '8', '7' . . . come on Trev, flick that switch . . . '6', '5' . . . hurry up you pillock, we're running out of floors here . . . '4', '3' . . . Trevor, if you're holding out for an even bigger drink this is definitely not the way to – CLUNK. The lift juddered for a second or two, and then settled into absolute stillness.

He'd done it! Trev had stopped the lift! What a star. Never doubted him for a minute.

'What's going on?' said Julia, looking a bit worried.

'God knows.' I jabbed a couple of times at the ground-floor button. Then at the one that opens the doors. But, would you believe it, nothing worked. Finally I hit the alarm button, and after a short delay Trevor's voice sang out to us, delivering his lines so convincingly that for an instant even I was convinced that the lift company really had been called.

Twenty-two minutes later Trevor spoke to us again, immediately prior to the lift jerking back into life and delivering us safely to the ground floor.

And yes, your suspicions as to why I'm not going to tell you what happened in the intervening period are correct. All I'll say is that at least a lift is a bit more salubrious than the floor of a cinema.

The flight this morning was at eleven. Having said goodbye to Julia when we changed Tube lines (we wrote our telephone numbers on each other's tickets), I somehow made it to the airport with slightly less than ten minutes to spare. Checking in, I was told that everyone else was already on the plane, and that Tim had kept the seat next to him free for me.

I hurried down the aisle, steadfastly refusing to catch anyone's eye. When I reached my seat, Tim looked up, nine hours' anxiety about whether I'd managed my 'L' playing cruelly on his features.

'Well?'

'Well what?' I said, cramming my bag into the locker.

'You fucking well know what,' he hissed as I sat down and put my seatbelt on.

I didn't say anything. Instead I reached into the pocket of the seat in front of me, picked out the 'What To Do If This Thing Ends Up In The Sea' laminated card, and pretended to read it as though it was the most fascinating document ever written. From the corner of my eye I could see Tim staring at me, hanging on my answer.

'Rob,' he said in a tone that denoted this was the last sentence he would feel able to deliver without shouting, 'did you or did you not manage to complete your task?'

Turning the sheet over, and still not looking at him, I quietly began to hum the chorus from 'Love In An Elevator' by Aerosmith. It took about five seconds, but when he registered what the tune was Tim harrumphed, and turned away in an unabashed fit of pique. Soon there came, from behind his complimentary copy of the *Daily Mail*, which he was rustling to a quite unnecessary degree, a muttered string of expletives. I was loving every minute of it.

After a while he lowered the paper. He seemed to have calmed down a bit now.

'You're still going to lose, you know,' he said.

'Oh yeah? Well, we'll see about that in due course. All I know is that Tim's "Rob can't do anything about Amsterdam" joker has been torn into a million tiny bits, and scattered over his head like so much confetti.' With my fingers I mimed the cascading descent of the pieces of card.

His mind thrashed around, desperately searching for an answer. In the end the best he could manage was: 'Cunt.'

I thought about the forthcoming weekend. Now that we were actually on the plane, and I'd got myself level with Tim in the Clare Jordan Five And Three-Quarter Feet Handicap Stakes, my mind was focusing on the question that, until the early hours of this morning, had been entirely academic: would I sleep with a prostitute in Amsterdam?

THOUGHTS ON PAYING FOR SEX

In many ways this subject is the crystallisation of every possible question you could ever ask about men's attitudes to
sex. As I thought about it this morning, a long-gone discussion came back to me. It had been started, as are so many of
the most interesting discussions in modern life, by the *Marie
Claire* sex quiz. Hannah and I had reached the inevitable
'would you pay for sex?' question, and I'd said that no, I
wouldn't.

'Why not?' she asked. 'You said last night that the thought
of a quick, no-strings-attached fuck is a real turn-on for men.'

This was true. We'd been watching one of those arty BBC2
dramas about a group of twenty-somethings, and it had
reached a scene where the gay guy ended up in a cubicle at a
club with another bloke. And I'd said, only half-jokingly, that
I wished straight girls could be like gay men. A woman's
instinctive response to the offer of sex is, 'Why?'; a bloke's
(gay or straight) is, 'Why not?' Of course there are many reasons why a woman will take up the offer, and many why a
man will decline it. But those are the initial reactions.

'I know I said that,' I replied. 'And it's true. But that only
appeals to one side of our make-up. And men know that that
side is the less important one. There, but less important.' I
tried to think of a way of getting this across to Hannah. It's
tied in with the need to increase your score, of course. But as
to why that need's there in the first place, that was difficult,
because I don't really understand it myself. Eventually,
though, I hit on a way of at least explaining to her how these
things make themselves felt to a bloke.

'If you really – and I mean *really* – want to simplify it,' I
said, 'it's a bit like the Spice Girls. The only two interesting
ones are Baby and Ginger.' This, you see, was back in those

innocent, far-off days when we thought there would always be five Spice Girls, and they would always rule the world.

Hannah then side-tracked us for a minute by asking about Posh Spice. You must fancy her, she said. But she's too thin, I explained. Nonsense, she said, a woman being 'too thin' is a contradiction in male terms. That's where you're wrong, I countered. Posh Spice is *known* for her thinness, and any girl whose defining quality is her thinness is too thin. Girls never believe this. They think that unless they can hide behind a telegraph pole they're too fat. Now obviously I'm not saying that blokes never think a woman is too big, but put it this way – if women knew what a lot of men think about Roseanne Barr, the dieting industry would collapse overnight.

Anyway, once I'd returned us to Baby and Ginger, I explained that I wasn't really talking about fancying. I didn't fancy either of them, what I meant was that they symbolise the two extremes of what men see in sex. Baby puts you in mind of tender, loving, gentle sex. Ginger makes you think of sex that's vulgar, rough and ready, tarty. It's love and lust. Making love and fucking.

'And yes,' I continued to Hannah, 'blokes can fuck without making love. The quick, no-strings-attached fuck increases your score by one.' (God, that sounds childish, I thought as I said it, but I was on a roll here, and honesty was chasing away my shame.) 'And so blokes will always be tempted by a one-night stand. But that doesn't mean they think the sex will be that good. In fact they know it almost certainly won't. They know that only happens when you really like someone.'

Hannah looked thoughtful. Not necessarily sceptical, just thoughtful. I realised perhaps I'd confirmed all her worst fears about men. But even though I couldn't really explain why men are made like this (if you have a God, perhaps you could go and ask Him for me?), I had at least tried to explain to her how it feels.

'That,' I carried on, 'is why a prostitute fantasy is only a turn-on if it's precisely that – a fantasy. Pretending to act that out with a girlfriend you care for. It's similar to – well, to the two most demeaning things you can do to a girl in bed.' (I named them for Hannah at the time, but as I tried to write them down just now I found I couldn't. They seemed excessively vulgar. Which, of course, they are. If you need any help, one of them's very good for the complexion, and the other one hurts like . . . well, it hurts like what it is.) 'Both of them are massive turn-ons, but only with someone you respect. The thrill is in the contradiction, doing something as degrading as that with someone who knows you don't really mean it.'

Hannah snorted, and said: 'Yeah, right Rob.' I don't suppose I can blame her. I can see, of course I can, why girls might listen to an explanation like that and think 'secondhand-car salesman'. All I know is that it's true.

As I thought about that discussion on the plane today, it reminded me of why I can't see myself sleeping with a prostitute in Amsterdam. It would be a tart fantasy for real, therefore no fantasy at all, therefore no fun. And quite apart from that, there's the fact that paying for sex is the ultimate sign of failure. To return to the football analogy from a while back, Gary Lineker wouldn't have got any pleasure at all from scoring a goal if he'd had to slip the keeper fifty quid to look away while he slotted the ball home, would he? It wouldn't have counted as 'notching'. A prostitute doesn't have sex with you because you're attractive, or funny, or charming, but simply because you've paid her. She'd do it with any bloke who paid her. And as blokes like notching because it proves they're better than the other boys in the playground, having sex with a prostitute doesn't count as notching.

But on the other hand, there's the Clare Jordan Five And Three-Quarter Feet Handicap Stakes to consider. And that gives rise to two thoughts. The practical one is: what'll have been the point of dragging myself back into contention if I'm going to stand idly by and let Tim retake the lead? And the moral one is: who the fuck do I think I am saying I won't sleep with a prostitute when I'm taking part in something like this race? If Tim and I are reducing sex to this purely mechanical level, wouldn't we be more honest to do it on a business footing? If my aim is to separate sex from its emotional significance, and sleep with someone because of the race rather than because they're them, then who better to go to than a prostitute?

Is Tim really going to go through with it?

And if he does, will I?

Sunday 9th May

11.40 a.m.

My body knows that I drank a lot of alcohol yesterday. And it's letting me know that it knows. But fortunately it has also, by and large, accepted my plea in mitigation, which was one of marijuana. We accompanied our drinking with so much smoking that the dehydration which should, by rights, have woken me at about five this morning, forcing me to suffer the grim dawn hours in Hangover Purgatory, was kept at bay by the dope-induced soundness of my sleep. So there's only a light-fisted timpani player at work in my head, rather than the full percussion section.

I wonder how Tim's feeling?

The afternoon started very peacefully. As we wandered into town, I reminisced about my two previous trips to Amsterdam. Well, maybe 'reminisced' is a bit over the top; neither of them was what you'd call memorable. The first was a sixth-form day trip from school, on which any exploration of the city's seedier side was prevented by a combination of Mr Bailey, the shortage of time, and the strange fascination teenagers have, no matter which city they're in, no matter how absorbing its cultural heritage, no matter how mind-bendingly different from their own home town it may be, with visiting McDonald's.

My other visit to Amsterdam was about four years ago, with my then girlfriend. (Lois, as it happens.) Actually she was only my girlfriend, if we're being strictly accurate, for the first day and a half of the weekend. Because it was that afternoon that Lois truly discovered cannabis's qualities as a truth drug. Halfway through our third joint her mouth suddenly decided, without any apparent permission from her brain, to tell me exactly what she thought of my mother. And, while it was on the subject, my taste in music. And my habit of using her expensive shampoo when I stayed at her flat. One or two other things made their way off her chest as well, although I can't remember what they were. But I do recall the girl on the check-in desk at Schipol Airport saying it was the first time she'd ever had a couple asking *not* to be seated together.

By the time Tim and I got into town it was nearly six, and the inadequacies of our 'lunch' on the plane were really beginning to hit home. Airline food isn't what you'd call substantial fare at the best of times, but this particular offering had put me in mind of a picnic prepared by a cost-conscious young girl for her anorexic teddy bears. So we stopped off at a restaurant in one of the crowded little alleyways between Central Station and the red-light district.

By now, just a few hundred yards from the scene of the evening's proposed activity, I was really beginning to worry. All the arguments I outlined yesterday about not using a prostitute were still in my head. I knew them all backwards. But I also knew that my competitive streak was hanging around as well, shouting occasional contributions to the debate. It was less than twenty-four hours since I'd drawn level in the Clare Jordan Five And Three-Quarter Feet Handicap Stakes. Would my joy at doing so, my determination not to fall behind again, make me change my mind? If Tim did it, and sought out a prostitute whose name began with 'A' (not, it had to be said, a difficult task in this city), how would I react? The first thing to do, I reasoned, was to establish the likelihood of it happening. How serious, really, was Tim about going through with this plan?

'When are you going to make your purchase?' I asked, tucking into my pizza, and trying to instil the question with an implication that he wasn't really going to do it.

'Oh, there's no rush.' He spoke in all apparent seriousness. 'The night is still young. I think that first we should savour a few of the other delights on offer.'

Was he putting it off? Or was he just taking his time? I got the feeling there was a hint of doubt in his mind, but Tim's such a practised bullshitter that I couldn't really be sure. Half an hour later we found ourselves in a café round the corner, on our third Heineken, and first joint, of the night. We enjoyed an odds-and-sods sort of chat, until Tim found himself drawing on the last of the spliff so that the glow hit the roach and disappeared.

'What are we going to do now then?' he asked.

Now, definitely, there was a sense of him avoiding the night's Big Decision. For the first time since the start of the Clare Jordan Five And Three-Quarter Feet Handicap Stakes, I felt in control. Not only were the scores level, Tim was in doubt about his next move. If neither of us slept with a prostitute (which, I felt confident, was how it was going to turn out), we'd stay level, but Tim would lose face because it had been his idea. I need all the help I can get in this race, and a morale boost like that would be very handy.

'I thought you were going to tell me what we're doing now,' I said, relishing the chance to tease him. 'Come on, Tim, you're in charge. You're the one who planned the mission. A mission to lose your dignity and pay fifty quid for the pleasure. Unless . . .' I left a pause for effect, 'unless you're having second thoughts, that is.'

'Of course I'm not.' He stood up quickly, as if to signal the fullness of his purpose. The effects of the dope made him sway a little once he was up, but soon he regained his balance and was heading for the door. 'Come on, no time like the present.'

This was getting better. Not only had I riled him, he was doubling his eventual shame by refusing to cut his losses now and admit he couldn't go through with it. We took our bearings and set off for Achterburgwal, the busiest street for the particular commodity that Tim was 'interested' in. The little glass-fronted booths in which the girls display themselves soon started to appear. Being a side street, though, these were the less impressive girls, and only every third or fourth booth was occupied. If Achterburgwal was Fortnum and Mason, this was Catford Market. Women who had hit fifty rather less well than Helen Mirren, but whose thirty years on the game had taught them the salesmanship that can shift sex just as effectively as any other commodity. Younger girls, in their twenties (but still not attractive enough for Achterburgwal), their underwear glowing detergent-ad bright in the fluorescent purple lighting. There was feeling of half-heartedness to it all, a sense of routine that I found deeply unarousing.

'Anything that grabs your fancy yet, sir?' I asked, rubbing a little more salt into Tim's open wound. He curled a disdainful upper lip, and strode determinedly on towards the hum of activity coming from Achterburgwal. As we hit it our mildly stoned attention was taken for a few seconds by the beauty of the canal that runs its entire length, the cosy little bridges that cross it every fifty yards or so, and the greystone buildings that line either side. In Paris this street would be full of romantic bistros, bohemian cafés and buskers playing moody saxophone. In Amsterdam, it's full of sex shows, cannabis museums and prostitutes.

The narrow pavement and the gawping mass of people dragged us down to crawling pace, so allowing Tim ample time to judge each girl. Just about every variation of the female form was on offer. Slim blondes with soft, downy skin and immaculate white suspenders. Formidable tattooed dominatrixes, clad in silver-studded black leather collars. Plump, full-breasted brunettes, cheekily teasing the passing boys. Peroxide Pamela Anderson clones, about as sexually alluring as a traffic cone.

We reached the top of Achterburgwal. Despite the multitude of options open to him, Tim had still not even made an initial enquiry. Instead, he crossed the bridge and started to wander back down the other side. I followed him. Just as I reached the far end of the bridge, a party of excitable Geordie teenagers veered in front of me, blocking my way as they tried to work out which of the alleyways they hadn't yet sniggered their way along. By the time I'd pushed past them, Tim had stopped a little way down the canal, in front of one particular booth. As I got closer, I saw that the girl was Chinese. The purple light gave her heavily foundationed skin a grotesque, unnatural appearance, rather like a porcelain doll going for a job on the Selfridges make-up counter.

When I reached Tim, I leaned with my elbows on the rail, and stared into the canal. Turning round, he copied my pose.

'Interested?'

He pretended to look confused for a second, before replying: 'Oh, her? Nah, not really.'

'Why not?'

'You know what it'd be like with a Chinese girl. I'd only want another one twenty minutes later.'

That was it. Conclusive evidence. Tim resorting to such a tacky line said everything. He was obviously having not just second thoughts, but some third and fourth ones into the bargain.

Opposite us, on the other side of the canal, a flashing sign caught his attention: 'Casa Rosso – Best Live Show In Town – Real Sex, Live On Stage.'

'Let's go and sit in there for a while,' said Tim. 'Now that I've had my first look at the goods, I need a bit of time to reflect, make sure that I pick the right one.'

'Oh I see – delaying tactics.'

'Not in the slightest. It's just that a hasty purchase is never a wise one. I'm not backing out, you know.'

'Of course not. The very thought.'

Two minutes and seventy-five guilders later, we found ourselves in the dark theatre. There were about thirty rows of seats, sloping down to the front. The place was roughly half full. As we decided where to sit, I thought back to being in the cinema with Julia, and chuckled. But there were some differences from Friday night. The location of the people having sex, for one.

A slightly threadbare red curtain was drawn across the front of the stage. Obviously we'd come in between 'acts'. One of the half-dozen or so waiters was walking back up the aisle with a tray of empties, so Tim caught his attention and ordered us a couple of beers. (Dutch dutch courage for later?) Some dire eighties Euro-pop was playing over the sound system. God knows who it was, but they made Roxette sound highbrow. Soon the curtain was pulled back, and the performers appeared, a guy from the left-hand side of the stage, a woman from the right. Both were in their early thirties, averagely attractive and wearing easily sheddable clothes. They started by kneeling in the middle of the moth-eaten bed, snogging and rubbing each other's arms, not so much like two lovers expressing their urgent desire as two apathetic paramedics trying to improve each other's circulation. After the regulation forty-five seconds of that they continued the snogging, but switched to him kneading her breasts and her kneading his crotch. Clearly the circulation problem had spread.

Already I was beginning to get bored. This display was as much about the erotic wonder of the human body as Richard Clayderman is about the beauty of classical music. All the components were there, everything was in the right place and doing what it should, but there was just no feeling to it, no sense that any of it was for real. A stupid statement, of course. Why would it be for real? This couple were doing what they were doing because they were being paid to, in entirely artificial circumstances, with dozens of complete strangers watching them.

All of a sudden something struck me.

'Come on, I've had an idea,' I whispered to Tim, and then I was out of my seat, heading towards the front.

'What the hell are you doing?' he said, but when I failed to turn round he got up and followed. Having reached the bottom of the aisle, I sat on the floor, facing the audience, my back supported by the six-foot high stage. Tim sat down next to me.

'See?' I whispered to him. The best thing to do at a sex show, I'd realised, is not to watch the sex show, but to watch the audience watching the sex show. The expressions on their faces are a lot more animated, and a lot less predictable. We watched a group of French teenagers, desperately trying to look blasé yet clearly spellbound. And a respectable American couple, finding just enough irony in events to stop them feeling uncomfortable. And a party of Japanese businessmen, whose lower jaws seemed to be caught in a super-strength gravitational field. I don't know whether Tim quite got my point, but I found it fascinating.

After a while, though, our backsides started to get sore (probably the first time any members of the *audience* have had that complaint in the Casa Rosso), so back out into the street we went. How was Tim going to execute his climb-down, I wondered?

By now it was getting on for eleven, and Achterburgwal contained a far lower proportion of respectable middle-aged couples, and a far higher one of rowdy young pissed-up males. Consequently there was far more banter being aimed at the girls in the windows. Experienced professionals that they were, though, they had standard put-downs for every uncouth suggestion thrown their way. The instant a lad was answered back to, he would clam up and shuffle away in embarrassment, his mates laughing at him to hide their relief that they hadn't been the one made to look stupid.

Time to set about calling Tim's bluff again. 'Look at all these hard-working ladies. Trying to ply their trade, but all they're faced with are time-wasters. They'll *leap* at the chance to do business with a genuine customer like you.'

No answer, although I was sure I heard the sound of teeth being gritted.

'They'll be glad,' I continued, 'of someone who's serious about this. Rather than someone who's just window-shopping.'

He stopped dead in his tracks. For a split second I thought I'd gone too far, and he'd taken offence. But then he marched straight over to one of the booths, and said something (I couldn't hear what) to the girl. She thought for a second or two, and then shook her head. He moved on to the next girl, who listened to his question and then leaned out of her booth, looking up and down the street. God – was he really asking them what I thought he was?

The girl pointed to a booth about ten yards back in the direction we'd come from. Without looking across at me, Tim went and spoke to its occupant, who was about thirty-five, with dyed blonde hair and an unsmiling face.

'Right, that's sorted,' he said, striding back to me in the manner of someone who's just picked up the keys to his Hertz rent-a-car at the airport. 'Anya. A hundred guilders. That's about thirty quid, isn't it?'

'For what?' I asked, dumbfounded.

'To have my palm read and a horoscope done. What do you think what for?'

'What, you mean for . . .' I'd turned into my grandma. One simple, three-letter word, and I couldn't bring myself to say it.

'Yes, for sex, Robert, for sex. She's a prostitute, you know. That's what prostitutes do. You give them money, they have sex with you.'

Jesus. He was going to do it. He was actually going to do it. *It*. With her. With a prostitute. Now. Here. In the tiny room behind her booth. She was going to draw the curtain across the window, take him through to the room, and . . . Jesus.

Tim took out his wallet. 'Eighty . . . ninety . . . a hundred. Right, there we are.'

We looked at each other.

'You not partaking?' he asked. 'No? Oh well, your loss. Not to mention your failure to keep up in the Clare Jordan Five And Three-Quarter Feet Handicap Stakes.' He pointed to a bar further along the street. 'I'll see you in there, all right?'

Before I could answer, he'd turned and walked over to the girl, who was standing in the open doorway waiting for him. He went inside. She closed the door, and then pulled the curtain shut.

I walked, in disbelief, to the bar, where I ordered myself a beer. For a minute I thought about trying to go through with it. I was annoyed at Tim regaining the lead in the race, especially so soon after I'd caught up with him. But as I sat down and watched the young, good-looking people all around me, laughing and flirting their way through another Saturday night, I knew in my heart that I didn't *want* to go through with it. They all served as a reminder of what proper sex is all about: the excitement of the chase, the intriguing uncertainty, the thrill of trying to read a smile, gauge what's behind a glance. If it happens, it happens. If it doesn't, you've still had some fun.

But what Tim was doing? No fun in it at all.

Sex is the least important part of sex. The physical act itself is not what brings the pleasure. At least not for me it isn't. The real kick comes from feeling close to a girl, and knowing that she likes you. At the heart of sexual stimulation, I realised as I thought it through, is the fact that she wants you as much as you want her. It doesn't have to be love, you don't need to be planning the rest of your lives together. But you do need to know that she at least likes you, that the sex is an expression of feeling (however mild and/or temporary) for you. Which is why sex with a prostitute, I now knew for certain, just wasn't an option for me. The woman's desire to sleep with you is conditional on payment. Therefore it's not really a desire. Therefore it wouldn't turn me on.

After a while Tim showed up, looking more than a little put out.

'Well that was a waste of thirty fucking quid.'

I couldn't believe my ears. 'What – you mean – you didn't . . . ?'

'No. I didn't.'

'Not even . . . ?'

'No. Not even. It was, not to put too fine a point on it – quite an apt expression, really – about as unerotic an experience as you could imagine. As soon as we got in there, she went all clinical and formal, like a really unfriendly dental assistant. She got out this box of condoms, and said that before anything else happened – and she meant *anything else* – I'd have to put one on.'

I was tempted to burst out laughing. But I didn't fancy getting thumped, so I managed to keep a straight face as Tim carried on. 'The whole way she went about it was a *complete* bloody mood killer, Rob. Being told to get an erection is like being told to make your fingernails grow faster. You can try all you want, but it's not going to happen.'

'So that was that, then.'

'Yeah, that was that. She said I could wait a while if I wanted, but I couldn't have my money back. End of story.'

As he stared miserably at the table, I wondered whether Tim saw what had just happened (or rather not happened) in the same way as I did. From my viewpoint, as I said before, the lack of erotic charge in paying for sex is exactly that – you're paying for it. But Tim gave the impression that he thought it had simply been a question of the woman's manner, as though if she'd said 'please' when she told him to put the condom on everything would have been all right. The emotional side of the issue didn't seem to have occurred to him. Merely the procedural.

But this was not the right time for sharing such thoughts, nor Tim the right person for sharing them with. So I contented myself with some medium-level taunting about the race still being level. And what with me celebrating that, and Tim drowning his sorrow, we drank very, very many bottles of beer last night.

Monday 10th May

12.40 p.m.

Coffee and orange juice swilled us through yesterday in Amsterdam. Hungover and crestfallen as he was from Saturday night, Tim's arrogantly pugnacious side began to show through again as the day wore on, and there were several barbed asides about the need for me to watch out once we got back to Blighty.

In the normal course of events, I'd be worried. After all, early form in the Clare Jordan Five And Three-Quarter Feet Handicap Stakes did prove that Tim has a certain advantage in the pulling stakes. But two things enabled me to maintain an inner calm yesterday. One was the pleasure I got from reminding Tim that the Jane option's still there. (Perhaps having learned his lesson from the previous evening about rising to the bait, he chose not to reply.) The other was much more important, and something that I kept to myself. It was, quite simply, Julia. I realised that with her as my willing assistant, those last three locations are mine for the ticking off. That was the risk Tim took when he plumped for names instead of places. So now all I have to do is make sure it comes back to haunt him. Give Julia a call when we're back in England, I thought, and start working my way through those letters.

This, needless to say, was one of my first acts this morning, as soon as I had five minutes free to nip up on to the roof.

Julia was working on reception at the production company, and so couldn't really speak. She's calling me back tonight.

9.10 p.m.

Just called Julia again – she apologised for not phoning, but said it had been manic at work all day, in fact she'd only just got home. She's busy tomorrow and Wednesday, but yeah, she said, she'd love to meet up on Thursday evening.

Can't wait to see her again.

Tuesday 11th May

11.40 a.m.

Something may have struck you as you read what I wrote last night. In fact it may well have struck you a long time ago. Call me a prat (go on, I know you want to), but it took me until about ten minutes ago to spot it.

My awakening to the uncomfortable truth came as I was taking an admiring (but subtle) glance at Clare Jordan. After the usual few seconds of aching to know the truth about her romantic status, followed by the equally usual seconds worrying that she likes Tim but not me, I was allowing myself a very unusual couple of seconds to relish the fact that I have got a clear route mapped out to victory in the race that bears Clare's name.

And my route bears Julia's name.

And involves sleeping with Julia at least (and probably more than) three times.

This would not, I suspect, be a problem for Tim, were he in my position. Use Julia for as long as necessary, then cast her aside to claim the prize that is Clare Jordan, or at least the chance to make a move for Clare Jordan. But I'm not put together like that. A less than pleasant side of me wishes I was. But I'm not. I've got an inkling that I'm going to develop real feelings for Julia.

Yes, you say – but that means that although you'll win the race, you won't then want to make a move for Clare, will you? Or if you do want to, and you end up sleeping with her, that'll show that you didn't feel as much as you thought you did for Julia.

Wrong, I'm afraid. There's a big chunk in the middle of the Bloke Feelings scale between 'meaningless sex' and 'I'm never going to look at another woman again'. Sometimes – in fact, most of the time – you're juggling two different things: Guilt and Temptation.

THE GUILT/TEMPTATION TRADE-OFF

If you're seeing a girl (say, someone called Julia), and you give in to the Temptation to sleep with another girl (let's pick a name at random – Clare), that doesn't mean you don't get any Guilt. You do. You get lots. As soon as Temptation trots happily off, sated again for a while, Guilt comes striding thunderously in to take its place. How men react to Guilt's terrifying presence varies. Some carry it around like an ulcer, a perpetual pain reminding them that they've done wrong. Some just can't take it, and confess to their partner what they've done. Some manage to forget about it almost totally, until once in a while they get a searingly painful shot of it, when they're playing in the park with their child and their wife smiles lovingly at them.

There is the argument (I've actually heard it expounded by women, though usually by men) that you shouldn't confess infidelities. At least not minor one-offs. What she doesn't know, they say, won't hurt her. Well, that may be true. But it will hurt him.

Oh come off it, you reply. If a guy knows that Guilt's going to come knocking (no, not even knocking, it's not that polite – it just breaks the door down), then why does he give in to Temptation in the first place? Because he does. Sorry I can't be any more cogent than that, but I'm concentrating on Bloke Feelings at the moment, not Bloke Logic. Which, in a way, is your answer. Concentrating on feelings instead of logic is precisely what blokes do when Temptation's hovering.

Look, all I'm saying is that there's a big grey area. That's why guilt is grey. Guilt is the grey-eyed monster.

And I'm staring it in the face right now. I know that my simple way of getting to 'E' is Julia. But if I do get to 'E', then Clare Jordan (who is, after all, the incentive for getting to 'E') is going to provide me with the Guilt/Temptation trade-off to end all Guilt/Temptation trade-offs.

Oh – *SOD* it. Why is life never simple?

Wednesday 12th May

10.35 p.m.

Yesterday's worry kept nagging me, until the point this after-noon where I decided to ring Chris and ask if I could go round for a chat about it.

All right, that's obviously a lie – to the point where I decided to ring Chris and pretend that I was bored, and didn't have anything to do tonight, so he'd invite me over, which would allow me to go round and slip my worry into the conversation as though it was just something to say, which would mean that we could have a chat about it.

I got there at about seven. Hannah had cooked a risotto.

'How are you doing in that race of yours?' asked Chris as soon as we were sitting down.

'All square,' I replied. 'Tim did "L" to go two–nil up, but I met this girl last week and I've managed to catch up.'

'Well done,' said Chris. 'Who is she?'

'She's called Julia.' I gave them a potted version of last Friday night's events.

Hannah shook her head in disgust. 'So I suppose this poor girl's going to get taken on a tour now, is she? Of places that begin with "A", "R" and "E"?'

I ignored her, hoping that my next comment to Chris would show her things weren't that simple. 'The thing is, I really enjoyed being with her.'

'Understandable, Rob,' he replied. 'Copious amounts of sex

with an attractive young girl. Always a useful little box to have ticked on the "enjoyable time?" questionnaire.'

It was at this point that Hannah gave a huff of disapproval, picked up her plate, and went to eat in the sitting room.

'No, it wasn't just that,' I said. 'It was . . . it was *fun*, you know what I mean? Julia was fun, we had fun, it was . . . fun. There was lots of sex, granted. But there was lots of cuddling as well.'

Chris shifted awkwardly in his chair. And not, before I hear any tuts from those of you with the Standard Male Attitudes manual you got free in a clutch'n'cleavage lads' mag, because he thinks cuddling is soppy. His awkwardness, I'm sure, was because he thinks cuddling *isn't* soppy. Sex without cuddling is like a bacon sandwich without ketchup – worth having, but not as good as it could have been. So his embarrassment at me using the word wasn't because he didn't know what I meant, but because he did. For me to mention something as intimate as cuddling will have told him that I must feel something for Julia. Or at least be worried that I'm going to feel something for her.

'Do you know what her favourite film is?' I continued. (We'd talked about it as we made our way to the cinema. I didn't report it to you on Saturday because I hadn't spotted its significance then.)

'Go on.'

'*Day of the Jackal*.'

He gave a little whistle through his teeth. '*Day of the Jackal*? God, when you said she was fun I didn't realise you meant that much fun.'

'She said Edward Fox is really sexy in it.'

'Edward Fox *is* really sexy in it.'

'That's what I mean. You know Edward Fox is really sexy in it, I know Edward Fox is really sexy in it, but a girl who knows that Edward Fox is really sexy in it? That's how much fun Julia is.' I stared at the floor. No, I stared right through the floor, right through to the other side of the world and beyond, to a spot about a million light years away where Julia and I were curled up together on a sofa, feeding each other Kettle crisps and sipping red wine as we watched Edward Fox painting a face on a watermelon.

Chris tentatively broke into my dream sequence with a question. 'So what are the implications of all this for the Clare Jordan Five And Three-Quarter Feet Handicap Stakes?'

For a second I looked at him as though he'd farted in the middle of the Remembrance Day silence. But then it dawned on me that he was only asking the question I've been asking myself – indeed the question I came round here to sound him out about.

'I don't know. I'm seeing her tomorrow night. How do you reckon I should play it?'

'There's nothing you can do. Except go with the flow. See how you feel. If you sit there with Julia tomorrow night, and can't imagine jettisoning her in favour of the race, then don't. And if you can't imagine jettisoning the race in favour of her, then don't do that.'

That's why I like Chris. No messing about. Straight to the heart of an issue, be it Viv Richards' batting or my emotional welfare.

'Yeah, you're right.'

'Look, Han and I are having a few people over on Friday night. Why don't you come round as well? Then if you're newly loved-up we can celebrate, and if you're planning your next move in the race we can discuss tactics.'

So that was that dealt with. Just have to see how it goes now.

Saturday 15th May

11.50 a.m.

My head hurts. In fact everything hurts.

I arrived at Chris and Hannah's just before seven last night. No one else was there yet, and Chris was upstairs getting ready. I parked myself on the sofa, and Hannah brought me a bottle of lager.

'Chris told me that you were seeing Julia last night,' she said warily. She clearly felt obliged to ask the question, but didn't really want to hear the answer. 'How did it go?'

Staring at the fireplace, I searched for the right words.

Hannah filled the silence herself. 'Oh, that look tells me everything. Our young lovers meet in a Soho bar, he takes one look into her come-to-bed eyes, her lip trembles with a week's accumulated passion, and he knows deep within his heart that what he could have with this girl is too important to throw away for some childish shag-fest. Desperate for each other's bodies, they rush back to his flat, where their burgeoning love grows more beautiful and more real with each insistent thru—'

'The cow's dumped me.'

'*What?*'

'Dumped me. Told me it's off. Ended. Finished. Over. No more. Finito. Kaput.'

'Yes, Mr Roget, I know what dumped means. But what happened?'

'She just came out with it. No preliminaries, just said it, drained her gin and tonic, gave me a peck on the cheek and fucked off.'

'Said "it"? Said *what*?'

I sighed, the impatient sigh of an eyewitness approached by his umpteenth news-crew. 'She was already there when I got to the pub. My first clue was staring me in the face the moment I walked in. Or rather not staring me in the face; she could hardly look at me. She'd already got me a bottle of Beck's. Touching that, eh, remembering what I drank? So I sat down, and before I could say a word she came straight out and told me she's got a boyfriend, and she'd been furious with him because she found out he'd had a quick fling with someone else, and I was—'

Hannah finished my sentence for me. 'You were Agent Revenge.'

'Yep, that's about the size of it. She wanted to get back at him, they had a big argument, but in the end they've sorted it all out and they're staying together. So bye bye, Rob.' Even as I said the words my memory flashed up the sight of Julia in the pub. Despite all the resentful thoughts I'd had about her over the last twenty-four hours, I felt that I wanted to be back there, spending whatever time I could with her.

Hannah sat down next to me. I sensed that whatever her misgivings about the race, she knew that now was a time for sympathy rather than admonishment. 'How do you feel about it all?' she asked. 'Used?'

I thought for a moment. 'Yeah, I suppose I do. But I quite enjoyed being used. She uses people very well. If you see what I mean.'

Hannah realised that my ability to see some humour in the situation was a good sign, and so set about encouraging me.

'Nice to know that, Rob. Nice to know that if you've got to be someone's plaything, tossed aside when your function has been fulfilled, at least you had a good time while she ran the batteries down.'

I laughed, almost despite myself.

'And you know, Rob, you can't really complain about what Julia did. It has been known, after all, for the odd bloke to be less than frank with a woman about his circumstances.' There it was – the admonishment fist in the sympathy glove.

'Mmm. I suppose so.'

At this point Chris came into the room. 'Hiya, Rob. How did it go last night?'

The way I was slumped down in the sofa gave him his answer. Hannah filled him in with a brief summary of the story.

Chris shook his head grimly. 'Not at all what the doctor ordered. Or rather, not what the Lurve Doctor ordered. His seedy backstreet colleague, on the other hand, Dr Give Me More Of The Clare Jordan Five And Three-Quarter Feet Handicap Stakes, is rubbing his grimy, calloused hands together in anticipation.'

Hannah cringed at this mention of the race, but realising that Chris was only trying to gee me up she bit her lip, and then continued with her own efforts. 'Now listen, Rob,' she said, 'your melodramatic moping around because you've been dumped by someone you only actually spent one night with is all very interesting. But if it's all the same to you we've got a party happening here tonight, and if your face stays as miserable and ugly as that then you'll completely put the mockers on it. So finish that beer,' she put the bottle to my mouth and tipped it up so violently that as much of the lager went down my shirt as down my throat, 'and start having a good time, will you?'

The beer spillage made us all laugh. Hannah went to fetch me a cloth.

'She's right, you know, mate,' said Chris. 'You've got a race to win and girls to find. You never know, you might even find your next one tonight.'

Soon the rest of the guests started to arrive. Of course none of them turned out to be even potential assistants for my continued progress in the Clare Jordan Five And Three-Quarter Feet Handicap Stakes. But that wasn't really what mattered. What was important was that I was up on my feet again, surveying the course.

Monday 17th May

Let it never be said of Chris that he leaves a job half-done. His keenness for me to progress in the race continued this morning, in the shape of an envelope that he biked round to the office. It contained an advert, ripped out of a Sunday supplement, for a dating agency. Chris had circled the opening line: *'Ninety-six per cent of people who join our agency are looking for a lifelong, committed relationship.'*

Paperclipped to the page was a note:

No surprises there, you think. But the sharper brain, the brain (let's be frank) of the person contemplating the Clare Jordan Five And Three-Quarter Feet Handicap Stakes, analyses that statistic a little further. 'If that's what ninety-six per cent of people are looking for,' it says, 'what are the other four per cent after?' Get working mate.

Chris.

I was touched by his desire to help me out. And the logic of his suggestion was clear to see. This agency looked thoroughly respectable. What their other four per cent are after is merely friendship. Old biddies who want someone to go to the bingo with, that sort of thing. But what if there was another agency that catered for . . . I'm not going to say 'less respectable' people – as I hope you've gathered by now, self-respect isn't a concept that's entirely alien to me. No, I think the best way of putting it is 'slightly more adventurous' people.

The internet is made for this type of situation. It took a while, but eventually I got there. Youngfreesingle.co.uk. The name was encouraging, as was the site's design. Lots of red everywhere, a very saucy-looking cartoon Cupid as a logo, and a caption that read: 'The site for people who want some excitement in their dating.' The words 'lifelong' or 'committed' didn't appear once. Exactly what I need. The one thing this definitely can't be about is falling in love. I've learned that lesson. I'm saving myself for Clare Jordan. (Well, sort of.)

The website offered a ten-day trial period for free. First of all you had to fill in your name, sex and age. Then you chose a 'handle', which is the name you want your ad to appear under. (You only have to reveal your real name as and when you want to, when you make contact with someone.) The examples they gave for suggested handles were mostly place-names with a number after them. 'Manchester 404', 'Norfolk 78', that sort of thing. Not wanting to appear too 'wacky' (working in an office with Graham always keeps you on your toes in that respect), I went for the same approach. The site told me that everything up to 'London 1247' had gone. Encouraging; lots of potential contacts out there. I went for 'London 1752', the number being five feet nine in millimetres. For my password I chose 'Jordan'.

Then you had to fill in a questionnaire, saying what you were like, and what you wanted in your 'match'. Eyes, for instance. I said that mine are brown, and I couldn't care less about my match. Or rather, I could; a girl's eyes are often (along with her smile) the sexiest thing about her (despite the usual female belief that blokes can't see any further than

breasts and legs). Window to the soul, and all that. But that's
not dependent on their colour, so I didn't specify one.

At the end was a disclaimer (essentially 'we're not responsible for anyone who ends up on the "I Stalked The Girl I Met On
An Internet Dating Site" Jerry Springer episode'), and then you
clicked 'send'. All I do now is sit back and wait for the replies.

4.45 p.m.

Tim's off for the day.

Claims it's a dental appointment. Do I believe him? Has he
got a plan up his sleeve, a female plan, whose name begins
with 'A'? Or is my enthusiasm for the Clare Jordan Five And
Three-Quarter Feet Handicap Stakes, cranked up by this
morning's web activity, making me see dangers where there
are none?

On second thoughts, why am I worrying about Tim at all?
I bet he doesn't worry about me. He just gets on and plays his
own game. Is that the real difference between us?

5.10 p.m.

Oh dear, oh dear, oh dear.

Whatever the reason for Tim's early departure, he's going to
regret it.

James, you see, has just asked if anyone fancies a quick
drink after work. And although he doesn't know it, his timing
was perfect. Because he happened to pose this question just as
I was standing at the printer. Which meant that I was halfway
between him and You Know Who. Which meant that I could
add my 'yeah, go on then' to the trickle of replies in a voice

just loud enough to make her look up, so allowing me to catch her eye and bounce the invitation down the office to her (I don't *think* my voice wavered too much). She thought for a moment (a Clare moment, that is – in Rob moments it was five and a half hours), before replying that yes, tonight, for the first time ever, she, Clare, Clare Jordan, the Clare Jordan of Clare Jordan Five And Three-Quarter Feet Handicap Stakes fame, would like to come for a drink with us. Her exact words, if you're interested, and believe me if you were Tim you would be, were, 'Sure, that'd be nice.'

God this is nerve-racking.

In the Small Mercies department, I'm just grateful for the fact that Tim isn't around to compete with me for her attention (i.e. win her attention).

He's going to kick himself. Or me. Or both.

5.35 p.m.

It's been decided that we're going to Bar 38, on the corner of Garrick Street and Long Acre.

I've just been to the loo to check my general appearance. As satisfactory as I could hope for, except that my hair was sticking up a bit at the back. So I tried to dampen it down. Got most of the offending clump, but a few strands remained near the vertical. Had another go, but this time used a bit too much water, and matted the whole back third of my hair to my head. So then I had to dampen all my hair, to get it to match the back third. But this made it too obvious that I'd been dampening my hair, and I don't want Clare to think that I'm that vain or that bothered about what impression I make in the pub, so I had to get rid of the excess water by standing crouched under the hot-air dryer.

Unfortunately this meant that my backside was right up against the door, so when Paul burst in he sent me flying across the room and into one of the cubicles. Only by throwing my hands out in front of me did I manage to stop my head disappearing round the U-bend.

I picked myself up, and turned to face a clearly confused Paul. 'Sorry, mate,' he said. And then, unable to contain his curiosity: 'What were you doing?'

'Just, erm . . . just . . . tying my shoelace.'

'Oh.' He started as if to ask why anyone would be so stupid as to tie their shoelace while crouching immediately behind a door that opened inwards, but his attention was distracted by something else. 'Your hair's wet.'

Stupidly, I plumped for the 'play innocent' option. 'Is it?' I asked, looking in the mirror. The dryer had sorted out the back of my hair, but the front half was still sodden. 'Oh yes, so it is.' I started to push it back from my forehead, in an attempt to spread the water around, and stop it dripping down my face. 'That must be from . . . from when I was washing my face. Just now. And my neck. Right up high on my neck, I mean. That's where the . . . the ink was.'

'I didn't notice you'd got any ink on you.'

'No, it must have happened on the way here. I think my pen was leaking, and I scratched my neck, in the corridor, on the way here, as I say, and that's what got the ink on me.'

'Oh, right,' said Paul unsurely as he moved across to the urinal. His presence precluded any more titivating on my part, so I was forced out of the loo in a worse condition than when I'd started. All I could do on my way back to the office was shake as much water as possible from the front half of my hair, and drag my fingers back through it to match up the wet and dry halves of my head. Why didn't I just leave well alone?

Off to Bar 38 it is then. With Clare.

And without Tim.

He's going to do his nut tomorrow.

9.40 p.m.

The turnout at Bar 38 was James, Lucy, Paul and me. And Clare, of course.

James and Lucy being such an obvious couple meant that the group's gender balance revolved around me, Clare and Paul. And Paul's quietness seemed to mark him as the odd one out, making it natural for Clare and me to talk to each other. This feeling was enhanced by (in fact perhaps subconsciously it led to) the seating arrangement at our oblong table – Paul at one end, then James opposite Lucy, then me opposite Clare. I felt like an unknown actor at a Broadway audition: desperate for the chance to prove himself, but also terrified of failure and wishing that he wasn't there. Thank God there's a table between us, I thought. Not because I was scared I'd lose control and throw myself on her, just because it would stop her noticing that my knees were knocking together.

At these close quarters I noticed, for the first time ever, that Clare has freckles. The very faintest sort of freckles, like minute flicks of cocoa-powder. They give her good looks a natural, girlish quality. You just know that she's always been this attractive. She would have been the one at school who made the six- and seven-year-old boys realise there was something different about girls, something apart from the fact that they wore skirts and used a different loo. A difference you couldn't quite put your paint-stained finger on, but one which gave you a funny feeling inside.

Paul got the first round in. Clare asked for a Budweiser.

'Is that your usual drink?' I asked, for want of anything less banal.

'Yeah, I guess it is,' she said. 'When I go out back home, say with girlfriends or whatever, we'll often get a jug of Bud between us.'

Already I was analysing everything she said as minutely as a Bletchley Park boffin trying to crack the Enigma code. 'Whatever' – what did that mean? Was it 'whatever' as in 'boyfriends'? And if so, was it as in 'my boyfriend who really exists at the current moment'? Or as in 'boyfriends as and when I have them, which at the moment I do not'? Or did she just mean 'whatever'?

While my personal Enigma machine set to work on that one, I got on with continuing the conversation. Was it my imagination, or did direct questions induce a slight wariness in Clare, an almost imperceptible raising of the conversational drawbridge? It's a thought that's certainly occurred to me in the office a few times. Perhaps I should try drawing her out with direct statements.

'The thing I always forget about drinking in America is tipping the barman . . . sorry, bartender.'

'I had the same problem the other way round, the first time I bought a drink in a bar, sorry, a "pub", over here.' The unfamiliar limey word came out as 'pob'. Usually Yanks' mispronunciations are annoying, like when they ask you the way to Lychester Square. But Clare's mistake was beguilingly, sexily sweet. Despite the fact that the e-mail announcing her arrival had mentioned a first in languages from Harvard, I fantasised that she was a naive linguistic virgin, who needed someone like me to place a strong, reassuring arm around her, and guide her through the minefield of English expressions. And while my arm was there . . . Stop it, Rob, concentrate. 'I got my change, and left a pound coin on the bar, and it's only when I'm, like, a few yards away that the guy calls after me, "Hey, you left some money." And then I noticed that no one else had been leaving tips.'

Non-Enigma part of the brain was directing traffic well enough to ensure that my smile remained convincingly interested, but Enigma itself had just spotted another question. A very alarming question. One that needed urgent attention. Just which pub, or pubs, had Clare been to over here? And when? And who with? And what had happened?

I always hate this, info-blindness about someone you fancy. Well, I hate it at the time, anyway. Afterwards, whatever the outcome, you reflect how it made everything more exciting. But that's a post-event rationalisation of things. At the time, your emotions are crawling up the bloody wall. And when Clare mentioned that she'd been to a pub my emotions weren't just up the wall, they were halfway across the ceiling towards the other wall. But just in time I remembered my theory about direct questions. Steam in there with, 'Which pub did you go to?' or, even worse, 'Who have you been to the pub with?' and Clare would clam right up. I had to be subtle here.

Subtlety when your knees are knocking together is a pretty tall order. But I managed it, after a fashion. 'Strange place, eh, the English pub? I suppose you're still not used to all those people drinking warm beer.'

She laughed. (It made the hairs on the back of my neck stand up – I had made Clare Jordan laugh.) 'Some of them look really weird, I have to say. Most of the men who drank . . . what do you call that stuff?'

'Bitter?'

'Yeah, that's it . . . most of the men who drank bitter seemed to have beards.'

This, I had to say, seemed a bit of a cliché. But I excused Clare on the grounds that she's from a different culture, and so the CAMRA brigade will be new to her. Sociological niceties aside, though, she still hadn't told me who she'd been drinking with. I was going to have to try again. Much more of this and my nervous system was going to short-circuit. 'I know. Not a pretty sight, are they? Mind you,' I gestured around at the other drinkers, 'you don't see many of them in central London nowadays.'

'No, I see what you mean,' she said, surveying the suit-and-tourist barscape. 'But this place is a real old pub, up in Hampstead. That's where my friend lives.'

Ker-ching! A lead! And it would be rude not to ask about her friend now that Clare had mentioned . . . him? Her? This wasn't sexually motivated prying any more, it was plain common courtesy. (All right then, it was sexually motivated common courtesy.)

'Oh, yeah? Who's that?'

'She's,' – you don't know how my heart leapt at that first word – 'the daughter of one of my mum's friends. We've known each other since we were children. She's doing a postgrad course over here.'

Because we were talking about someone who wasn't a romantic rival for Clare, I managed to relax a little, and build up some conversational steam. 'Must have been nice to have someone in London you already knew.'

'I suppose so. Nicola's been great, picking me up from the airport, helping me unpack, things like that. But . . . oh, this sounds unkind, and I don't mean it to be, but she's kinda boring, you know what I mean?'

'Really?'

'Yeah. She's a sweet girl, don't get me wrong, but . . . Well, we just don't have that much in common any more, that's all.'

'Oh, that's a shame,' I replied. Then, realising what I was

about to say, my apprehension resurfaced. 'You should come out with us more often, you know.'

Clare smiled back at me. She didn't say anything in reply, but then neither did she fall off her chair in hysterics shouting: 'Go out with you, Rob? Because when you said "us" you meant "me", didn't you? Don't make me laugh.' And the state I was in, that counted as a victory.

I carried on. 'Admittedly there's Graham around most of the time, but apart from him we're a fairly acceptable bunch. And what's more, we make a point of never going to pubs where there are men with beards drinking bitter.'

Her smile broadened into another little laugh. 'I'll look forward to it.'

I was convinced, as I walked to the Tube later, that there was a three-inch gap between the soles of my feet and the ground.

Tuesday 18th May

10.40 a.m.

Left Tim a Post-it note first thing this morning. 'Something to report. Coffee Place at one?'

He looked a bit worried when he got in and read it. This was satisfying to see. But let's hope he hasn't got anything of his own to report from last night.

11.05 a.m.

Have just logged in to my 'postbox' on youngfreesingle.co.uk.

It took a couple of seconds to come up on the screen, but when it did there were sixteen replies. *Sixteen*! Ten days of that, I thought, would be a hundred and sixty! My finger twitching excitedly on the mouse, I opened up the first one. Which particular young, free and single respondent would it be?

'Earn extra £££ today!' the message started. 'Just forward this message to ten of your friends, and we will send you a cheque . . .' Idiot. Imagine joining a dating service just to send out chain messages. I hit 'delete'.

'XXX Hot Teen Action!' began the next one. 'Visit www.teenageslut.com for the most explicit . . .' It was at this point that it started to dawn on me. Opened the next one – yup, another porn site address. And the next – an American book entitled *How To Make a Million on the Stockmarket in Under Three Weeks*, yours for a mere $19.95 . . .

Wonderful. Absolutely fucking wonderful. Every shyster on the Net has cottoned on to the fact that sites like this are great for searching out your next load of victims.

But one of my last messages did offer a ray of hope. It was a genuine reply, from someone called Sally. Twenty-six, and a trainee teacher from Manchester. Too far away to be suitable for the race (when someone would have to travel on two motorways to reach you the odds are they're looking for a bit more than an uncomplicated one-night stand), but at least it showed there's some real interest out there.

I felt a bit rude in not replying to her. But if girls can Flirt Without Intent then I can Post An Advert Without Intent.

Must keep an eye on this postbox.

2.40 p.m.

Tim had a Grande Iced Latte at the Coffee Place, as his new filling was still 'a bit sensitive' to hot drinks. So he was telling the truth yesterday. If the early exit had been to meet a girl, you can rest assured I'd have been told about it by now.

Once we were sitting down I regaled him with an account of my Out-Of-Office Clare Encounter. Not an entirely accurate account, I have to admit. That would have been: 'She only stayed for a couple of drinks, and I didn't really find out that much about her, but even so, it was very pleasurable to sit and admire the sexiness of her freckles for half an hour.' I didn't lie about anything, though. I just left Tim enough space to wonder.

At first he threatened a fit of anger at my breaking the 'no inviting her along to collective social functions without asking the other contestant first' rule. But I countered that it had been James's invitation, not mine. And if Tim had gone to the dentist's then that was just his bad luck.

'Did she mention your selfless act of bravery again?' he asked sarcastically.

'No, Tim, as it happens she didn't.'

'I bet you found a way of worming it into the conversation.'

'Don't judge me by your own desperate standards. I'm just letting that particular fact float around in the file marked "background knowledge", playing its part in the overall impression she's forming of me.' I was trying my damnedest to get him worried.

'What do you mean, "fact"?'

Oops. Time to change the subject. 'Come on, don't be small-minded. I've pooled last night's info, haven't I? That she hasn't got a boyfriend on this side of the Atlantic.'

'Yeah, that's encouraging,' admitted Tim. 'But we still don't know about her situation back home.'

He was right. Despite my best efforts last night, we didn't.

I stared thoughtfully at the ceiling. 'You know what we need, don't you?'

'What?' Now we were on the same side again.

'Some female assistance. If that had been a girl Clare was talking to last night, instead of me, they'd have been on to boyfriends before you could say "Johnny Depp".'

Tim looked slightly lost.

'I think we should get Lucy on the case.'

'You *what*?!' he spluttered, horror sending some latte down the wrong way. 'And let her know that we fancy Clare?'

Not for the first time I marvelled at the fact that Tim, who spends so much of his life chasing (and indeed catching) girls, can sometimes miss the finer points about how they operate.

'Tim, that's precisely what I'm saying. Lucy's a girl. Girls notice these things. She'll have spotted that we fancy Clare ages ago. Probably the day that Clare walked into the office. In fact, probably before you and I worked it out for ourselves.'

Although he didn't look that convinced, Tim nevertheless agreed to the plan. We're going to ask Lucy to dig around, all subtle like, and find out whether Clare's got a boyfriend. Which, in Girl Speak, just means having a normal chat with her.

'Anyway,' he said, 'what about the race itself? Have you got a lucky girl lined up to help you with "A"?'

How could I best hide my risible lack of options? By coming out fighting, that's how. 'Oh, you know me, Tim. Always got a plan I'm working on, always scheming away, always plotting life's next little detour.'

'So that's a no then?'

I opened my mouth to tell him about the website, but decided not to in case it alerted him to the very desperation I was trying to conceal. (Not that it is desperate. Is it?) Instead I turned the spotlight on to Tim's own endeavours.

'How about you? Is there a Miss "A" waiting in the wings?'

'No,' he said matter-of-factly. 'Not at the moment.'

'Never mind, something'll turn up eventually.' I pretended to think for a minute. 'Oh, in fact it already has turned up, hasn't it? Good old Jane.'

Tim held out his closed fist, and waited until I was looking at it. Then, very slowly and very deliberately, he extended his middle finger.

Pleased as I was with my quip, I couldn't (and can't) help wondering about Tim. He doesn't seem that bothered about not having any options on the horizon. By which I mean he *really* doesn't seem that bothered. Of course he's going to be careful not to seem bothered, to present an outward display of indifference. But underneath he seems indifferent as well. I get the impression he's perfectly happy to wait for his next pulling opportunity to come along, without feeling too much need to engineer it.

And here I am filling in questionnaires on websites.

Wednesday 19th May

11.35 a.m.

Clare today. Wow. For the first time ever she's worn the dark red skirt and the black high heels together, and they're combining to make her look fantastic. But the thing that really knocked me out was the way she mouthed 'hi' as she passed me on her way in this morning. Mouthed, mind you, not said; I was on the phone at the time. Which is why it was so memorable. As I said the other week, less is more when it comes to sexiness. Plus there's the fact that a silent 'hi' looks very much like a blown kiss. And as she accompanied it with an especially friendly smile (due, no doubt, to being in a good mood rather than because it was aimed at me, but still, I didn't care), it fair set my heart a-thumping.

12.25 p.m.

About half an hour ago Lucy caught Tim staring at Clare, and gave him an 'oh yes?' look. So, after an enquiring glance at me, to which I responded with an auction-room nod of approval, Tim seized the moment. He e-mailed both me and Lucy, convening a meeting up on the roof. We staggered our disappearances from the office, Lucy covering hers by saying she was taking an early lunch to do some shopping.

'You may have noticed, Lucy,' said Tim, when we were all up there, 'that Rob and I are both, shall we say, somewhat attracted to Clare.'

Lucy guffawed. 'That's a bit like Danny DeVito admitting to being small.' I knew she'd already have picked us up on her Female Love Radar.

Tim looked a bit startled by her frankness. 'Yeah, all right, if you want it spelt out – we both fancy the arse off her.'

'You can almost see her arse with some of those skirts she wears,' sniffed Lucy.

I wanted to put my hand up and dissociate myself from this part of the conversation, on the grounds that my appreciation of Clare Jordan is based on far more meaningful factors than her (admittedly very attractive) posterior. But I thought this would complicate matters unnecessarily, so I let them get on with it.

'Whatever, Lucy,' said Tim, his desire to get to the point bubbling over into mild impatience. 'All we wanted to know was – could you find out for us whether she's got a boyfriend or not?'

'Are you really that bothered about her?' asked Lucy, realising for the first time that we were serious about this.

We both nodded.

'God,' said Lucy, genuinely surprised. 'And there was me thinking how boring she is.'

Tim and I looked at each other, as shocked by this as Lucy was by our request.

'Well, if that's what you want,' she continued, 'yeah, I suppose I could find out for you.'

And so our curious little meeting was concluded.

8.45 p.m.

That's it. Another would-be suitor gets his red card from Helen.

'I felt awful telling him, Trudi, I really did . . . he was *such* a nice guy . . . but, you know, I just wasn't *sure* . . . and I told him it would be lovely to be friends, because he really is an interesting guy . . . but I think . . . yeah . . . a while . . . at least.'

And then she was into the bathroom for another of her marathon candlelit soaks. The aromatherapy oils will be putting in an appearance as well, I'll wager.

Shouldn't a girl like that be making more of her sexual prime?

Oh, leave it, Rob. You've got enough on your plate as it is, without worrying about other people's love lives as well.

Friday 21st May

11.25 a.m.

Just checked my youngfreesingle postbox.

Almost all junk. But there was another genuine reply (or at least one that looked genuine). Someone called Kay, from Northampton. So still not close enough for the purposes of the race, but nevertheless a sign that results could well be obtained here. And results, I'm telling myself, are what the Clare Jordan Five And Three-Quarter Feet Handicap Stakes are all about.

Sunday 23rd May

6.20 p.m.

The garden fence is looking lovely after its new coat of varnish. Simpson's deafness has got a bit worse, but the vet says there are a good few years left in him yet. And extensive study of the timeshare brochure has led to a preference for Tenerife in October, although Gran Canaria in September remains an outside possibility.

These were the highlights of today's news bulletin on Parent FM. An old friend's sixtieth-birthday celebration lay the other side of London from them last night, so they stopped off on the way back today and bought me a very agreeable lunch. As always I found it easy enough to play my part in a couple of hours' conversation with them. The couple of days that Christmas usually requires tend to be slightly more challenging, but that's not for any want of love or appreciation on my part. It's simply down to the fact that, like a lot of people my age, I don't have an awful lot in common with my parents.

But as I stood and waved goodbye to them, the late afternoon sun glinting off the back window of their Mondeo, I thought of their cosy, slipper-clad stability, and wondered. What were they like at my age? I did the arithmetic, and realised (with a real sense of shock) that I am now older than my father was when I was born. Two months and seventeen days older, if you want the precise figure.

So, OK, not what my father was like when he was my age. But what about in his mid-twenties generally? What about the years before he met my mother? Did he have the same thoughts as me, the same attitudes to life, the universe and everythi— all right – to sex? Not something that I could ever discuss with him, of course, even if Mum wasn't there, which she always is. Telling my parents over Sunday lunch (or indeed ever) that I am at present engaged in a furious attempt to sleep with girls in five locations with certain initials before my mate can sleep with five different girls with the same certain initials to decide which of us gets the first chance to make a move on the girl whose name is spelled out by those initials . . . just thinking about it makes me shudder. They know about Sarah, of course, and the momentary awkwardness that passed over the table when Mum mentioned her today told me that they've guessed a little of how badly all that hit me. But that's about the limit of such talk between us.

Got back to the flat to find that Helen was out. I made myself a cup of tea, and sat down at the kitchen table. The kettle hummed and clicked gently as it cooled from boiling point, and gradually it came to monopolise my attention. Once it had completed its long journey to silence, I pressed a floorboard with my foot, causing it to creak. That too drew me in, until once more everything was perfectly still, and I felt completely alone. My parents were probably deciding which was the best route home now, or if that had been settled they'd be on to what to have for dinner tonight. Small, boring decisions, but ones that they took together, which was what kept them happy.

And I am all alone. Free, yes, free to take my own decisions. But isn't free just another word for alone?

Monday 24th May

10.55 p.m.

Good turnout in the pub after work tonight. Well, any turnout of which Clare forms a part is a good one. (Yes, another trip to the pub for Miss Jordan. She was wearing the dark blue outfit that I maintained we first witnessed on her second day in the office; Tim swore it was the third.) But it was good numerically as well, mainly because James and Lucy had insisted that everyone come along. Even Simon, who'd tried to back out citing a dinner with Michelle's friends (not his friends, you note, Michelle's), had eventually been cajoled into attending.

Irritation at having to vie with Tim for Clare's attention began to bubble around inside me. But before very long it got pushed to one side.

'If I could just have everyone's attention for a moment,' said James. We all stopped talking. Not that we really needed to listen to the rest. There's only one announcement a bloke can be about to make when his girlfriend is beaming at him the way Lucy was just then. 'I'd like you all to know that at the weekend I asked Lucy to marry me, and I'm delighted to report that she's said yes.'

There was that half a second of silence you always get at moments like this, when it suddenly seems rude to be the first one to say anything, before everyone steams in at the same time with the backslaps, the hugs, the handshakes, the kisses, the ohthatswonderfuls and the congratulationsImreallyhappy-foryous. Then there was the mini Twister session as arms reached out for whichever half of the happy couple people hadn't yet congratulated. Paul, pointing towards the bar like Columbus spotting America, shouted the single word 'Champagne!', which attracted the attention of just about everyone else in the pub, and a fair few came up to add their own congratulations. Then the whole mass of bodies started to rugby scrum towards the bar.

And then something very strange happened. If this had been a Martin Scorsese film, it would have been one of those moments when the action suddenly goes into slow motion, and the sound echoes, as though you're hearing it from the other end of a long metal tube. Robert De Niro (who's playing me, of course) is standing on his own, a little way away from the others, who are all crowded around James (Ray Liotta) and Lucy (Uma Thurman) at the bar, and the camera zooms right up on De Niro's face, and then on James's face smiling lovingly down into Lucy's, and Lucy's face smiling adoringly up into James's (this is all in slow motion, remember?), and then it cuts back to De Niro's face, looking all distant and meaningful and lost in thought, and gradually the cheering fades into a seismically cool record from the sixties or seventies, probably something by Ray Charles or The Who or Jimi Hendrix, and you know that De Niro's completely cut off from everything happening around him, and he's having a Really Important Thought.

My lone, moody thought was . . . well, I can't decide what it was. It was definitely lone, it was definitely moody, but as for what it actually was, it's one of two polar opposites, and I can't decide which. James and Lucy are turned towards each other, framed in the centre of the picture by everyone clustering round them, but they're not really aware of any of them, they're staring right into each other's eyes, perfectly, unshakably happy in their love for each other. And part of me is looking at them thinking: 'Sod that. Sod that for a game of matrimonial marbles. Who wants to have eyes for only one other person? There are, as people always tell you when you've been dumped and need cheering up, plenty more fish in the sea. So why is that only true when you haven't got a fish on the end of your rod, eh? Why does catching one fish stop you looking at all the others?'

But the other part of me, the polar opposite part (don't worry, it's De Niro, he'll be able to do them both with one look), is thinking: 'That is so beautiful. That is what true happiness is all about: just losing yourself in one other person, and not ever finding your way out, not ever wanting to find your way out.'

Leave the seismically cool record to play through for a bit (ideally until it gets to the guitar solo, so you're not fading out on vocals – very unprofessional), and then bang in a bit of dialogue that knocks us out of slow motion, jerking the sound back to normal. When the line gets repeated for a second time you realise it's someone talking to De Niro.

'I said, are you going to put your hand in your pocket for this bleedin' champagne or what?' It's Tim. (Nicholas Lyndhurst, and that's if I'm feeling generous.)

'Oh, yeah, sorry,' I said, handing over my fiver.

Things calming down a bit, we all found a table in the corner, and started making inroads into the bubbly.

'Needless to say you've all got to come,' said Lucy. 'It's in Dulwich. The ceremony's at the church, and then the reception and evening do are at my parents' place. They're putting up a marquee in the garden.'

'It's on July the tenth,' added James. 'We know that's a bit soon, but once I'd proposed we decided on all this very quickly. My grandparents are over from Canada then, the church was free, so we thought why not?'

'You do realise,' said Tim, topping up everyone's champagne glasses, 'that we'll have to start thinking about your stag night, James.'

From the corner, Graham gave a horrible little Vespa-start of a snigger. Everyone turned to look at him.

'Yes, Graham?' asked Tim. 'Do you have something to say?'

Graham assumed what he obviously took to be a knowing, man-of-the-world expression. 'You know – James's stag night.' And then, with an even more lecherous glint in his eye: 'James's *stag night*.'

Tim put down his glass, and took an exasperated breath. 'Look, Graham,' he said. 'In the unlikely event that you ever get married – and I can only assume that will happen if some poor foreigner is *particularly* desperate for her immigration appeal to succeed – in that event you will be free to make whatever plans you wish for your stag night. But if you think that James's stag night is going to feature foam, females disrobing for cash, or even the vaguest inkling of handcuffs meeting railings, then you are sadly mistaken.'

James looked a tad crestfallen, but Graham kept quiet after that. Pretty soon the champagne ran out. (As indeed did Simon, the terror at having to explain his lateness to Michelle already causing him to sweat visibly.) We reverted to normal drinks, and slowly, imperceptibly, the conversations forked further and further apart, until Lucy was huddled up in the corner with Clare, having a right girly gossip, while the boys talked stag nights.

Tim and I soon twigged what Lucy was up to. And once we'd twigged, the waiting was agony. We tried to pay attention to our discussion, but Tim and I were just killing time, waiting for Lucy's report. I remember the suggestions starting at ten-pin bowling. The dogs got mentioned, as did the horses, as did paint-balling. Someone got surreal and said something about backgammon, although the details escape me. In the end everyone came back round to what we all knew from the start would be the consensus: a really pukka restaurant followed by serial drinking.

One by one people peeled off and went home. Graham. Then Clare herself (I couldn't decide if I was sad to see her go, or relieved that Tim was now unable to make any more inroads with her). Finally Paul departed, leaving just me, Tim, James and Lucy.

'If I pay for the next round will you go and get it, love?' asked Lucy. What a darling.

As soon as James had gone, Tim and I launched a perfectly stereoed 'Well?' at her.

'So you both fancy her?'

'You know we do,' I said impatiently.

'And you want to know whether or not she's got a boyfriend back in America?'

'Come on, Luce,' said Tim, 'stop arsing around. These are serious matters of the heart you're on about here.'

Lucy raised a sceptical eyebrow.

'All right,' I conceded. 'Maybe not as serious as some matters that have been discussed tonight.'

'And perhaps there are more relevant parts of the body I could have mentioned than the heart,' added Tim.

'Apology accepted,' said Lucy. 'OK, I'll tell you. Clare Jordan let me know, here, tonight, not half an hour ago, that back in San Francisco, she has the sweetest, most devoted, most gorgeous . . . labrador in the whole wide world.'

'But no boyfriend?'

'No. I got the feeling that she might be interested in someone at the moment – but no, she hasn't got a boyfriend.'

Tim slapped the table. I punched the air. And for the second time in a minute we uttered a single syllable word in unison.

'Yes.'

My heart, though, had registered Lucy's suspicion about Clare being 'interested' in someone – and it added an 'oh no'.

11.25 p.m.

Reflecting on tonight's discovery, I realise it's made everything even scarier. I'm glad Clare hasn't got a boyfriend, of course I am. But up until now there was a temptation, even if it was only a small one, to think that losing the race wasn't something to get too scared about, because even the winner of the Clare Jordan Five And Three-Quarter Feet Handicap Stakes might end up stymied by Clare Jordan being unavailable.

Now that safety prop has been taken away, the contest seems more frightening. For the first time ever I think I understand what people mean when they talk about the 'heat of battle'. I know it depends on Clare finding us attractive, but it really could be winner-takes-all.

Tuesday 25th May

10.35 a.m.

I'm saying half an inch.

Tim insists it's three-quarters.

Either way, Clare's haircut has done what I for one thought was a physical impossibility, which is make her even more captivating. It's given her a fresh, youthful, first-day-back-at-school tinge. Remember what I said last night about the heat of battle? Well, to mix my metaphors, this has turned the gas up even more. And my worry is that Tim's going to respond by making another move. On somebody else? On Clare herself?

10.50 a.m.

My worry was not without foundation.

Tim turned to Clare as he passed her on his way to the coffee machine. 'Oh, you've had your hair cut.'

Shit, I thought, now he's going to compliment her on it, which means that I won't be able to, because it'll look like creeping. I might as well put a note on her desk saying, 'Just wanted you to know that I fancy you as much as Tim does.'

Sure enough, in he waded. 'It looks really good.'

She smiled. It was a sudden smile showing how the compliment had pleased her, rather than a perfunctory smile just to be polite. 'Thank you.'

Bastard. Him, I mean, not her. But then – and I still can't quite believe that this happened – Tim made his fatal mistake. 'Not that it didn't look really good before.'

Now that sort of line works if you get the tone *absolutely* spot on, deliver it as a throwaway spoof of a howler. But Tim didn't. Something about the way the line came out meant it really did sound as if he'd tried to reassure her about her previous appearance. I gripped the edge of my desk, unable to express to anyone (least of all Clare herself) my joy at this turn of events.

'No, no, I didn't think—' she began, formality flooding back into her voice as she dealt with the awkwardness.

Tim interrupted her. 'What I meant was it looks even better than . . .' But there was nothing he could do now. If the irony had been missing from the initial comment, there was no way he could introduce it at this stage. He was in a lose–lose situation. Clare was still smiling, but now it was an embarrassment-covering smile rather than a pleased-at-your-flattery one. I was about to pull a chunk out of my desk in utter jubilation.

'Anyway,' said Tim, having to clear his throat slightly, 'I'm getting a coffee – would you like one?'

'Erm . . . yeah, OK then, thanks,' she said, turning away.

Painfully obvious that she was only saying yes to be nice to him.

I've just, under cover of dropping a pen, examined my desktop, almost hyperventilating with euphoria. You can clearly make out the marks left by my fingernails.

7.15 p.m.

Lucy made a point of leaving at the same time as me tonight. Once we were out of the building I found out why.

'You like Clare, don't you?'

'Yeah. We told you that the other day.'

'No, I don't mean "you" as in you and Tim. I just mean you. You really like her, don't you?'

I felt flattered that Lucy could detect something in my thoughts and feelings about Clare that she doesn't see in Tim's. But then I started to worry what that distinction meant.

'I do, yeah. Why do you mention it?'

Lucy stopped. 'I'm sorry, Rob. Maybe it's not my place to mention it.'

'No, go on.'

'I just think you should be careful. You're not Tim. And in many ways that's a good thing. Don't get me wrong, I like Tim. He's lovely. In his way. But I think he . . .' Lucy stared into the distance, searching for the right words. 'I think he's very good at not getting hurt. Which is fine if you want to be like that. But I don't think you are, Rob. And that's a weakness as well as a strength. So just be careful.'

Then she spotted her bus, and ran to catch it. Is this more serious than I thought? Am I falling for Clare? I mean *really* falling for her?

Wednesday 26th May

2.45 p.m.

'Rob, I can see why you were buoyed by my haircut compliment backfiring yesterday.' We were in the Coffee Place, and Tim's dander was up. 'But that did NOT give you the right to try and salvage matters by inviting Clare to the parachute jump!' On the word 'not' he thumped the table so hard that his Tall Mochaccino sloshed all over my Mediterranean Vegetable sandwich.

'You're just annoyed because I didn't tell you first.'

'Too fucking right I'm annoyed. You've broken one of the rules.'

'I was going to tell you, but I didn't get a chance. I only got the idea after you'd left last night. She'd left as well, so she only read my e-mail this morning.'

And Clare had wandered down to us (well, to me) to deliver her reply in person.

'Hey, thanks for the invite,' she'd said cheerily. 'A parachute jump – sounds like real fun.'

I smiled, relishing the chance to breathe in the Jean-Paul Gaultier. (I was passing Dickins and Jones on Saturday, and thought I'd nip in and do some research at their perfume counter. Just in case it ever comes to it, you know.) 'Yeah, it should be. Do you think you'll be able to make it?'

'Well, that's the thing – I'm not really sure. You see, I might be doing something that weekend. Can I double-check and get back to you?'

Disappointment overtook me as I replied that yes, of course she could. But when I looked across at Tim and saw the fury in his eyes, I realised that disappointment was going to be the least of my problems.

And here we were at lunch, his anger at last able to find a voice. 'Haven't you worked it out yet?'

'What?' I asked, dabbing at the Fried Beetroot crisp fragments with my one remaining bit of dry sandwich crust.

'There might be some attractive girls on that parachute weekend. Attractive girls that could perhaps be of interest to us in connection with the Clare Jordan Five And Three-Quarter Feet Handicap Stakes.'

I stopped mid-dab.

'Yes,' he continued. 'It's going to be rather difficult to pursue the Clare Jordan Five And Three-Quarter Feet Handicap Stakes if we're in the presence of Clare BLOODY Jordan, isn't it?'

I looked at him in horror. 'Tim, I am *really* sorry. It never occurred to me.'

For a few seconds we stared despondently at the soggy sandwich.

It was me who broke the silence. 'I know why you're so bothered about it. You're the one who's definitely got an option lined up for that weekend.'

'Rob, what part of "I'm not going to sleep with Jane" don't you understand?'

3.30 p.m.

This is torture. All we can do is wait for Clare's answer.

Thursday 27th May

11.15 a.m.

Tim's coped with the tension since yesterday afternoon by playing games on his computer. I know this because the comments from those who can see his screen have included 'Which level's that you're on?' (James), 'Red seven on black eight,' (Paul) and 'Do you ever do any work?' (Lucy).

My approach has been to whittle away at Tuesday's fingernail marks. There's now a minute pile of sawdust directly underneath them. If Clare doesn't give us an answer soon, my whole desk's going to collapse.

12.55 p.m.

Clare's just passed us on her way out to lunch. Jean-Paul Gaultier again.

'Oh, I meant to say, Rob,' she said, 'that thing is on the Saturday evening, I'm afraid, so I won't be able to come along.'

'Oh, that's a real shame,' I replied.

'Yeah,' chipped in Tim. 'That's really bad news.'

'I know,' said Clare, turning to him. 'I'd have loved to come along as well.'

'What a pity,' he said, putting on an expression of disappointment that had even me convinced for a second.

'Yeah, well. Thanks for asking me anyway.'

And with that she was off. Tim turned his head away from the rest of the office so that only I could lip-read him: 'Thank GOD for that.'

1.15 p.m.

About thirty seconds after Clare had left, Tim's expression of relief changed in an instant to one of horror. He stood up and left the office. Soon my mobile beeped to denote a text message: 'Roof. Now.'

'What "thing" is she going to?' asked Tim as soon as I got up there. 'And more importantly, who's she going with?'

'Christ, I hadn't thought of that.'

'What can it be, that they can't rearrange it? Must be a concert or something.'

'Concert?' I said. 'You mean she's been asked out by a posh guy?'

'All right, then – gig or whatever. What I meant was it isn't just dinner or the cinema – then he could have changed the date for her.'

'Assuming she asked him to. Maybe she was lying about wanting to come on the parachute jump.'

'What's he got that we haven't?'

We returned miserably to our desks. A small fog of gloom has now descended over us.

Friday 28th May

3.50 p.m.

Ingrid. I've just met a girl called Ingrid.

Well, cyber-met her.

Yes – at last, and just when my ebb was lower than the average professional footballer's I.Q., youngfreesingle.co.uk have delivered the goods.

Dear London 1752,

I've seen your profile on the site, and wondered whether you might be interested in meeting up for a drink.

I'm 28, dark hair, medium height and build. I work for a Central London estate agent, but that doesn't make me a bad person.

Best wishes,

Ingrid Macleod.

When I read the message, I had an overpowering desire to leap up and do a victory lap of the office. Well, almost overpowering. I did just manage to stay in my seat. Clearly my fear of losing the race has got a bit of a kick to it. Or is it the joy of having a date to look forward to? Or both?

Thought about replying to her this afternoon, but decided that would make me appear too keen. Dating websites may be unchartered territory for me, but I'm sure the usual rules still apply. I've tried never to call anyone (or return their call) too early or too late. The same day implies you're desperate (which might well be true, but you don't want them to know that), whereas a week later implies they're a last resort.

I'll get in touch with her on Monday, I think.

Sunday 30th May

Popped over to Chris and Hannah's this afternoon. Took a printout of the message from Ingrid. I'd been thinking about it, you see, and wanted a bit of advice.

Hannah, who was cutting some recipes out of the Sunday papers, gave a contemptuous shudder. 'A website?' she sneered. 'A dating webs—'

'Look,' interrupted Chris, 'we know what you think of this race. There's no need to keep going on about it.' He refrained from mentioning that the idea had actually been his.

Hannah snatched the message from my hand. I thought for a moment that it too was going to fall victim to the scissors, but after she'd read it she smiled at me as though I was to be pitied rather than scorned.

'Ingrid Macleod,' she said. 'Swedish-Scottish. She'll be gorgeous, but expect you to pay for everything.'

'Now could I have the serious answer?'

'Hmmm. It's not exactly groaning with clues. I suppose you could say the estate agent comment shows a sense of humour.'

'But she's not what you'd call flirty, is she?' I replied. 'If all you're after is a bit of a fling then surely you start off more saucily than that?'

'Perhaps. Why does that matter though?'

'I've got to be sure I don't get anyone who wants a big romance. Or, more to the point, anyone who might make *me* want a big romance. Apart from it being unfair on them, it'd lead to all the complications I thought I was heading for with Julia.'

Hannah put the message down in exasperation. 'For God's sake, Rob, she's replied to you, hasn't she? Which is the whole point of you being on this website in the first place. Take her out for a drink. There's no obligation after that. If you're going to insist on competing in this race then at least have the courtesy to bloody well get on with it.'

'OK, OK. You're right. I'll send her a reply.'

'I just hope you feel proud of yourself,' she said, rebusying herself with the recipes. 'Really proud of how you're treating this girl.'

I wish she wouldn't say things like that. I'd tried explaining my worries, hadn't I?

Monday 31st May

3.10 p.m.

Clare's out of the office, meeting a supplier. Although I miss her, it does at least mean I've been able to compose my reply free from distraction.

> Dear Ingrid,
>
> Thanks for the message, and indeed for admitting at the outset that you work for an estate agent. Admitting you've got a problem is always the first step on the road to conquering it. I should know – I design computer software.
>
> Shall we discuss our social inadequacies over that drink you suggested? When are you free?
>
> Rob

I like this way of working. Non-Real-Time Chatting Up, I suppose you could call it. A chance to think about everything you say, make sure it's funny/intelligent/whatever effect you're trying to achieve. I wish post-work drinks with Clare could be conducted on the same basis.

I've hit send. Now I'm keeping the webpage on my screen (being careful to minimise it if I leave my desk), and waiting for it to flash up an indication that a new message has arrived.

3.53 p.m.

Hi Rob!

Great to hear from you – I'd love to meet up. I'm busy for the rest of this week. But how about next week? Wednesday?

You can explain megabytes to me, and I'll teach you all about stamp duty.

Best wishes,

Ingrid

Reflections on the above:

1. Forty-three minutes to reply. Therefore I should leave it until about half-four to get back to her. A micro-version of the 'not the same day, not a week later' rule. Don't appear too keen.

2. Busy for the rest of the week. Either she really *is* busy for the rest of the week, and therefore socially competent, or she has got nights free this week but doesn't want to admit it for fear of not looking socially competent, which in itself implies social competence. But the fact that she's on a dating website in the first place shows that she's not overly competent. Good. I think Ingrid and I could be on a level in this respect.

4.32 p.m.

Next Wednesday's fine. Where shall we meet? And
how in-depth will this stamp duty thing be? Should I
bring my notebook?

4.55 p.m.

Hi again!

I work quite near Oxford Circus – shall we meet in the
Argyll, opposite the Palladium? About six-thirty?

Yes, bring your notebook, and have all your pencils
sharpened as well. But be warned – I'm very strict, and
I always insist on lots of homework!

Ingrid.

Reflections on the above:

1. There is only one reflection: bloody hell! And unlike either
of Ingrid's, my exclamation mark is fully justified. Because if
that last sentence isn't the 4.55 Express to Flirt Central, then
I don't know what is. Let me open the window, so that those
worries about someone wanting a big romance can make their
escape.

At the back of my mind, yesterday's criticism from Hannah is
playing, very quietly, on a loop. Should I be careful here?
    No, I deserve this. Six months of misery mean I deserve
this.

5.02 p.m.

The Argyll it is. I'll be the one carrying a satchel.

Tuesday 1st June

2.15 p.m.

Clare's just got back from her lunch hour carrying an L.K. Bennett bag. More shoes?

Are they for Mr Saturday?

Grrrrrrr.

Tim could hold him down while I punch him, I suppose.

That fog's back over our desks again. And now it's a pea-souper.

Wednesday 2nd June

11.05 a.m.

Clare's wearing the new shoes already.

They're black (how many pairs of black shoes does one girl need?), about halfway, heel-wise, between most of her others and That Pair, and they have a little 'v' cut out of the front, which allows you to see a bit of the top of her feet.

Tim hit the keyboard almost as soon as she'd got into the office: 'What you'd call Fuck Me shoes, don't you think?'

Ignoring his tender sense of romance, I e-mailed back with my tactical thought: 'The fact that Clare's wearing them today is a good sign. It means she hasn't bought them to impress whoever she's spending Saturday evening with.'

'Maybe she's just breaking them in for him?'

Why does he always have to ruin everything?

11.10 a.m.

Anyway, I've found that today my attention hasn't been taken so much by her shoes as by her shoulder blades. As I stood at the photocopier, which is slightly further down the office than Clare's desk, I glanced across at her and noticed, for the first time ever, how feminine her shoulder blades are. I'd never really considered how that part of the body could be markedly feminine or masculine. But Clare's made me consider it. As the copier churned out its mundane load, I had a dreamy couple of minutes imagining the end of a long, tiring walk, with me massaging Clare's shoulder blades for her.

Thursday 3rd June

2.45 p.m.

Didn't really feel hungry at lunchtime. I think it might be the nervousness I'm starting to feel about this parachute jump. Until today it's just been a theoretical event on a very distant horizon. But now it's getting close, I've realised that what I'm going to do this weekend is throw myself out of a perfectly safe aeroplane at two thousand feet. Even though (according to Paul) more people are killed by fishing each year than by parachute jumps, I've got a creeping sense of fear.

Graham's not helping matters. He's changed the ring on his mobile to the theme from *The Dambusters*, and is calling it from his landline at ten-minute intervals to 'get us all in the mood'. Just what I need. Quite apart from anything else, *The Dambusters* wasn't even about parachuting. It was, when you consider it, very much about staying *in* the plane. To point this out to Graham, though, would be to start a no doubt intensely inane conversation with him, which in turn would encourage him to be even more irritating than he already is, so I'm ignoring him.

4.10 p.m.

I've eased off the Abigail comments in the last few days, as I don't want to provoke Tim to the point where he makes certain of finding an 'A' before the weekend. But I couldn't resist it just now. Lucy had asked whether we were all looking forward to our jump at the weekend. I caught Tim's eye, and pathetic as the double-entendre was, I could see he was fuming.

His getting stuck between Jane and a hard place on Saturday will, I think, have much the same effect.

7.50 p.m.

Helen's just answered the phone.

'Oh, hi there . . . no, I was thinking about doing some tai-chi, but I hadn't started yet, you're all right . . . oh, yes, about who? . . . what, *really*? . . . [screams as though she's seen a mouse] . . . when did he say that? . . . oh my *GOD*! . . . yes, I thought he was yummy . . . and *really* interesting, you know? . . . did you give him my number? . . . [screams as though she's seen a nest of mice] – no, no, he hasn't called . . . oh, Trudi, this is *soooooo* exciting . . . when did he say he would call? . . . oh, I'm so nervous now . . .'

Bet the tai-chi's on hold for a while.

8.40 p.m.

I was right. The telethon only ended two minutes ago.

And the truth of the matter is that listening to Helen dissect her meeting with Yummy Really Interesting was actually quite sweet. I hope he calls her. She's got to engage in some romantic activity sooner or later. Hasn't she? Watching a normal, straightforward courtship would make a pleasant change from the convolutions of the Clare Jordan Five And Three-Quarter Feet Handicap Stakes.

Saturday 5th June

7.15 p.m.

Larks are stupid.

I know, because I was up with the little sods this morning, and any creature that voluntarily puts itself through what I suffered at five-thirty is clearly not all there.

Actually, my suffering only lasted for the first ten minutes or so, before water, via the shower-head and the kettle, shocked me into life. After that my growing sense of dread at the jump resurfaced. But I also got the virtuous glow of worthiness I always feel on the (thankfully very rare) occasions I'm up that early. Instead of the comforting womb it had been a short while before, bed was now a pit in which everyone else was rotting, while I, the Intrepid Early Riser, was up and about, relishing the crisp dawn air.

Just after six, Tim pulled up in the 1982 Mercedes he inherited when his father got a new one. Next to him sat Graham.

'Morning,' I said, climbing into the back.

''lrite,' muttered Tim.

'Good Mornington Crescent,' warbled Graham.

Dawn car journeys always present my imagination with the same role to play. I'm Tim Roth (don't know why, he just seems to fit), driving a beaten-up old Chevy along the desert highway, the sun beginning to creep over the Colorado mountains in the distance, my eyes filling with tears of love as I motor my way to the girl I'm meant to be with. *Blackbird* by the Beatles comes on the radio, and carries on playing as the helicopter camera pulls back and the credits begin to roll.

'What number's Paul?'

'Seventy-eight.'

Before I know it, *Blackbird*'s finished, the screen's saying 'Copyright Twentieth Century Fox' and Paul's sitting next to me on the back seat.

'Morning everyone.'

'Morning.'

'Hiya.'

'Greetings to you, Paul, on this bright and glorious morn.'

Within ten near-wordless minutes we were outside the flat of our last passenger – Jane. Tim's shoulders tensed visibly as she appeared. The early hour had kept her make-up use to quite modest levels, and an old sweatshirt (the parachute centre advised 'practical clothing') was far less revealing than her usual choice of top, but even so, the way she pouted down her garden path was pure, undiluted Jane.

She opened the offside back door and climbed in. Paul and I received the obligatory smacker on the lips, Graham was given a friendly squeeze of the shoulder, and then Tim got a kiss that Jane transferred to his mouth via the tips of her fingers. Although it spared him the sink-plunger treatment, it was in a funny way even more provocative, because she'd had to go out of her way to do it. As Tim checked his mirror to pull out into the road I caught his eye. He responded to my smirk with a scowl.

We gradually woke up as the journey progressed, and by the time we reached the dirt-track that led to our destination, conversation was flowing smoothly. After about a mile and a half of pot-holed Leicestershire had severely antagonised Tim's suspension, we pulled up outside the biggish, low-ceilinged shed that contained both the parachute centre's office and its canteen. Next to the shed was an enormous, and slightly decrepit, aircraft hangar, its corrugated-iron roof splotched with patches of rust. In the field, on the far side of the hangar, were two twin-engined planes. They were the same size as the ones Buster Keaton used to hang off, but thankfully a bit more modern-looking. About a hundred yards beyond them were pitched half a dozen or so tents of various shapes and sizes.

It was ten past eight. Not bad timing at all. We registered our presence with the office, got some tea and toast from the canteen, and took it outside. After a while, James and Lucy arrived. Paul, Graham and Jane went off to show them where to sign in, leaving Tim and me on our own.

'In fine form today, our Jane,' I said.

'Certainly is.'

'Or should I say Abigail?'

He kept quiet.

'Yes, of course I should say Abigail. That is, after all, her name. Isn't it, Tim?'

Still he didn't rise to the bait. I noticed his fist clench a couple of times, but that was about it. He was in the same position as I'd been in that night in Amsterdam; he wants to win the race, but equally there are certain things he just won't do. How could I pass up an opportunity like that to rib him? Especially when the thought of my forthcoming date with Ingrid was there to boost my confidence?

Before I could say anything else, though, the antiquated PA system coughed feebly into life. 'Attention everyone, attention everyone. Would all those on the beginners' course please make their way to the hangar. Beginners to the hangar.'

About thirty of us gathered there, and soon our instructor appeared, a sturdy, practical-looking guy who introduced himself as Tony. After about forty-five minutes of the basics, he let us out into the sunshine for a tea break.

'Great hobby this, isn't it?' said Graham as we all stood there. 'You can guarantee it'll always get you sky-high.'

A couple of girls, who I hadn't really noticed until now, turned to see who'd been responsible for this pathetic comment.

'Sorry about that,' said Tim, cringing. 'That's Graham. He's harmless. Irritatingly unfunny, but harmless.'

The girls smiled. 'Why's he with you?' asked one of them. She looked quite young, but spoke with the ageless self-assurance of the truly rich. Halfway between blonde and ginger (blinger?), she was quite chubby, in a very attractive way. For some reason, I knew instantly that in the car park around the corner was a brand-new Golf GTI, which was a twenty-first birthday present from Daddy, and which early this morning had made its way along the Fulham Road.

'We work with him,' replied Tim, wandering over to the girls. As he did so, though, Blinger kept directing her smile at me. Drawn by it, I followed Tim across. Her friend, darker and thinner, was smiling as well. But somehow it didn't seem quite as warm. At least not to me it didn't.

'God knows how it happens,' I found myself saying, without having to think about it, 'but he always manages to cling on to us outside the office as well.'

The girls laughed. Both sets of parents were worth millions, that was clear enough from the designer jeans, the pearl earrings, the cashmere cardigans. But neither daughter seemed to have developed the patronising frostiness you usually get in Spoiled Sloanes.

Blinger spoke. 'I'm Francesca. What's your name?'

'Rob.' My heart went on a little sprint, and I realised it was because she'd introduced herself just to me. Initially, that is;

straight away she turned to Tim, who announced himself, and then we both looked at Francesca's friend, who told us she was called Sophie. But the first point of contact had just been with me. It gave me an adrenalin rush, and that drug, as it often does, opened my mouth. 'You looking forward to jumping out of the plane, then?'

Francesca grimaced. 'Not really. I'm still not convinced I should be here. I only agreed to it to keep her company. It's a birthday present from her brother.'

'Oh, many happy returns,' I said, turning to Sophie. But she was saying something to Tim, and didn't hear me.

'It's her twenty-first next Wednesday,' continued Francesca. (Knew it. This was only confirmation about Sophie, of course, but they were almost certainly the same age.)

'We're the same,' I said. 'It was Tim's twenty-first last week.'

Francesca laughed. Tim, now involved in a conversation with Sophie, half-registered that I'd just made a joke at his expense (and, to be fair, at my own as well), but was unable to do anything about it. And as I looked at Francesca, I realised that I fancied her. Nothing physical that I could specify for you, it was just something about the way we'd clicked. Already the suspicion (the hope?) had come to me that I wouldn't have to work at chatting her up. The best sort of chatting up isn't that at all – it's just chatting. It negates the need for 'lines', you know, the 'what's a nice girl like you . . .' catalogue. They always sound corny, which is why I've never used them. (All right, I've never used them since I discovered they never work.) No, the most exciting times are when you don't have to think of things to say to a girl, because they occur to you naturally. That's the surest sign that you'll get on, that she's your sort of person. And I had a nervous feeling there might be a chance of this with Francesca. It wasn't that we had a lot in common. Clearly we didn't – age, background, money, in all of these respects we differed. But that didn't matter. There was an easiness between us. It animated me.

'Come on, you lot,' Tony shouted from behind us. 'Back inside.'

Francesca and I walked back in together, with Tim and Sophie just in front of us. And a thought came to me that, even as I prepare myself to commit it to paper now, shames me. But if that last paragraph (about Francesca) was the truth, then this next one is the whole truth, and I think you'd better have it. My thought was about the Clare Jordan Five And Three-Quarter Feet Handicap Stakes. If the easiness I already felt with Francesca (and which, I sensed, she felt with me) managed to develop to . . . oh, you know what I mean, then the fact that we were on an airfield (think about it) was really quite good news. Unless you were Tim, in which case it was pretty terrible news. Especially in view of the fact that your only immediate route back to parity in the race, a route you were deeply reluctant to take, was on the airfield as well.

Glee. I think that's the best word I can find for my feelings just then. Glee, mixed with a nervousness about whether I could manage to advance things with Francesca to . . . to the required point.

The next bit of training was all about the parachute itself. Tony showed us a packed one, and then led us out on to the field so we could see it opened out. Everyone gathered round him as he lifted up a long nylon chord that was secured to the parachute's outside.

'This is the static line,' he said. 'We attach this to the plane, so when you jump out it unravels . . . and unravels,' he achieved this manually as he spoke, 'until it goes taut and then – WHOOSH – it pulls your parachute open for you.'

The package came apart, revealing something the size of about thirty duvet covers stitched together.

'Could a couple of you give me a hand?'

Francesca and I were nearest. Stepping forward, we each grabbed a handful of parachute, and started shaking furiously to open it out. Soon it caught the wind and ballooned, floating up at about forty-five degrees to the ground.

'I don't know what you're so worried about,' I whispered to Francesca. 'You're clearly a natural with these things.' She smiled.

Tony kept hold of the parachute by two straps down at the 'passenger' end. 'These are what you steer with. That's the arrow you'll be aiming for, over there.' About two hundred yards further out into the field, flat on the ground, was a piece of metal, painted white and cut into an arrow shape, about ten feet long. 'We move that according to which way the wind's blowing, so you know which way to steer.'

As Tony droned on, I turned to Francesca again. 'You probably knew that already,' I muttered under my breath, 'what with being a natural and everything.' She giggled, and pushed me away in light-hearted reproach. Looking up at the rest of the group, I noticed Tim and Jane standing next to each other. Jane raised her eyebrow at me to signify that Francesca's response hadn't gone unnoticed. Tim refused to look at me, but the grimness of his expression showed that he too had spotted what had gone on. I couldn't help treating myself to another spoonful of glee.

The rest of the morning was filled with further sessions in the hangar. At lunchtime, Tim, Jane and I found ourselves in the canteen queue together.

'Come on then,' she said. 'Tell us about her.'

'Who?' I was, I'll admit, relishing every moment of this.

'Who?' parroted Jane. 'The girl you've been talking to for the last two hours, that's who.'

Tim opened his mouth to say Francesca's name, but then stopped himself to avoid giving me the satisfaction.

'Oh, *her*,' I said, rather like Bill Clinton saying, 'Oh, *that* Monica Lewinsky'. 'She's a very nice girl.'

Jane laughed. 'Yes, Rob, she's a very nice girl – and you're so in there you'd need a map, and possibly a St Bernard, to find your way back out.'

Then she turned to Tim, whose face was now so thunderous it had probably come to the attention of the Met Office. She pinched a finger-and-thumbful of his cheek. 'Poor little Tim. Rob's gone and found a girl, and left him *all* on his own. What *is* he going to do?'

All three of us knew the implication behind Jane's teasing. It was just that one of us was a lot less happy about it than the other two.

The afternoon session was all about landing. We had to practise this by jumping off five-foot-high platforms, making sure that we hit the ground with our feet and knees tight together. Otherwise, according to Tony, you can very easily break your ankles and/or legs. Not a nice thought. At about four we stopped for tea. Tim, I sensed, was by now really irritated at just how much Francesca had been laughing at my comments during the afternoon. I couldn't help enjoying both her continued interest in me and his reaction to it.

Tony stuck his head round the door of the canteen. 'Looks like the wind's going to be too strong for you to go up tonight, I'm afraid. But we'll carry on with your practising, and get you all assessed and ready to jump for tomorrow morning. See you round at the hangar in five minutes, all right?'

'Fabulicious,' said Graham. 'I'm gonna get to use my tent.' And with a tuneless rendition of 'Gingangooly' he was off to the loo.

Paul stood up. 'I asked in the office at lunchtime about hiring tents. It's twelve quid a night, and they sleep two.'

Tim and I opened our mouths at the same time. I got there just before him. 'Shall I share with you?'

'Sure,' said Paul. 'I'll go and book it now.' He went off to the office. Only with the very maximum of concentration did I stop myself shouting 'checkmate' at Tim. Who, I noticed, had gone a light shade of purple.

'James and Lucy said they had a tent, didn't they?' asked Jane.

Already Tim was on a path whose destination, while he couldn't bring himself to look ahead to it, was glaringly obvious. But there was no way he could get his feet off that path. 'Er, yeah, they did, that's right.'

'Well, that just leaves us two, I guess.' She looked straight at him. He knew what was coming next. But there was no way it was going to be him that actually said it. 'So what do you say, Tim – shall we be canvas chums for the night?'

'I have to warn you that I snore,' he said. 'Quite badly.'

She laughed, and squeezed his knee as she stood up. 'I'm sure I can live with that.'

Sunday 6th June

10.40 a.m.

The skies await. Wind speed is acceptably low. We're behind some others who were also kept on the ground last night, awaiting our turn to jump. I'm in the canteen, writing this. Trying to ignore the question that I forgot about in yesterday's machinations, but which has been breaching the perimeter fence of my thinking since first thing this morning: who did Clare Jordan spend last night with, and is she still with him?

I can't answer that, of course. But I suppose you want to hear what I do know. Namely what happened last night in a particular bit of Leicestershire.

Training finished for the day, we all set about pitching our tents. After about ten minutes, Francesca came across. 'Sophie's done something wrong with ours,' she said. 'You couldn't give us a hand sorting it out, could you?'

Being utterly impractical, I was letting Paul take charge of operations on our tent, and merely holding down guy ropes or passing him pegs as and when instructed. 'That really wouldn't be a very good idea,' I replied. 'I'm useless with my hands.'

'I'm sure that's not *completely* true,' she said, the faintest of grins playing across her mouth.

For a second I matched her with a grin of my own, letting her comment hang heavy in the air. Then I said: 'Your certainty flatters me, ma'am. But when it comes to mundane tasks about the house, or indeed airfield, I've got a man who takes care of business. Just let him finish up here, and I'll send him across to you post-haste.'

Paul emerged from our nearly completed tent. 'Anything you say, your lordship,' he said, playing along with the joke. Laughing, Francesca returned to Sophie.

I glanced across at Tim. The look of aggravation that had been scarring his features for much of the day now seemed to have departed. Instead, he appeared quietly determined. For the first time, the possibility entered my head that he might actually be thinking of going through with it. He might sleep with (as opposed to just sleep with) Jane (or, as she is known to the Clare Jordan Five And Three-Quarter Feet Handicap Stakes, Abigail). For a second I felt annoyed with myself, for having pushed him too far.

But then my emotions checked themselves. So what if he did sleep with her? Quite apart from the fact that I was now in with a distinct chance of doing 'A' myself, I also had my date with Ingrid lined up next week. For a while during the afternoon I'd toyed with the idea of (if things went as I was hoping last night) seeing Francesca again when we both got back to London, and trying to do 'R', and maybe even 'E', with her. But two things put a stop to that. There was my worry about a repeat of the Julia situation. Francesca was much younger than me, granted, and despite our attraction we weren't likely to be boyfriend–girlfriend material. But even if my feelings didn't need considering, hers did. I don't want those sort of complications on my conscience. And secondly, Francesca had mentioned that next week she and Sophie are off to the Far East, to go travelling for 'a few months'. In fact, thinking about it, that had removed any doubts my conscience might have been having – if Francesca and I were going to end up having sex this weekend, she clearly wouldn't expect it to lead to anything more long-term.

My thinking, spelt out like that, seems pretty coarse. All I can say in my defence is that it was obviously Francesca's thinking as well. And if I was *really* that coarse I wouldn't have been bothered about her feelings at all, would I? There are men who operate like that. One of them, for instance, was pitching a tent about forty feet away from me.

But enough self-justification. Tents sorted, Francesca and Sophie joined our group in the canteen, and we decided to see what the local village had to offer. It turned out to be small and pretty, and to have the thing that appears every-where in Britain where seven or more domestic dwellings gather together – a Chinese takeaway whose decor hasn't changed since 1973 and which serves chips the size of housebricks. Resisting the temptation I always get in a Chinese takeaway on a Saturday night (namely to order that week's winning Lottery numbers and see what you get), I plumped for my usual (sweet and sour chicken, egg fried rice).

Jane and I got our food first, armed ourselves with plastic forks, and went out on to the village green to wait for the others. 'Have a word with my man,' I said to Francesca as we went. 'I'm sure he'll carry your food out for you.' As I said this Tim pretended to be studying the menu in great depth.

'I'll do that,' replied Francesca. And then, just before she turned to Sophie: 'But I hope he doesn't do *everything* for you.'

'Bloody hell, Rob,' said Jane when we got outside. 'She might as well have a sign on her forehead saying "take me now".'

'I wonder what she sees in me?' I replied, sitting on the banks of the River Compliment with a fishing rod in my hand.

'A few extra birthdays.' Jane must have seen the disappointed look on my face, because she carried on: 'Oh be honest, Rob. She's clearly not inexperienced in the ways of the flesh, is she? But most of her crowd are going to be the same age as her, hanging out in the same tapas bars and ski resorts. So getting attention from a real, proper, grown-up older lad is probably making her feel all big and clever. Especially with Sophie around to show off to.'

I mused on this as I chased a piece of chicken around the silver foil container. Not quite the confirmation of my all-round irresistibility to women I'd been hoping for. But then you can't really grumble at failing to get verification of something you never thought existed in the first place.

'I suppose you've got a point,' I said. 'Were you like Francesca in your early twenties?'

Jane considered this for a minute. 'In a way, yeah. I certainly didn't restrict myself to youngsters. But not because I needed men to make me feel big and clever. I've never used them for that. I just enjoy them for what they are.'

I chuckled. 'If a bloke talked about women like that he'd be called a sexist.'

'Not by me he wouldn't,' said Jane. 'If it feels good, do it.' And with that she devoured a spring roll so graphically that I was forced to look away.

The others soon joined us out on the green, and a very pleasant time was had taking on board our monosodium glutamate in the setting sun. After that we had a couple of drinks in the village pub. As soon as we got back to the airfield, which was by now totally deserted, Paul and Sophie executed diplomatic withdrawals to their respective tents. The evening's creeping progression to double-date symmetry was now complete.

Francesca offered Jane a cigarette. While they leaned against the fence, their Marlboro Lights glowing pluckily against the dark night, Tim and I went back to his car to fetch our sleeping bags.

'Committee meeting?' I said.

'Looks like it, doesn't it?'

'I take it my "A" is "Airfield"?'

'In a sense, Rob, in a sense.'

'What do you mean, "in a sense"?' I asked suspiciously. 'It either is or it isn't.'

'Well, obviously, assuming that you and Francesca are heading towards the fulfilment of your by now day-long courtship, and that that event is going to take place within a two-mile radius of this spot, then yes, your location is destined to be the airfield, isn't it?'

'Right,' I said. 'So it's airfield.'

'No, it's not *exclusively* airfield. That very two-mile radius to which I refer makes your challenge just too straightforward.' I couldn't really argue with that. 'So it has to be a particular part of the airfield.'

'What do you mean?'

'Think, Rob. A part of the airfield. That begins with "A". That was mentioned to us this morning.'

I racked my brains. But they failed to rise to the occasion. 'Give me a clue.'

Tim pointed out over the field. 'It's big, it's white, and it's ten feet long.'

The answer smacked me horrifically round the head. 'The *arrow*?'

'Why not?' he said, grinning in satisfaction at his own inventiveness. 'You'll be aiming for it tomorrow, so you might as well get some practice in tonight.'

I looked around, playing a solitary game of I Spy for

another, easier 'A'. Eventually, though, I was forced to give up.

'All right, agreed.' I paused. 'And what about you?'

His grin disappeared like a shot. 'No comment.'

Back outside the hangar, Jane had gone.

'She's turned in already,' said Francesca, exhaling the last of her cigarette smoke.

Instant transformation of Tim into gooseberry. 'Oh, right.' Manufactured yawn. 'Well, I think I'll join her. See you in the morning.' He set off for the tent.

''Night,' said Francesca as she ground her fag butt underneath her heel.

'Sleep well,' I chirruped provocatively. But Tim didn't even reply.

Once he'd gone, Francesca looked across at me. 'So. It's just the two of us.'

'Seems to be, yeah.' There was a buzz of anticipation between us. It excited me, but equally I couldn't help feeling stressed. The sheer length of time we'd spent flirting had managed to dissipate some of my nerves, but I was still unsure about how much intent lurked within Francesca. Would she sleep with me or not? And more than that, would she go the couple of hundred yards out into the field where that arrow was?

I tried to make my legs move me across to her. They resisted for a couple of seconds, but eventually I got an attack of courage, and suddenly Francesca was in my arms, and I was kissing her. She responded with a zeal that only served to heighten my desire even more, which in turn increased the fervour of her kiss, and so we locked in mutually intensifying passion until soon Francesca's body was pressed against mine, pushing me back onto the fence. Somehow the setting made everything even more charged. With nothing around us except countryside, no other options for things to do or places to go (no pubs, no taxis, no nothing), what we were doing became urgent, vital, compelling.

'Come on,' she whispered impatiently. 'Let's find somewhere quiet.'

One obvious solution was to go round the corner to the car park. But I blocked that option by pointing out that someone might need something from their car. 'Let's head out into the field,' I said.

'OK,' replied Francesca.

Blimey, that was easy, I thought. Before I knew it we were hurrying away from the tents, in the general direction of the arrow. The night was quite cloudy, so it didn't take long before the field enveloped us in almost total darkness. For a minute I began to worry that this might mean I wouldn't be able to find the arrow at all. But soon, as our eyes got used to the conditions, I could make it out, about a hundred yards further ahead. If I could just keep us . . .

'This'll do,' said Francesca, stopping abruptly and seizing my hand.

'No, I, er . . . think we should . . . erm, go a bit further. People might still be able to see us from the tents.'

'Don't be silly,' she replied, pulling me towards her. 'They couldn't possibly see us from there.' There was nothing I could do except respond in kind to the kiss that Francesca was planting on my mouth. And immensely pleasurable as that was, my twin worries were still there: would she, and if so, where would she? I had to think of a way of temporarily halting our embrace and decamping it another hundred yards out into the field.

'What's that?' I whispered, tearing my lips away from Francesca's.

'What?'

'I'm sure I just heard something. From over there.' I pointed towards the tents.

We both stayed perfectly still, listening for any signs of activity. Needless to say, signs of activity came there none.

'You must have imagined it,' said Francesca, cupping her hand at the back of my neck and trying to drag me back down into another kiss.

'No, no, I definitely heard something.' I pulled away from her grip, and waited another few seconds. 'There – there it was again.' It wasn't at all easy to pass up the opportunity I was being presented with here, but the demands of that bloody race called for it.

'Are you sure?'

'Yeah. Come on, let's get a bit further away.'

Before Francesca had a chance to object, I was on the move again. Not having much choice, she followed me. And indeed overtook me. Which was my mistake. It allowed her to turn round after only another fifty yards or so and stop in front of me, blocking my path to the arrow.

'Right, that's better,' she said, smiling.

'No, just a few more yards, let's be absolutely sure that there's no chance of anyone seeing us.'

Was what I wanted to say. But before I could, Francesca's arms were round my neck, and her mouth was covering mine again. Worse than that, we had dropped to the ground, and were lying together.

'Worse than that'? I can't believe I've used that phrase about that event. But so great was my distress at being blocked from reaching the arrow that that was how I felt. In a desperate attempt to seize the initiative from Francesca and give myself some more time to think, I lifted myself up and rolled us over so that I was now on top of her. Our snogging (and my brain-racking) continued apace. But after just a few seconds

Francesca decided she wanted to execute a roll as well, and suddenly I was on my back again. Briefly the farcical idea entered my head that if we carried on like this, I could, within no more than about nine hours, succeed in rolling us all the way to the arrow.

It was about the only amusement I could glean from the situation, though. Even if Francesca did want our kissing to proceed to sex, I couldn't see how to move us from where we were to the arrow. Making an issue of moving away from the tents again would be just too suspicious. What in God's name was I going to do?

In another attempt to buy some thinking time, I broke away from the clinch, and let my arm, which had been around Francesca, fall away so that it was lying stretched out on the ground.

'Like night into day.' That's the phrase we agreed on afterwards. It was like night turning into day, in an instant. Suddenly dazzling light was bathing me and Francesca, as well as every inch of the field between us and the hangar. An alarm was going off which, judging by how loud it was where we were, must have been jeopardising the eardrums of everyone in the tents.

'What the hell . . . ?' shrieked Francesca.

I looked down at my hand. A tiny red pinprick of light was playing on it. Christ – I must have set off some kind of alarm. I rolled out of the red light's path, and Francesca scrambled across to join me. We looked around us, petrified by the shock of what was happening. The illumination was coming from a row of lights along the top of the hangar, and reached about twenty yards past us. Within seconds a fresh source of horror emerged: the voices of people coming out from their tents. I could see the first of them starting to appear, although I couldn't make out who they were, largely because of the distance but also because the lights were behind them (it reminded me of that scene in *Close Encounters of the Third Kind* when the aliens first appear from the space craft). There was also the hysterical barking of a couple of dogs.

Like all true cowards in an emergency, I persuaded myself that the safest thing to do was nothing. 'Stay put,' I hissed to Francesca. 'Just get as flat as you can.' We both pressed ourselves against the ground, like the ones who had nearly made it out of Colditz but not quite. Francesca's mouth was positioned over a nice soft clump of grass, but mine found itself thrust, while it was still partly open from the word 'can', into an especially rich mound of soil. I'm sure it would have been perfect for potatoes, but my teeth felt far less at home in it. Once I'd got into this position, however, I didn't dare look up, for fear of attracting the attention of the people whose shouted requests to 'turn that fucking alarm off' were floating across to us. After a couple of minutes, someone managed to achieve that feat, and quietness, if not darkness, returned to the countryside. Not only could I feel my heart pounding, I could hear it.

Amid the gradually decreasing chatter of people returning to their tents, I managed to make out two voices in particular.

'I told Tony he'd set the bloody thing all wrong,' came the first, who I recognised as one of the instructors. 'I bet it's just another fox.'

'Three nights this week,' said his colleague. 'He is *such* a twat. What's anyone going to nick from this place, anyway? There's only the planes, and they're hardly going to start those up while we're kipping here, are they?'

'Let's keep dead still,' I muttered to Francesca, soil spraying out with every syllable. 'They'll be gone in a minute, and as long as we don't move I'm sure they won't notice us.'

She grunted her agreement, keeping her mouth firmly shut for fear of it ending up full of grass. Sensible girl.

And then I heard a voice that I recognised only too well. 'Don't you think you ought to check the field, just in case?'

You *absolute* bastard, Tim.

'No, it's all right, mate. It's another false alarm. You can go back to bed now.'

Yes, Tim, go back to bed. Jane's getting lonely.

'I'm not so sure, you know. You can never be too careful.'

Tim, you are the wanker's wanker. If you'd been in Colditz, you'd have shopped your mates to the guards for an extra helping of rice pudding.

The two instructors paused. 'What do you think, Jeff?'

I held my breath, although quite what difference I thought that was going to make from a hundred and fifty yards I'm still not sure.

'Nah, it's the third time it's happened this week.'

'Well, I appreciate that,' said Tim, 'but I think it would be better if you checked. For our peace of mind, you know.'

He'd adopted his vaguely supercilious tone, the one he sometimes uses with waiters and cabbies. Which was his mistake.

'Thanks for the advice, *pal*,' said Jeff, clearly angered by one of the punters trying to boss him around. 'But I can assure you there's nothing to worry about. So goodnight.'

Hah. Serves you right, you duplicitous little fucker.

After about another thirty seconds the lights went out, and wonderful, comforting darkness enveloped us once more. Francesca and I gave it a little while longer, just to make sure, and then stood up.

'Are you all right?' I asked, spitting out the last of my earthy supper.

'Yeah, I think so. A bit shaken, but I'll live.'

'We'd better get away from this beam,' I said. 'The last thing we want is to set the bloody thing off again.'

As we walked further away from the tents, something occurred to me.

'And, you know, I think we'd better get *right* away. We should be out of the reach of those lights, just in case another fox or something sets it off again.'

'I suppose so. But how do we know where the lights reached to?'

I pretended to think for a couple of seconds. 'You know what? I noticed that the big arrow they told us about was out of reach. We'll be safe there.'

'OK.'

Five minutes later, Francesca broke off from our kiss. 'Were you frightened back there?' she asked.

'You could say that. Why?'

'Well, I've heard people say this before, and I never knew if it was true or not, but – fear is a real aphrodisiac.'

And you can put your hand down at the back there. You know I'm not taking questions of that sort.

11.25 a.m.

Tim and I haven't been able to speak to each other on our own this morning. But even so, what's just happened will have given him all the information he needs. One of the instructors, who'd been out to move the arrow so that it was in line with this morning's wind direction, has just shouted: 'Hey, Tony, I think one of the jumpers must have landed on that arrow yesterday. There's a big bend right in the middle of it.'

11.35 a.m.

Tim's just sidled up to me.

'Congratulations,' he whispered out of the corner of his mouth. 'You managed it.'

'Yeah, no thanks to you, you little shit.'

He grinned. 'But you're still not in the lead, you know.'

I can't say it came as much of a surprise, so I wasn't overly disappointed. And in case I had any thoughts about the details of what Tim did being broadcast in salaciously detailed Jane-o-sound, he went on to explain that tomorrow she's off to Greece for a fortnight with a couple of girlfriends.

11.50 a.m.

That's it.

We've just been called.

We're doing the jump.

Now.

Wish me luck. I feel like I need it.

8.55 p.m.

The only ones from our group in my plane were Paul, Tim and Jane. There didn't seem to be any embarrassment between the last two about what they'd done. Which come to think of it, and Jane being Jane, and Tim no doubt being happy to follow her lead, wasn't that surprising. What was it she'd said? 'If it feels good, do it.' Well, it had felt good, so she'd done it.

It didn't take long for the plane to reach the right altitude, and being first out I soon found myself sitting with my legs dangling over the edge, ready to jump. Maybe it was nerves, but I can't remember making the decision to leap. Somehow, all of a sudden, I just found myself in the air. I'd love to furnish you with a fuller description of what it's like to float towards earth underneath a parachute, the isolated, magisterial wonder of the sky, and all the rest of it, but I can't. Because no sooner had I got used to being in the air than the ground was coming up to meet me. It only takes about ninety seconds to reach terra firma from two thousand feet. Someone, it appeared, had put a gigantic hydraulic platform underneath the field, and was powering it up towards me. In the last couple of seconds they cranked it into top gear, and before I knew what had happened I was on the ground.

Later, as everyone was getting ready to go, Francesca and I executed a discreet farewell. I gave her my phone number, which I think surprised her a little. She said that she didn't know where she'd be staying when she got back from the Far East, whenever that was, but she'd 'hang on to the number and give me a call'. We both knew that she wouldn't, but it didn't feel too awkward. And if I felt a twinge of regret about that, equally I knew what last night was about and what it wasn't about.

And so yesterday morning's car combinations reloaded themselves, and headed back towards a rematch with the M1. Funnily enough Tim seemed less uncomfortable about being in the same car as Jane on the way back, after they'd shagged, than he had on the way there. And in turn she seemed more relaxed. There was a sense that on her list of things to do Tim now had a tick by his name.

Now it's Sunday evening. Helen's out somewhere, so I've got the flat to myself. And I've been thinking about Francesca. Of course I have. Tim might be able to forget girls as soon as he's slept with them, but I never can. (Nor would I want to.)

A Sunday evening sadness came over me as I reminisced how much I'd enjoyed being with her. But it passed when I forced myself to remember that last night wasn't a deeply meaning-ful episode for either party, and that we could never realistically be relationship material for each other. Instead my thoughts strayed to the race. Still level with Tim. Might even be able to take the lead on Wednesday if things go well with Ingrid.

11.50 p.m.

It's an assault course, not a menu.

Life, I mean. (Don't worry, this bout of philosophising won't be too heavy. It's really just a thought about my para-chute jump.) The experiences that fill your life aren't dishes on a menu that you choose from, they're obstacles on an assault course.

You finish the course not when you get to the end of it, but when the Grim Reaper blows his whistle. And however many obstacles you've completed when that whistle goes is how well you've done. They're a measure of how full and varied your life has been. The obstacles can be whatever you want them to be – they might include going to Peru, learning karate, sleeping with someone of your own sex, robbing a bank. Or doing a parachute jump.

And they don't necessarily have to bring you pleasure in themselves. Just having done them can be what counts. Like my jump. I can't remember too much about it, and even the bits that my memory did manage to photocopy weren't really that much fun. They weren't really that much not fun, either. They just were. I did them, and that was that. No real physi-cal kick, no real emotional high – I just did them.

But looking back I'm *glad* that I did them. Glad that I'm able to say I've done a parachute jump. I've experienced that bit of life, now I can get on with some other bits. The jump is something new under the belt. Another memory for the dotage. Another defence witness should I ever face trial for Having Had A Life Full Of Television Watching And Occasional Cinema Visits.

Always regret the things you've done, not the things you haven't. You should try everything once, they say, except incest and folk-dancing. Or you could find that, before you know it, life has made your plans for you.

Monday 7th June

3.45 p.m.

The shadow that descended on my consciousness in the first few seconds after waking this morning was a little bit darker than the one you usually get on realising it's Monday. Because I remembered that Clare had spent Saturday evening with an as yet unknown companion, and that today was going to be a tortuous mix of attempting to find out who it was and not wanting to find out who it was for fear of not liking who it was. In a funny way I almost didn't want Clare to be in the office. Never thought I'd say that.

Not only was she in, she came with us to the Lunch Pub, keen to hear from everyone how the parachute jump had gone. She was, I could tell, a little disappointed with the replies, such as, 'You know, it was fun,' and 'I was really nervous, but in the end it was surprisingly easy'. As none of us had very much to say about the brief time we spent in the air, the flow of information in that direction petered out fairly quickly. And although Clare didn't know it, the flow in the other direction, about how her weekend had been, was far more interesting, at least to two of us.

The answer?

'Nicola – you remember, my friend who's doing the postgrad course over here? – well, she was having a dinner party for her birthday. And as she was so nice when I flew in, I really felt that I had to go.'

'Was it a real bore?' I asked, as Tim listened in.

'You know what? It actually wasn't too bad in the end. Nicola told me she's joined a sports team at her university, and they play . . . oh, what do you call it? Yeah, that's it – rounders. So she ran me through the rules, and how the game differs from baseball, and it was *really* interesting. We ended up chatting for ages. Maybe I was too harsh on her when I first got here.'

So in the end we were worrying about nothing. Or at least that's my conclusion. Tim asked me on the way back if I thought she might have met any blokes at the dinner party. What *is* he like?

3.51 p.m.

I wonder if she did meet any blokes at the dinner party?
    That fog's back.

4.45 p.m.

Tim and I have decided not to bother with a committee meeting. No doubt he's keen to make sure that his dalliance with Jane is forgotten about as soon as possible. Plus I bet he's annoyed about me managing to stay level with him. Imagine how he'll react if I manage take the lead.

Wednesday 9th June

11.20 a.m.

More stirrings in the jungle (well, neatly trimmed lawn) of Helen's love life last night. A phone call from an unidentified male. Bet he's the one she was tipped off about last week. I answered the phone – he was well-spoken, intelligent, a slight charmer if I'm not mistaken ('May I speak to Helen, please?' as opposed to 'Is Helen in?'). But despite putting on some dance music (no lyrics to distract me) and keeping the volume down, I still couldn't make out much of what she said to him. Not that there was a lot to make out. She spent most of the conversation giggling. Although I didn't see her, I bet you a Robbie Williams to a Gary Barlow that she spent the entire call with her finger wrapped round the telephone cord and one foot kicking the other. A date of some description was fixed for Sunday.

Any prospects of battle finally being joined this time? We can but hope. This guy must be in with a decent shout; Helen put on the *Titanic* soundtrack after finishing the call. She only ever does that when she's really keen on them.

It's funny, you know, but I've realised that I quite enjoy keeping track of this one-woman soap opera. Helen's only doing what everyone does. We all look for love, for a lover, for the lover, for whatever it is that makes us happy. She's got her own particular way of skinning the cat – so what?

On the subject of less coy females, I've just sent a quick e-mail to Ingrid to confirm tonight. She's (and I quote) 'really looking forward to it.'

So am I. Bring on that homework.

Thursday 10th June

11.20 a.m.

Boys will be boys. The thing is, so will men.

Like we needed you to tell us that, chorus the half of the species who never have been, and never will be, boys. But hear me out. This is no cheeky plea of gender-inevitable roguery. Rather it's something that occurred to me last night, a thought about how a man feels when a date's really successful.

'Went that well then?' comes the new chorus. Well, in a word: no. And, in twenty-four words: if there's a way that last night could have gone any more disastrously, arse-clenchingly wrong than it did, then I can't spot it. The only thing that's stopped me thinking about it too much is purposefully remembering dates from my past that have gone well. Hence the philosophical bon mot about boys.

THOUGHTS REGARDING FIRST DATES AND WHAT THEY TELL YOU ABOUT MEN

When a first date's going well, when the conversation's zooming along, when you're both having fun, when you both sense that you fancy each other but there's still that delicious uncertainty – you know the score – when all that's happening, a man feels like he did at primary school. The pushed-out chest, the swelling (stop tittering, this is serious) pride in his performance, the 'look at me the world's telling me I'm brilliant' grin. It's the desire for approval, for the flattering pat on the head. The same feeling you get when your painting wins first prize, when all the parents cheer your egg-and-spoon victory, and when your grandma says you're a musical genius for playing *Greensleeves* on your recorder almost perfectly.

The adult world doesn't have recorder pieces, of course. (One of its many advantages over childhood.) It has Tall, Dark and Handsome. And it has Funny. Funny is the last, hidden quarter of the get-them-to-fancy-you equation. A bit like Charlie in *Charlie's Angels*. Never seen, doesn't get a starring role, but vital to the plot. Just as the Angels depended on Charlie for their instructions, so Tall, Dark and Handsome have to wait for Funny to come along before they can get working. In fact, more than that, Funny can often make up for Tall, Dark or Handsome not being there at all. Dudley Moore, for example. Dark, yes, but not classically handsome, and certainly not tall. Funny as hell, though. Hence the women.

Comedy, of course, is subjective, which is why a good first date depends on you sharing the same sense of humour. But when that happens, and when the conversation's zooming etc, you never want the feeling to end. Which is one of the reasons for men's mortal fear of settledown. (Settledown is to a man what meltdown is to a nuclear power station, namely the end of its normally functioning state. It happens to most men eventually, but only when they're ready for it – see Initial Thoughts On The Clare Jordan Five And Three-Quarter Feet Handicap Stakes.) Settledown means No More First Dates. And so no more feeling like a schoolboy.

Don't get me wrong, I've been very close to settledown, a couple of times. And when those relationships have ended, I

haven't just cantered happily off looking for the next conquest. There's been hurt as well, a lot of it. Because going out
with a girl is lovely. Pretending as you leave her flat together
that you've forgotten something, so you can put a surprise
note on her pillow, is thrilling. Making her a Sunday morning
fry-up, followed by an intertwined-arms walk in the park,
then going back home for more of what immediately pre-
ceded the fry-up, is wonderful. Explaining the LBW rule to
her as you lie cuddled up on the sofa watching cricket is fantastic. And none of these records are available in the stores;
they can only be purchased by dialling the Having A
Girlfriend phoneline.

But sooner or later, I'm afraid, the boy inside you starts
stamping his feet and bawling his eyes out for more attention.
I wish it wasn't true. Really I do – life would be a lot simpler.
But it's pointless to deny it. A successful first date sows the
seeds of destruction for what it leads to. It gives you the thrill
of knowing that you really get on with this girl, that you've
got enough in common to feel comfortable with each other,
enough not in common to stay interested in each other, and
that there's a healthy desire on both sides to spend vast
amounts of time in bed with each other. And so that means
you'll end up going out together, and feeling something for
each other, and so that will stop you having any more first
dates that give you the thrill of knowing that you really get on
with . . .

All of which has gone halfway to filling you in on what
happened last night with Ingrid. Simply reverse everything
I've just said. And multiply it by ten. And set it to a particularly morose Leonard Cohen song. That should just about
give you the flavour of things.

We met, as agreed, in the Argyll. I was six minutes late, my
attempt at implying a vaguely devil-may-care approach to

time-keeping without actually appearing rude. Ingrid was already there. I didn't have any difficulty in spotting her, as she was well within the boundaries of her self-description ('twenty-eight, dark hair, medium height and build'). Not in the best-looking corner of the territory defined by those boundaries, admittedly. My initial reaction might even have been that she was in the plainest corner. But that didn't matter. Books and covers and all that. Besides which, risqué e-mails about homework were still powering my imaginative juices.

'Ingrid?'

'Rob, hi!'

We shook hands. This being my first ever blind date, it was only then that I truly realised how artificial they are. You shake hands with business colleagues, friends, girlfriends' brothers, even (when you get to an age when such a thing seems appropriate) your father. But shaking hands on a date? Come off it. Normally when I've been on dates things have reached a cheek-kissing stage. This was like going for an interview.

What do I mean, *like*? It *was* going for an interview. A dating agency gets you romantic interviews in the way an employment agency gets you job interviews. You both know the reason you're there. And that reason sits, blatantly obvious, on the table between you, like a hideous great turd that you're not allowed to mention.

'Sorry I'm a bit late.'

'That's all right.' She said it entirely functionally. Pleasantly, but functionally – it was nothing more than a simple communication of the fact that she didn't mind my being late. No bouncing off my apology, no reference to (for instance) something she'd been reading in the paper while she waited. All right, bad example – she hadn't been reading a paper. She hadn't been reading anything. Not a book, not a magazine, not even a label on an empty beer bottle. She hadn't been on her mobile to anyone. She hadn't been doing anything. It was as though she was just sitting there waiting for our date to start, much as one would sit at a bus stop waiting for the bus.

A little thrown, I stumbled into an enquiry as to whether she wanted a drink.

'That'd be lovely. Could I have a dry white wine, please?'

'Dry white. Sure. The Pub Landlord would be proud of you.'

Blank look on her face. 'Sorry?'

'The Pub Landlord. Al Murray, Pub Landlord? No? He's a comedian, does a mickey-take of . . . well, of a pub landlord. His catchphrase is "pint of lager for the feller, dry white wine or fruit-based drink for the lady" . . .' My attempted explanation ran full-tilt into the incomprehension on Ingrid's face and bounced back, lying bruised and winded on the floor. 'You should see him, he's great,' I gabbled, cutting my losses and heading for the bar.

As I waited to get served, my mind ran over Ingrid's e-mail last week and tried to reconcile it with the person I'd just met. How could someone who wrote such leadingly suggestive comments about strictness and homework exude such ordinariness in the flesh? It was a bit like finding out that Muhammad Ali's fight poems had been written by Gordon Brown.

That's the power of e-mail, I reflected sadly. Gives no clue as to the nature of the person sending it. No voice tone, no handwriting, no nothing. And thinking back on it, Ingrid had had just as much time as me to think about her replies. What was it I called our exchange? 'Non-Real-Time Chatting Up.' Well now we were on to the Real-Time stuff. And as I've said before, that's a two-way process. It depends, in the final analysis, on how well you get on rather than how good you are with words, and it's either going to work or it isn't. I already had a horrible feeling that I knew what tonight's answer was going to be.

'What can I get you, mate?' asked a cheery barman with a New Zealand accent. Well, to me his accent could have been either Kiwi or Aussie, but the Auckland University T-shirt he was wearing pointed towards the former.

'Bottle of Beck's and a dry white wine, please.'

'No worries, mate.'

I took the drinks across to Ingrid's table.

'You'll never believe it – that guy working behind the bar's from New Zealand. What are the chances of that in a London pub, eh?'

Now I'm not claiming that Oscar Wilde, had he been around today, would necessarily have delayed the publication of his memoirs to make sure they got that one in. But I felt confident enough that it was all right for a throwaway line on a first date, at least worthy of a response in the same vein.

'Oh, I come across lots of bar staff who are from New Zealand,' replied Ingrid cheerfully.

Christ, no. Please let it not be this bad. How could I have allowed myself to be so misled by one poxy e-mail? Not even bothering to point out that it had been a joke, I lunged hopefully at the nearest conversation-opener my brain had in stock. 'Good day in the housing market, then?'

'Yes, not too bad, I suppose.'

I stayed silent, a trick I picked up from a minor radio presenter I met in a pub once. If an interviewee gives you too short an answer, he said, you should keep your mouth shut. That way they feel obliged to carry on talking, flesh out their response a little. Eventually, and I do mean eventually, it worked on Ingrid. She started to tell me about a couple of the properties her firm have on their books at the moment, and from the way she was talking I gathered that hers is a secretarial role, providing clerical back-up to the estate agents themselves. The more junior ranks in an office are often the most interesting. They're relatively unconcerned with the back-stabbing minutiae of office politics, and can instead keep an eye on who fancies who, who's shagging who, and who hates whose guts. I rallied, and for a brief moment thought I might be in line for a rundown on the assorted deviancies of Ingrid's colleagues.

But she was not such a member of the junior office ranks. As her answer went on, it became clear that it really was going to be all about gas central heating and numbers of bedrooms.

Don't get me wrong, she was a perfectly nice person. Nothing offensive, nothing weird about her. That was the problem. Weirdness can be fanciable. Blandness can't.

After a while my brain registered that there had been a couple of seconds' silence, and that her answer had come to an end. Time for another prompt. (Oh for a Julia, or a Francesca, or even, God bless her, for dear Jane. Wonder if her holiday's claimed its first scalp yet?) Certain that if I had to listen to another syllable about property prices I'd fall asleep, I changed tack. A puzzle had started to form in my mind, a puzzle as to what someone like Ingrid was doing on a website like youngfreesingle.co.uk in the first place. I set out on a diplomatically phrased search for the solution.

'How long have you been using the website?'

'This one? Oh not too long, really. Only six weeks or so. Normally I give each site about three months.'

'Normally'? 'Each site'? A faint ringing sound came to my ears. The distant, though unmistakable, sound of alarm bells.

Radio-interviewer technique again. After a couple of seconds, Ingrid elaborated on her answer. 'I think dating websites are a tremendous idea. So much more immediate than the old-fashioned type. I haven't registered with a postal dating agency for about two years now.'

The ringing got louder.

'So you've used quite a few agencies then?'

'Oh, yes. This one seems very good, I have to say. I was meeting people every night last week.'

By now, one of the bells was about three inches from my right ear, and being clattered by Quasimodo on steroids. So the reason Ingrid hadn't fixed a date for last week was not that she was playing it cool with me, but that she was playing it at whatever temperature she could manage with whoever would reply. And without being cruel to the girl (do I have to say again that she really was a lovely person?), I can't imagine that last week's contestants would have been any more interested in going for the jackpot than I was.

I felt it time to communicate to Ingrid that perhaps she and I had different approaches to the whole dating agency question. 'Blimey. You make me feel terribly inexperienced. This is the first time I've ever done anything like this.'

'Really? You should get into it more. It's great fun, you know.'

Someone had just given Quasimodo a great fat line of angel dust. Things were starting to make sense. For Ingrid, dates had ceased to be a way of meeting a partner, and had become an activity in themselves. I got the feeling that she collected dates like other people collect train numbers. Dating agencies were her hobby. Better than torturing small animals or making obscene phone calls, I suppose. But still – a bit offputting. The thought flashed into my head of someone filling in a dating agency application form, and putting 'using dating agencies' in the hobbies section.

'You meet all sorts of people,' continued Ingrid above Quasimodo's frenzied efforts. 'But I'm always totally frank. I tell the men that if they don't want to go any further, you know, if they want to walk out there and then, they should do it. There's no point being anything but honest, is there?'

'No, of course not.' At that point my throat stopped letting words into my mouth, and so I found it impossible to say what Ingrid had clearly given me the opportunity to, should I so wish. What I wanted to say was: 'And being honest with you, Ingrid, I have to say that there is absolutely no chance of us ever so much as speaking to each other after tonight, let alone sleeping together, so why don't we just bid each other a polite farewell and leave it at that, no hard feelings?' What I actually said, after my throat relented and allowed certain, permitted words into the open, was: 'Of course not. Honest. Got to be honest.'

Ingrid smiled. Then, noticing that my Beck's was nearly finished, she stood up. 'Another drink?'

My throat and I both knew which were the only words it would allow past at this point, so I didn't even bother trying to force any others out. 'Yeah, that'd be lovely. Same again please.'

But with Ingrid gone, I was once more a free verbal agent. And those verbals were going to be directed down my mobile, straightasoddingway. To a mate. A reliable, sensible, quick-thinking mate. As I dialled Chris's number, I gave a quick glance over my shoulder to the bar. Packed. Good. It would take Ingrid a while to get served, thereby giving us time to sort out an escape plan.

After five rings, the phone was answered. By Hannah.

'Han, it's Rob.'

'Hi there. Where are you?' That silly question which people always ask when they hear you're on a mobile, despite the fact that the whole point of mobiles is it doesn't matter where you are.

'In a pub. Listen, I need help, and I need it quick. I'm trapped in the blind date from hell – yes, *that* blind date – and I need a way out. Pronto. Please, Hannah, please help me.'

Like Harvey Keitel in *Pulp Fiction*, Hannah took a few seconds to assess the situation, and then pronounced her solution with composure and authority.

'I take it she's not with you now?'

Another glance at the bar. No sign of Ingrid. She must have gone up the other end, out of my field of vision, where perhaps it was a bit easier to get served. 'No, she's getting the drinks in. We're fine for a minute or two.'

'Right, here's what we do. I'll wait five minutes, then call you. I'm going to be a friend, whose boyfriend's roughed her up and left her somewhere. I'll ask you to come and fetch me. There's no way any girl would object to you—'

'There we are, one bottle of Beck's.' FUCK! How the *hell* had Ingrid managed to get served that quickly?

Proving (even if I say so myself) a much better pupil than either Samuel L. Jackson or John Travolta, I sprang into action. 'It's all right, it's all right . . . Look, try and calm down, give it ten minutes or so, and if you're still upset, call me back then, all right?'

Hannah sensed what must have happened and stayed silent, allowing me a clear run at my acting job. What a star. In much the same way that you can fall off a bike if you think too long about how difficult riding it is, I tried not to analyse what I was doing. Instead, I carried on in soothing tones. 'Yeah . . . no, don't be silly, it's all right . . . yeah, that's it, everything'll be perfectly all right, I promise you . . . OK, speak to you soon. Bye then . . . Yeah, bye.'

Ingrid, by now seated and sipping her wine, looked at me with a dutifully worried expression.

'Sorry about that,' I said. 'Flatmate. Splitting up with her boyfriend. Been happening for a while. Getting quite nasty now. Big argument. Somewhere. Sounded like a street.'

Come on, Rob, start talking in proper sentences for fuck's sake. Any more of this and you might as well hold up a card saying, 'I'm making this up as I go along.'

'I think he's pushed her around a bit, and just left her.'

That was better. I stopped and took a sip of my beer, partly to avoid rambling on any more and losing credibility, partly because the thought of Helen allowing a shark like that through her ultra-fine net was in danger of making me laugh.

'Oh, that sounds *awful*,' said Ingrid.

Did she believe me? Hard to tell. Her words were the standard ones anyone would feel obliged to utter in the situation, but there wasn't much in the way she'd said them to convince me her concern was genuine. It was a bit of a coincidence, wasn't it? Being 'called' by my 'flatmate' at the very moment Ingrid had gone to the bar. Oh well, nothing to do but carry on and pray that things didn't get too embarrassing. For the next few minutes we chatted about this and that. Or rather Ingrid chatted, while I put my head on automatic nod mode, and yearned with all my heart for that mobile to ring as soon as possible.

Mercifully, Hannah was as good as her word. My phone trilled into action. I made what I hoped wasn't too theatrical a job of examining the number being displayed.

'Oh God, it's her again.'

Ingrid didn't say anything.

'I think I'd better take it.'

'Of course, of course you must.'

Click. 'Hi again. Are you OK?'

On the other end of the line, Hannah did what she had to do. Magnificently. An Oscar-winning performance. Or at least a bloody-big-drink-the-next-time-I-see-her performance. All the drama I needed to bounce off and more. With, of course (she wasn't going to let me get away *too* easily), a little sting in the tail for fun. 'Rob, oh Rob, oh Rob, *please*,' she cried, 'you've *got* to come and help me. I just don't know what to do, and he's been so awful to me, he really has, and now he's run off and left me, and I really don't know how I'm going to get home. It's horrible, Rob, it's really horrible, and I'm really scared. This is so rotten of . . . Tarquin.'

I pressed my lips together in a furious attempt to avoid laughing.

'It's all right,' I said after a moment, flashing a look of apologetic despair at Ingrid. But she had turned away, as if to avoid intruding on private grief. 'Calm down, Helen, calm down. Do you really want me to come and collect you?'

'I'm sorry, Rob, I know you're having such a wonderful time on your blind date,' Hannah was starting to push her, or rather my, luck a bit here, 'but really I do need you to come and get me.'

I sighed just enough to pre-empt my apology to Ingrid, but not so much that I'd look like I was being insensitive to my supposed caller. 'OK then, I'll come and get you. Where are you?'

'I'm in Venezuela.'

Hannah, we're nearly home and dry here, don't make me crack up now.

'Right. Whereabouts exactly?'

'Near the Burger King.'

'OK, I'll jump in a cab now. Just stay where you are.'

'Thanks, Rob. You're a star. Give your delectable companion a huge kiss goodbye from me.'

I hung up before she could push me any closer to the edge.

'Ingrid, I'm really sorry about this . . .' I paused, hoping
she'd fill in the gaps herself, so letting me off the task of actually saying that I was bringing our date to an end after fifteen
minutes. She didn't. I got the feeling she knew full well what
was happening (not that you had to be in Mensa to work that
one out), and was determined to at least get the satisfaction of
putting me through the wringer a bit.

'I'm really sorry,' I repeated after a few seconds of her
silence, 'but Helen wants me to go and pick her up. She does
sound in a bit of a state, I have to say.'

'Don't apologise, please don't. I understand, of course I do.
If I was in that position I'd want someone to come and get me.
Where is she?'

I started to say 'Venezuela', but stopped myself just in time.
'Brixton. I said I'd jump in a cab.'

'I see. Oh well, that's a pity.'

'I know. I really am sorry about this. But . . .'

Again, Ingrid didn't say anything. She just gave a shrug of
the shoulders, which *might* have been 'it's a pity your flatmate has had to drag you away from our date', but was in all
probability 'too bad you didn't just have the courage to tell me
the truth and say you wanted to leave'.

I started to back away, leaving her on the other side of the
table. 'I'll have to, er, get in touch . . . rearrange for another
time . . . perhaps.'

'Yeah, sure. Hope everything's all right with your flatmate.'

'Thanks.' By now I was a good few feet away. 'I'll, erm . . .
see you then.'

Ingrid, having just taken a sip of her wine, couldn't say
anything, so she merely raised her glass in farewell. As I made
my way out into the evening sun, I felt more than slightly
ashamed that I hadn't been mature enough to accept her invitation to be honest. Plus, I'll admit, there was a touch of

irritation that my chance of taking the lead in the race had gone begging. But mostly I was just relieved to be out of that pub.

Today, though, that relief has evaporated against the window of Tim's attractiveness, and is running down it in great fat trickles of worry. Perhaps it's because last night was such a catastrophe that all day long he's seemed unusually cool. The knot of his tie is casually askance in his unbuttoned collar, giving him an offhand sort of charm. Everyone's laughed at his jokes. And, most infuriating of all, Clare laughed at one particular joke, a joke that I didn't hear because they were at the coffee machine together, but a laugh that I did hear because it carried all the way down the office. No one ever laughs *that* enthusiastically, unless the enthusiasm being signalled is for more than the joke itself . . .

No, I'm imagining it. The anxiety is just me giving myself a hard time about how badly last night went. All I have to do is accept that it didn't happen. Sometimes things click, sometimes they don't. They did with Francesca, they didn't with Ingrid. And it isn't as though I'm behind in the Clare Jordan Five And Three-Quarter Feet Handicap Stakes. All I did was lose an opportunity of taking the lead.

Friday 11th June

11.55 a.m.

Do I detect the faintest increase in Clare's sexiness today? This week, even? Has the smile in her eyes been a fraction more dazzling? And if so, what can be inferred from that vis-à-vis last Saturday night? Did she meet someone whose attention has made her feel even more attractive, and so act accordingly? Or did the disappointment of *not* meeting anyone make her all the more eager to do so, which is why, maybe even subconsciously, she's put more of a sparkle into her eyes?

Immediate preference, of course, is Option Two. Clare Jordan not having met anyone else is always the preferred option.

But then that opens up the unnerving possibility that her laughter at Tim's joke yesterday was indicative of something else after all.

Hence the fact that I'm unnerved. And I don't care for it. Not one tiny bit.

12.15 p.m.

In a way I think I'd rather Clare *had* met someone else, because at least that would stop her getting interested in Tim while the Clare Jordan Five And Three-Quarter Feet Handicap

Stakes was in progress. Then, if I'd (somehow) managed to emerge victorious, I could get on with an attempt at wooing her away from that someone else.

5.05 p.m.

Clare has just cried off from post-work drinks, saying that she's 'really tired'. The truth?

Realised I'm not quite as amenable to the idea of her having met someone else as I thought I was.

5.10 p.m.

Now Tim has said he's not coming to the pub either. His brother's up in London for the weekend, and he's got to get back to the flat to let him in.

5.12 p.m.

No.

They couldn't be . . . could they?

Sunday 13th June

6.50 p.m.

Even before my phone had completed its first ring, I knew something was amiss. And I knew it was going to be Tim.

'All right, mate. How are you?'

I gave a non-committal grunt.

'Fancy coming over?'

Three little words. But three very ominous little words. My horrible worry from Friday afternoon reappeared.

'Why?'

'Oh, you know . . . just for a chat.'

He couldn't have. Could he? No, it's against the rules. But then if you've slept with Clare Jordan, the fact that you've broken the rules of the Clare Jordan Five And Three-Quarter Feet Handicap Stakes in the process doesn't really matter.

On balance, though, I didn't think Tim would have done that. By 'chat' he must mean 'committee meeting'. And by 'committee meeting' he must mean 'committee meeting to chalk up the girl I slept with last night whose name begins with "R".' This was a right pisser. Only four days ago I'd been dreaming of going ahead in the race. Now Tim had done it.

I wasn't going to let him know how annoyed I was, though. 'Mmm. OK. I'll be over' – I yawned for effect –'some time.' Then I put the phone down, and tried to think of things to do. But it was no use. The fact that Tim had retaken the lead kept slapping me around the face like a wet flannel. And I wanted to get round there to learn the worst, like when you're irresistibly drawn to looking at a bad road accident.

Even though I took the bus instead of the Tube to kill time, it was still only half past three when I sat down on Tim's sofa. He'd already taken down the *Scarface* poster, and replaced it with the chart, on which the words 'Abigail' and 'arrow' lay side by side. He picked up the black marker pen.

'Gentlemen, this meeting of the Clare Jordan Five And Three-Quarter Feet Handicap Stakes committee is hereby declared' – he uncapped the pen, which made a tiny popping sound – 'open.' Then he turned to the chart, and in the space underneath 'Abigail' wrote 'Rebecca'.

Although I'd known what was coming, the horror I felt still surprised me. Because it hadn't occurred to me until now exactly what Tim's latest success meant – he was only one step away from outright victory. If a girl called, say, Emma were to walk through that door now and have sex with him, he'd have won the Clare Jordan Five And Three-Quarter Feet Handicap Stakes. (Not to mention severely embarrassed me, but that was beside the point.) And my alarm got even worse as I realised just how many girls' names begin with 'E': Elizabeth, Esther, Elaine, Emily, Eleanor, Estelle, Emma, Erica, Eileen, Esme, Ellen, Eve, Eliza, Ella, Enid, Elsie, Eva . . . oh God.

Then came the brief, irrational thought that perhaps we'd got it wrong – perhaps Clare wasn't Clare after all, but Claire. If we had, in fact, been conducting the Claire Jordan Five And Three-Quarter Feet Handicap Stakes, Tim would just have done a letter out of order, and so disqualified himself.

'Brief' and 'irrational' indeed. Within nano-seconds, e-mails from 'Clare' and memos about 'Clare' were leaping out of my memory. But still I refused to appear bothered. 'Well done. Who is this lucky Rebecca?'

'She calls herself Becky, actually. Met her in a bar in town last night. And Gary met her friend. Those two have gone down the pub together, but Becky had to get off somewhere. She's a secretary, and her friend works in the postroom at the same firm. Or is it Becky who works in the postroom, and her friend . . .'

As Tim struggled to remember the answer to this vital question, I gazed round at the night's debris. Empty and half-empty bottles of Pils, overflowing ashtrays, some of whose cigarette butts were stained with lipstick. Some girls get wined and dined, this pair had been lagered and fagged. No doubt they'd been more than willing to accompany Tim and his brother back here. I'm not judging them at all. I'm not even judging Tim. But I couldn't help contrasting this scene with my memories of Wednesday night. I failed to fancy Ingrid because she didn't interest me. Without that spark of attraction, the evening was going (and indeed went) nowhere. I wondered what Tim and this Becky had talked about, what he thought of her as she came back here, how interested he was in her as they . . .

I realise this might sound like bitterness at Tim's success, dressed up as some kind of supposed moral superiority. And yes, if you want the totally honest answer, part of it probably is. But at the same time I couldn't help feeling that the thought of spending a night like that genuinely – what do I mean? Offended me? No, that's ridiculous. I hadn't turned into Mary Whitehouse. It's a free country, we're all grown-ups and people can sleep with whoever they want to for whatever reasons they want to. I think what I mean is that it bored me.

The thought of trying to 'get the shag' for its own sake bored me. This is not, I repeat, a judgement on Tim. I've done it myself, for all the reasons that I've told you about before. Now, though, for the first time ever, it struck me as a little bit boring.

Monday 14th June

12.35 p.m.

Tim and I have just been visited by Kerry.

Kerry is great. She works upstairs in admin, and is easily the best person at their job in this whole building. She's twenty-two, about five foot three, and could organise anything, anyone, anywhere. Nothing ever flusters her. Give Kerry a major currency crisis, a cholera epidemic and a serious outbreak of civil unrest to deal with at nine in the morning, and by teatime she'd have them all wrapped up and be asking if you've found those receipts she needs for your expenses claim. I've long been telling Kerry she should be running this firm. Not in the patronising way that office workers sometimes do when talking to their admin staff, to make themselves feel better about the obscenely inflated salaries they get for sitting on their fat arses doing next to nothing of any value. I simply think she should be running this firm.

There's no way, for instance, that Kerry would have come up with the latest piece of lunacy being foisted on Tim and me by the people who really are in charge, and which was the reason for her visiting us today. It's another 'intra-firm conference'. These are get-togethers which occur every six months or so, and which despite their billing as 'discussion forums about the future direction of the company' are nothing more than officially sanctioned opportunities for people to network their way up the corporate pole. Our offices from all over Europe send representatives, who then sit around for a couple of days in a hotel somewhere 'discussing' things, most notably their own career advancement.

This one's in Bristol, next week. Needless to say, no one in our department is at all interested in going, but for complex political reasons (with which I won't trouble you, mainly because I don't understand them myself) someone high up in our office always wants us to be represented. Paul went to the last one, so he's been excused this time. James and Lucy have made the not unreasonable plea of wedding plans. Simon has been pre-booked by Michelle for a family gathering back home in the Land That Vowels Forgot, and Graham is . . . Sorry, everyone. I actually bothered to start explaining to you why Graham is never even considered for attendance at the intra-firm conferences. Please accept my apologies for nearly insulting your intelligence.

So it was down to Tim and me. Knowing as we both do that these events are easier to face with some moral support at your side, we'd engineered a joint nomination. The afore-mentioned someone high up was only too glad to agree to this, of course, as it gives 'his team' even more of a profile on the company stage. We've both been studiously ignoring Kerry's memos about the subject, asking us various questions about the trip. They want us, for example, to provide a short outline of our recent projects within the firm, to put in the laughably pompous brochure that accompanies the weekend. (Tim suggested including the Clare Jordan Five And Three-Quarter Feet Handicap Stakes, saying it counted as company business because its aim is to further relations with our San Francisco office, or at least one specific section of our San Francisco office. I told him to shut up.) And so today Kerry, as she always does when you ignore her memos, came to see us in person, and informed us in her usual jocular fashion that unless we gave her the information she needed now she'd break our legs. Tim and I answered all her questions like timid schoolboys, until she got to the last one.

'You won't have any preferences about which hotel you stay at, will you?'

We gave cursory shakes of our heads, and turned back to our computers.

Then, just as Kerry was walking away, something came back to me from one of her memos. 'Actually, what are the choices? Of hotel?'

She consulted her notes. 'They've got block bookings in a couple – the Metropole and the, erm . . . Regency.'

'Oh, now that you say that, I'd much rather stay at the Regency.'

Kerry and Tim both looked at me in confusion.

'Why?'

'Erm, some friends of mine stayed in Bristol once. At the Metropole. Said it was an absolute nightmare. The staff were useless. The rooms were tiny. And . . . and . . . the trouser press didn't work.'

Kerry looked predictably unconvinced by this, but nevertheless gave a shrug of her shoulders. 'Fine, if that's what you want.' She turned to Tim. 'I suppose you'll want to stay at the Regency as well then?'

I kept my head down, praying that Tim wouldn't have worked out what I was up to. I should have known better.

'Just a minute, Kerry. Rob, these friends of yours – when exactly did they stay at the Metropole?'

Panic seized me. 'Erm, last year some time. Why?' Stupidly, I coated the last word with menace, to signify that I'd take a very dim view of him derailing my plan. That only egged him on even more.

'Last year? Oh, well, that's all right then. I read a couple of months ago that the Metropole had been taken over. New management, complete refit, the lot. The reviewer said he had a thoroughly pleasant time.'

My face suddenly felt as though I'd spent the morning on a very hot beach. 'Ah, well, you see, yes, erm, I know what you mean, sort of, but . . .' On and on I blabbered, Kerry looking at me as though I'd gone mad, Tim trying hard not to snigger. Eventually I stumbled across a thought. 'You see, although he had, as you put it, a "thoroughly pleasant time", that's not really too high a recommendation, is it? I mean, the Regency's bound to be at least pleasant, and it'll probably be a lot better than pleasant. So I really do think we should go for the Regency.'

'With respect, Rob, I have to pick you up on your reasoning there. We *don't* know that the Regency's going to be better than pleasant. It might be, but then again it might be a nightmare, as indeed was the old Metropole. But we *do* know for a fact that the Metropole is pleasant. I can't see that it's worth taking a risk on one hotel when we've got definite information on the other.'

Kerry looked back to me, as though following a tennis match. A particularly obtuse and illogical tennis match, if the baffled expression on her face was anything to go by.

'But come on, Tim,' I said, telegraphing him a 'this is your last fucking chance to keep your mouth shut' look, 'isn't life all about taking risks?'

Underneath my desk, the fingers of both hands were tightly crossed. Tim gave me a couple of seconds to sweat, and then brought my suffering to an end. 'Yeah, I suppose you're right. OK, Kerry, stick us down for the Regency, would you?'

'Of course,' said Kerry. And then, as she walked away, 'I don't know why you two have to make everything so bloody complicated.'

Now I can't decide whether I'm relieved that Tim allowed us to get booked into a hotel beginning with 'R', or infuriated that he's so confident of winning that he doesn't mind us getting booked into a hotel beginning with 'R'.

8.20 p.m.

I bring further news of the woman who has turned celibacy into a martial art, my darling flatmate Helen.

Owing to an especially loud appointment with the Rolling Stones' greatest hits, I missed the start of her report to Trudi on how last night's date went. She hadn't even made/answered the call when *Honky Tonk Women* started, yet when *Midnight Rambler* got to its quiet bit her familiar tones came singing into my room. I was across to the volume control in less time than it took Charlie to go from his snare to his floor tom.

'I'm so excited, Trudi . . . yeah, we're seeing each other again tomorrow night. We're going to the cinema . . . That new Kevin Costner film . . .' (Didn't even know there was one. It's probably about baseball.) 'He is *such* an interesing person . . . He works in an art gallery, only in the gift shop, but he wants to write about art, he knows so much about it . . . He's got incredible eyes . . . They just make me melt . . .' Lots of giggling at this point. 'Well, I'm not making any predictions, but . . .' Trudi finishes the sentence for her. More giggling signals Helen's agreement.

Let's hope those eyes do some serious melting tomorrow night. Could this finally be the dawning of Helen's sexual heyday?

Tuesday 15th June

11.20 a.m.

A postcard from Jane arrived at the office this morning.

'Dear All – Having a nice time out here with the girls. (And indeed boys!) Weather great, food wonderful . . .' And on it went. One of Jane's companions had drawn an arrow pointing to the word 'boys', and written 'four at the last count!' (It was postmarked Saturday.) She might have done that with or without Jane's knowledge. Either way, I'm sure the girl herself didn't mind us being informed.

'Business as usual for Jane then,' said Paul.

I grinned at Tim, who merely looked away.

8.30 p.m.

Helen's out at the flicks with her man. I'm club-videoing.

This is a self-invented hobby. I took the name from that thing clubs do when they show incongruous images (Laurel and Hardy movies, public information films, that sort of thing) on screens at the edge of the dancefloor. The post-modern humour this achieves can be recreated at home by watching random videos with the sound turned down while you play a CD. You'd be surprised how often it works. Tonight, for instance, I've slotted my everyday-use tape into the VCR, and put the Prodigy on my stereo. Highlight so far has been a Noel Coward documentary accompanied by *Smack My Bitch Up*.

11.50 p.m.

I think the eyes have it.
   I really do.
   I really really do.
   Helen's still not back. Surely that means she's gone back to his place?
   Surely?
   Please let there be more than just coffee on the menu.

Wednesday 16th June

11.30 a.m.

I know what they say about chickens and hatching, but I didn't get to sleep until gone one last night, and Helen still wasn't back.

If she hasn't cracked this time I am going to brain that girl.

7.30 p.m.

Oh for *God's* sake.

Why doesn't Helen just have done with it and become a nun? Last night's timetable, as surmised from the latest report to Trudi, was roughly as follows:

The film, followed by dinner at Café Flo, over which it emerged that Jonathan (as it transpires his name is) disagreed with Helen over the film's merits, followed by a coffee at Bar Italia, over which some further, equally earth-shattering differences of opinion took place, followed by some more coffees over which Helen decided that she 'really wasn't that sure about him after all', followed by a 'hug goodnight' on Charing Cross Road, followed by Helen waiting fifty minutes for the night bus. Which is why she didn't get home until nearly two.

I can't spell the noise that I want to make right now, but it's the one that geezer in *The Scream* by Edvard Munch is getting his throat round.

Something has got to be done about that girl. I hadn't realised until now how much I've come to care about what happens in her private soap opera.

Thursday 17th June

12.15 p.m.

Nothing to report on Clare Jordan herself, although the race that bears her name has been marked by a particularly annoying couple of hours in which every sentence uttered by Tim has begun with the letter 'E'.

Going to the coffee machine: 'Everyone all right for drinks?'

Talking to himself as he tidied the files on his computer: 'Empty wastebasket. Except for those two documents.'

During a discussion about films: 'E.T was a bit like that, wasn't it? Even though it was a kids' film, adults could really get into it. Enjoy it as much as their children.'

2.10 p.m.

Have just got back from the Coffee Place. Tim and I went there with Simon.

All morning he'd seemed a bit distracted. Kept going to the coffee machine, or the loo, or the stationery cupboard, anywhere for a wander. Even when he was at his desk he contributed not one jot to the office banter. At about a quarter to one, when the first Lunch Pub murmurings had started to circulate, we found out why. An e-mail from him to us both: 'Are either of you available for a chat at lunch? I need a bit of advice about something.'

Hello. What was all this about? His use of e-mail clearly meant he wanted to keep this to himself, so I replied in the same way, ccing Tim as well. 'Sure. Tim and I know just the place, don't we?'

A few seconds later, Tim's reply hit our screens. 'Let's meet in reception at five to one.'

By five past one we were queuing in the Coffee Place, engaged in that slightly forced small talk you always fill in with in situations like this, when somehow it doesn't seem right to start the serious stuff until you're sitting down face to face. We paid, and shuffled along to the little table at the end where you receive your chosen drink. The other two got theirs pretty quickly, and went off to bagsie a table. But I'd plumped for a mocha (which, Tim assured me, is just a posh word for hot chocolate), and the new coffee-maker hadn't been taught that one yet. The turnover of staff at this place is unbelievable. Every time you go in there you can guarantee that at least one table will be taken up by the latest recruit being talked through an A4 ring-binder of the firm's 'customer service philosophies' by a veteran of ten days' standing.

As I waited, someone asked for a small semi-skimmed cappuccino to take away. 'Tall semi cap to flee,' yelled out the hyperactive girl at the till, whose manic grin and bouncing enthusiasm reminded me of those films you see of Hitler Youth members trying to get noticed by the Führer.

To flee? If you want a two-word proof that these places are irretrievably up their own frappiatoed arses, then there it is. No doubt they think the phrase creates that 'hey, we're all so crazy in here because we all love coffee so much' party atmosphere that they're after. Well it doesn't. In my book it creates the 'look, you're really getting on my tits so can I please just have that fucking hot chocolate I ordered five minutes ago?' atmosphere.

At last my drink arrived. Overjoyed that I'd discovered a weak spot in the armour of the Coffee Place's pretentiousness, I bounded across, keen to relay my thoughts to Tim and Simon. But as I got about three steps away, and caught sight of Simon's despondent expression, and Tim's (unusually for him) paternally concerned one, I bit back the comment. Probably better not to intrude on such an evidently serious moment with flippant remarks about the significance of sales patter. Instead I sat down as respectfully as possible, adopted a thoughtful but slightly quizzical look, and waited for an explanation.

It clearly wasn't going to come from Simon, who was staring sombrely into his Tazo Chai Tea. So Tim filled me in. 'Michelle has suggested to Simon that they arrange their marriage,' he said gravely.

Normally, of course, mention of the word 'marriage' has people scrambling over the congratulatory parapets to offer their best wishes. As, for example, when James and Lucy announced theirs the other week. But this was not a normal mention of the word 'marriage'. If you hadn't worked that out from the look on Simon's face, then plenty of other clues were available. The fact that Tim had had to tell me, rather than Simon himself. The request for advice in Simon's e-mail, rather than a statement that he had something to tell us. And the final pointer, of course, was the replacement of the wonderfully emotive word 'proposed' with the mundanely routine word 'suggested'.

Even so, it was difficult to know how to play this one. Simon was clearly wrestling with the question, but if his doubts were only marginal ones, and he was just checking with a couple of his mates that marriage was the correct decision, it would be inadvisable to steam in there with: 'No fucking way, Simon, tell the po-faced battleaxe that you've been living under her thumb for far too long, and that far from marrying her you're telling her to piss off and find someone else to henpeck.' Equally, though, if being forced to make the decision was crystallising in Simon's head the realities of his position (flat on his back, with Michelle's size four jackboot firmly on his chest), then talking him into it would be like throwing a drowning man a breeze block.

So I tried to gauge the wind's direction. 'What do you think about the suggestion, Simon?'

He shrugged his shoulders. 'Don't know, really. I can see why she's saying it. Makes sense, in a way. What with having been engaged for so long, and that.'

Oh, the romance of it. And that was the obvious first answer, to point out to Simon that if the strongest argument he could come up with for marrying his girlfriend was an ill-defined feeling of it 'making sense', then perhaps it wasn't a decision crying out to be made. Certainly when you put his melancholy appearance next to the elation James and Lucy had shown, it was an uninspiring sight. But it would have been pointless to bring that to anyone's attention, least of all Simon's. OK, so a marriage between him and Michelle wouldn't have 'Made In Heaven' stickers slapped all over it. But plenty of marriages don't. Some marriages are made in heaven. Some are made in the bathroom with a pregnancy test. Some are made in the estate agent's office when you realise that your salary multiplied by three won't cut the mustard on its own. And some are just made by the inevitability of life's conveyor belt. If Simon's inclination to get hitched belonged to that last category, then he was no worse than a lot of people.

I gave him another rattle, to see what information would fall off the shelves. 'It may make sense, Simon, but you still don't seem all that sure.'

'I'm not, to tell the truth, lads. I've just got this feeling, see, that something's missing.'

'What?' I asked.

'I don't know – it's missing.'

'Have you got an inkling as to what it *might* be?' asked Tim, who was clearly starting to lose patience.

Simon leaned forward, elbows on knees and the fist of his right hand in the cupped palm of his left. This proved of no help in summoning forth an answer, so he switched to tapping his outstretched fingers on the table's edge. Still nothing. Finally he tried revolving his mug first clockwise, then anticlockwise. Eventually it produced a reply, of sorts.

'I feel as though there's some unfinished business. Something I should have done, or seen, or . . . oh, I don't know, just *something* that should happen. Before I make a decision, like.'

Tim and I looked at each other. We both knew what had to be said, but I was worried that leaving the job to him might mean Simon ending up in tears. The requirement here was a persuasiveness that was tender without becoming patronising. 'I'll tell you what I think it might be,' I said. 'It might be a case of needing to . . . how can I put this, Simon . . . erm . . . look around a bit before you make your decision. I don't know how much experience you've had of girls apart from Michelle . . .'

I deliberately left a tiny gap, in case Simon wanted to say anything. Being of the male persuasion there was no way I could come straight out with: 'How many girls did you sleep with before Michelle?' So it had to be done this way. As it happened, Simon did respond. 'Not a lot,' he mumbled. I got the distinct feeling that in this case not a lot plus one would equal one.

'Well,' I continued, as Tim stifled a yawn, 'maybe that's the something that should happen. You never really spend time with other women without Michelle being there. Perhaps if you did a bit of that you'd find it easier to make up your mind. Highlight your thoughts about Michelle against your thoughts about another girl or two, and you'll see the whole thing a lot more clearly.'

Pausing, I realised that I was doing pretty well here. Bubbling underneath the surface of my comments was an unspoken, *Don't just go with the first choice life offers you.* To spell it out like that, though, would have sounded crude. On this form, I was a serious loss to the diplomatic service.

'But I don't know how to talk to girls,' said Simon, as though someone had just asked him to take control of the space shuttle in mid-orbit. Looking down at the floor, so that Simon wouldn't notice, Tim gave a huge smirk. No doubt it was intended as a dig at me, implying that someone who was currently trailing so badly in the Clare Jordan Five And Three-Quarter Feet Handicap Stakes was hardly the best person to ask for advice on talking to girls. Well, next to him, I might not be that hot. All right, next to him I'm definitely not that hot. But next to Simon, I'm Warren Beatty.

'Rubbish, of course you do,' I carried on, ignoring Tim. For inspiration had just given me a sizable whack in the kidneys. 'And you've got the ideal opportunity next week. The Saturday of next week. Which is . . . ?'

'James's stag night,' answered Simon. He thought for a moment. 'Are you sure? I mean, if you really think that's what I should do . . .'

'Of course it is,' replied Tim, leaping into the debate. 'Just have a laugh, a drink, a chat with someone other than that . . . someone other than Michelle, and I bet you everything will start to make a lot more sense.'

Simon seemed to perk up a bit after that.

2.25 p.m.

I've just had an idea.

I think there's scope for progress on the Helen question here as well.

Saturday 19th June

11.30 a.m.

I returned to my humble abode last night feeling pretty humble myself, as Clare had laughed at three of Tim's jokes in the pub but only two of mine. Found Helen lying on the sofa, drinking a bottle of still water (she's switched from fizzy as 'it can give you cellulite'), watching *Frankie and Johnny* on video. Having fetched a beer from the fridge, I sat down to watch it with her. Of course I did – it's got Al Pacino in it, and despite the fact that at the moment he reminds me of my failings in the Clare Jordan Five And Three-Quarter Feet Handicap Stakes, I'd watch a film of Al Pacino reciting the Wolverhampton telephone directory. My only decision would be whether to have salty popcorn or sweet.

We'd just reached the bit where Pacino and Michelle Pfeiffer have their first little bicker, and it struck me that that's why the film is so good: it's realistic about how relationships start. Most of them have fairly unpromising beginnings. You've just got to give them a chance, water them regularly, point them towards the light and hope for the best. That's how Michelle ends up with Al. If only people like Helen would do the same, I found myself thinking . . .

Which is when I remembered about the other day, and how I felt sorry for Simon, and wanted to help him. And I realised what a gift this film was. I sat tight, and waited.

'Aah, isn't he lovely?' cooed Helen after a while.

'Mmm. But Michelle hasn't spotted that yet, has she?'

'No, I suppose not.'

Leave it a while, Rob. Let that one stew for a bit.

Eventually Michelle softened slightly, and we got to the first kiss.

'Aaahhh.'

'She'd have missed out on that if she'd stuck with her original opinion of him.'

'Mmm.'

At that point I stopped watching the film, and started watching Helen's reflection on the screen instead. Was it my imagination, or was there some thoughtfulness creeping into her expression?

Time to lay it on a bit thicker. 'When was the last time you gave a bloke the benefit of the doubt?'

'I can't remember, really.' I bet she can't. For the same reason I can't remember the last time I won an Olympic gold medal.

'You should do, you know. Maybe you'd end up with someone as lovely as Al Pacino.'

She laughed.

'All right,' I continued, joining in with her merriment to try to keep her onside, 'maybe not quite as lovely as Al Pacino. But even "not quite as lovely as Al Pacino" is still pretty good.'

'Do you think so?'

'Of course I do.' I pretended to think for a second or two. 'For instance, there's a bloke in my office, right, who's really sweet. Now if you were to meet him, you could probably pick out a few little things you didn't like about him. But I bet if you put them to one side for a while, gave him the benefit of the doubt, you'd see soon enough just how lovely he really is. Like Michelle does with Al.'

'Are you sure?' said Helen.

'Dead sure. Look, what are you doing a week tomorrow?'

'Nothing.'

'Right, put it in your diary. Someone else I work with is having his stag night, and Simon's going to be there. We're having a meal at L'Escargot, then going on somewhere else for the rest of the night. You be at the somewhere else, and we'll take it from there.'

Helen considered the proposition. Thankfully Al and Michelle were kissing again by now, and I think that tipped the scales. 'OK,' she said, 'I'll give it a go. No promises, though.'

Result. Simon's got his girl to talk to, Helen's got her chance to practise doling out the benefit of the doubt. Nothing's going to happen, of course. Nothing sex-wise, anyway. They might have a quick snog, if alcohol has removed enough inhibitions, but that'll be it. And even if anything does happen, it'll only be because Simon wants it to, which will mean that he's not sure about marrying Michelle, and discovering the answer to that question is the object of the whole exercise in the first place.

Sunday 20th June

2.45 p.m.

Just had a bit of a shock.

Wanted to take soundings on how best to play the Helen–Simon thing, so I phoned Chris and Hannah. The lady of the house answered, and I asked her what they were doing this afternoon.

'Splitting up,' replied Hannah, her words interspersed with tiny sniffles.

What? Where had this come from? She picked up on my puzzled silence. 'Don't worry,' she said, with an emotionally exhausted sigh. 'There's no big drama. Not really. That's the whole point.'

'How do you mean?'

'There's no drama left between me and Chris. I suppose that's why we're splitting up.'

'What's happened?'

She sighed again. 'Chris went and shagged someone from work on Friday night. I could tell there was something wrong the minute he got in. Particularly as it was four a.m. Even through the alcohol fumes it was clear he was worried. And I suppose I'd already guessed what had happened. But I didn't say anything. I waited for him to raise it. Which he did, yesterday afternoon. In the food hall at Marks and Spencer.'

'Suppose that was tactical. Reduce the chances of you making a scene.'

'No, I don't think so. He really was being eaten up by the guilt. You could tell.' What did I tell you? Guilt and Temptation . . . All right, I'll get on with it. 'And even if he was trying to avoid the saucepan-round-the-ear treatment, he needn't have worried. To tell you the truth, Rob, I'm not that bothered. Our relationship has been comfortably crumbling away for ages. This was just the rubber stamp.'

How was I meant to react here? Sympathy didn't seem very appropriate when the sympathisee wasn't that upset. 'Well, Han, I don't know what to say. I—'

'There's not a lot *to* say,' she interrupted. 'It's a shame and all that. But Chris and I have become too cosy. Stale, if you like.'

'Where is he now?'

'At his cousin's, asking about staying there for a while. He'll be back this afternoon, to start packing. I'm doing us a roast dinner.'

'Quite a civilised end to a relationship, I suppose.'

'A bit too civilised. I think the rows are still to come. I mean, quite apart from anything else we've still got to divide up the CD collection. *Abba's Greatest Hits* stays with me, that much I'm sure of. And if he thinks there's any bargaining power in U Bloody 2 he can think again.'

Funny, isn't it, how you assume some relationships are rock solid? Richard Burton and Liz Taylor – yeah, you could see the divorce coming there. Both divorces, in fact. But Chris and Hannah? It's strange to think of them not being together any more. Made me realise that I'd come to think of them as a single entity, with a four-syllable name: ChrisandHannah.

Anyway, I'd better get some things in a bag for tomorrow. When I'll be staying at the Regency Hotel, Bristol. As, of course, will Tim. Once more unto the breach, dear observers of the Clare Jordan Five And Three-Quarter Feet Handicap Stakes.

Monday 21st June

11.55 p.m.

Today has been a dark and dishonourable day in the history of the Clare Jordan Five And Three-Quarter Feet Handicap Stakes.

It started at Paddington Station, at a disgustingly early hour. Tim and I got our tickets stamped in Pleb Class, waited for the guard to leave our carriage, then strode authoritatively into First Class, just in time to blag a complimentary breakfast. Quick snooze after Reading (we'd got a table for four, which allowed a diagonally opposite, feet-up-on-the-seats configuration). At Bristol we got a cab from the station to our hotel, flicking through today's agenda on the way. Everything was happening at the Metropole. The Regency, it seemed, was just an overflow place. Good call by me, then. We were safely out of the eye of the networking storm, with a ready-made bolt-hole should things get unbearably dull. Not that I'd made the call for those reasons, of course.

Having dumped our bags, we turned the five-minute walk to the Metropole into a ten-minute saunter, arriving just in time for our first session at ten o'clock. This was in the Churchill Room (others included the De Gaulle, the Kennedy, the Adenauer . . . you get the picture, and I'm sure you're just as depressed by it as I was), and was entitled 'New Horizons: Corporate Decision Making In The Twenty-First Century'.

Of course what it should have been called was 'Some Overpaid Management Lecturer Combines Blindingly Obvious Common Sense And Meaningless Jargon For Two Hours In An Attempt To Lend This Pointless Conference Some Academic Credibility'.

If Churchill had had to direct any of the Second World War from the room which bears his name, Germany would now finish at John o'Groats. It was a windowless, reproduction-pine-laminate nightmare, whose carpet wanted to be maroon but was really brown. Several tables had been arranged into a horseshoe, at the open end of which was an easel-type stand, bearing a pad of A2 paper. Tim and I took our places, and surveyed the dozen people with whom we were to share this morning of air-conditioned hell. Nothing very encouraging, either in terms of the Clare Jordan Five And Three-Quarter Feet Handicap Stakes, or simply someone to have a laugh with to help us get through the session. The company line ran all around the room, and twelve big toes were tied securely to it.

At five seconds past ten o'clock, Judy appeared. We knew she was called Judy, because a white plastic badge on the lapel of her immaculately clean pastel-green jacket told us so. Underneath the jacket was the perfectly arranged ruff of a pristine white blouse. The professionalism with which the make-up on Judy's nondescript face had been applied was undeniable. But despite her faultless appearance (in fact perhaps because of it), it was clear that thirty-odd years as a member of this species had done nothing to teach Judy how to act like one. There was something so unhuman, so unreal about her look that in a strange way it made me feel sorry for her.

My sympathy was short-lived, however. It didn't even survive her first sentence, which was delivered in a voice so

smothered in nasality that her accent was completely uniden-
tifiable, although for some reason my mind kept flashing up
the word 'Stevenage'.

'Good morning, everyone, my name is Judy, and I am from
Brook Davies Management Consultants.'

Perhaps the other sessions had got lecturers as wooden as
this, but I doubted it. (We'd been split into several groups for
the morning. From the look of it, ours was the 'keep the kids
out of the way while the forty-somethings start their heavy-
duty networking' group.) Judy's voice seemed to bypass lungs
and larynx, starting straight from her sinuses. 'This morning's session *will* be quite intense, and we *are* going to cover
quite a lot, so you might like to take notes in the folders provided.'

I knew it. Unnecessary emphasis on verbs. The sure sign of
a brain-dead script-slave. Why did she need to emphasise
'will'? 'This morning's session *will* be quite intense.' None of
us had said it wouldn't. You get it everywhere nowadays. 'Our
flying time today *will* be one hour forty minutes.' 'There *are* a
number of payment options available on this model.' My
mind wandered back to Winston. Imagine if he'd delivered his
speeches in the same manner. 'We *shall* fight them on the
beaches . . .' 'Never in the field of human conflict *was* so much
owed . . .'

'. . . improve your decision-making in today's business
environment.'

How did she get her voice to sound that nasal? It was
almost as though there was a clothes peg on her nose, but I
couldn't see one. Maybe it was a really tiny one, flesh-
coloured so you couldn't . . .

'And the first question that we need to consider is, "What
initial step should we always take when confronted by a
decision?"'

Or perhaps she'd had some kind of internal clip fitted, that pinched the top of her nose from the inside? That way you'd get the nasal quality without anyone seeing the . . .

'So let me "throw" that one over to you, as it were. Anyone got any ideas?'

Judy signified the quotation marks around 'throw' with a double-handed waggle of her index and middle fingers. As always when anyone does that, I had an almost uncontrollable urge to use my own index and middle fingers, one in her left eye, the other in her right. So it was at that point that my sanity erected a defence shield around itself, and stopped my memory from recording any more of the session. As a result, all I can tell you is what's in my notes. They read as follows: 'nasality', 'lapel badge', 'neatly arranged pens', 'originality, completely lacking in', 'Debenhams', 'anal', 'Nissan Micra' and 'Celine Dion's Greatest Hits'.

Eventually we reached the end of the session. Judy thanked us very much for attending (as though we'd had any choice in the matter), and expressed her hope that we '*had* found the session of value'. She then went a little way towards ruining my lunch appetite (which was by that stage approximately the size of Kent) by revealing that those of us attending the afternoon session on 'Market Positioning – A Fresh Perspective' would be seeing her again, as she was taking that one too.

'Be still my beating heart,' muttered Tim under his breath as we scraped back our chairs.

Down in the lunch room, grazing contentedly on a table of our own, Tim and I assessed everyone turning up from the other sessions. All was as we'd feared. Politics aplenty, but not one drop of genuine friendliness.

And then *they* appeared. At that precise moment Tim was gazing out into the room, chewing away while I spoke to him. And I swear to you, I swear on anything you care to have me swear on, that his jaws stopped moving. For at least three seconds. Needless to say this reaction caused me to turn round, and follow Tim's sightline until I spied the cause of his wonderment.

The mousy blonde was taller than the blonde blonde (about five seven to five six), and they were both, I have to admit, very good-looking. Inevitably they were surrounded within seconds, a forest of Boss and Armani shielding them from our gaze. I turned back to face Tim. And as I watched him attempting to watch the girls, I realised that my heart felt heavy rather than excited. More talk of girls, now. No doubt we'd be endeavouring to chat them up before the day was out. The same old routine was to be acted out once more. Yes, the possibility of a further step in the Clare Jordan Five And Three-Quarter Feet Handicap Stakes was there for me. If either of those girls had a name beginning with 'E', though, that possibility was there for Tim as well. And a further step for him meant the final step. I was annoyed. But I couldn't tell how much of it was annoyance at my rival's possible progress in the race, and how much at the race in general.

'Our age?' asked Tim.

I did my duty. 'Yeah. Maybe a bit younger.'

'Good. They didn't look the sort to go for older men, did they?' Tim reflected for a moment before answering his own question. 'Nah. They might flirt a bit with Club 38–50 over there, but only on a keeping-in-with-the-bosses basis.'

Even as he spoke the group began to move along the buffet table in a single mass, like a celebrity and their press pack after a court case. The competing males then vied with each other to sit with the girls. In the end five of them secured the honour. Tim gave a running commentary, which I let wash over me.

'They're laughing with one of them . . . but it looks pretty routine . . . now they're just talking to each other . . . blanking the guys . . . hang on . . . you know the really smooth-looking one, with the tan and the slicked-back hair? . . . well, he's offering Mousy his napkin – she's just knocked a bit of her wine over . . . *yes*, she's ignored him, she's using Blonde's . . . now she's pretended to notice him at the last minute . . . "oh sorry, didn't see you, it's all cleared up now, thanks anyway" . . . he's blushed a bit, the others are looking smug, they know he's out of the race . . .'

And so on. Tim was obsessed. Even after his initial commentary stint, he kept going back for updates. Despite the occasional midfield tussle, at no point was there any change in the score.

Soon two o'clock loomed, and our next session. This, being a slightly larger group, was in the Roosevelt Room, at the back of the ground floor. On the way Tim said he needed a pee, so he'd see me in there. When I'd got to the room, found my seat and sat down, I looked up and saw something that, initially, made my heart even heavier than it had been at lunch. It even bred a little boredom within me. But then a sense of mischief sprang up, rebelling against that boredom and giving me an idea. Within thirty seconds I'd acted on it, and was back out of the room. Thankfully Tim hadn't yet got there, so I ducked into the Gents straight over the corridor.

When I came out again, a couple of minutes later, Tim was waiting for me just outside the Roosevelt Room.

'Where did you get to?' he asked.

'Same as you. Except I went to the one just there.'

'Oh.' A grin appeared on his face. 'So you haven't been in there yet?'

'No. Why?'

He grabbed me by the shoulders. 'Bountifully has the Almighty blessed us today with His gifts.'

'What?'

'They're in there.'

'What, *the girls*? *They're* in our session?' Mischief, I was discovering, can make you a pretty good actor when you need to be.

'Indeed, Robert, indeed. And, if you please, seated directly opposite us.'

By now Tim's grin was almost coming off the edges of his cheeks. I gave him a gentle slap across the face. 'Well, for God's sake, play it cool then. I'm not having you scaring them off by looking like the bastard love child of Jack Nicholson and Carol Smillie.'

Tim took a deep breath. 'Sorry mate. But you've got to admit – it's bloody good news, isn't it?'

'Of course,' I said coolly.

'And you don't know the half of it yet.'

'Don't I?'

Tim was too keyed up to notice the implication behind my comment. Although he didn't know it, I was in control here. And I was loving it.

'You'll see, you'll see,' he said, turning and heading into the room. I followed, and saw the girls sitting at top-left of the horseshoe. The door was at bottom-centre, and Tim and I turned to the right, to reach our seats slap bang opposite them. In front of the girls, on the desk, were their place cards. The blonde blonde's, on the right as Tim and I looked at them, said 'Orianne', while the mousy blonde's bore the name 'Elena'.

'Wow, even their names are pretty,' I whispered to Tim. 'Funny, isn't it,' I began to treat him to one of my pet theories, 'how many attractive people have unattractive names? The

Hollywood sex symbol Miss Stone, for instance. Or the heart-throb actor Mr Firth. Or . . . Hang on.' I looked back at the place cards. The one on the left in particular.

Tim's grin had reappeared. 'Yes, Rob,' he muttered. '*That* was the half of it you didn't know.'

I swallowed hard, and set my face in as determined an expression as I could manage. 'You're assuming that Elena's going to fancy you,' I hissed dramatically. 'If she does, then fine. But if she doesn't, Tim, and if I can get Orianne to the Regency . . .'

'We'll see,' he chuckled.

Before either of us could say anything else, Judy marched in to the room.

'Good afternoon, everyone. For those of you whose company I did not have the pleasure of this morning, my name is Judy. I'll be taking your session this afternoon on "Market Positioning – A Fresh Perspective".'

Then she started her spiel. About fifteen minutes in, I managed to catch Orianne's eye. At first I wasn't sure whether she was smiling, or if her features had merely glazed over into vacant boredom. But when I ratcheted up my own smile a fraction she followed suit, and soon I realised that those blue eyes were shining back at me, if not suggestively then at least warmly. We locked stares for what felt like the ideal amount of time, then looked away simultaneously.

After that we settled into smiling at each other every few minutes. This was good, as it gave me time to get used to the idea that Orianne might actually be interested in me before I had to do anything as complicated as talking to her. And I got a further boost of confidence from the fact that Tim hadn't yet managed to get himself on smiling terms with Elena.

The session continued for another half an hour or so, at which point Judy suggested that we break for coffee, which was to be served in the buffet room. Everyone rose, and the mild hubbub of a dozen conversationettes began to fill the room.

The girls' progress down their side of the room was quicker than Tim and I could manage down ours as a huddle of senior managers had formed, blocking our way while they feverishly discussed a point Judy had raised in one of her babbleogues. By the time I'd edged my way round them, Orianne and Elena were out of the door and well down the corridor. As I dodgemed my way between the dawdlers to catch up with them, Tim got trapped by a subsidiary huddle that was trying to ingratiate itself with the main one. He flailed his arms through them like a man wrestling an octopus, but eventually he broke free, and I only just had time to introduce myself to the girls before he came bounding up behind us.

'Hi there,' he said.

I took up the reins of social responsibility. 'Orianne, Elena, this is Tim.'

Both girls smiled at Tim as charmingly as they had at me a few seconds earlier.

'It was pretty heavy going in there,' said Orianne, in what appeared to be a perfect English accent.

'Think yourself lucky you've only had to endure Judy this afternoon,' I replied. 'Tim and I had her this morning as well.'

'Really?' said Elena. 'You two must have done something awful in a previous life.' Her accent was pure Radio Four too.

Tim was obviously as puzzled by this as I was. 'Where are you from?' he asked.

'Switzerland,' replied Elena. 'We work in the Geneva office.'

'Your English is superb,' said Tim. 'Both of you.'

'Thanks. My father is English, so we speak it all the time at home.'

'With me it's just natural talent and hard work,' said Orianne cheekily.

Just then we reached the buffet room. Tim, level with Elena, paused to let her through. Orianne and I, now finding ourselves just behind them, fell into a conversation of our own.

'You must have studied English at school, I guess?'

'Yes. And of course films and television keep you up to speed.'

We picked up our coffees, and followed Tim and Elena over to a table in the corner. 'I always feel guilty about the rest of the world speaking English. We're so lazy over here. I can just about get by in French, as long as I don't want anything more than a cup of tea and a ham sandwich. And I only know one word of German.'

'Really? Which one's that?'

'*Gesundheit.*'

'Ah. Not much use unless you're talking to someone with a cold.'

I laughed. 'No, I suppose not.' I'd already known that Orianne was good-looking, but now, despite the vague sense of ennui I'd felt on first seeing the girls, I really found her quite sexy. There was a liveliness about her that was drawing me in.

'There's nothing to stop you learning a foreign language now, you know,' she said.

'I said I felt guilty. I didn't say I felt guilty enough to do anything about it.'

'Ah, typical male. If you want something said, ask a man. If you want something done, ask a woman.'

'That's unfair. We just save our energy for the important things in life.'

'Such as?'

'Erm . . . All right, I can't think of anything off the top of my head. I'll let you know if anything occurs to me.'

'I don't think I can face another bout of Judy,' said Elena.

'Come on,' I said. 'Where's your spirit? Tim and I have had a whole day of her, and look at us. A few scars, maybe – but we're still in there fighting, giving our all.'

'You're forgetting that we're Swiss,' she countered. 'We never get involved in wars.'

'Well, now's your chance to change all that,' said Tim. 'If you learn nothing else from this conference, and let's be honest that's not much of an if, at least you'll have been schooled in the ways of good old British backbone. Standing firm in the face of disaster, all that sort of thing.'

'What's happening tonight?' asked Orianne.

'The usual,' said Tim. 'Dinner on the firm, then several hours of drunken corporate bitching.'

Elena cast an unimpressed eye over the hordes. 'With that lot? You have *got* to be joking. I'll do the dinner if we have to, but there is no way I'm wasting my evening swapping opinions I don't have with people I don't want to talk to.'

Tim leapt into action. 'Shall we all do a bunk after the meal then? Find a decent bar in town?'

'I'm game,' said Elena.

He turned to Orianne. 'Want to join the escape party?'

'Sure.'

'That's that sorted then.'

I was a bit miffed at the way Tim had spoken to Orianne without asking my permission first, but that aside, the anticipation of spending an evening with her meant that Market Positioning II proved a relatively easy sequel to sit through. By about half past four even the discussion's most enthusiastic contributors had tailed off. Thanking us for our input, and hoping that this afternoon '*had* alerted us to some of the

considerations that *can* alter one's approach to market positioning', Judy sent us all packing.

'I need a rest after all that,' said Tim as soon as we were out
of earshot. 'I'm going for a lie-down, I think.'

'Which hotel are you two staying at?' asked Elena.

'The Regency.'

'Oh, really?' she said. 'So are we.'

The great cake-maker in the sky had done himself proud
with that particular bit of icing.

'We're going for a walk round the town now,' said Orianne.
'See you both at dinner, OK?'

Tim and I bade them farewell, and set off to our hotel.

'Well, would you believe it, Tim? They're staying at the
Regency as well.'

'Doesn't matter, Rob.' He was irritatingly unriled. 'If Elena
likes me as much as I think Elena likes me, then the race
could be over by tonight. Just think – you could be hours
away from defeat in the Clare Jordan Five And Three-Quarter
Feet Handicap Stakes.'

My mouth opened. I really had to tell him now. But at the
very last second his arrogant, prancing victory boast got to
me. It genuinely pissed me off. *No*, I thought, *if that's how
you're going to be, I fucking well won't tell you*. Instead I settled
for a vague: 'Mmm, we'll see.'

By seven we were at our predetermined places in the
Metropole's main dining room, on different tables, as indeed
were Orianne and Elena, though neither of them was on
either of our tables. Although I knew that our post-meal
escape had been agreed, it was still frustrating to watch
Orianne chatting to the blokes seated next to her. My worries
were only eased by looking at Tim, who was clearly thinking
the same thing about Elena. But all we could do was get ourselves on the outside of the rack of lamb and the peach torte,

knowing that afterwards we'd be whisking the girls off into the Bristol night. As coffee was being served, four separate excuses were made at four separate tables, and within sixty seconds Tim, Elena, Orianne and I were through reception and on our way to freedom.

The clouds were swirling, the evening pulsing with the threat of rain. Down by the docks we found a pedestrianised street full of old pubs that would be called 'quaint' were there not so much real life still going on inside. We had drinks in a couple of them, and soon enough the conversation split into two factions: Tim talking with Elena, me with Orianne. The next place we tried was a modern bar, right on the water's edge. We found a table near the window. By now it was getting dark outside, and the warm, fuzzy glow from a street lamp lit up the huge raindrops that were starting to fall. As each one hit the water it sent out swelling circles, and I reflected how dramatic it made the night seem.

'This place is great,' said Orianne. 'I wish we had bars like this in Geneva.'

'You mean you don't? I thought Geneva was supposed to be glamorous.'

'It is. That's the problem. It's too glamorous. No one seems real. Lots of designer clothes everywhere, but people never relax and have a good time in the way they do over here.'

'Really?'

'Really. And the men are so boring over there. All they want to talk about is which investment bank they work for, how much their apartment is worth, and what make of car they drive.'

'Did I mention my new Audi?'

Orianne laughed, giving the dimmer switch in her eyes a momentary tweak upwards. With every minute I was finding her more and more attractive. She intrigued me, she was funny, and she made me feel relaxed. But as much as I fancied her, guilt about what I should be saying to Tim was beginning to creep up on me. I looked across at him. His body language with Elena told me everything I needed to know. But their conversation was so obviously intense that it stopped me from interrupting them. All I could do was carry on talking to Orianne. Not an unpleasant task, of course. The very opposite, in fact. But as I say, a task on which I couldn't really concentrate.

At about ten o'clock, Orianne excused herself and went to the loo. And because some customs are truly international, Elena went with her.

'Well?' asked a notably chipper Tim. 'How are you getting on?'

'Great,' I replied. 'Really great. But, Tim—'

'I'm glad for you, of course,' he said, 'but unfortunately, Rob, I have to tell you that I'm getting on "really great" as well. In fact, I might even go so far as to say that I'm getting on "really, really great". So you see, if I'm correct in my feeling as to how the rest of tonight could turn out, then the Clare Jordan Five And Three-Quarter Feet Handicap Stakes might very well be in its last few hours. The only question will be whether you came second with one fence left to jump or two.'

I stared at the table, waiting for him to finish. As he paused for breath, I summoned up my courage and—

'Shall we get back to the hotel then?' boomed Orianne cheerfully. 'Wow, look at that rain. Let's get a taxi.'

I'd lost my chance. Before I knew it we were outside and into a cab that had appeared as quickly as they always seem to in films (is that what being a blonde girl with a blonde friend can do for you?). By the time it deposited us at the entrance to the Regency my stomach was churning.

Elena was ferreting about in her handbag. 'Damn. I must have left my key in my room. Just hang on while I get a spare from reception.'

Orianne and Tim waited patiently while Elena went across to the desk. I, on the other hand, idled across to a noticeboard right on the other side of the lobby, and started reading (or rather pretending to read) about the facilities offered by the hotel's gym. I knew, you see, that we were fast approaching what might be termed 'a moment of some drama', and my stomach was doing a convincing impression of a tombola.

'Yes, madam?' said the girl behind reception to Elena.

'I'm afraid I've very stupidly left my key in my room. Would it be possible to have a replacement for tonight? It's room number four one five.'

'Certainly, madam.' The girl set about encoding another plastic card. 'Could I just check the name?'

'Of course,' said Elena. 'It's Lehman. Orianne Lehman.'

It took Tim something like a third of a second to position himself next to me. But he was clearly so shocked that he couldn't speak. Instead he just faced the gym poster.

'I am *really* sorry,' I whispered. 'I tried to tell you in the bar.'

My voice box offered a set of jump leads to Tim's. 'What?' he growled. 'What did you try to tell me in the bar?'

'This afternoon, right, when we got to the second session? When I went ahead, but then went for a pee and actually got to the room after you?'

'Yes. With you so far.'

'Well, that was actually the second time I'd got to the room. The first time, when you were in the loo, I saw that the girls were there. And the guy who was sitting next to them jolted the desk as he sat down, and their place cards fell onto the floor. As I was sitting right opposite, and it was difficult for them to reach, I went across to help. And then I . . . I mean, I thought it'd be a laugh to . . . erm . . . to . . . well, you see, what I did was . . .'

'You swapped the cards around?'

'Yeah. I was going to tell you early on this evening. After we'd chatted to the girls for a while, obviously, but well before now. I never got the chance, though. I only did it for a laugh.'

I turned to look at him. He was eyeballing me with a ferocity that was immense, but coldly, perfectly under control. 'You say, Rob, that you did it "for a laugh". The question I want you to answer now is: can you detect, anywhere in my expression, anywhere at all, the remotest sign of amusement?'

'Tim, I am really, really sorry. I honestly didn't mean it to go on this long.'

He looked away, obviously thinking back over the course of the afternoon and evening. The first introduction (a vague wave of the hand, 'Orianne, Elena, this is Tim'); neither of the girls being on his table at dinner, thereby denying him the chance of seeing their place cards there; the conversations in the bar that had forked off from each other, negating the need for names. I, meanwhile, was feeling ashamed. But not so much at the way I'd cheated in the race. My embarrassment at that was tempered (albeit in a thoroughly immature manner) by the reality that my cheating had worked, and Tim couldn't now win the race tonight. No, my shame was at the insult I'd paid the girls by involving them in the race at all.

'Are you two going to read about that gym all night?' It was Orianne. And, yes, I do mean Orianne, the mousy blonde, the one that up until then Tim had thought was Elena. She was holding the lift doors open.

Tim and I clicked back to display mode in an instant.

'Sorry girls, just coming.'

'It was him, he wanted to read it. He's the one out of shape, not me.'

We all got out at the fourth floor, the unspoken assumption hanging in the air that Tim was going back to Orianne's room and I to Elena's. Sure enough, at a right angle in the corridor, and with the briefest of 'goodnight' swapping sessions (a keen observer would have noticed the absence of one between Tim and myself), our paths diverged for the final time today.

Elena and I went into her room. She opened the minibar and took out a bottle of Perrier. I stood by the window. The lights of Bristol twinkled in the drizzle, the odd one prisming out sharply as it passed through a droplet on the pane.

'Some water?'

I answered without turning round. 'Please, yeah.'

The sound of two glasses being poured. Then Elena coming up behind me. I turned round, and took my water.

'Thanks.'

Our eyes locked. She took a half-step closer, smiling nervously. I reached out for her. Our lips brushed softly against each other. I put my glass down on the windowsill, as did she. We embraced, and this time instead of kissing her lips I bowed my head and kissed her neck. It tasted as wonderful as I'd known it would. But it also settled once and for all the question that had been bobbing around in my mind. Elena, I could now sense, was a very different girl from Orianne. She put the decision into words for us.

'Rob,' she murmured, her head resting on my shoulder, 'I don't want to go to bed with you.'

'I know,' I whispered, holding her close, 'I know.' Pouring over me was a sense of relief. As much as I wanted to draw level with Tim in the race, I was glad that things were going to stay simple. The Clare Jordan Five And Three-Quarter Feet Handicap Stakes hadn't made too much of a mess of the day.

'I'm sorry,' she said.

'Don't be silly. You've nothing to be sorry for.' She really couldn't have known how much I meant it.

'It's not you. It's . . .'

'Ssh. You don't owe me any explanations.' I rocked her gently in my arms, gave that gorgeous blonde hair one last kiss, and stood up straight. 'I guess I'll see you at breakfast.'

She smiled. 'I guess you will.'

'Night then.'

'Night.'

Tuesday 22nd June

7.35 p.m.

Grand total of words uttered today by Tim to me – eleven.

None of these was at breakfast. I was the first down there. The simple brevity of my encounter with Elena had been a relief, and had helped distract me from my sense of self-reproach. Sleep, therefore, had taken me in its arms just as quickly as Orianne had no doubt taken Tim in hers, but with completely the opposite effect on our energy levels this morning.

After a while the girls appeared, and came across to sit with me. Strangely, I felt perfectly relaxed in Elena's presence because of what we didn't do together last night, but a little uncomfortable in Orianne's because of what she did do with Tim. Five minutes later (nice touch that, for appearance's sake) the man himself joined us, his eyes distinctly panda-like. He said a 'good morning' in my direction, rather than with my name attached to it. Conversation was as forced as it usually is at breakfast, and as soon as good manners allowed, we all vanished back to our rooms. I said goodbye to the girls there and then (we were in different sessions this morning). I presume that Tim's farewell to Orianne took place in her room, and wasn't entirely verbal.

The first seven of his eleven words weren't uttered until half past one this afternoon. We were at Bristol station, and had just settled into our seats on the train.

His words were: 'I'm going to sit in another carriage.'

The start of my reply trailed in his wake like futile bullets after a man on a motorbike: 'Tim, come on, I'm really sorry, it was a joke that went on a bit too long, that's all. Can't we just talk ab—'

I don't suppose I can blame him for being angry. I realised that he was still thinking that Elena and I slept together last night, and so will be furious at me catching him up, as well as denying him victory. But even if I hadn't swapped the cards round, and he'd got the right girl, would Elena have slept with him? As I said last night, I don't think she's that sort of girl. But you never can tell with Tim in these matters. And if his spells had achieved their usual success, how would she have felt about it afterwards, as she flew back to Switzerland? Thinking it through that way made me even more glad that I didn't try to persuade her into having sex last night. And that went a little way towards helping me get over my shame at how the Clare Jordan Five And Three-Quarter Feet Handicap Stakes made me behave yesterday. A little way, mind you.

Neither of us was going back to the office this afternoon, so as he got the cab in front of me at Paddington Tim completed his word quota: 'Right, see you tomorrow.'

Wednesday 23rd June

6.20 p.m.

Détente with Tim today. Playing Reykjavik to our Reagan and Gorbachev was the Coffee Place. By this time I think even Tim could spot that I'd been an inept practical joker rather than an out and out Judas. But working on the 'if you're holding cards you might as well play them' principle, he took advantage of my continued penitence by making me pay for lunch. His selection comprised their most expensive sandwich, plus a monumentally overpriced chocolate bar, all washed down with the biggest Frappuccino in discovered space.

'In view of your kind offer,' he said, indicating the feast laid before him, 'and bearing in mind the fact that you're of inferior intellectual calibre, I have decided to view Monday's transgression as an act committed not with malice aforethought, but with stupidity all-the-bloody-time-thought. Accordingly, you are forgiven. But should anything similar ever happen again your bollocks will hit the blender, and pronto.'

'Right.' One interpretation of my reply was, *Right, I understand, Tim, and I'm grateful to you for finding it in your heart to grant me this pardon.* But to avoid losing too much face I tried to steer my tone more towards, *Right, that's your childish temper tantrum over with, can we get on with being adults now?*

'So parity's restored then,' he said, trying not to sound too irked about it.

It took me a second to work out what he meant. 'Oh – you mean Elena?'

'Yes, of course I mean Elena, you cretin. Elena. In the Regency.'

'Well, no actually. Not Elena.'

He looked at me in confusion. 'What, you didn't . . . ?'

'No.'

He stared at me. For a second he was literally dumbstruck, and then jubilant. 'Haha, she didn't fancy you. Elena didn't fancy Rob.' He punched the air.

This got on my nerves. Not because it was a reminder that I'm still behind in the race. Well, all right then, maybe a bit. But mainly I was aggravated by the way Tim dealt with it. Perhaps Elena fancied me, perhaps she didn't. That wasn't the issue. I'd enjoyed the time I'd spent with her, irrespective of any sexual agenda. I knew why Tim was reacting in the way he was. I've been through all those feelings in my time, so I'm not claiming that I'm purer to my very soul than he is, or anything ridiculous like that. It's just that watching him made me feel detached from all that.

Explaining that to Tim, however, was not an option. Firstly, he would have interpreted it as sour grapes. And secondly, he wouldn't have understood. I just knew it. He wouldn't have seen what I meant. So I changed the subject instead. 'Simon looks a bit under the weather today, don't you think?'

'That'll be weather spelt t-h-u-m-b. No doubt Her Dragonship has been pressing him for an answer on the marriage front. You probably noticed the curvature of his ear.'

Let's hope Saturday helps straighten it out.

8.35 p.m.

Have just collared Helen, and checked that she's still revved up for Saturday. She is. Good.

8.50 p.m.

I gave Chris a call just now. On his mobile, of course. Didn't say anything as overt as, *Wanted to see how you were after splitting up from your girlfriend*, but I hope he interpreted my ringing in itself as a sign that that's what I was doing. He sounded rather low, said he wished he hadn't done what he did on Friday, and it does feel strange not waking up next to Hannah in the mornings. But I think he knew, like Hannah, that the end had been in sight for a while.

Then he asked how it was going in 'the stakes', and could he join in? I laughed, and started marshalling my thoughts to tell him about everything that's happened. But then I thought better of it. 'There's a lot to catch up on,' I said. 'I'll fill you in when I see you.'

Sunday 27th June

6.20 p.m.

A proper landlord would have gone for it.

A proper landlord, with a proper pub, his own pub, lord and master of all the optics he surveys, would have looked me up and down and thought, yeah, why not, there's his money, there's my tape, his story holds just enough water to sound feasible, no harm in giving him half an hour with the remote.

Nigel, on the other hand, the sixty-six inches of graduate-entry respectability who carefully kept the bar between himself and me (a trick gleaned, no doubt, from some Judy-clone), was having none of it. Or rather, it was with regret that he informed me he could not depart from company policy on this matter, as Thirty Something Bars'R'Us (or whatever it is they call themselves), can under no circumstances allow anybody other than the police, or a suitably authorised representative of a government agency, to view their closed-circuit television footage for any purpose whatsoever.

And so it is with equal, although in my case genuine, regret that I inform you that I cannot offer a full and exhaustive explanation of just how the hell what happened last night happened. Helen, it is true, may throw us the odd scrap of detail from her table, but the full three-course explanation with wine and coffee will inevitably be reserved for a girl-friend. All I can tell you, in the absence of a video replay, is what the outcome was. I saw the evidence with my own eyes this very afternoon.

Come to think of it, Nigel's intransigence was doubly frustrating. Not only would the tape have cleared up how Helen did what Helen did, but I'd have loved to watch myself doing what I did. Not because I can't remember what I did. I can, give or take the odd memory-edge haze, which is par for the course on any decent night out. No, my self-voyeuristic desire comes from wanting to see how I appear to other people. In grainy black-and-white, maybe, but still, it would give me an idea. I can fill you in on last night's events as they appeared to me at the time. But wouldn't it be interesting to see how you operate, how your body language works, how you stand, move, react to other people – all as they see it? Wedding videos sometimes give you a taste of this, but only when the shot pans across you in the background, unaware that you're being filmed. Knowing you're on film shifts you into acting mode, which isn't the real thing at all.

But I should tell you about things from the beginning. Which occurred in my bath, at about half past five, when I picked up the soap. Having worn away to a mere sliver, it squirmed from my hand. Bugger. Soap always takes ages to find. It usually ends up behind your back, unless of course you go there first, when somehow the little sod knows that's what you'll do and so goes straight to the tap end to double-bluff you. Last night, though, a miracle occurred – my hand located the soap at its first attempt.

This might sound silly, but it felt like a lucky sign. Would this be a night when things went well for me? It was hope that I was in dire need of, not least because I was finding it hard to get motivated. Yes, it niggled me that Tim was so close to winning the Clare Jordan Five And Three-Quarter Feet Handicap Stakes, but at the same time the race had begun to

Mark Mason

feel like a weight round my neck. Part of me yearned for the simple pleasure of sleeping with a girl in somewhere as straightforward and normal as a bed.

I finished my bath and wrapped myself in two enormous, freshly laundered towels. Bathroom Traffic Control had Helen stacking outside the door, ready to prepare for her appearance later on in the evening. Knowing that I'd be gone well before she re-emerged, I administered a final, rousing pep talk about the need to 'go for it', and handed her a three-quarter-full bottle of wine she'd started the other night, with instructions that she was not to turn up at the club until she'd quaffed the lot.

Just over an hour later, as I strolled down Greek Street to the bar where we were congregating for a pre-meal snifter, I thought back to the sliver episode and felt enlivened. I was in my one really good suit (Kenzo, since you ask). Soho was mixing the palette of its day, melting late afternoon subtly into early evening. Boozy laughter filled the streets. The night stretched temptingly before me. My nerves were still there, but at least I was in a frame of mind to contend with them.

Paul was the only one there before me, just finishing his drink, so I got him another and myself the same: Japanese lager in a metallic bottle, which I wouldn't normally be seen dead with but which last night somehow felt right with the clothes we were wearing and the event we were celebrating. In fact I'd have been disappointed if it had cost less than the three quid a bottle it did.

Relayed the sliver incident to Paul. Being Paul, he knew that the Kurds have a word for that useless sliver of soap: 'binesk'. What, I asked, was the point of such a word? Paul replied that if English had had an equivalent word, it would have saved me the hassle of explaining to him that my bar of soap had been worn away to a sliver. He then went on to make a convincing case for other words that need inventing. For instance that action you have to engage in to open a cupboard neither of whose doors has a handle, when you push one of them really firmly shut, so that the other one pops out a bit, allowing you to grab its edge with the tips of your fingers. That took him forty-odd words to describe. But if we had a verb for it – say, 'to gribble' – all that verbal toiling would be unnecessary. You could just say, 'The handle had fallen off, I had to gribble the cupboard open,' and everyone would know what you meant.

Presently our ruminations were interrupted by the arrival of someone for whom there are plenty of words – Graham. I don't suppose I'd ever really believed that he would buy a second suit for James's stag night. But my hopes had risen almost despite myself, and so it was a disappointment to see him standing there in his faithful old work suit, its familiar relief-map of creases spread before us. The only saving grace was that he was wearing a normal tie. Any sign of a cartoon character and I think I really would have lost it.

Simon, on the other hand, was a revelation. A more-than-usually-severe haircut had lent a mean edginess to his appearance. His suit, shirt and tie were all dark, which made him look a bit like Joe Pesci in *Casino*. As long as he kept his words to a minimum it was an impression he stood a fair chance of maintaining. If Helen obeyed her instructions properly (i.e. kept talking at him) there'd be every chance of his quietness continuing. And if Simon's attire/haircut double whammy wasn't enough to keep her talking at him, then nothing would be. All in all it was the start of what I hoped would be a beautifully virtuous circle.

Tim soon joined us, as did the Star Of The Show himself. By now it was getting on for half-seven, which was when the table was booked at L'Escargot, so we finished our beers and set off. Inside the restaurant we were shown upstairs and to our table so efficiently that we were seated and had ordered our drinks before we knew where we were. Only top-class maître d's have that ability to distract you from what's being done to you. Them and pickpockets.

Gazing round the room, I reflected that this stag night was reassuringly grown-up. No bawdy displays of laddishness, no drinking games, no puerile pranks. Just a wallet-bursting blow-out meal, followed by some elegantly bacchanalian excess in a club we didn't normally go to. A night to remember, without the need for any medical attention in the early hours.

After we'd polished off our starters, and were well into the Shiraz, James tapped his knife, a little unsteadily, against a nearby glass. 'Thank you, everyone,' he intoned after silence had descended. 'No big speech, but I just want to say how glad I am that you're all here, and thanks for coming along to make my stag night the huge success I'm sure it will be.'

Murmurings of mutual appreciation, which Tim scooped together in a reply: 'And on behalf of everyone here, James, I'd like to say how chuffed we all are for you. In the absence of a proper bloke, Lucy has settled for the best specimen she can find, and I'm sure that you'll make her a thoroughly adequate husband. To James and Lucy, everyone.'

We raised our glasses. 'To James and Lucy.' The sense of this being a meaningful occasion hit us all I think, even Graham, who managed not to fuck it up with one of his customary comments. James was getting married, a first among last night's group. As I looked at him, the glows from six red wine glasses bathing his contented face, I was reminded of that night in the pub when he told us about the marriage in the first place. And I had the same mixture of feelings. Part of me saw myself as I was right at that minute, taking hungry bites out of a young London night. I had a momentary vision of James and myself in a boxing ring, a referee standing between us, our fight just finished. As the ref lifts my arm in triumph, James can only slump back in his corner. For this, you see, is a world full of others. And James has to forsake them. I don't.

But then another part of me had a vision of James on the gangplank of a huge luxury liner, turning to give one final wave to the crowd on the shore. I was in that crowd, waving back at him, shouting my farewells, wishing him all the best. Didn't know where the liner was heading, but it looked a comfy one all right. And I was staying in the familiar city. A lively city, yes, whose lights dazzled and whose stories gripped, but a familiar city nevertheless. I knew its streets, its bars, its sounds and its tastes. James, though, was going off to something unfamiliar, something new. He was going on an adventure.

The meal, as meals do in expensive restaurants, ploughed through a huge chunk of the evening without us noticing. Expert service was one reason for this, vintage brandy another. And so it wasn't until about ten to eleven that we found ourselves, seventy quid lighter apiece, shuffling through the entrance to the evening's second venue. Helen had been told eleven, so that was all right.

We'd picked a club in Covent Garden, admittedly part of a chain (they've got a few in the richer parts of London, plus some in cities like Manchester and Edinburgh), but nevertheless inhabiting that hard-to-define territory where cool remains cool without becoming poncy. The girls are neither It nor Essex. You can afford to get drunk there, but you wouldn't go every week. We descended the burgundy-carpeted stairs, the walls either side of us hewn from the rock on which London is built. The whole place is like a subterranean playground in which small side-caves branch off from a central dance-cave, with dark wooden tables and lushly upholstered banquettes. Not a single light-fitting above neck height. Easy to lose someone (or indeed yourself) in there, should you so wish. The DJ helps in steering the middle course between mainstream and elitist; he'll play Primal Scream, for instance, but it won't be *Loaded*.

The first wave of music and shouting that hit us as we entered felt like a wave that I wanted to surf. There was a good time to be had here. OK, the wine and brandy may have aided this euphoria, but isn't that part of their job description? As we eased our way through the crowded (but not too crowded) club, a buzzing sense of anticipation had me by the guts, the throat, the balls. Progress in the Clare Jordan Five And Three-Quarter Feet Handicap Stakes was part of it, I'm sure. But this felt like a night in itself, when anything could happen for its own sake.

First, though, there was business to attend to. I moved over to Simon. The pensive 'got to get the next train home' look he normally displays any time after seven was refreshingly absent. He'd clearly taken confidence from the fact that not even Michelle could begrudge him a full evening out for his friend's stag night.

'All right, mate?' I shouted above the throb of the speaker in front of which we'd all settled. 'Having a good time?'

'Yeah, not bad like.'

'Is that all? "Not bad like"? Come on, Simon, this isn't a bloody golf club dinner and dance in Prestatyn, you know. This is James's stag night, in central London, and you're going to do better than "not bad like", all right?'

He smiled. 'Yes, sergeant major.'

'And route one to doing better than "not bad like", young Simon, is having a drink and some fun with your mates. And with any attractive young girls who may happen to catch your eye.' I realised I was enjoying taking an interest in Simon's love life. So much simpler than coping with my own.

He looked uncertainly around the club. 'That's the bit I'm not so sure about, Rob.'

'Nonsense. We'll have none of that defeatism. Even if no one else here wanted to talk to you, which, trust me Simon, they do, but even if they didn't, you'd still be in luck, because my flatmate Helen's coming down here tonight, and she doesn't know anyone, and—'

'Have you set this up?' he interrupted suspiciously.

'No,' I replied, slightly too emphatically. And then, to pacify my conscience, I crept a little way back towards the truth. 'Not as such.' I winced at my Grahamism, but ploughed on regardless. 'Helen said to me this afternoon that she had nothing to do tonight, so I said if she wanted to she could come along here. I knew you'd be here, of course, but I wasn't matchmaking.' Simon was giving me a half-convinced look. 'You'll get on with her, I know. She's Scottish, so you can gang up in an all-Celts-together sort of way.'

'Scottish? Oh God, that's got so much more cred than being Welsh.'

'Bollocks. If she starts any of that just remind her that you've got Tom Jones and she's got Marti Pellow.'

At that point Paul and Graham reappeared from the bar laden with bottles of Grolsch, and group life recommenced. I chatted to James for a while, until at one point I realised he was staring straight past me at a girl on the dance floor. I turned round; there was no denying it – she was stunning.

'Oi, stop it,' I said to him. 'You're an about-to-be-married man.'

He grinned. 'That's what my stag night's for, isn't it? Get it all out of my system.'

I volunteered to get the next round in. While I waited to get served, contentedly tapping the bar with a twenty-pound note I'd creased lengthways down the middle, someone at the far end of the room caught my attention. It wasn't anything physical about her that did the catching. Rather it was her apparent remoteness from the bedlam going on all around her. She was with a group of girls, but while they were joking and dancing and flirting and shouting, she was just standing there, quietly sipping a white wine, her face set either in relaxed detachment or sheer boredom, it was hard to tell which. No sooner had the question formed itself in my mind, though, than I sensed a member of the bar staff hovering into my catchment area, and so to avoid missing out I had to jump into action.

'Six Grolsches, please.' The clock behind the bar (one of those light-projection ones that isn't really there) showed a quarter past eleven. Call that ten past in the real world. Helen was late. She'd better get here soon, I thought, or Simon'll have the women flocking round him like . . . On second thoughts, Helen, there's no hurry. Take your time.

I carried the drinks across. Tim and James were deep in conversation about cars, while Paul had managed to get into a good-natured argument about David Beckham with a couple of girls standing near by. I latched on to Simon and Graham, who had depressingly, but not altogether surprisingly, started talking about work. Turning this to my advantage, I began firing technical questions at Graham at the rate of two a minute, purely so that Simon would have nothing to say, thereby ensuring that he drank his beer all the quicker. If ever anyone needed the confidence that alcohol imparts, then it was Simon last night.

By half eleven there was still no sign of Helen. Come on, girl, I thought, there's the dramatic late entrance and there's too fucking late. Another half an hour and Simon turns back into a pumpkin. Needing a pee by now, I made my way over to the Gents. Fortuitously, my route took me past the detached/bored girl I'd noticed earlier. Even more fortu-itously, a minor bottleneck in the doorway through to the loos meant that I had to stop right by her. Or at least it did after I'd been careful to let a couple of people through before me.

Up close she was interesting-looking. And I mean that in the literal sense rather than in the way it's often used, namely as a euphemism for ugly. She wasn't what you'd call good-looking, but then she wasn't what you'd call bad-looking either. She just looked interesting. As well as detached/bored.

I gathered my courage. 'Not having such a good night then?'

She didn't even look at me. Surely she must have heard? I'd shouted as loud as you can shout an opening line without risking total dignity loss. So it must have been a blank. I took the risk that it had been a Vodafone blank. ('The girl you have addressed does not respond. She may respond if you try again.')

'So bad that you've lost the power of speech? God. That is bad.'

Still no reply. Oh well, I thought. Nothing ventured, and other clichés. But as I set off again, a voice sounded from about eighteen inches behind my left shoulder: 'Don't mind her, she's always like that.'

I turned round. The voice's owner was quite a bit shorter than her friend, but good- rather than interesting-looking. Red hair, not one of nature's reds, but deep and full rather than brash and punky. Rich brown eyes flickering cheekily in a small round face. Her cheeks were freckled, and a silver stud earring nestled cosily on one side of her nose.

'I don't even know why she bothered coming tonight, the miserable cow.'

Almost involuntarily I found myself laughing at her directness. There was something about her voice (Scouse, I'd pinned it down to on the second sentence, but gentle, lyrical Scouse) that was utterly . . . well, the word I reached for first was 'enchanting', but the women in Evelyn Waugh novels were always called enchanting, and this girl was most definitely not from an Evelyn Waugh novel. No, I'd have to say 'compelling'. The way she spoke was almost like singing. It made you listen to her.

'You're not her biggest fan, are you? I can tell.'

Her smile was twice as cheeky as her eyes. 'We call her Pilot Light.'

'Eh?'

'She never goes out.'

'How come tonight's such a special occasion then?'

'It's Andrea's birthday.' She indicated one of her friends, who, along with a couple of the others, was out on the dance floor, drunkenly oblivious to the male attention their gyrations were attracting. 'Twenty-fifth. So we're having a weekend down in London. And Her Ladyship over there got all excited at the thought of Harrods and Selfridges, so she thought she'd come along for once.'

'Are you having a good time?'

'Yeah, great. Drinks cost a bloody fortune though.' She held up a nearly finished Bacardi Breezer.

'Am I allowed to take that as a hint?'

'Do you mean you want to buy me a drink?'

I nodded.

'Well then why didn't you just say so?' If this girl was any more down to earth she'd bury herself. 'Yes, of course. Why do you think I spoke to you in the first place?'

I gave another laugh. 'Same again? Rightio. Back in a sec.'

Quick dash to the Gents, nifty bit of shoulder work at the bar, and the Bacardi Breezer was being presented within three and a half minutes.

'I'm Rob.'

'Karen.'

'You from Liverpool then?'

'Well spotted.' Her smile reassured me she was being playful rather than sarcastic.

'What else have you been up to in London?'

'Drinking, mainly. We went to have a look at Oxford Street, but the shops were so soddin' crowded that after half an hour we gave up and found the nearest pub. How about you?' She gave the lapel of my jacket the tiniest tweak with her finger and thumb. 'Special occasion, is it?'

'Stag night.'

'Who's the unlucky bloke?'

I pointed to the other end of the club. 'James. I work with him. He's the tall one, dancing with that shorter guy and those two girls.' Paul and his Beckham opponents were indeed strutting their stuff. 'And the guy standing behind them near the speaker is our equivalent of . . .' I indicated Pilot Light, who was continuing her Greta Garbo routine.

'Valerie.'

'Graham's our equivalent of Valerie. Except that Valerie doesn't want to speak to anyone, whereas with Graham it's more a case of no one wanting to speak to him.'

She squinted through the darkness to make him out. 'Fucking hell, that moustache looks *shite*. Has no one ever told him?'

'Frequently. But he never listens.'

Karen shook her head in appalled bewilderment. 'And who's that next to him?'

'That's Ti—' As I looked across, I saw that Tim was now talking to the girl who James had spotted earlier. An almost automatic sense of fear seized me momentarily, but I ignored it. 'That's Tim. Don't know who the girl is. The guy behind them is Simon.'

'Aaahh. He looks a bit of a gooseberry. I feel sorry for him.'

'No need to, Karen, no need to. His maiden in shining armour is on her way.' My watch showed a quarter to twelve. 'At least I hope she is.'

No sooner had the words left my lips, and been replaced by a bottle of Grolsch, than Helen came bouncing through the doorway. Disorientated by the crush of people and the volume of the music, she failed to notice that I was standing about ten feet away.

'Helen,' I shouted, stepping into her line of vision. As she focused on me, I realised that her disorientation wasn't just due to the crowd and the noise. She really was quite drunk. She was moving towards the person standing next to me. And there wasn't anyone standing next to me.

'Hello, Rob,' she slurred, grinning inanely.

'Hello. You finished that wine then?'

'Mmm. It was lovely. I had a couple of Tia Marias as well.'

I held up three fingers of my right hand. 'Before you're allowed to speak to Simon you've got to tell me how many. And I must accept your first answer.'

Very slowly and carefully, she counted. 'Fo— three.'

I decided to give her the benefit of the doubt. It would have been silly to abandon the plan at this late stage, and after all a few drinks inside her could only help things along. I just hoped that at the other end of the room Simon had been acting along similar lines. Warning Karen, who seemed most amused by the whole episode, that I'd be back shortly, I guided Helen around the undulating boundary of the dance floor until we reached my group. To avoid making things too obvious, I introduced her to Tim first. He in turn introduced us both to his newfound friend.

'Rob, Helen, this is . . .' I realised that my fear was back. Was she? Could she? Did her name begin with . . . 'Elaine.' Tim could barely disguise his glee. Doing my best to disregard him, I said hello to Elaine. As I said earlier, she was undeniably good-looking. But not, I couldn't help thinking, all that sexy. She struck me as one of those women who are so attractive in the basic, physical sense that they feel no need to complement it with any effort in the personality department. I'm not saying that she wasn't perfectly polite when she returned my greeting. It's just that she didn't seem to have much about her other than looks.

Next I introduced Helen to Graham, and finally we got to Simon. He and Helen shook hands.

'Where's the guy who's getting married?' she shouted.

James, Paul and the Beckhamettes were still giving it plenty on the dance floor. Pointing at the groom-to-be, I took a step back so that Helen was nearer to Simon than to me. Fortunately, at exactly the same time she shifted her weight to her other foot, so getting even closer to him. This made it much more natural for him rather than me to answer her question, and under the further cover of saying something to Graham my retreat was concluded. My work here is done now, I thought to myself. Simon and Helen are on their own. Having lit the fuse, all I could do was stand back and hope that the firework wouldn't turn out to be a dud.

By the time I'd worked my way back over to Karen she'd restocked our drinks.

'What was all that about?' she asked, handing me my beer.

I filled her in on Helen wanting a man, and Simon wanting to know if he wanted his woman. She seemed to approve of the plan.

'Anyway, enough about my lot,' I said. 'What do you do?'

'I work for the council,' said Karen. 'In the housing department.'

'Must keep you busy.'

'Too right.'

'But quite satisfying, I suppose, knowing that you're helping people get a roof over their heads.'

She pulled a face as though the mouthful of Breezer she'd just swallowed was two-day-old dishwater. 'Get to fuck is it. Ninety per cent of the letters I deal with are from ungrateful, scheming bastards who just want to screw a better place out of us than they've already got. All they ever do is moan. They complain if they don't like the colour of next door's dog.'

'Oh right. Not that satisfying then.'

I was rapidly coming to the conclusion that Karen was a top girl. Or maybe not top, as I've got a feeling that's a Manc rather than a Scouse term, and I'd hate to get on the wrong side of her. But anyway, she made me laugh, and I liked her. A lot. She knew I was chatting her up, and in her own enchan— roguish way she was chatting me up as well. It didn't really feel like that, though. We weren't flirting, we were having a laugh. All right, they're the same thing. But our chat wasn't loaded or angled or spiced. It was honest and open and fun. Karen had a complete absence of bullshit about her.

The Breezers and Grolsches flowed. We danced a bit, and chatted to Karen's friends, and at one point even Valerie joined in (with the chatting, not the dancing – she hadn't loosened up that much). At about half-twelve a table in one of the side-caves became free, so those of us who were on a dancing break nipped in.

As we sat there, observing the jollity outside, Helen wandered past on her way to the loo. I shouted after her, and she came back to us.

'How's it going?' What did she think of Simon? And what did he think of her?

'He's *lovely*,' she cooed. Mercifully her intoxication level seemed to have plateaued, inducing relaxation rather than collapse. 'We're having a really *lovely* time.'

'Great. Have you been chatting?'

'Mmm. We've had a *lovely* chat.'

'And dancing?'

'Yeah. We all have. It's all so *lovely*.'

Karen giggled, turning it as quickly as she could into a cough. Helen looked at her.

'Helen, this is Karen.'

'Hi, Karen,' said Helen. 'Are you having a nice time with my flatmate?'

'Mmm. I think he's lovely.'

Fortunately Helen was too 'relaxed' to notice the ironic undertone of Karen's reply. Beaming cheerfully, she resumed her journey.

'Well well well.' I felt quite pleased with my first proper attempt at matchmaking. 'I've never seen Helen like this. Perhaps there might be something on the cards after all.'

The mention of sexual intrigue reminded me – how was Tim getting on with Elaine? Excusing myself from Karen, I shot out of the alcove and headed for the other end of the dance floor.

I won't deny it – the sight of Clare Jordan was a shock. But halfway between my end of the room and Tim's there she was. The surprise stopped me in my tracks. She was dressed in a

Little Black Number, and was dancing with a man. He was tall, with dark, expensively cut hair, and tanned skin. Good-looking? It'd have been hard to argue otherwise.

Instinctively I ducked behind a pillar. Thankfully she hadn't seen me. The subdued lighting, together with the sheer number of dancers between her and the stag night group, meant she hadn't spotted them either. But that could only be a matter of time. Now that I was starting to recover from my initial astonishment, I took stock of the situation. Clare Jordan's presence in the same establishment as the two competitors in the Clare Jordan Five And Three-Quarter Feet Handicap Stakes, both of them accompanied by young females, was clearly a complication. For the same reason that her attendance at the parachute weekend would have been a complication.

But that, I realised, only applied if she caught sight of a competitor with his girl, and made the appropriate conclusions.

Time for a little fun.

Emerging from behind the pillar, and keeping my face turned to the wall until I was well away from Clare, I carried on down the room. Tim and Elaine were dancing with the rest of the group. I tapped him on the shoulder.

'Hello, stranger,' he shouted over the music, turning round but continuing to dance. 'What have you been up to?'

'What have I been up to?' I carefully positioned myself so that no one else in the group could hear. 'I've been spotting people.'

Tim looked puzzled at my obtuseness.

'Look over there.'

Still dancing, he turned round. 'Where?'

I stood behind him, and despite the fact that he still wouldn't stop dancing I rested my arm on his shoulder, so that my outstretched finger acted as a telescopic sight for him. 'There . . . in a line with that speaker.'

'Who? The girl with the curly hair?'

'No – a bit to the left.'

'The guy with the orange shirt on?'

'No – a tiny bit more to the left.'

As soon as his brain registered who he was looking at, Tim dropped to the floor as though he'd been shot. I quickly retired to the side of the room, and watched in amusement as Tim scrambled across to join me. We were well out of earshot of our group and (just as importantly) out of sight of Clare Jordan.

'I suppose you think that was funny.'

'I do actually, yeah.'

'What in Christ's name is *she* doing here?'

'Same as you and me, Tim – having a good time.' Clare turning up in the club was a headache, sure. But to my surprise I found that I was far more relaxed about it than Tim. Not that that was difficult. The average Russian roulette player looks more relaxed than Tim did at that moment.

'And who's that bloke she's with?' he glowered.

'How the hell should I know?'

'He's a bloody good dancer, isn't he?'

'I hadn't really noticed. But yes, I suppose he is.'

'Bastard.' Tim's whole body bristled with murderous intent, before he realised that what the situation called for was careful planning. 'What are we going to do? If she sees me here with Elaine it'll be game over before it's even started. If there's a game to be played with her at all, that is, what with Fred Ableedingstaire over there.'

As he hopped anxiously from foot to foot, I realised that he was reacting emotionally to the sight of Clare with another man, far more intensely than I'd ever seen him react before.

But I was genuinely unconcerned by it. My only concern was about the logistical difficulty her being here presented in the Clare Jordan Five And Three-Quarter Feet Handicap Stakes. And even that didn't bother me as much as it should have done.

Tim turned to me. 'And anyway, where have you been?' When I didn't reply, his eyes widened in horror. 'What – you mean . . . ?'

'If you're asking whether I too have found some female company this evening, Tim, then the answer is yes.'

He groaned. 'Oh, you're *fucking* having me on.'

I couldn't help laughing at him. For the first time since this whole thing started, I felt utterly calm and at peace with myself. 'No, Tim, I'm not.'

He rolled his eyes towards the ceiling. For a moment I thought he was going to scream his lungs out, but after mouthing a silent 'one . . . two . . . three' in order to compose himself, he looked down at me.

'All right then,' he said doggedly. 'Let's sort out your "R".'

'Actually, Tim, I don't really care—'

But he was on a roll. 'Or rather let me tell you what it is. This one's non-negotiable, because of last Monday. Your penance for stealing my "E" is that you lose bargaining rights on your "R". So here you go: it's "river".'

'Tim—'

'All right, I don't expect you to commandeer a yacht. You can have "within five yards of the river". You can't grumble about that being too difficult.'

'Look, Tim, I'm—' But just at that moment a very sweaty, very out of breath and not very sober James bopped up to us. 'Hey, Tim mate – I think you've lost your chance there.' Out on the dance floor, Elaine was disappearing away from our group towards the bar. With a man.

This time Tim couldn't control himself. The howl came from the depths of his soul.

In time, I knew, he'd realise that it was probably for the best. On the assumption that sooner or later Clare was going to notice him, it would be simpler for Tim if he wasn't caught with a smoking Elaine. But I'd leave him to work that out for himself.

A few feet away, Simon was taking a rest from the dancing. 'Still enjoying yourself?' I shouted in his ear.

He raised a glass of whisky in salute. 'I'm having a great time, Rob, a GREAT time. Eh, listen – thanks for that advice last week. It's really helped sort my head out.'

'Any time, any time. Glad to be of service. You know, if you can't be arsed getting all the way back to Streatham tonight you can always kip over at my flat.'

'Yeah, I know. Helen mentioned it.'

I'll bet she did, I thought, as I carried on back to Karen. Sneaking a look at Clare and her man on the way, I noticed that Tim had been right about his dancing – he was superb. Git. I hate blokes who can dance well.

Tim's challenge came back to me. Should I go for it? Should I try and get Karen to the river? No. I just couldn't face all that any more. Going to bed with a girl was, I decided, to have a literal meaning for once.

When I reached the alcove I noticed that our booze gauge was bouncing off empty.

'Another Breezer?'

'No, I'm all right, ta,' said Karen. Then she picked up her handbag. 'In fact, I'm getting a bit fed up of this place. I think I'll be off.'

I couldn't believe my ears. 'Oh – right.' I felt as though someone had suddenly pulled a curtain down on the performance, and I was trapped behind it, frantically searching for an opening that could get me back on stage. And in the echelons of great openings, 'oh – right' doesn't rank that highly. I'd have to come up with something better than that. And quickly – Karen was already on her feet, adjusting the strap of her bag so that it felt comfortable over her shoulder. Think, Rob, you're down to a matter of seconds here, and if you don't say something soon she's going to be out of that door and—

'You coming then?' Karen asked the question as though surprised that she'd had to. The subtitle in her expression read: *We've been joking and dancing and drinking all night, what else are we going to do now except leave together?* Normal codes were redundant here. Don't get me wrong, there was nothing slaggy about Karen. Her prettiness was far too great for that. It was just that she was as direct as she was attractive. None of the usual half-hidden, half-teasing invitations for her. She'd liked me, so she'd let me buy her a drink. She'd carried on liking me, so we'd carried on drinking. And now she wanted to leave with me, so she was leaving with me. Assuming (as even the least confident bit of me now did) that sex was a possibility, it would be sex as an extension of friendship. That's what the best sex always is in the long-term. Sometimes it can apply in the short-term as well. And I felt relieved, liberated almost, by the fact that I was doing this for its own sake, rather than because the Clare Jordan Five And Three-Quarter Feet Handicap Stakes was telling me to.

"Course I am.'

As we moved across to the exit, I took one last look at the other end of the club. Clare and her man had indeed caught sight of our group, and gone across to them. This had interrupted everyone's dancing, and introductions were being made all round. I chuckled at the sight of Tim shaking hands with Clare's companion. Despite an extremely forced smile it was obvious he wanted to drag the guy down and knee him in the face.

Karen and I emerged into the warm night air. 'Which hotel are you staying at?'

'Can't remember its name,' she said. 'But it's near that bloody great castle-type place . . . oh, what's it called?'

'Buckingham Palace?' I asked hopefully. That was only a couple of minutes by cab.

'No, it's not that. It begins with a "T", I think. Got it – the Tower. The Tower Bridge hotel. You'll love my room – it looks right over the river.'

It was just gone eleven when I got back this morning. As I turned the front-door key I noticed that my hand was shaking. There was every likelihood that on the other side of that door were Helen and Simon. Together. In my flat. In her room. In her . . . And I, Rob, Simon's friend from work, who has only ever known him as the prisoner of the Creature From The Valleys, was about to see him emerge from Helen's room as a new man, bathed in a post-flagrante glow. The tension holding me at that moment was far greater than any I'd ever suffered about a sexual experience of my own. In a funny way it felt as though it *was* a sexual experience of my own. Simon and Helen had been connived together by me, given their pre-bout lectures by me. I was responsible for all this.

Two wine glasses and a nearly empty bottle glared up from the living-room table, defiant beacons of the truth. But I persuaded myself that I had nothing to feel guilty about. All I'd done was introduce them to each other. Just how many of Simon's thoughts were of Michelle as Helen cast her teddy-bear collection from the bed was a matter between him and his conscience.

The feeling of wearing yesterday's clothes was starting to bother me, so I went upstairs and ran a bath. I decided to put the radio between myself and any temptation to strain for aural clues from Helen's room, so an advert for car insurance jingled away as I lowered myself gingerly into the hot water (having remembered just in time to replace the binesk with a fresh bar). And then 'Rocket Man' by Elton John.

Heaven. Say what you like about the diminutive buffoon, but when I was still in nappies he wrote some corkers, and 'Rocket Man' corks more than most. I floated off on the song's beauty, thinking of Karen, and the fun we'd had, and the way she'd told me not to be 'soft' when I asked for her number this morning, and the joke I'd made about the word 'soft' which was the obvious crass one but which at the time somehow made us both laugh. And then I thought of the Clare Jordan Five And Three-Quarter Feet Handicap Stakes. Despite my best intentions, we were level now. I'd caught up with Tim. Both of us were one step away from victory.

As I wondered how I felt about that, it hit me that the race seemed like the most vulgar thing in the world. OK, Karen had been part of it. But even if she hadn't been I'd still have fancied her, and liked her (a lot), and gone back to the hotel (if not the river) with her. For a one-night stand, admittedly. She'd made that plain this morning. Her farewell had a distinct finality to it, and there was no reference to any possibility of meeting again. But the perfection of our single night together, its lack of complication, was nevertheless beautiful, in its own way.

Back in my room I put on some knocking-about-the-flat clothes, and then went downstairs. Helen's door was now slightly ajar; one or other of them was obviously up and about. I knew it was only one of them because from inside the room I heard a faint duvet rustle. Through the gap I could see

Helen's clothes piled carelessly on the floor. A hint of lacy black bra strap showed from one side, as if to underline the nature of last night's goings-on.

I found the girl herself in the sitting room, watching TV. Her hair, you could tell, had been ruffled by more than just sleep, and her face was flushed the deep pink that recently deflowered girls always have in film dramatisations of Victorian novels. Half embarrassment at the loss of their virtue, half pride in the attainment of their womanhood. And although you can't lose your virginity twice, what Helen had done last night was, in view of her recent abstinence level, a pretty good try.

Her head shot up when she heard me come in, and then just as quickly turned back to the television.

'Morning,' she said in as normal a voice as she could muster.

'Morning. Good night, then, was it?'

She cleared her throat, obviously aware that her unprepared voice wouldn't have held out for the full sentence it was facing. 'Yes, very good, thanks – how about you?'

'Great.' I noticed she'd got her trainers on. 'You going out?'

'Yeah, we're going out for breakfast.' Realising that she'd answered in the plural caused her face to complete a substantial leg of the journey from deep pink to scarlet.

'Ah, that's nice.'

A few minutes later came the sound of footsteps on the stairs. This was it. What was I going to say to Simon? Obviously any thought of mentioning Michelle had two words written all over it: 'no' and 'no'. Apart from anything else I didn't know how much he'd have told Helen about his current 'situation'. I elected to keep it simple. A nice, lightweight, throwaway, 'Hello, fancy seeing you here, Simon.'

Enough humour to break the awkwardness, but not too direct a reference to last night, as that would appear crude.

The feet ran out of stairs. They started on the hall floor. A turn to the left and they began to eat up the carpet behind me. Then a rush of air past my cheek signalled that he was standing right next to me. Mentally rehearsing the line one last time, I looked up.

'Hello,' I said, 'fancy seeing you here . . . Graham.'

Monday 28th June

12.30 p.m.

By the time I got into the office this morning everyone else was at their desks, with the exception of Graham himself. And the news had clearly spread. They'd all witnessed the beginnings of the romance while I'd been alcoved away with Karen. Graham and Helen were the last ones dancing when the rest of our party had departed, leading to a great deal of intense, if drunken, gossip on the street outside. James had reported events to Lucy, who by five o'clock yesterday after-noon just hadn't been able to control her curiosity any more, and had rung Graham on his mobile. His stilted reply about not being able to talk at the moment had told Lucy everything she wanted to know.

Helen hadn't come back last night, so I threw that in to the pot as my contribution to the general theorising. Simon's role in events, of course, was known about only by me, Tim and Simon himself, so amid the general hilarity concerning Graham I e-mailed both of them to convene a Coffee Place meeting at one. Quite how the motorway of Helen–Simon had led to the B-road of Helen–Graham was a mystery I wanted to solve, and soon.

Tim's reply to my e-mail, it won't surprise you to learn, con-cerned more than just our lunch arrangement. He obviously wanted to know whether I'd done my 'R'. As I was, albeit by accident, still in the race, I couldn't resist the opportunity to annoy him, so I gently began humming 'Old Man River'. He was noticeably unhappy, and fired off another e-mail calling a committee meeting for seven tonight. He also relayed his 'hunch' about Clare's companion in the club. Which is, for the record, that he is 'ninety per cent sure that the contestants in the Clare Jordan Five And Three-Quarter Feet Handicap Stakes have nothing to fear in respect of their prize still being up for grabs.' But you can tell that he's itching to deal with the other ten per cent. He keeps looking at Clare, trying to spot when she's going to visit the coffee machine so that he can follow. It's quite sweet really.

Anyway, back to Graham. He still hadn't appeared by ten o'clock.

'She must really have tired him out,' said Paul, to widespread tittering.

'I wonder if he's told her his "prostitute and the Archbishop of Canterbury" joke yet?' asked Lucy.

'No, that would be spoiling the girl,' replied James.

We continued along similarly mature lines until twenty past ten, when the door slowly opened and a very uneasy-looking Graham made his way across the office to his desk, eyes fixed firmly on the floor as he bid us a communal 'morning'. Our response was as restrained and sympathetic as you would expect from a group of people aware that one of their number, not overly familiar with the opposite sex, had spent most of the previous day engaged in carnal activity.

'DUM, dum-dum-dum dum DUM . . . DUM, dum-dum-dum dum DUM . . . I believe in miracles . . . where you from . . . you sexy thing?'

We did attempt the next line as well, but well before the end of it every last one of us was laughing so hard that we couldn't speak, never mind sing. For a moment Graham looked a little hurt. But soon enough he realised that we were only teasing, and stood up to take a small bow. Our applause was hearty and enthusiastic.

'Nice of you to join us, Graham,' said Tim. 'Hope we weren't dragging you away from anything.'

The same half embarrassed, half proud blush appeared on Graham's face that I'd seen on Helen's yesterday.

Lucy went over and ruffled his hair affectionately. 'When are you seeing her again, Graham?'

'Tonight,' came the muttered reply.

'Your place or mine?' I shouted over. 'If you see what I mean.'

'Mine. I'm cooking her dinner.'

We all exchanged uncertain glances. God knows what Graham's cooking is like. But then again I get the feeling it won't really matter.

2.20 p.m.

Simon appeared thoughtful as we sat down at our table in the Coffee Place. Engrossed even. But not at all anguished. He wore the look of a man who has travelled across the arid desert of heart-search and arrived at the oasis of self-knowledge.

'I just couldn't do it, lads,' he said, shaking his head firmly. 'Couldn't do it. Don't get me wrong, Helen's a lovely girl. Really nice. And if I was going to leave Michelle for anyone then she'd be first on the list. But that's it, see: I'm not going to leave Michelle.'

Tim and I exchanged a disappointed look, like social workers who'd just been told that one of their charges had reoffended. Simon read our thoughts. 'No, don't be like that, lads. You've done your bit. And I want to thank you for that. I came to you for advice, you gave me the best advice you could, I acted on it, with your help, and it resolved matters.

That's what I meant on Saturday night, Rob. Going out with you lot, and meeting Helen, and having a drink and a laugh and seeing how the other half live, it really did sort my head out. You haven't failed – you've succeeded. Succeeded in proving to me that down the aisle is where I'm headed. Yes, the thought of going off and having some fun with Helen, or whoever it might be, was attractive. *Is* attractive. But is it worth ditching everything I've got with Michelle? For some people I'm sure it would be. Not for me, though. Life with Michelle might not be perfect, but who ever said that life was going to be perfect? As long as it's a simple life, that's enough for me. All I was missing before was someone to point that out to me. And although you didn't mean to, lads, you did the job. So thanks, eh?'

He raised his cappuccino in salute.

Tim looked disillusioned. 'Cheers,' he said, a little grudgingly, as he chinked his mug against Simon's.

Although I too was disappointed by what Simon had said, I couldn't help being touched by it as well. 'Yeah, cheers, Sime,' I said. 'I hope you and Michelle are very happy together.'

'Well I don't know about "very",' he smiled. 'But at least now I'm sure I'm making the right call.'

So we drank our caffeine toast, not to a happy marriage, but to Simon knowing that he's made the right call. Two office weddings on the way then. Makes you think. Is marriage, or at least settledown, stalking us all?

3.15 p.m.

Tim's finally collared Clare. (Not at the coffee machine, in the end, but at the photocopier.) Came back to his desk desperately trying to suppress a grin, and gave me a thumbs up that was hidden from everyone else by his computer. Then he mouthed the words 'tell you tonight'.

He's like a little kid, bless him.

4.25 p.m.

Phone call from Hannah.

'Do you want to come round on Friday night? I'm having a few people over for dinner. Nothing special.'

'In other words it'll be the best food I've ever tasted.'

'One of the people I've invited is this designer who's been freelancing at the office. I want a second opinion.'

I laughed. 'And I don't suppose you're talking about his capabilities as a designer.'

Hannah's silence was the only answer I needed.

'And exactly how long have you had your eye on this particular chap?'

'Mmm, well . . .'

'Since before you split up with Chris, perhaps?'

Another wordless answer.

'Yes, of course I'll come. My second-opinion services are at your disposal.'

9.30 p.m.

The speech started as soon as Tim opened his front door.

'Everything's fine Rob he's a friend from the States who was over here on business and had an evening to kill before his flight home yesterday morning so he rang Clare and she said yeah she'd like to go out that'd be fun so they went for a

few drinks and then they went for a meal and then they went
to the club to go dancing because he'd read about it in *Time
Out* I was sure there was nothing between them even though
I couldn't be sure without prying didn't I tell you in the e-mail
you could sense they were just friends and that was it even
though they left with each other I was still pretty confident
pissed off because Elaine had got off with that shitbag who
nicked her from me but anyway confident about Clare and
Doug that's her friend confident that they weren't going home
to shag so there you go the point is everything's fine.'

'Great. Do you mind if I come in now?'

'Oh, sorry mate, yeah.'

As we went through to his sitting room, he continued, this
time pausing for the occasional breath. 'But do you want to
know the best of it? The pièce de résistance? My favourite
part of the whole tale, as revealed to me this afternoon by the
photocopier?'

'What?'

'He's gay. Gay, gay, gay, gay, gay.'

I laughed. 'He was such a good dancer, I suppose we
should have guessed from that.'

'So even if she had been interested in him as more than a
friend, there was no danger of him reciprocating.'

'Wonderful,' I said. 'Wonderful news, Tim. But what would
be even more wonderful at the moment is a cup of tea. If you
don't mind.'

His manic grin faded a little. 'Oh, tea. Erm, yeah – I'll just
go and make us one.'

Sitting down on the sofa, I got the feeling that this confirmation of Clare's continued availability had enthused Tim far
more than it had me. There's no doubt that her sexiness is still
apparent when I look for it. But it doesn't seem to get to me in
the same way any more.

'So you got your "R" done then?' said Tim, returning with our drinks.

I felt a twinge of exasperation at him labelling the time I'd spent with Karen 'getting my "R" done', but nevertheless I confirmed that yes, I had complied with the rules of the race. Tim reached under the television cabinet for the chart, and fixed it to the wall. Then, in the space next to 'Rebecca', he wrote the word 'river'.

He stood back. 'All level, final straight.'

I didn't have the energy to remind him that I'd tried to bow out of the race. But still I felt obliged to say something. 'You got any ideas for "E"?'

'First time anyone's ever asked me that and meant a girl.' He sat down. 'Nothing immediate, no. You?'

'Nope. Haven't even been thinking about it, to be honest.'

He took a sip of his tea. 'Well you'd better think about it, sunshine. Saturday night was your warning shot. I was one unlucky break away from victory. Next time you won't be so fortunate. Are you feeling the pressure?'

Strangely enough, I found that I wasn't.

Sunday 4th July

5.20 p.m.

Do you have your betting slips to hand, those of you who risked a little of the hard-earned on this curious contest? Because it is my duty to announce that there is, as of last night, or rather the small hours of this morning, a winner. The Clare Jordan Five And Three-Quarter Feet Handicap Stakes has run its course. The better man has won. Not necessarily better in any moral sense, of course. Indeed I'm sure there are those among you who disapprove heartily of the whole tawdry idea and everything it's led to. To such people I can only offer my apologies, and my appreciation of your continued presence in the stands. No, I simply mean 'better' as defined in the rules of the race.

Having undertaken my usual wine-choosing ritual on the way round to Hannah's (more than a fiver, less than a tenner, nicer label winning in the event of a tie), I presented myself on her doorstep at 8.07 p.m. prompt. Everyone else was there already. Hannah pointed me straight at her potential quarry, with a whispered instruction to see what I thought of him.

I can tell you his name: Richard. And I can tell you what he looked like: tallish, light brown hair, clean shaven, intelligent face. But that's about all I can tell you. He was so shy that he kept filling any gap in the conversation, however small, with questions. Consequently we ended up talking about me all the time, no matter how much I tried to turn it round by quizzing him. A pleasant enough bloke, was my verdict, and no doubt a very talented designer – but more at home with drawing boards than people. Just as he was about to ask me yet another question (which by that stage could only have been about my grandparents' blood groups, such was the paucity of subjects left open to him), a be-aproned Hannah strode into the room.

'Right, everyone, do you want to sit yourselves down? Anywhere you like. Rob, you can come and help me bring the food through.'

As soon as we were in the kitchen, I reported my findings. Hannah looked disappointed. 'Really?' she said. 'I know he's always quiet in the office. But I do fancy him quite a bit. I was hoping there might have been some hidden depths lurking somewhere.'

'Not that I can find, I'm afraid.'

Hannah's face fell. 'Oh well.' She picked up one of those over-complicated culinary implements made from impossibly shiny metal that go for about twenty quid a throw in the Conran shop, but which I can only describe as a stirrer. (Where's Paul when you need him?) 'How's your stakes thing going, by the way? You haven't told me anything for ages.'

This, it suddenly struck me, was true. As Hannah whizzed around the kitchen, effortlessly bringing every component of the meal perfectly to the boil (or whatever its state of perfection was) at exactly the right moment, I filled her in on the intrigues and manoeuvrings that had taken the Clare Jordan Five And Three-Quarter Feet Handicap Stakes to its current state of equality. Despite her concentration as she peered under saucepan lids and into ovens, Hannah seemed to register everything I was saying.

'I bet some disaster's going to befall Tim,' she said.

'How can you be so sure?'

'He will be punished for his arrogance.'

'By who?'

'God. The God of Love. You know, thingy . . .'

'Barry White?'

'Aphrodite.' And with that Hannah thrust a bowl of pasta at me, and dinner was set in motion. As usual everyone went into raptures, although Richard made the mistake of adding that 'even Jamie Oliver would be proud of this'. Hannah caught my eye, and I knew instantly that Richard had just blown his last chance. Hannah and I are both anti-Jamie Oliver. Her because she once disapproved of his use of coriander in a recipe, me because he's an annoying little bastard who needs a good smack.

It cropped up in the after-dinner talk that virtually everyone there (including Hannah herself) had set their videos for *Frasier*, and as formality had long since been vanquished by red wine it was agreed that we might as well watch it there and then. Being the one who necessitated that 'virtually' in the last sentence, I felt a little left out. I've never got those slick American programmes: *Friends, Larry Sanders, ER*, all that lot. But I did my bit for the common dinner (television?) party good, and sat there trying to laugh in the right places.

Eventually came that time-for-the-last-Tube shadow that creeps across London every night, bringing days to an end, people to their homes. The Northern Line was relatively kind to me, and as it trundled along I thought of everything and of nothing. When I got in the phone was ringing. Dashing across the room, I made it with about half a ring to spare before the answerphone clicked on. It was Hannah. She told me to put the telly on quickly, as there was a programme on BBC2 about the making of *The Muppets*. We watched the last five minutes, chatting away at the same time.

The programme ended. We carried on chatting, filling twenty minutes more of my night. Then Hannah said she was tired, so I said thanks again for the lovely food, and she said thanks for putting up with *Frasier* (she knows my feelings on the matter), and we said goodnight.

Pleasantly boozed, rather than drunk, I armed myself with the remotes, swung my feet up onto the sofa, and settled back for some electronic entertainment. Too can't-be-bothered to pick up the paper, I checked the telly listings on Ceefax. Now that its high-powered cousin the Internet has taken over, I reflected, no one really bothers with Ceefax any more. It's been usurped, just like Etch-a-Sketch was by the Playstation.

Handy when the newspaper's on the other side of the room, though. But not even Ceefax can turn a crap night's telly into a good one, and last night's was a crap night's telly. So I hit 'play' on the CD remote. A brief whirring as the mechanism kicked in, and then 'Controversy' burst into life. Prince's *The Hits 2*. Great. The perfect album for club-videoing. Highlight of the session was an unusually ill-tempered Dennis Wise sending-off to 'Kiss'.

At just gone one Helen rolled in from a night out with her girlfriends. It was only her second evening off from Graham this week, so no doubt she'd had to stay out that late simply to fit all her gossip in. Looking happy but exhausted, she went across to the answerphone.

'Who's the message from?'

Eh? I hadn't even noticed there was one. Helen pressed 'play', and after the weird electronic voice telling us the message's time (hasn't Stephen Hawking made enough from his books without getting that answerphone gig as well?), my own voice crackled out across the room: 'Hello?' Then Hannah: 'Hi, it's me, quick, put BBC2 on . . .' Obviously I hadn't got there in time after all, and the machine had clicked into record without me noticing. Helen stopped the message, and was just about to hit 'delete' when I asked her to leave it.

'Sure,' she yawned, and went off to collapse into bed.

Turning the telly off, I went over to the answerphone and pressed the play button again. Hannah's voice and mine came out of the tiny speaker like two actors in a radio play. No, not a play. It was a real recording. A real conversation, that had taken place between two real people. And bizarre as it may sound, neither of those people was me. I was listening to two people I had never met before, and I was judging them as I would judge strangers, evaluating their comments, their personalities, trying to guess what emotions were passing between them.

And my conclusion about these people, as I listened to their conversation ramble on? They were the two happiest people in the world. They knew each other, they understood each other, they made each other laugh. In the ocean of human uncertainty they were sitting on their own tiny island, just the two of them, watching contentedly as the ships sailed by and the waves crashed against the shore. Nothing could touch them.

Our answerphone doesn't have a maximum message length, so the whole conversation played itself out. All the time Prince was singing away in the background, although I have to admit that I didn't take much notice of him.

Not until he got to the last track, anyway. Then he made me sit up and take notice of him. Because the last track was 'Purple Rain'. And as the first chord rang across the room, hitting the answerphone voices like a spotlight of sound, I snapped back into myself, and once again I was me and Hannah was Hannah. And I remembered the first time I ever compared her to that song. It was a Sunday afternoon, and we were in her kitchen, making a cup of tea to take back to bed.

(Yes, it had been that sort of Sunday.) I was standing behind her, hugging her while we waited for the kettle to boil, when the opening chords of 'Purple Rain' came on the radio. My head was buried in her neck, and I was breathing in her wonderful smell, and the fact that she was as beautiful to me as those chords were just came into my head and my heart and my mouth all at the same time, and before I knew what had happened I'd said it.

As the song played over our voices on the answerphone, I thought of Green Park one achingly hot day seven summers ago when our ice creams melted almost before we could eat them. I thought of the evening of our college ball, and how the way Hannah had looked had made me catch my breath. I thought of a Saturday afternoon in Waterstone's when she'd kissed me softly on the shoulder as we waited for the sales assistant to swipe a troublesome book.

And I cried the most peaceful, soothing tears I have ever cried.

And then I knew.

I'm tempted to sit here and tell you that life sometimes has a way of letting you know that you're moving on, that one chapter of your life is ending and a new one opening up. That sort of talk, though, is for sixty-eight-year-olds, not twenty-eights. But I can tell you that at that moment the 'sometimes' happened to me. As I sat there, listening to my voice and Hannah's, 'Purple Rain' soaking everything we said in the perfection of a thousand memories and a million hopes, life told me that Hannah was the one.

When the band hit the final chord, our conversation was nearing its end. It takes another two minutes and eight seconds for the track to actually end. I know this because I sat there and watched my CD player count the time away. As I said thanks for the food, and Hannah made her *Frasier* comment, the piano and the strings were cascading away on their final notes. And then we hung up, leaving me alone with the song's dying embers and the last tear trickling gently down my cheek.

The CD mechanism whirred, and there was silence. I had a couple of calls to make. I picked up the phone and dialled.

Tim, at two in the morning, wearing a dressing gown, his eyelids still half glued together with sleep, is not a pretty sight.

'Couldn't this wait until the morning?'

'Shut up and get me a drink. A strong one.'

While he did that, I kneeled down by the television and retrieved the chart from its by-now traditional storage place. Then I stood up and took down the poster. 'One last time, Al,' I said, placing him on the floor. 'One last time, and then it'll all be over. No more getting messed around for old Scarface.' Then I pinned the chart to the wall.

Tim returned with a whisky for me and a tea for himself, and sat down on the sofa. Hypnotised by the steam coming from his mug, he barely seemed to notice what I was saying.

'Gentlemen,' I began, 'we are gathered here tonight for a meeting of the Clare Jordan Five And Three-Quarter Feet Handicap Stakes committee.'

Tim yawned, and groggily scratched his head.

'It is my solemn and momentous task,' I continued, 'to inform the committee that this will be the last ever such meeting. Because one of the contestants in the Clare Jordan Five And Three-Quarter Feet Handicap Stakes has secured victory, thereby earning himself the right to attempt on Miss Clare Jordan an approach of a familiar and intimate nature.'

This finally woke him up. '*You what?*'

Holding up my hand for silence, as if affronted by his gross infringement of committee etiquette, I turned towards the chart. Very deliberately I wrote, in the one remaining blank space underneath my name:

'Ex-girlfriend's flat.'

I turned back to Tim. His mouth was silently forming the words over and over again. After ten seconds or so he gave up. 'No, it's no good. You've lost me.'

'Ex-girlfriend's flat, Tim. The flat where my ex-girlfriend lives. That's my "E".'

'That's cheating. That's an "F", not an "E".'

'Tim, you don't understand. I'm putting that down *because* it's cheating. And if you want another infringement of the rules, I haven't even done it yet. I'm claiming it in advance. So there are two counts of foul play. And therefore Rob the judge is disqualifying Rob the contestant, and awarding victory to Tim. Which, in case you've forgotten, is you. Congratulations. You are hereby declared victor of the Clare Jordan Five And Three-Quarter Feet Handicap Stakes.'

I held out my hand. Tim stood up and examined the chart, his sleepified brain trying to catch up with my reasoning. I knew that further explanation would be pointless. Even if he knew which ex-girlfriend I was talking about, he simply would never understand why I wanted to concede the race to him. Finally he gave up trying to work it out, and decided that he might as well just enjoy his victory. Turning to me, he grinned broadly and shook my hand. 'Thanks, mate.'

Half an hour later I was standing on Hannah's doorstep. But as she looked back at me, not inviting me in, in fact not saying anything at all, just standing there with a questioning expression on her face, I realised suddenly that my script had blown away in the wind. I'd taken for granted that she thought the same way as me, but now I wasn't so sure. I tried desperately to come up with a clever remark, some witty comment that would get me where I wanted to be – through that doorway and into Hannah's arms. But it was useless. The more I tried the more I panicked, and the only thought that entered my head was how Tim would have come up with something to say in an instant.

Eventually Hannah broke the silence. 'Yes, Rob? What do you want?'

'I don't know. I don't know what to say.'

'Try telling me what you're thinking.'

'I . . . I just thought . . . I wanted to be with you.'

She reached out and took my hands in hers. 'Well, now you are.'

And then we kissed. A soft, tender kiss, but not at all unsure. It was the kiss of two people who are sure, who know that their kisses belong to each other. Somehow all those years that I'd spent not kissing Hannah any more were a hill that I had climbed, and down whose other side I was now freewheeling. Not kissing her had been right then, kissing her was right now.

'Sorry,' I said. 'I didn't explain myself very well then.'

Hannah smiled. 'You explained yourself perfectly. The only thing I wanted to hear was that you didn't know what to say. If you'd come out with some crap one-liner, I'd have known this was just a game for you. But the fact that you couldn't say anything . . . well, it said everything.'

Then she pulled me into the hallway, and closed her front door. We hugged, and I felt as though I was holding on to my past and my future at the same time. Then our lips met again, this time the softness and tenderness firing up into passion and longing. Hannah pressed me back against the wall, and our bodies met. We slid, by degrees, to the floor, our kisses now straying to each other's temples and necks.

And then we made love. Hannah and I undressed each other, more hastily than caringly, but then the longing was a very desperate one, and we made love. And if there were words to tell you how it felt, I'd write them down for you now. But there aren't. The best I can do is ask you to think back to the closest you have ever felt to someone as you made love to them, and remember that. Because that's how I felt making love to Hannah. If the feeling you're remembering is any-where near as wonderful as the feeling I had then, and for your sake I sincerely hope it is, then you'll appreciate the lack of words to describe it. A poet I read once, or a writer, or someone like that, said that sometimes if you put a word to something you can't help but diminish it. I think I know what he meant now.

We went to bed, and spent much of the night reprising our performance, at greater length, with greater variety and in greater comfort. But it's that first time that still floods my memory.

So there you go. I've broken my 'don't mention the sex' rule. Admittedly my account wasn't overburdened with details, but then graphic accounts of which body parts met which body parts for how long and in which order really don't add that much to things, do they? (If your answer to that was yes then you're reading this for all the wrong reasons.) I'm sure you can imagine most of them anyway.

No, the bit you need to know about is how it felt. It felt the best ever.

During the hour or so around dawn that I spent watching Hannah sleep, my thoughts roamed back over the Clare Jordan Five And Three-Quarter Feet Handicap Stakes.

It was a T-shirt, I think. As in been there, done that, got the . . . Everything I wrote about boys and what they think about sex, and how they differ from girls and what they think about sex, all of that was true. But it's a phase they grow out of. I always knew that would happen to me. It was just that I'd never known how. And now I'd found out.

As it went on, I realised, I talked less and less about Clare Jordan and more and more about the Clare Jordan Five And Three-Quarter Feet Handicap Stakes. The race became a crucible in which I could burn up my energy, a catalyst to hasten the day when I could sit back, contented and secure in the knowledge that I've seen everything youthful adventurism has to offer. (And it has much to offer.) Clare was the starting point, her sexiness and the mystery of everything we didn't know about her. And the sheer, naked (in some cases literally) excitement of the challenge that was formed from her name gripped me, as it did Tim. But now that race has been run. My road of excess has led to my path of wisdom.

That moment of inarticulacy which Hannah said was the most articulate I could have been – that wouldn't have happened with anyone else. Sarah, as much as I loved her, would have been waiting for a one-liner. Which shows she wasn't the one for me. We didn't really understand each other, not in the way that Hannah and I do. Maybe Hannah being part of ChrisandHannah stopped me seeing that. But I see it now.

Remember what I wrote on the evening after my parachute jump? About having tried that bit of life, and now I can get on with some of the other bits? Well, I feel a bit like that now. Je ne regrette un single thing I've done in my sex life. In fact I'd regret it if I hadn't done them. But they're gone now. It's time for something new.

Different people settle down at different times, for different reasons. James and Lucy have always been happy with each other. Simon wasn't so sure about Michelle, but he got there in the end. Graham had to wait, and maybe in Helen he's found someone who can see the goodness within him that no one else spotted.

And Tim? Tim's still out there, grabbing as many goals as he can. One day he'll retire. But not yet. Next in his sights, of course, is none other than Clare Jordan. I can still see why I thought she was sexy. It was because – and only because – I didn't know anything about her. The longer she spent in the office, the more I realised there wasn't anything about her that interested me – and I patently didn't interest her. So she stopped being sexy. Which isn't to say that she stopped being good-looking. (God, it seems a lifetime since I wrote those first notes.) It's just to say that now I don't want to do anything about it.

Hannah woke at about seven. As we lay cuddled up, the closeness of the other the only thing each of us needed, I murmured to her: 'Did you always know this would happen?'

She brushed a gentle kiss against my forehead. 'I think so, yeah.'

'What about the guys you've seen since me?'

'I had feelings for them. Like you had feelings for some of the girls you've seen since me.'

'But you always knew we'd come back to each other?'

She smiled, a Hannah Smile. 'Yeah. Even if it was just at the back of my mind, or my heart, or wherever – yeah, I knew.'

For the first time ever, I understood it. I gave a Hannah smile myself.

Monday 12th July

1.45 p.m.

Quick bit of advice.

Courtesy of Tim. Who's learned it the hard way.

It'll come in handy if you ever find yourself in the following position.

For several months, you have been lusting after an American girl in your office who is so sexy that she inspired a competition with your friend for the right to ask her out. You have painstakingly ploughed your way through four-fifths of that race, bringing yourself level with said friend as you approach the final hurdle.

But then circumstances, and your friend, have altered in such a way as to hand you victory in the race, giving you the right to pursue the object of your affections.

Over the course of several days, you have nurtured and developed your relationship with that girl. You have assiduously chatted to her by the coffee machine in the office. You have danced with her at your workmates' wedding reception, and then gone over to your friend, showed him the Ivy's number programmed into your mobile phone, and told him that at some point in the next few days he's going to have to get busy with that chequebook.

Later on in the evening you and the girl have engaged in a slightly drunken discussion about ex-lovers. Then, as the sun sets on the day's festivities, you have suggested to her that the two of you slip away and travel back into town on your own. She has said that would be nice, she was just thinking the same thing. When the train reaches Waterloo, you have invited her back to your flat for coffee, and she has accepted the invitation. As you have drunk that coffee, kneeling together on your sitting-room floor and discussing the films you have on video, your eyes have met hers for slightly longer than mere friendliness normally permits. You have leaned across and initiated a meeting of lips, and, after an initially shy and unsure response, the object of your affections has responded with an ardour that is keen and vigorous.

Soon you have found yourselves lying together on the floor, stretched out in a kiss whose intensity is growing by the second, and she has turned her head to let your eager mouth play on her irresistible neck. As she does so her hand has stretched out in a particular direction . . .

If you find yourself in that position, there's one thing that it's a really, really, *really* good idea to make sure you've done first.

Get rid of any bits of paper that might still be under your television.